THE

LOST

EXPERT

THE

LOST

EXPERT

A Novel by

Hal
Niedzviecki

Cormorant Books

Canadian Heritage / Patrimoine canadien   Canada Council for the Arts / Conseil des arts du Canada

 ONTARIO CREATES | ONTARIO CRÉATIF ONTARIO ARTS COUNCIL / CONSEIL DES ARTS DE L'ONTARIO / an Ontario government agency / un organisme du gouvernement de l'Ontario Ontario

We acknowledge financial support for our publishing activities:
the Government of Canada, through the Canada Book Fund and
The Canada Council for the Arts; the Government of Ontario, through
the Ontario Arts Council, Ontario Creates, and the Ontario Book
Publishing Tax Credit. We acknowledge additional funding provided
by the Government of Ontario and the Ontario Arts Council to address
the adverse effects of the novel coronavirus pandemic.

LIBRARY AND ARCHIVES CANADA CATALOGUING IN PUBLICATION

Title: The lost expert / a novel by Hal Niedzviecki.
Names: Niedzviecki, Hal, 1971– author.
Identifiers: Canadiana (print) 20210212144 | Canadiana (ebook) 20210212209 |
ISBN 9781770866348 (softcover) | ISBN 9781770866355 (HTML)
Classification: LCC PS8577.I3635 L67 2021 | DDC C813/.54—dc23

Cover photo and design: Angel Guerra / Archetype
Interior text design: Tannice Goddard, tannicegdesigns.ca

Printed and bound in Canada.
Manufactured by Houghton Boston in Saskatoon, Saskatchewan, Canada
in October 2021.

CORMORANT BOOKS INC.
260 Spadina Avenue, Suite 502, Toronto, ON M5T 2E4
www.dcbyoungreaders.com
www.cormorantbooks.com

To the lost.

A ROOFLESS MINIBUS HAULS its load of ten tourists, a driver, and a guide up a steep hill on a narrow bend. The guide, sporting safari shorts and wraparound sunglasses, stands in the front reciting a canned script into a microphone.

"We come now to home of star of big screen," he tells the tourists through a heavy Eastern European accent. "Thomson Holmes! One of world's greatest star, known to whole world!"

A man flanked by a young daughter and a wife jumps up. "*Condor Air!*" the man yells, pumping his fist. "*Condor Air!*"

The vehicle lurches to a stop in front of a gate. Set back from the gate is a low-slung, compact house mostly obscured from view by the barred entrance and the verdant bushes strategically planted throughout the compound. The tour guide, after a slight pause to let their proximity to greatness sink in, continues his spiel. "Thomson Holmes lived here since ... Fourteen movies already so far including ... Is been romantically connected to leading ladies of —" Suddenly, he breaks into a yell. "Him! It is him! People! Him!?! Coming out!?!"

The gate to the compound is slowly sliding open.

The tourists leap to their feet, phones outstretched, furiously capturing video of the event. The gate recedes to reveal a circular driveway and the front of a modernist stack of cubes, a sci-fi domicile perched on the edge of the Hollywood Hills.

"It's him!?!" The tour guide is frantic now, his mouth too close to the cheap microphone, his words breaking into static. "Him! Him!"

The man and his family lean over the side of the bus and wave their hands. "Thomson!" the man yells. "Thomson Holmes! How about an autograph? *Condor Air*! Yeah! Man! *Condor Air*!"

"Thomson," his dark-haired, cherubic daughter tries out quietly, a tentative smile on her round face.

The gate, almost fully opened, jerks to a stall. Then it begins to close.

"Thom-son Holmes!" the guide moans. "Thom-son Holmes!"

Sombrely, the passengers take up the plea: "Thom-son Holmes! Thom-son Holmes ..."

The house and the driveway disappear. The gate locks with an audible click.

The tourists chant, their litany continuing as the van hauls them up and around the next tight turn.

PART ONE

CHRIS WOKE INTO THE usually soothing cloud of sound: Laurie's breaths, the laboured hum of the kitchen's ancient refrigerator, the murmur of the next-door apartment's always-on TV. But he was tense, his body tight. He'd been out with Krunk last night. Laurie had been long asleep when he'd staggered home just before three. Laurie didn't like Krunk. She didn't like the drinking and the late-night greasy Chinatown snacks. She especially did not care for the way Chris's best friend since third grade lived his life: hand to mouth, getting by on small grants and odd jobs — his primary energies focused on screening movies no one had ever heard of.

At her mostly unspoken behest, Chris had been cutting back on his Krunk outings. But it had been Midnight Madness at the Royal, and he'd promised Krunk he'd definitely go this time. He'd cancelled the last two months in order to avoid, maybe even put off altogether, what he knew would be coming: Laurie, annoyed, pointing out once again that Chris needed to get serious about his "life choices" and stop "wasting so much time messing around." Serious people did not get Thursday-night drunk with a basement-dwelling self-proclaimed video anarchist. But there were only so many times you could say no to Krunk before you'd find him standing outside your apartment throwing empty beer cans at your second-floor window while chanting, "Pusseee whipped. Pusseee whipped."

Scooping up yesterday's clothes from the floor, Chris clicked the bedroom door behind him as quietly as he possibly could. He tiptoed to the kitchen, which also doubled as the living room. He dressed quickly in the dark. A sudden image: His girlfriend unhurriedly scrubbing out a small soup pot. The scene pained him. Laurie's kitchen, with its tiny stove and ancient buckled floor illuminated by a single bulb set in a dulling light fixture of dusty, brownish glass. Laurie, meticulous, rubbing the soup pot until it shone silver despite the gloom. She could afford a nicer place, but whenever something went wrong with the apartment's clanging radiators or spotty internet connection, she dismissed it, reminding Chris that she was saving for a down payment on, maybe, a small condo ... She usually trailed off at that point, looking just past him with a half wistful, half pained expression.

Even Chris, who Laurie said was "on cloud nine half the time," got the hint. If he could just figure out his shit, they would, as Laurie liked to say when one of her coupled friends bought a place or got engaged, "progress to the next phase."

Progress. Chris struggled into his black waiter's pants. They were getting too tight. His thighs pushed against the fabric. He had muscles now.

At first, he'd resisted Laurie's workout regimens. He'd always been a bit on the scrawny side and had never really been much for sports or exercise. But Laurie's urging bordered on insistence. He started doing push-ups and sit-ups and going for the occasional jog. That had been enough to convince Laurie that he was all in on the plan. Without further ado, she presented him with a weekly regimen to follow.

So, progress. And the occasional sleepovers that had gradually turned into regular weekend stays, which finally turned into Laurie presenting him with a key and suggesting that he give up his apartment to "save money." Chris remembered walking to work that morning with unfamiliar propulsion, a goofy grin on his face as his long, skinny legs slid him toward the future.

Practical, utilitarian, sensible Laurie, drying the dishes, carefully stowing them away in the crooked cupboard, humming to herself all along. He hadn't yet admitted to her that despite the hefty reduction in his expenses (Laurie had asked him to pay only $200 a month), he hadn't saved a cent. Things like that were hard to discuss with Laurie. She had plans. Workouts and co-habitations and next-level progress.

Chris padded down the dark alcove to the front door. He tripped over his trusty, battered Blundstones. He froze when he heard Laurie stepping into the kitchen. She turned on the overhead light. Chris watched from the foyer as, humming quietly to herself, she put the kettle on the burner. She looked out the tiny window over the sink with its view of the next building's bricks. She stretched her arms above her head. Completing the habitual gesture, she took the elastic out of her hair. She'd been letting her hair grow. Blond and wavy, it spilled over her shoulders. Chris, watching without being seen, felt like he was spying on a stranger.

"Laurie," he said.

Laurie, gasping, spun around.

"Hey! It's just me."

"Jesus! Chris!"

Laurie had grown up in the shelter of her conservative, church-going parents. She'd attended a Catholic school, been actively discouraged from "cussing," as she still called it. Her parents were polite, even kind, to Chris, though he knew they did not understand why their daughter wanted anything to do with him.

"I thought you'd gone to work!" Laurie laughed loudly, as if seeing him had jarred something loose in her. Chris felt his big smile blossom. Relief, or something else: a warm heat through his chest. He stepped toward her, conscious now of the poor state of his outfit. The black button-down, untucked, still moist with spills of coffee, beer, and black bean sauce. His black pants, stiff, literally crusted with dirt. And yesterday's socks, so filthy and redolent of rot that Chris imagined he was leaving soiled footsteps, as he padded along the sloped, worn but clean, linoleum kitchen floor toward his girlfriend.

"I'm sorry," he said. "I didn't mean to scare you."

"What are you still doing here?" Laurie didn't give him a chance to answer. She moved toward him and pulled him into her, her arms strong around him. "I thought you'd left," Laurie murmured against his neck.

"Laurie," Chris breathed. "I —"

"It's all right, Chrissie. I know ..." Laurie slid her hands down along his newly muscled abs. "And what's this?" she asked, squeezing a bicep. "So buff now ..."

Laurie pulled Chris into a kiss. Her tongue against his felt strange at first, but then it felt like it always had — her shape, her taste. Chris tried to say something, to explain, to protest, but she just shushed him and pulled him back down the hall. In the bedroom she discarded her pajama shirt, groaning as his hands moved reflexively to her breasts. They kissed again, falling onto the smooth comforter.

AFTERWARDS, LAURIE LAY WITH her head on his chest. Chris was going to be late for work, but he couldn't bring himself to move.

It was like they'd had makeup sex without fighting first. He lay there feeling awkward and anxious, looking away from her, looking at the top of her dresser, empty except for her phone and a picture of them all dressed up at Laurie's cousin's wedding. Chris gangly in an ill-fitting jacket and tie combo, Laurie floofy in her forest green bridesmaid gown. They were both smiling toothily, out of their element, arms around each other, holding each other up.

"Hey, uh, Laurie."

"I know," Laurie said. "You and Krunk." Her voice hardening, just a bit.

"Yeah. I was going to call, but —"

Laurie was looking at him, waiting for him to continue.

"Laurie ..." Chris said again, starting and stopping. He couldn't find the words. Something about him and her and Krunk and how he was trying, really trying. "I know you don't —"

"It's all right," Laurie said impatiently. "It's fine, Christopher." She got out of bed and pulled on her robe.

"But, Laurie —"

She leaned over, her clean lemon soap smell enveloping him. She kissed him on the cheek.

"You should go. You'll be late for work." Her smile was vacant and firm, like a teacher who had already made up her mind to report him to the principal. She tightened her robe. She had light brown eyes flecked with yellow. "Time to go," she said.

He nodded, smoothing at the creases in the comforter. Decisively, Laurie moved to the bathroom and shut the door. Sighing, Chris got out of bed. For the second time that morning, he pulled on his clothes. He hurried into the kitchen, hunting around for the keys to her — their — apartment. He found them in the foyer, on the rickety side table. He paused for a second, holding them in his palm, gauging their weight. Should he say something? Goodbye or something?

CHRIS WALKED PAST THE still-slumbering row houses of Beaconsfield Avenue, feeling the chilled air on his forehead. It was still mostly dark, morning a distant gleam over the Great Lake. He ran a hand down his face, the pads of his fingers catching on his stubble. He was hungover. He smelled of sweat, stale popcorn, and sex. Luckily, he was working the breakfast shift, and the boss didn't stumble in until he was long gone. Later, after he worked out following Laurie's program, he would take that much needed shower. He would shave. The wind blew. Chris shivered. It was fall now, time to dig out his coat. That's the way it happened: suddenly and unexpectedly, though it was the same thing every year.

Shoving his hands in the pockets of his tight black pants, Chris pushed on. But he came to a full stop where Argyle hit Ossington. The Vietnamese restaurant, the pho place on the corner, seemed to have been replaced overnight. There was a new shop, apparently called Motzie's Bagels. The Motzie's sign was cracked and faded, the raised cursive letters weathered and slightly buckled. It was as if the bagel shop had always been there, a recalcitrant holdover from some other era. Chris rubbed at his eyes. Then he noticed the corner Portuguese bakery he was standing next to had also transformed. The display window was piled high with golden breads twisted into elaborate braids. Painted on the window were letters from a foreign alphabet he vaguely identified as Hebrew.

ענעש ןיא עטיג רהאז
תבש ףיוא תולח
תולח רעייא ךיוא

Two new Jewish bakeries? Mechanically, Chris pulled out his phone. He saw the time and hesitated. It was far too early to consider calling Krunk, who was always talking about how he was half Jewish on his father's side. "Which, technically, means I'm a goy," he liked to say. "But I can feel it" — he'd thump his chest — "in here." Anyway, he had to keep moving or he'd be late.

HURRIEDLY, HE PUT THE coffees on to brew — Colombian Supremo Organic Dark Roast. Antigua Caribbean Smooth. Kenyan Jungle Fair Trade. Then Chris laid out the baked goods: muffins, cookies, fudgy gluten-free paleo brownies. The door opened, letting in a cold breeze. In his rush, he'd forgotten to lock it behind him.

"Hey, sorry, we're not —"

Turning, he saw it was Krunk in his greasy trench coat. Krunk marched in, dramatically kicking up the bright yellow high-tops he'd found — brand new! — hiding on a street corner in the waning darkness of a long, hot August night bordering on morning. Chris had been with him. It had been just before he'd moved in with Laurie. A few months ago. An eternity.

"Seen that fricking film shoot?" Krunk demanded. Krunk hated film shoots. As soon as he identified one setting up its ubiquitous fleet of trailers, he immediately began agitating for the fire-bombing of craft trucks, the stealth removal of pylons reserving blocks of parking, and the pie-ing of Hollywood poseurs pretending to be actors. Krunk claimed that as a committed guerilla filmmaker, part of his job description included actively opposing the "brain-dead corporate studio idiots that teach people how to chew their cud." He thought big and respected no compromise. He had yet to complete a project longer than six minutes.

Krunk helped himself to an extra-large takeout cup of the organic dark roast. He reached for a fancy brownie. Chris slapped his hand away.

"No way. Those always sell out. You can have a raisin muffin."

"Raisins," Krunk moaned. He took a huge bite.

"What are you doing up?"

"Never went to bed," Krunk said, muffled through the muffin and large slurps of coffee. *Figures*, Chris thought. Krunk had no gainful employment, no Laurie, no structure. "I saw them setting up that abomination in the park and decided to stake it out for future action." Krunk spoke like he chewed, with enthusiastic intensity, spewing muffin crumbs and stray raisins.

Future action, Chris thought, a low-level dread adding to the low-level nausea that had already made camp in his empty stomach. Future action meant Krunk roping him into some asinine scheme under the guise of anarchist aesthetics or guerilla video or DIY cultural resistance or some other sobriquet. Future action meant silly stakeouts punctuated by the draining and crushing of endless cans of Old Milwaukee and Labatt 50 and trying not to think about the pings of Laurie's increasingly annoyed texts.

"So," Krunk demanded, "Laurie mad at ya or what?"

"Something like that," Chris muttered.

Krunk made his usual "whipped" gesture-and-noise.

"Fuck off," Chris managed. "You gotta get out of here. We're opening in a few minutes."

"Me? Your best customer?" Krunk feigned anguish and took a seat at one of the three small round tables. "Man ..." He shook his head half despondently.

Chris grabbed a rag and swiped at the tabletop, somehow already covered with crumbs and coffee dribbles. "You can stay for, like, five more minutes." Turning deliberately away from

Krunk, Chris poured himself a steaming cup of freshly brewed Kenyan Jungle Fair Trade.

"All right, all right, geez ..."

It was just Krunk being Krunk. What nagged at Chris was something else. He'd felt it when he woke up, and he was still feeling it. It wasn't Krunk and it wasn't Laurie and it wasn't another movie shoot taking over Trinity Bellwoods Park. It was all those things. *Motzie's Bagels*. All those things put together and jumbled up and dumped out like one of those thousand-piece puzzles Laurie liked to do. Puzzles! Maybe Krunk was right. Progress. He watched the steam wisp up from his mug. And Laurie. Last week, casually asking him, "Are you still thinking of going back to school?" There were basically two people in his life, Chris thought. They didn't particularly like each other, they were opposites in every way, but both seemed in agreement: It was time for him to do something.

The door opened, and the first customer of the day walked in. He was a regular, dressed for work, chinos and a tucked-in light blue dress shirt accessorized by an upscale take on the peacoat. "Getting cold out there," the guy said, steadfastly ignoring Krunk. Chris thought his name was Andrew. Andrew rubbed his hands together in mock defrost. Smooth-shaven Andrew, in his early thirties — worked in tech, Chris recalled. Probably figured Krunk for one of those homeless guys who goes from coffee shop to coffee shop asking for handouts. Chris filled a large dark roast and added a splash of oat milk and a single spoon of sugar.

"Brownie today?"

Andrew nodded. "Gotta have it."

Chris bagged a paleo brownie.

"Thanks," Andrew said heartily.

"No problem."

"No problem," Krunk imitated in an unctuous falsetto as soon as Andrew had departed.

"That's it," Chris snapped. "Time to go."

There was a problem. Chris felt it. A miscalculation in the cosmos, particles separating, dissolving, solute into solvent, another day's solution — same as the last. Only, somehow, different.

RACHEL SHOWED UP TWENTY minutes late, wild-eyed and disheveled, her blond hair frizzy, her pale skin so translucent she looked almost grey. "Oh my god," Rachel moaned as she tied on an apron. Chris poured her a coffee.

"You're late," Chris said to her, smiling sardonically to show that he didn't really care. Last week, he'd had to stay on for the lunch shift two days in a row. Rachel had been increasingly erratic, drinking and partying, showing up at work complaining of vicious headaches, code, as Chris well knew, for killer hangovers. Rachel came around the counter. She gulped at the coffee then looked up at Chris, managing a grin.

"Sorry ..." Rachel said, sounding anything but.

Up close she looked greedily sensual, her hangover or come down or whatever it was only serving to enhance her gravitational pull. Pretty girls could be late, unkempt, hungover, slow to make lattes, and terrible at cleaning up. They still got good tips, requests for their phone numbers, the occasional leer courtesy of Carlos the owner/manager as he amiably ambled in and took up his position in the back office.

"Don't worry about it," Chris said.

"Okay. Thanks for covering for me." The shorter girl looked up at him with dark eyes shining. Chris didn't move. Rachel leaned in. For a second, he thought she was going to kiss him. Or he was going to kiss her. They stared at each other.

"I should go." Chris looked at his watch. As if he had an appointment or something.

Rachel raised her hand and did a slight wave.

"Bye," she said.

ON THE STREET, THE day had brightened. Where there had been shadows and fog, there was now revealing sunshine. Chris moved aimlessly along Queen. At the steps leading to the park, he hesitated. Maybe he would go around, skirt the perimeter, take the long way? No. Why take the long way? What was he avoiding? He loved movies. His best friend was a filmmaker of sorts. Lately, he had been toying with the idea of getting into the business himself, taking a course, becoming a sound man or a lighting grip, something like that. He could ask his mom to help him out with the tuition money. Tell Laurie that he was getting series about a career. Progress. Or something.

At this hour, Trinity Bellwoods was mostly patronized by dog walkers and stroller pushers. If Chris noticed them, he pitied them. The moms looked desperate, and the dogs looked ridiculous, dressed more often than not in an array of sweaters, jumpsuits, and booties, as if they were extras from some failed *Best in Show* sequel. Chris picked up the pace, warily keeping watch for signs of the film shoot. Just past the playground, he stumbled and almost fell. Surprised, he looked down. A bundled snake of cables stretched along the path. He followed the clustered cords. The wires twisted along the paved walkway then split apart at a colonizing huddle of trailers, abrupt fungi glowing white against the dark grass. Chris edged toward this sprawl of lunar flora. There it was again — that feeling. Unease and disruption, growing inside him.

Down the slight incline toward the bottom section of the

park, a lone security guard lolled against a trailer set slightly
apart from the others. Through shadows and beams of sunshine, Chris caught flashes of the man's teeth masticating a wad
of gum. Beside the security guard stood a tower of orange
pylons awaiting ubiquitous deployment. It was just another
movie shoot. The same slovenly, disinterested security guard
eying passersby, the same ragamuffin band of headset-wearing
crew, the same hurriedly scrawled signs pointing to the catering
truck and the gathering point for extras. The shoots were so
common in the summer and fall months that most people barely
even noticed them, let alone bothered to find out what masterpiece was soon to grace screens big and little or see if there
were any stars hidden away in the giant buzzing trailers that
narrowed already narrow streets, blocked alleys, and crushed
random slabs of urban parkland grass. Motzie's Bagels! And that
other shop with the Hebrew writing. It was part of it. It was part
of the set. How could he not have seen that straight away? Some
kind of old-world Jewish village. A shtetl? It hadn't looked particularly *Fiddler on the Roof.* More of a retro vibe, modern nostalgic.
Krunk would know. Just another movie set …

It was almost noon. The intermittent sun had just about burnt
off the last of the glistening morning dew that clung to the white
walls of the trailers. Krunk often claimed he could tell what kind
of piece of crap was in production with a single glance. Cop
cruisers next to a gritty alley off Queen meant a crime proced-
ural for TV, fake NYC taxis driven straight out of that warehouse
where they keep everything you need to turn Toronto the Good
into the Big Apple. Trucks and trailers outside ivy-encrusted
University of Toronto halls meant a college boys gross-out
comedy, the perfect setting for fraternal high jinks aimed at
disrupting a corrupt university president presiding over middle

America's youth with the earnest zeal of the well-fed kleptocrat. And, of course, if they were filming on Bloor Street, that meant a hotel penthouse rom-com scene offering panoramic skyscapes evoking the limitless possibilities of love — but watch out for the CN Tower! Ah, no worries; make it disappear in post.

"Ah, there you are! Finally!" Chris felt a hand on his forearm, strong fingers circling. "I won't even ask where you've been. Boys will be boys!"

The speaker barked a laugh. She held a clipboard and wore a headset. She seemed frazzled, relieved, and pissed off all at once. "I've got him," she blurted into the headset. "He's here. No, no, he just showed up. I don't know. I *don't know*. We're going to makeup." The woman pulled him along through the park. Chris noted passersby eyeballing him. He felt his legs moving. He heard the woman's chatter, a kind of passive-aggressive non sequitur babble. "You had us worried. Beautiful day out. Bryant's meeting us. He just got here too. How does he do that? It's like he knows. How does he know? Oh, you boys!"

She pushed Chris up the stairs of a trailer. The interior was dominated by a giant vanity mirror of unforgiving high-wattage light bulbs. Chris blinked against the glare, and when he could see again, a guy with aggressively blond highlights was attacking his face with an oversized powder puff. Chris felt his feet. They hurt from five hours of pouring coffees and bagging buttered multigrain bagels. Suddenly tired, he leaned back into the chair and closed his eyes.

"I've got to do something with the hair," the makeup guy said to the clipboard lady.

She shrugged. "He's already been to wardrobe, I guess." Chris felt cold spray dew his scalp.

"Leave it!" a commanding voice insisted.

Chris jerked upright. Makeup guy froze, his finger on the trigger of a squirt bottle filled with liquid shine.

"It's perfect!" the voice said again. "Doing your own hair now, huh, Holmes?"

The man laughed a big, booming laugh. The makeup guy's eyes narrowed. The voice put hands on Chris's shoulders and leaned in. Chris surveyed the new arrival in the mirror. He was short and stocky, his wide forehead deeply furrowed. A faded Pittsburgh Penguins cap was pulled over what was most likely a serious case of male pattern baldness. He was smiling, but his brown eyes, absorbing the blinding hot lights, exuded cold.

Bryant Reed, Chris thought or said. The director.

"At your service," the man boomed, laughing again.

He was one of Krunk's heroes. Well, it was kind of a love-hate thing. Krunk hated Reed's later work, ranted about how he had lost his edge and was cozying up to the establishment. But he loved his earlier movies and still talked about him as one of a handful of American directors who had once managed to "get something real" into the theatres.

The movie, Chris thought. *It must be his.*

"Holmes! Your little disappearing act cost me, what, sixty grand? Probably more! But, hey, what's a few lost days between friends? Beggars can't be choosers!" Reed boomed another murderous laugh. "At least he looks the part," he said to the clipboard woman. "It's like he just did a stint at the local diner." Reed waved the smell from Chris's hair into his face, inhaled it as if he was contemplating the bouquet of a fine wine. "He even smells like it."

Clipboard lady sniffed, made a sour face.

Chris shifted his gaze from Reed's reflection to his own. People said he was handsome. He had short blond hair, blue eyes, straight white teeth, a square jaw, and stood just a sliver under six feet tall. Krunk said he'd have been perfect in *The Great Escape* — "Nazi or canny Brit POW with a knack for tunnelling, take your pick!" Take your pick, Chris thought. He cultivated no particular style, made no attempt to either blend in or stand out.

"Holmes?" barked Bryant Reed. "Earth to Holmes?"

Holmes. He keeps calling me Holmes. Then it came to him. Thomson Holmes. An A-list action star Laurie liked to claim he resembled. Laurie went to his movies with her girlfriends. She admitted they were predictable, juvenile, meaningless — the kind of movie Krunk hated more than anything else in the world. "We don't go for the *plot*," she said coquettishly. *They think I'm Thomson Holmes.* What was Holmes doing in a Bryant Reed movie? Wait until Krunk found out. He'd go ballistic.

Maybe he did look like the guy? A skinnier, paler, infinitely more disheveled version. In the mirror, his face and his blue eyes stared back, clear and hopeful.

"Ready?" Reed said.

"They're on their way to set," clipboard lady announced into her walkie-talkie.

"I, uh —"

"Don't talk, just listen," Reed growled, ushering Chris out of the trailer and into the early afternoon sunshine. "You've wasted enough of my time already. As of this moment," Reed half hissed, half whispered, "you're someone else. You're a young man with an astonishing gift. You're a penniless waiter with a gorgeous new wife and baby. You're a visionary about to discover your nascent powers for the first time. Your whole life is ahead of you. So don't speak. Don't *say*. Just *feel*. Feel what it's like to find yourself as you really are, as you were really meant to be. From this moment on, you're not Thomson Holmes. You're him. You're that guy. The Lost Expert."

EXT. URBAN PARK — MORNING (1928)
A large urban park still slightly misted by the
morning chill. People, many dressed formally in
suits and dresses, stroll along the paths past
benches under mature trees, their leaves just
beginning to curl and turn. THE LOST EXPERT, in
black trousers and long-sleeved black shirt,
walks through the nexus of several paths where
three ROUGH LOOKING YOUNG MEN, their ragged
newsboy caps pulled low over their broad
foreheads, hand out fliers: "Join Allan's Army
— Harold Allan for President." One of the men
tries to hand a flier to the Lost Expert.

                    CANVASER
        Mister, hey, mister! America first and
        jobs for all! C'mon, mister, take one,
                    read all about it!

The Lost Expert ignores the proffered flier and
walks on.

EXT. URBAN PARK — MORNING
THE LOST EXPERT walks along the west side of
the park, following a thin dirt path that moves
behind a series of benches overlooking a sharp
drop into an area that is densely treed and
overgrown.

> GIRL
> Missy? Missy! Where are you, Missy?

The GIRL, nine years old, fashionably clothed in
a wool dress, matching short sweater, and velvet
cloche hat, runs to and fro frantically along
the top of the ridge above the forested area.
Finally, she throws herself on a park bench and
begins to bawl. The Lost Expert, walking past,
veers off the path and approaches the girl.

> THE LOST EXPERT
> Are you okay? Are you lost?

> GIRL
> (sniffling)
> I'm not supposed to talk to strangers.

> THE LOST EXPERT
> Well, then, I better introduce myself.
> I'm a waiter at Sutton's Hotel. I'm on
> my way there right now.

                    GIRL
You are? My daddy takes me there for
                 breakfast!

              THE LOST EXPERT
I bet you like the crispy bacon,
              don't you?

                    GIRL
            (nodding seriously)
            How did you know?

              THE LOST EXPERT
Ah, well, just a lucky guess.

                    GIRL
Can you help me find my cat?

              THE LOST EXPERT
Sure. Sure, I can. I'm good at
            finding stuff.

EXT. URBAN PARK — TOP OF THE RIDGE
THE LOST EXPERT stands on the ridge overlooking
the thick woods below. It's early fall, the
colours just emerging: green blending to red
and yellow. The sun shines brightly. The Lost
Expert peers down into the tangled bush, deep in
concentration, taking everything into account.
He stands straight, his arms folded against
his chest, his senses active, alive. The sun

comes out from behind a cloud and catches the
Lost Expert in a ray of pure light. The GIRL
is revealed, standing behind him, watching,
almost awestruck. The Lost Expert holds up his
index finger as if to test the wind. Slowly,
purposely, he lowers his finger until he's
pointing at something in the woods below,
something, perhaps, only he can see.

                    GIRL
          Is that her? Is that Missy?

The Lost Expert lopes down the hill and
disappears into the trees. The girl waits,
alone, anxiously peering down the slope.

EXT. URBAN PARK — IN THE WOODS
The woods are crowded by a thick copse of spiky
fir trees, low-lying bramble bushes, and semi-
mature maples spreading their limbs to the sky
and casting everything below them in shadow. The
ground is covered with leaves and branches in
varying states of decay. THE LOST EXPERT walks
silently through the dense brush, almost seeming
to float. He appears and reappears through
boughs and bushes until, suddenly, he stops.

EXT. THE SOUTH RIVER CONSERVATION AREA — SUNNY,
LATE MORNING (FLASHBACK — 1903)
MOTHER trots down a nicely groomed path past
woods of birch, maple, and conifer. It is early

fall, and the trees are just beginning to turn.
She jogs awkwardly, and we see her well-used
brown Oxfords press down against the reds,
yellows, and oranges, fresh leaves lightly
covering the trail.

> MOTHER
> (sing-song voice, smiling)
> Where are you, sweetheart? Sweetheart,
> where are youuuuuu?

Mother turns a bend. There is a clearing of
grass with two picnic tables overlooking a
slowly moving river. BOY LOST EXPERT, in plaid
shorts and shirtsleeves, hides behind the trunk
of a fir growing out of the soft, dark earth
bordering the river. Mother approaches the bank,
pretending not to see him.

> MOTHER
> Hello? Anyone?

Mother shields her eyes and sweeps her gaze up
and down the river as if she's scanning the
opposite bank. She steps slowly toward the fir
tree then suddenly whirls around and grabs the
boy.

> MOTHER
> Got ya!

BOY LOST EXPERT
(laughing, but also annoyed)
How did you find me?

EXT. URBAN PARK — IN THE WOODS — MORNING (1928)
THE LOST EXPERT's eyes shoot open. He looks
around in confusion. Then a faint sound.

MISSY
Meow.

Instantly, he is back in the present moment,
taking it all in, fixing in his mind the
whereabouts of all creatures great and small
living in this tiny cluster of woods. The Lost
Expert steps toward the source of the purring,
a dark crevice of thick thorn bushes competing
with waist-high, sharp-needled adolescent pines.

MISSY
Meow. Meeeow.

Blocked by the tangled underbrush, the Lost
Expert gets down on his hands and knees
and pushes through. He crawls slowly and
purposefully toward the cat.

MISSY
Meo—

A dead branch under the Lost Expert's knee, grey
wood snapping loudly. The cat swings her head

toward the source of the noise, back arched,
poised to run. Dark cloud settles above, casting
the urban woodlands into gloom. The wind picks
up. Tree limbs brush against one another,
pine needles rustling. It starts to rain. Not
torrentially, but slowly, steadily.

                    MISSY
                 (woefully)
                 Me-ahwwww.

The Lost Expert shoots forward. He rolls through
the underbrush and comes up with the cat cradled
in his arms.

                    MISSY
                (protesting)
                  Rowww!

EXT. URBAN PARK — TOP OF THE RIDGE

     (The GIRL jumps up and down, clapping.)

                    GIRL
                Missy! Missy!

THE LOST EXPERT gently hands the cat to the
GIRL, who tucks her into the crook of her arm.
The girl strokes the cat affectionately, and
the cat purrs.

                    GIRL
        Why did you run away? Why did you do
          that? Don't you do that again,
                you bad kitty.

               THE LOST EXPERT
                She's not bad.

The girl looks up through the light rain,
surprised.

               THE LOST EXPERT
           We all get lost sometimes.

The girl nods dolefully. On the verge of tears,
she pulls the cat closer to her.

               THE LOST EXPERT
        You go on home now. It's getting cold.

The girl doesn't move. She stands, petting the
cat and staring up at the Lost Expert.

               THE LOST EXPERT
                 Go on now.

She turns and runs off. The Lost Expert is alone
in the rain, the sun pushing rays through the
ominous grey of the looming sky.

"CUT AND WRAP," BRYANT Reed barked.

Rivulets of water ran down the sides of Chris's face. Could it have rained? He craned his neck, and the sun flooded into eyes, blinding him. He blinked, bright spots in his pupils. He was standing at the top of the hill, in a semicircle of frantic activity of which he was the languid centre. White screens encircled the small space, reflecting bright, blinding spotlights visible even in the bright day. Overhead, microphones on booms were retreating. The woods below quietly dropped leaves. And beyond the cameras, a little girl was being led away by a prim woman wearing red gloves. Her mother, Chris thought.

"Are you all right?" An elegant young woman appeared next to him. She was holding a towel and a square glass bottle of water, a brand he'd never seen before.

Chris watched the girl and her mother slowly moving away. The girl looked back, smiled fleetingly at him. Uncertainly, Chris raised a hand.

"Thomson? Are you okay? Would you like some water?"

Chris brought the surprisingly heavy bottle to his lips. He drank. The water was sweet, fresh, tasted of some faraway, unspoiled place.

"What is this?"

"It's —" the young woman said hesitantly. "It's your water. Would you prefer something else?" She asked the question with a note of worry, tucking an escaped strand of dark hair behind her small, white ear.

"No. No. I was just —"

He inspected the solid glass bottle: *Artesian Spring. Chilean Andes.*

"It's the one you always drink," the young woman continued.

"Of course," Chris murmured. His legs felt weak. He needed to sit down. "Hey, uh —" He turned to the woman. "What's your name again?"

"My name?" He was really scaring her now. He could hear it in her voice. "Thomson, are you okay?"

He didn't answer.

She put a hand on his arm. "Thomson?"

"He's fine! He's fine! Aren't you, Holmes?" Reed slapped Chris hard on the back. He was wearing a wide smile the way a cowboy wears a ten-gallon hat.

"He asked me my name," the woman said worryingly.

"He's still in the movie," Reed said. "It's like waking up from a dream." He took the towel from her and brusquely patted Chris's forehead. "Let's get him out of those wet clothes. He'll come around."

Reed threw his arms over Chris's shoulders. He pulled him down so that Chris, stooped, was face to face with the shorter man.

"That was it," Reed hissed. "That was exactly it, Holmes. You disappear for three days, show up two hours late on set, *don't* have a clue what's going on, and it's fucking great." Reed kissed him on the lips then shoved Chris away.

Members of the crew chuckled. Chris blinked and straightened.

"Great work everyone," Reed yelled randomly. "Let's get back to it!" Then, looking between him and the young woman: "Holmes, this is Alison. Remember her? She works for you." Without waiting for an answer, Reed strode off into the cameras.

CHRIS STOOD BEHIND AN ornate screen contemplating the pants and shirt neatly laid out along with tight white briefs, silky striped socks, fancy leather loafers, and a fluffy towel. There was also a sports jacket, a very expensive-looking tan number, like something Colin Farrell would wear on a casual stroll with his latest model girlfriend. "You should change," the assistant, Alison, had told him after leading him into what was apparently his very own trailer. Not knowing what else to do, he started pulling on the clothes in front of him. Then he stopped, his fingers fumbling with the buttons of the shirt. What was he doing? He would get arrested. There must be a law. Multiple laws. He'd acted in somebody else's movie. How had he done that? Reed had told him. More or less. What to do. What to say. He'd just done it. Sweat broke out on his forehead, on his upper lip. What if the real Thomson Holmes walked in right then and saw Chris standing in his trailer wearing his silky briefs? He'd be arrested. He'd go to jail.

"Thomson?" The assistant again, Alison.

"Be right out!"

His hands shook as he buttoned himself up. What next? How to get out of this? He couldn't think.

Alison looked at him critically. "You've lost more weight," she said flatly. "You'll need some new clothes until you bulk back up again." She pulled out a phone. Chris was aware of the jacket dangling from his shoulders as if to emphasize the muscles that had suddenly gone missing.

"No," he said hurriedly. "That's okay."

She stared at him.

"I mean," he said, "that's good! Great! Okay."

She nodded and went back to her tapping.

What had Reed said? It was like waking up from a dream. Only he hadn't woken up yet. He needed to get rid of her, Alison, and then make a run for it. He'd never tell anybody. Not Laurie. Not Krunk. Maybe when the movie came out. Maybe then.

Alison put the phone away and was once again openly considering him. Chris ran a nervous hand down his cheeks, felt his stubble. His stomach rumbled.

"I'm hungry," he blurted.

"Should I get you your plate?"

"Uh, yeah. Could you?"

Alison seemed more annoyed than perplexed now.

"Please?"

Without another word, she spun and left.

Chris walked over to the bar. He should wait a few minutes, at least until she was out of sight. He pulled his shaking hands out of unfamiliar pockets and considered the trailer's glimmering selection of alcohols. He picked up a bottle of vodka. Like the water, it was a brand he'd never seen. He drank straight from the bottle, feeling the liquid pool, a heat in the cold of his belly. Somehow, Bryant Reed had liked it. His acting. *But when they find out the truth, it'll be a different story. They'll look at the rushes. They'll see a scared, confused boy standing there with his mouth hanging open and the rain falling in.* Chris felt the alcohol spreading. Liquid courage, Krunk called it. Liquid courage.

SAFELY ON DUNDAS STREET, Chris stopped his half-jog half-speed-walk. He hunched over, breathing heavily, hands on his thighs.

A streetcar rumbled by, encased in a scrim of fabric, an ocean and a beach rolling slowly through the city. Chris watched it go past. *Cuba*, he read on the streetcar's rear end. He should have gotten on. It was going the wrong way. He straightened up and looked behind him, as if he'd felt a tap. Clipboard lady or Alison, the assistant. The little girl with the big eyes, tugging on his hand and leading him back. To where?

No one was following him. Yet, he told himself. With forced steps, he moved down Dundas toward Laurie's apartment. At Ossington, he stopped for the red light. He surveyed the intersection. The small drugstore. The community centre. The Portuguese fish store under new management. No Jewish delis or synagogues or bagel bakeries. Now that he was out of it, he realized how strange, how ridiculous it was. What a joke. You have to laugh. He didn't feel it. He didn't feel like laughing. He would tell Krunk. Of course, he would. And Laurie too. They had actually thought he was a movie star. He took off the sports jacket. The lining was slippery, shimmered. He draped the jacket jauntily over his shoulder.

Chris brazenly crossed the street, pausing to take a long, suspicious look down Ossington in the direction of the ersatz bakeries. But by the time he was on the other side, his flash of cocky confidence was already dissipating. Nervous again, he ducked into the Communist's Daughter, a dive bar that had taken over the guts of a former workers' luncheonette. He'd drunk there once or twice with Krunk. It was dark and cheap and got pretty loud. It was not the kind of place anyone would think to look for a Thomson Holmes. The door jingled as Chris slipped inside. Tom Waits played loudly. The lone employee looked up from arranging glasses behind the bar and openly stared at him. What? Chris wondered. Oh yeah, he realized. I'm dressed like a

rich asshole. He put his hands in his pockets, trying to act the
way a guy like Thomson Holmes would act when confronted
with a dismissive bartender with a helix piercing, bedhead, and
a faded John Deere T-shirt. But, with his hands in his pockets, he
felt even more ridiculous.

The bartender's lips curled in sardonic friendliness. "What
can I get you, bud?" he said. That's when Chris realized it. His
pockets were empty. His wallet, his keys, his phone. They were
still in his black waiter's pants. Back in the Thomson Holmes
trailer. "You all right there, buddy?" the bartender asked just a
bit less dismissively. Chris's stomach turned. He spun on the
slippery heels of his loose leather loafers and fled back to the
scene of his unbelievable crime.

ALISON LOOKED UP AS he entered the trailer. Her hair shimmered,
caught in the lamplight, everything else in the rectangle space
reduced to gloom. She gazed at him curiously, her white teeth
like pearls. Chris wiped at his forehead with his sleeve and tried
to grin at her. "What is it?" she asked him cautiously.

"Nothing," Chris said too quickly. "It's nothing." Alison
pushed that errant strand of hair behind her ear. Chris reflexively
ran a hand down his stubbled cheek. For the first time he realized
how perfect she was. She *glowed*.

"I've got your plate," Alison said. She gestured at it, sitting on
the small table next to the leather armchair.

"Great. Thanks."

She was still looking at him quizzically.

"I just —" The words stuck in his throat. "Needed some air."

He cringed inside. *You're staring at her. Stop staring at her.*

"Ohh-kaay," she said. "Well, you eat. I'll, I'll see you later."

As soon as she left, Chris rushed behind the screen. His

clothes were in the heap he'd left them in. Chris fell to his knees. He fumbled at the pockets of his pants, retrieving his wallet and his keys. He flipped open his cell phone and scrolled through the messages. Laurie had already called five times. Probably checking up on him, making sure he was working out, following the routine. What if his cell had rung while Alison was in here? What if she'd answered? Chris poked at the phone with a wobbly finger, finally managing to turn the ringer to silent before the next call came through, his girlfriend and best friend both wondering: Where are you?

The Lost Expert is lost, Chris thought, feeling on the verge of hysteria. Anyway, you have your stuff. Now get out of here. But he stayed there, crouched next to his filthy waiter clothes. That scene he'd shot. It was ludicrous. A little girl, some guy called the Lost Expert rescuing her cat. Everyone dressed like extras in the next failed remake of *The Great Gatsby*. Krunk would die. He'd just about kill himself laughing.

But it hadn't been funny. It had been — Chris searched for the word, his fingers tracing an invisible stain on his work pants, still damp from the sudden rain of the film shoot. How could he explain it to them if he couldn't understand it himself? It hadn't been funny. Not at all. Instead, it had been glorious.

Outside, a walkie-talkie burst of static followed by a loudly barked reply. Chris dropped the pants and calmly stood up. His stomach gurgled. He hadn't eaten since cramming two handfuls of Honeycombs down his throat at half-past five this morning.

His plate sat on a table next to the armchair. The voices outside got louder, then quieter. Chris slid into the armchair and took the cover off. A cold skinless, boneless grilled chicken breast next to a bright green sauce. A bed of baby vegetables. A light dressing in a small side thimble.

Laurie always said he was a terrible liar. But nobody seemed to even suspect him. Not even his assistant, Alison. Voices again, this time closer, getting louder. He felt the barely perceptible shake as someone ascended the steps of the trailer. Chris hurriedly put down the fork. There was a rap at the door of the trailer. Probably Alison, back from wherever she had gone off to. He looked down at the plate again. If it was Alison, he didn't want her to think that he was the kind of guy who sends someone to get them food and then doesn't even bother to eat it. There was a small garbage receptacle unobtrusively squeezed into the corner. Chris grabbed the plate, swept the food into the bin. The knock again. "Mr. Holmes?" A deeper voice. It wasn't Alison. Chris grabbed a napkin and reflexively swiped at his dry lips. A few more raps. He hurried over and yanked open the door.

It was clipboard lady. She looked him over disapprovingly. "Where's Alison?" she said to the crackling void on the other end of her walkie-talkie. And then, to him, "Where's Alison?" He shrugged. Her mouth was open, showing barracuda-like lines of small, sharp teeth. "Let's get you to wardrobe."

THE INTERIOR OF WARDROBE featured a long room full of clothing stands on wheels staffed by a frizzy-haired, middle-aged redhead wearing elaborate green eye shadow and too much blush. "Let's see here," she said, ignoring him. She consulted a printout on a clipboard. Then she turned to him. "Now, Mr. Holmes," she said playfully, "you've been a naughty boy, haven't you?" He didn't know what she meant, so he kept quiet. "Yes, you have," she said wagging her finger at him. Still, he looked at her blankly. "Come on now," she teased. He thought for a minute that she knew the truth, knew who he really was. For some reason, he didn't care. A faint smile played on his lips. "There you go," she said, "you know what I'm saying, don't you?" Again, she wagged a manicured, painted nail at him. "Showing up in costume," she tsked. "You're going to put us out of work." Her real tone, accusatory and hostile, was starting to creep in. "I know that Mr. Reed takes an unorthodox approach. But we have rules, Mr. Holmes. We have a union. And there's continuity," she pronounced. "You can't just show up in whatever you feel like." She stopped, suddenly looking worried, like she'd gone too far. Then she turned away. "Now then," she said brightly, "let's get you suited up." She rustled through the clothing racks that occupied the bulk of the trailer. She emerged with a garment bag, held the hanger out to him. "Here we go," she said. "The pajamas, for the bedroom scene." Her smile was strange. It was a very particular kind of look, an uncertain gaze that broke before it set and reflected a shifting set of emotions back at him — fear, jealously, rage, want. Chris had seen it a few times already. People looking at him as if he were something not quite human. What was it? Chris wondered. What was it they thought he was?

INT. APARTMENT — BEDROOM — MIDDAY
A small bedroom, shabbily furnished with a
second-hand bed and dresser, but spotlessly
clean. The view through the window of this
second-floor walkup apartment is of the
long, low single brick building of attached
establishments across the street. THE LOST
EXPERT, in his pajamas, his eyes bright and his
hair tousled, watches through the closed window
of his bedroom. Directly across from him is
the Quick Lunch with its Orangeade canopy and
its Blue Plate Ham Special sign in the window.
Next to it is the Malt, Grain & Hops store, the
Cushman Shoe Repair and Shine, and the Busy Bee,
its sign offering butter and eggs. A BUM sits
with his back against the thin strip of bricks
between the Quick Lunch and Cushman Shoe Repair.
The waitress at Quick Lunch — Romanian WIFE OF
THE COOK-OWNER — appears with a broom and swipes
at the homeless man.

                    QUICK LUNCH WIFE
        Hey! You shoo! Shooo! Get out of here!

The homeless man wanders off, muttering to
himself. Before turning the corner, he stops
and makes a crude gesture. The Quick Lunch wife
curses in Romanian, though the Lost Expert,
watching through the window, can only see her
lips move.

EXT. LUNCHEON STAND BY SIDE OF ROAD — MIDDAY
(FLASHBACK — 1903)

                        MOTHER
                 (smiling bravely)
      So, it's just going to be us for a while,
                  I guess, kiddo.

BOY LOST EXPERT impassively opens a Hershey's
Milk Chocolate bar.

INT. APARTMENT — BEDROOM — MIDDAY (1928)
THE LOST EXPERT lies on his back on the bed, his
hands folded under his head. Still in pajamas,
he stares up at the cracks in the painted
ceiling. Enter SARAH, in a long, shapeless
nightgown covered by a drab flannel robe. Sarah
stops at the window. Outside there's the sound
of something falling over, several long blasts
of a car's klaxon (AHOOGA!), and then the shouts
of the police. Sarah sighs and draws the curtain

over the view. She pulls her robe around her, as
if she's caught a chill.

> SARAH
> You don't want to know what's going on
> out there. It's disgusting.

The Lost Expert closes his eyes.

> SARAH
> (turning to him)
> Aren't you getting dressed? Don't you
> have a shift soon?

The Lost Expert breathes languidly. The car
horn blasts again, longer and more drawn out
this time, and there is, again, the sound of
shouting. The baby in the bassinet next to the
bed starts crying.

> SARAH
> Oh, that's just swell! They've woken the
> baby!

Sarah picks up the baby and soothes him. The
Lost Expert lies inert on the bed. The muffled
shouts from outside fade. Then, from the
apartment upstairs, there is the slow timbre of
a cello playing the same three notes over and
over again.

INT. APARTMENT — KITCHEN — AFTERNOON
SARAH sits at the kitchen table idly listening
to music on the radio.

                    THE LOST EXPERT
          (entering from the bedroom, wearing his
                    waiter outfit)
          Are you sure you're going to be okay?

                         SARAH
                   (smiling bravely)
          It's just colic, right? We'll survive.

                    THE LOST EXPERT
                 Maybe I should stay?

                         SARAH
          No, no, I'm fine. We need the money.
          I mean — It's fine. Get going. You
                 don't want to be late.

INT. LUNCHEONETTE ON RUNDOWN STREET NEAR
APARTMENT — LATE AFTERNOON
THE LOST EXPERT sits at a table in the back
of a dimly lit, shabby diner. It's afternoon
and almost empty. THE WAITER, jaded and bored,
occasionally passes by and refills his coffee.
The Lost Expert, still in his waiter clothes,
has the sections of four different local papers
strewn around him. We catch various headlines
as he flips impatiently through the paper:

*Unemployment at 30-Year High; Allan's Upstart
Maverick Party Makes Gains; Lindbergh's Speech
Warns Against Foreign Influences.* He arrives at
the classified section.

>   THE LOST EXPERT
>   (under his breath)
>   Butlers, laundresses, photographers,
>   stenographers …

He pauses at one ad in the full page of
classifieds printed in tiny type. He reads the
ad:

>   THE LOST EXPERT
>   Mystic. Speak to your Lost Loved
>   Ones; "Where Are You Going and
>   How Will You Know When You Get
>   There?" Ancient Knowledge for
>   Modern Times.

Inspired, the Lost Expert picks up his pen and
begins to write on the yellow legal pad beside
him.

>   . THE LOST EXPERT
>   (speaking slowly while writing)
>   Have you lost someone? I can help. No.
>   (crossing out the "I") The Lost Expert
>   can help. He provides a unique service.
>   No. (crossing out the last sentence)
>   A man with unique talents. No. (crossing

out talents) Skills. Discretion
guaranteed. Contact …

The Lost Expert looks up, catching the eye of
the waiter wiping down the counter.

WAITER
You need somethin' pal?

THE LOST EXPERT
What's the address here?

"CUT!"

Chris stayed where he was. *Something's coming.* He knows it. He feels it. Sarah, his wife, she feels it too. But she's afraid. She's afraid to change.

"Thomson?"

Chris smelled her, her skin.

"Thomson? It's over."

It's over, Chris thought.

"We should go."

Chris sat up. The bed creaked. He could feel the thin mattress under him. His pajamas were pinstriped and elegantly simple. It was obviously the Roaring Twenties, Chris thought, the Jazz Age on the cusp of the Great Depression. But what about the Jewish bakeries, then? How did they fit in?

"Thomson?" Alison said. "We should get going."

Alison was looking down at him, her impatience softened by a quizzical half-smile. Chris swung his legs off the bed and stood up. He could feel his bare feet on the rough floor rug.

"Was that okay?" He was leaning in, whispering.

"It was great," Alison said, almost reluctantly. "You really ... I mean ... I really got it."

A thrill ran through him.

Then Reed was there. "Amazing, incredible. You're killing me. Absolutely killing me." Reed theatrically threw his arms up in the air, as if beseeching God. Reed, it seemed, was capable of only two types of interpersonal communication: yelling his head off for the benefit of everyone within a half-mile radius or close-quarters barely audible whispers, the words not even grazing the world before slipping directly into your auditory canal. "So ... Sarah, huh?" Reed continued, his big voice dominating the room, which was, Chris suddenly noticed, boiling hot and filled with lights, cameras, and action. "Where did that come from? We'll go with it. Why the hell not? Biblical, right? If you want to call her Sarah, that's fine by me. Maybe it'll get us in the mood for the big Jew scene tomorrow? Hey, don't get all offended, people! I'm a Jew boy, right! I can go there! Me and half of Hollywood. Coen brothers shmoen brothers. We'll out-Jew them! We'll out-everything them! Well," Reed said, slipping his arm around Chris and drawing him down into one-on-one mode, "Darlia wasn't so crazy about the name change, not to mention the rest of it. All that silence you put in there. Loved it! Like I always say — less is more." Reed paused, as if expecting a response. He didn't get one. "Look at you. You're as pale as a ghost. I guess there's not enough of that California sun around here for you. Seriously though. The way you stand, the way you move. The way you are. It's just like I imagined him. You're a different person." Reed stared into him with menacing intensity. Then, suddenly, he pivoted. "Alison, a word please?" He pulled her into the corner of the room. Chris stood uncertainly in the middle of the set, acutely aware of the powder on his face and the thin fabric of his pajamas.

ALISON USHERED CHRIS INTO the town car and climbed in beside him. The car pulled away smoothly. Chris slumped in the back seat. He watched Queen Street go by. They passed the café. Chris idly wondered what time it was. The windows in the car were tinted, and the city looked different and distant, vague and dark. It's Friday, he thought randomly. You're off work tomorrow. They rolled west toward the heart of downtown. Alison near him, a scent of fresh flowers. Chris let himself slide closer to her.

"What did he say?" he asked hesitantly.

Alison looked at him. "Oh, nothing really." She tucked hair behind her ear. "We were just talking about arrangements. Tomorrow's shoot. That kind of stuff. That's what you have me for, right?"

"Right," Chris said.

Alison smiled, encouragingly, ironically. Chris couldn't tell. The smooth back seat of the car between them, a gleaming distance.

"There is one thing."

"Oh yeah?" Chris said.

"He doesn't want any more — absences."

Alison's hard stare, as if she could see right through him.

"Right," Chris said nervously.

"I don't want any more either."

The car turned, and Chris pretended to slide a little, hoping they might touch. Absences, he thought to himself.

"You know, Thomson," Alison said, a trace of a warning in her voice. "I almost didn't take this job."

"You didn't?" He tried to keep his tone casual, but he felt suddenly desperate: desperate to know something, anything, about the life of Thomson Holmes.

"I was worried about what people say about you," Alison said, turning to gaze out her tinted window.

"So why did you?" Chris asked quickly. He didn't know. He didn't have a clue. *What people said about him?*

"To be honest, Thomson, the money. I thought, okay, how bad can it be? And if he tries anything, I'll just walk away. It's not like I'm some young starlet who'll do anything for a chance. And then, when you went missing, I thought, great, I never even had a chance. I was surprised. I felt so cheated. And you should have seen Reed." Alison laughed gently now. "He was losing his mind. Just completely freaking out. He kept texting me. As if I knew where you were. As if it was my fault."

"It wasn't," Chris protested. "It had nothing to do with you!"

"You just up and disappear without a word to anyone. And I was like, well, they warned me, right? I can't say they didn't warn me."

"I — that was —"

"Park Hyatt," the driver announced.

"We're here," Alison said.

A doorman opened the side door. Chris hesitated, then reluctantly stepped out. *You've come this far.* They were up on Bloor Street. Chris tilted his head to take in the twenty or so floors above him. The Park Hyatt. He pictured a drugged-out Thomson Holmes, lying naked on a plush oversized bed, watching old black-and-white reruns of *The Twilight Zone*, a full ashtray balanced on his taut stomach. Going into his hotel room. That would be too much. That would be really crossing the line. Where the hell was the guy? He'd disappeared. That much was obvious. They thought he was back. He wasn't back. But he would be.

Alison gently tugged on his arm and gave him a beseeching look that seemed to sum it all up. Be normal now, okay? Chris reluctantly followed her into the posh lobby. He blinked against some anticipated change of space and light that didn't quite

materialize. The lobby, like the interiors of the town cars and the
trailers, was dimly lit. Night in perpetuity. House lights falling.
Art deco tiled floors and a giant Persian carpet. Dark wooden
panels and vaguely modernist, uncomfortable-looking couches
and armchairs. The lobby, too, was a liminal space possessing
the incongruous, timeless feel of a movie set. They could be anywhere, in any time. A manager appeared out of nowhere and
greeted them. A couple checking in looked behind them and
whispered. Before Chris had a chance to assess his escape options,
they were whisked through several ornate lobbies and into an
elevator. Chris had only ever been in the Hyatt once before, when
he was still in high school. Krunk had wanted to sneak into the
once glamorous, now abandoned ballroom left over from the
hotel's glory days. He'd read in a zine called *TOUE — Toronto
Urban Explorers* — that you could reach the floor hiding the
decrepit hall with relative ease. Following the instructions of the
zine, they'd slipped in and taken an elevator to the ninth floor.
They'd wandered through several nondescript hallways until
they'd found the door they thought they were looking for. The
door led to a side staircase, which took them up a short flight of
stairs before ending in another door that was supposedly always
open but turned out to be locked. Krunk had wanted to break
the lock. Chris had convinced him that trespassing was one
thing, breaking and entering was another beast altogether. "Fuck
it," Krunk had said. Instead, they'd wandered the city guzzling
from a jam jar of mixed boozes Chris had siphoned from the
dusty bottles in his parents' liquor cabinet.

The bellhop held the open-door button and gestured them into
a long hallway. Chris followed Alison. Footfalls were muted on
the heavy carpet. Nobody spoke. Chris found himself slowing
down, forcing himself to put one loafered foot in front of the

other. He'd been up since five. He was exhausted. "Here we
are," the bellhop said quietly. Alison unlocked the door with a
key card. The bellhop grabbed the doorknob and held the door
open for them. Chris winced in expectation, half closing his eyes.
Alison moved into the room. She looked behind her. He stepped
forward. The room was dark. It felt empty. The bellhop let go
of the door and rushed ahead to turn on various lamps. Chris
stood in the foyer as his digs were revealed. He saw an expansive suite complete with a living room dominated by a massive
flat-screen TV and a fully stocked, glimmering bar. Patio doors
offered a panoramic view all the way down to the lake. Behind
soft grey clouds, the sun was just a sliver, the scene all but set.

"Thank you," Alison said to the bellhop. She handed him a
twenty. "I'll talk to you later, Thomson," she said, and, before
Chris even realized what was happening, the door closed with a
soft click and they were both gone.

Chris closed his eyes, rubbed them against the palms of his
hands. The room muted the busy city below. Everything seemed
far away. He felt his eyeballs rolling against his palms. He heard
a faint sound, distant laughter, breathing, footsteps. He blinked
furiously, spun around. There was no one. He was alone.

He opened the French doors to the balcony. The city in front
and below, twinkling twilight. Chris traced the outlines of
massive skyscrapers leading down to the black lake, then honed
in on individual office windows randomly flickering into darkness as harried salary workers reluctantly packed it in and
headed home. Chris followed them; scurrying, ant-like in gait
and size, toward the subway. He stared intently, willing himself to be mesmerized by their rhythmic synchronicity, as if they
were part of some gigantic stage direction, extras in their own
lives. But not him. Not the Lost Expert. He goes his own way.

Ha ha, Chris thought nervously, self-consciously. *Where did that come from?* The Lost Expert. Everything has its pattern, its way of being in the world, an inevitable slope that determines how it will roll, in what direction it is most likely to disappear.

He was tired. Exhausted. He'd sit for a minute. Maybe he'd watch a little cable. Five minutes. Ten minutes. Then he'd go. It was time to go. Laurie didn't have cable. She said it was a waste of money. It was the rare thing she and Krunk agreed on. But when Chris went home to visit his mom in Mississauga, the small industrial city half an hour west down the highway she'd moved to after the divorce, he relished in it, whiling away the hours switching between the Weather Channel, obscure European League soccer games, and cheaply made reality shows chronicling the exploits of hoarders, pest controllers, hillbillies, and bounty hunters. Chris stepped toward the couch. *Just for a minute.* Who would suspect him? He didn't know the actors or the director or anyone even remotely related to anything Hollywood. North or otherwise. He could leave now, vanish into thin air, and no one in the world, even once the deception was uncovered, would have any reason to suspect that he, Christopher Hutchins, was the culprit. Krunk was more likely to be questioned. This was the kind of thing he'd love to have staged. Chris smiled at the image, his friend in pedantic mode, lecturing bemused detectives on Hollywood's persistent motif of inner decay, a tired façade covering up the truth of their own complicity in celebrity capitalism's destructive consumerism. He should call him. And Laurie too. Chris leaned forward and picked up the television remote lying on the coffee table in front of him.

A knock on the door. Chris froze. Another knock. "Mr. Holmes?" The voice was tentative, worried about interruption. "Excuse me, Mr. Holmes?" Chris stepped quickly to the door and peeked through the peephole. A man in hotel livery. Chris opened the door. "Good evening, sir," the waiter said. He wheeled in a tray, lifted the silver lid to reveal a single glass of champagne, the bubbles coalescing and popping around a sole red raspberry. "Your cocktail, sir," the waiter said importantly.

"Oh. Ah ... thanks."

"Will there be something else, sir?"

"Ah ..."

Chris looked up at him, actually noticed him for the first time. He wasn't young like the bellhop. He was an older gentleman, in his late fifties, older than Chris's father. Dark complexion, a hint of an accent, maybe South American. The waiter stood in his perfect uniform, a white napkin draped over one arm, and regarded him curiously, one eyebrow raised.

"Sir?"

"Just, uh, just a second ..." Chis said. He dug into the pockets of his new pants and pulled out his battered wallet. His hands were shaking again. He dropped the wallet, and it burst open, spilling old receipts, change, the tips from work he had cashed out into a five and a fifty from the register. Lately, Chris had started converting his tips into bigger bills, the idea, Laurie's idea, being that he would be less likely to break a fifty to buy a coffee, a pint, a popsicle, or a tattered copy of last year's Murakami novel. Laurie said he was terrible with money. Laurie said that he should be saving a minimum of one-third of everything he earned. Laurie could never figure out why he was always one shift away from being broke. The answer, of course, was Krunk, who borrowed twenty or forty bucks off him once a week and seemed to be under the impression that the least Chris could do — if he was going to sell out with his bourgeois job and banker girlfriend — was buy the tickets, post-movie drinks, and greasy Chinese snacks a night out with the great *artiste* required. Sheepishly, Chris scrabbled in the carpet, snagging change and streetcar transfers. The waiter watched, dignified, expressionless, as Chris straightened up, wallet's contents in hand. Chris avoided looking at the motionless older man. Quickly he grabbed a bill, waved it in the air. The waiter took the crumpled bill gingerly in his fingertips. *Shit*, Chris thought as his fifty disappeared.

"And good evening to you, sir," the waiter finally breathed, retreating into the cloistered hallway.

Fifty bucks. An entire morning shift, practically. Chris shrugged. What could he do? It was probably worth it, right? For the day he'd had? He sniffed at the champagne. The bubbles tickled his nose. He'd never had real champagne before. On his and Laurie's one-year anniversary he'd wanted to buy a bottle, but he couldn't afford it, so he'd settled for the next shelf over, cava from Spain. "Also very nice," the guy at the LCBO had assured him with studied dispassion. They'd drunk it out of juice glasses. This was a different beast altogether. The glass was thin and delicate in his big hand. When Chris brought it to his lips, he had the absurd urge to bite down. He drank instead. The taste: sour and dry, then wet and sweet. Had Alison sent this? He imagined her sitting across from him on the settee, looking impassive and perfect, an actress from the age of silent film, big eyes full of mystery watching him drink.

Chris drained the champagne. He'd acted. He'd done it. And the character — the Lost Expert. He had seemed so real.

In the Italian loafers he was quickly becoming accustomed to, Chris padded over to the closed door that led, he assumed, to the bedroom and bathroom. Tentatively, he opened the door. The room was occupied by exactly the kind of bed he'd imagined, an oversized king bulging with gold pillows. It was the kind of bed James Bond would wake up in, a blond and a brunette on either side, both spies, both not what they seemed.

There was a closet and a nightstand and a dresser and another closed door leading to the bathroom. Chris put the champagne flute on the nightstand and inspected its single drawer. Maybe he'd find a bit of cash. *Fifty bucks*, he thought, *and we'll call it even. After all, Holmes, I did your job today*. The drawer was empty. Which was just as well. He wasn't a thief. He didn't even like to jaywalk. He opened the wardrobe. It was filled with clothes, linen suits and tight European jeans dangling off wooden hangers. Weird. No money, no personal effects, just clothes. Where the hell was this guy? All day long, Chris had dreaded the inevitable appearance of Thomson Holmes. Now he kind of wanted him to show up. Just get it over with. They'd get drunk, they'd laugh their asses off. Thomson Holmes would give him the diamond watch off his wrist as a combination memento and bribe — nobody needs to know. Nobody would ever know.

So where was Thomson Holmes?

THE PHONE RANG. CHRIS jerked to awareness. He was sitting, half awake, on the toilet. The soft seat exuded a gentle warmth. It was heated. The phone kept ringing, a trilling over his left ear. Then he noticed it, a cordless mounted above what looked very much like a platinum toilet paper dispenser.

"Hello?"

"Thomson! What are you doing?"

It was Alison.

"Uh."

"Reed is downstairs. He's waiting for you."

"Reed?"

"Why aren't you answering your cell?"

"My cell?"

"I called you three times. What's going on?"

"It didn't —" Chris realized, just in time, that she wasn't talking about the ancient Nokia flip phone with the cracked screen. She was talking about *Thomson's* cell. "I lost it," he blurted.

"You lost it?"

"Yeah. Someone call The Lost Expert." He winced at the lameness of his own joke.

"I'll have another delivered tomorrow," Alison said tonelessly. "I'll arrange for them to transfer your contacts and data."

"Thanks."

"Did you see your new clothes?"

"Yeah, I —"

"Wear the black suit with the turquoise shirt. I'll text him that you'll be right down." She was about to hang up.

"Why?" Chris blurted.

"Why what?"

"Why does Reed want to have dinner with me?"

Alison sighed. "I don't know, Thomson." She hung up.

Chris slumped. Laurie would be heading home; maybe she was already there, getting dinner together, a simple, wholesome meal — arugula and avocado salad topped with yesterday's leftover roast chicken. Champagne swirled around Chris's stomach. *Get up*, he told himself. *Wake up.*

THE ROOM WAS STARK white with a projection of softly tinted lights in varying shapes — stripes, prisms, globes — on the west wall. Chris and Reed sat in a corner table set somewhat apart from the other diners watching the lights rotate through barely perceptible renditions of pinks, purples, and yellows.

"What's this place called again?" Reed demanded.

Chris shrugged. How was he supposed to know? He had no idea where they were. If he got up and walked out the door, he'd probably be as lost as his alter ego Thomson Holmes. He should have been uncomfortable, intimidated. But it was all just too ridiculous. Ignoring Alison, he'd picked out the most movie star outfit he could find in Thomson Holmes's closet — a shark-grey Italian suit showing flashes of a Florida orange T-shirt. He'd posed for himself in the mirror. He looked silly. He looked kind of amazing. It was dress-up, he realized. Krunk on some movie star or other: "It's just clothes! The clothes make the man!" It was fun being Thomson Holmes. The realization gave him a sudden confidence. Brazenly, Chris gazed around the room. Moneyed older couples stared docilely at their plates. *They don't want to be caught looking*, Chris realized.

"And to start, gentlemen? A cocktail, perhaps?"

"Champagne," Reed said to the waiter. He looked over at Chris. "What are we celebrating?"

Chris felt the emergence of a self-satisfied grin. His old self was a million years away. Light-years, he told himself, watching the wall glow and fade, lavender slowly dissolving into a radiant bath of canary yellow.

The waiter returned with a bottle. He said something in French. He was talking to Reed, but looking at Chris.

"Good, good," Reed agreed. With a flourish, the waiter opened the bottle.

"To the new you!" Reed proposed when the glasses were filled and the waiter had retreated a safe distance.

"Yeah," Chris muttered, suddenly ill at ease. Their glasses clinked. Chris could feel the eyes of the other diners. But if he looked around, he knew he'd see nothing but their shadowed profiles.

"So, what's the deal?" Reed blurted.

Chris stared back questioningly, trying to maintain the fixed grin on his face.

"Today. On set. Since you've been back. The way you move, the way you look into the camera, the way you speak. It's like you're a different person."

"I am a different person," Chris said. He felt his heart beating. But he smiled coolly. "I'm The Lost Expert."

"That's just it," Reed grumbled with what Chris was coming to understand as his trademark delighted gloom. "That's just fucking it."

Both men hit the champagne.

"You know, I was going to make changes."

"What?"

"I was going to get rid of you."

Chris willed himself to look up, to look Reed in the eyes.

"Really?"

"Cut the crap, Holmes. Man to man, you knew from the beginning I didn't want you in this thing."

Chris nodded.

"Nothing against you, okay? Did they really think I was going to ruin my movie? Just piss it all away because someone upstairs had a hard-on for Thomson Holmes and the second phase of his so-called career?" Reed peered at him, his eyes angry and piggish beneath his ball cap. Chris stared back. "What, Holmes?" Reed barked. "You gonna cry now?"

Chris smiled genuinely. Something about Reed reminded him of his grandfather. Grandpop had been confident and blunt, a siding salesman prone to saying exactly what he thought — which was usually something preposterous, hilarious, and at

least half true. But when Chris's parents had split up, Grandpop
held his tongue. At the house for dinner and a game of chess
with his grandson, he stared at a crack in the ceiling as Chris
and his mom talked interminable, depressing logistics: what days
he'd be at his mom's, he could call whenever he felt like it, it's
not forever (whatever that was supposed to mean), don't forget
your gloves at your dad's place again. For his part, Chris knew
that Grandpop would get quite the kick out of "Dad's place," the
cheap, undecorated bachelor pad Chris was now consigned to
for half-weeks at a time. But it wasn't funny, really. At his
dad's, he spent his time watching TV and eating freezer-burnt
pizza heated in the microwave. His dad, meanwhile, hid out in
the bedroom, working on an old laptop. Chris pictured himself
and Reed, sitting hunched over the cardboard chessboard, their
faces — young and old — nearly touching.

"Your move, Grandpop."

*"Mine? Already? Ah … okay … lemme see … there it is … I got ya
now, ya little bugger …"*

Reed stopped talking. Or maybe he'd stopped a while ago?
He reached over and filled up Chris's glass. It was empty. Empty
again, Chris thought. He had the sudden urge to giggle. More
champagne, the tiny bubbles popping on his brain making it
hard to think. Reed was going to get rid of Holmes? So maybe
Holmes took off before he could get fired? Or maybe Reed …?
Reed what? Chris's stomach growled. Was there bread or something? He looked around for the waiter. Weren't they VIPs?

"What? What's the problem?" Reed was like an over-percep-
tive animal, a purebred gun dog. He noticed everything. "Drink
your champagne, Holmes. Relax."

Out of nowhere, the waiter appeared, picked up the bottle,

and pointedly topped off their just refilled flutes. Before Chris could ask him for something, a piece of bread, a bowl of nuts, a menu, he was gone again.

"Look," Reed continued. "They wanted you. The money men. The bean counters. I couldn't fight them on it. I knew I couldn't. Not after last time. I lost a lot of their cash on that one. Shit." Reed shook his head ruefully. "I honestly do not know why I bother. Does it even matter anymore? What's one more movie gonna do? So maybe it doesn't matter. Movies don't change the world anymore. They're just entertainment. So I gave in. What choice did I have?" Reed was whispering again. Chris felt heat on his cheeks. He was blushing. It was like being on the subway, a disheveled stranger abruptly crying on your shoulder. "I'm being honest with you, Holmes, which is more than you've ever done for me. I told them, fine, we'll cast him. And here you are, you little prick, making the movie of your life."

Reed gulped champagne; the lights burnt a bright red oval for a few seconds before fading to a pyramid of sombre olive.

"But that's it, Holmes. That's the only thing I'm changing. The last two movies were crap," Reed said. "Really crap. Studio garbage. I kept trying to meet them halfway. Not this time. You got that, Holmes?"

"Sure," Chris said.

"Sure," Reed said. He shook his head, perhaps in disbelief. "Anyway, what if it does matter? There's a chance, right? This could be the one. Couldn't it?"

Reed looked at him, defiant and pleading. How old was Bryant Reed? Chris was bad with ages. Maybe sixty? Seventy? The way he was looking at him, the lines around his eyes, the loose skin pulling his cheeks down, suggested a much older man.

"I want to make one more," Reed said. "Just one more great

one." It was like he was begging. Chris felt the urge to turn away, to lose himself in the blurred mist of colour. But he couldn't. Reed was enlisting him, summoning him, beseeching him.

The restaurant turned blood orange. The waiter set a long, rectangular plate in front of each of them. "Trio of foie gras," he said importantly. "The chef describes this one as a play on the American hamburger, with deep-fried panko onion coating on a fresh-baked mini sourdough. And this one —"

"Just leave the food," Reed barked. The waiter froze. He didn't seem to know what to do. Reed giggled, a jovial, high-pitched whinny. The waiter spun on his shoes and walked off.

Foie whatever, it was delicious. Slimy and meaty, heavy yet weirdly insubstantial. Would they bring more? Who had ordered it for them? Alison? Maybe that's the way it was at this kind of restaurant. Nobody ordered. Nobody asked about the price. Things just arrived. Chris hungrily eyed Reed's plate. The director had taken a tiny nibble of the one on the bun, then grunted and pushed the whole thing to the side.

"What?" Reed said. "You want 'em?"

Chris shook his head, no.

"Go ahead," Reed said, pushing his plate over to Chris's side of the table. Unable to resist, Chris picked one up and demolished it in a single delicious bite.

"So where did you go, anyway?" Reed asked casually.

"What?" Chris said through bulging cheeks. He chewed slowly, buying time.

"What?" Reed scoffed. "Remember when you took off for three days while we sat around on the set pissing money? And you can bet that's coming out of your pay, you little fuck." Reed giggled again. He was a little tipsy now, Chris thought. Chris laughed too.

"No. Seriously. Where did you go?" His bulgy eyes narrowed.

Chris was at a loss. He tried to smile mysteriously.

Reed shook his head. Dismissive? Disgusted? "You got off the plane. You checked into the hotel. And then nothing. Nada. Gone like the wind."

Reed's lips suggested a smile, his beady eyes blazing angrily.

"To the new me," Chris said. He lifted his flute, toasted himself, and drank.

WHEN CHRIS WAS THIRTEEN, the backyard fence had burst into flames. It was just after Halloween, early November, 6:30 p.m., already dark. For as long as he could remember, he'd been a latchkey kid, his parents both working long hours downtown, returning, in their separate cars, rumpled and exhausted. That evening had been no different. He'd done his homework, except for the math. He'd do the math later. Or not at all. Ian, the kid across the street, did his math for him when he asked. Increasingly, Chris had been asking. Things were changing. The wheat separating from the chaff. His parents, once a single, immutable entity, MomandDad, were transforming — ignoring him, fighting with each other, coming and going randomly, unpredictably. Last month, after a particularly voluble dispute, his father hadn't come home from work for several days. Though it upset Chris more than he could understand, it hadn't been that big of a change. The house, which framed the space of his life, remained as it had always been: filled, but weirdly empty.

With Krunk encouraging him, they'd started catching the bus to the west side of downtown. Krunk, pre-contacts, in oversized specs that at least somewhat covered up his burgeoning acne; the both of them gawky and awkward in faded T-shirts and dirty sneakers. In the city, they would browse used bookstores, share heaping platters of cheap Chinese noodles, sneak into R-rated movies. His friend was beefier then. With his pimply face bathed in movie glow he looked like an awkward baby, ugly and bulgy-eyed and beautiful the way only a teenager can be. But that didn't stop him from leaning back nonchalantly, putting his feet up on the back of the seat in front of him, and generally acting as if he'd seen it all before. Chris was the opposite — already tall and lean for his age, but sitting with his arms crossed, his back straight. The movies, replete with every manner of drugs, drinking, and sex, filled him with a sense of expectant dread. Is that what comes next? But how to get to it? And what is it, exactly?

The night of the fire, Chris had been sprawled on the couch, half watching TV. He hadn't had any dinner and had been thinking about microwaving something or maybe even working himself up to scramble some eggs. That '70s Show came on, an episode Chris had seen before. He was ambivalent about the show. The loving Formans were always finding time to bring Eric's wayward group of misfits into the family; no one ever had to be alone, and any other potential outcome turned out to be the result of a momentary misunderstanding. The laugh track spun into a commercial for frozen pizza pockets. The doorbell rang. Expecting some sales pitch, Chris reluctantly padded down the dark, carpeted hallway and into the tiled foyer. The bell rang again before he got there. As he approached the white front door, he noticed there was a strange pattern, a jumpy origami shadow projected against it. It made him turn. A line of bright orange flames cut through the darkness, through the kitchen's bay windows, illuminating the gloomy front hall. The back fence that bordered the small woods behind their house was burning. Chris stared. The doorbell rang again. Sirens swelled in the near distance. It's like something from a movie, he thought.

Chris walked slowly into the kitchen, drawn to the fire, mesmerized. The voices on the other side of the front door got fainter
as he drifted away. He slid open the back screen door and stepped
out onto the patio. Outside, the fire was loud, crunching the air.
Chris stepped off the concrete patio and onto the grass, stiff and
cold under his sock feet. He walked five, six, seven, eight steps
forward. The fire filled his vision. The back fence was in a full
burn. He could feel the heat on his cheeks. He stepped closer.
A cinder hung in front of him before landing on the grass, spark-
ing then smouldering. He put his arm on his forehead, as if to
shield his eyes from a fierce sun. The heat enveloped him. He
tasted smoke.

A hand on his shoulder pulled him back. Chris turned and
saw his mother. He abruptly buried his face in her shoulder,
sobbing. She walked him back to the patio, where they watched
the fire crew arrive and extinguish the blaze.

Now, once again, red flames danced. Thirteen years had
passed. The fire had been traced to a couple of high-schoolers
carelessly discarding their blunts in the dry leaves heaped against
the fence. The house had long since been sold. The sound he
remembered was of his parents splitting apart, like a burning
log suddenly cracking in half. And his grandfather, gasping for
breath. He'd died quickly, it seemed, though the whole thing
happened over a matter of months. Chris mainly remembered
his sense of betrayal followed by keen, irreversible loss. He died.
Just when Chris needed him most, he died. Chris could still feel
it: the heat dancing on his cheeks. It had never left him, never
faded; it had only been waiting, latent in his neurons. Here it
was again — a heat, shocking and distant. An empty void.

The projected blaze turned blue. Chris turned away from the
soft, liminal scene that had gently played with their senses

throughout the dinner of small, strange offerings, elaborately alien foods that seemed designed to evoke the flavours of not just other places but other worlds altogether.

"Earth to Holmes?" Reed said, grimace-smiling. "Usually, they can't get you to shut up. Now I can't get you to say two words in a row."

Chris nodded affably in agreement. Throughout the elaborately drawn-out dinner, Reed had occupied the conversation. Among other things, he'd told Chris the story of the giant trout he'd almost bagged fly-fishing in Colorado. The story was long and involved. It included the exploits of a minor character actor, plus a local stripper, a Comanche guide, peyote, vodka, beer, and a dog, maybe Reed's dog. The longer the story went on, the less Chris followed it. High on champagne, he was content to just be in the rhythm of the words, rolling along with the guttural baritone of Reed's folksy morality play. But Chris was listening carefully now, Reed's change of tone catching his attention. "— thought I was screwed. *Thomson Holmes wants to do a serious picture,*" Reed said, mimicking some self-important executive. "I choked on my coffee. I thought they were shitting me. I thought it was a practical joke. *He really admires your work.* Seriously, I was looking for the hidden camera." Reed grabbed his champagne flute, waving it around, his gravel voice reaching a crescendo. "I didn't know you meant it, Holmes!"

Reed drank. Chris drained his glass. He felt the cold liquid sluice into him, separate him; he wasn't there, not really.

"There it is again!" Reed barked. He slapped the table, and their glasses rattled. Other diners paused their quiet conversations but couldn't quite bring themselves to stare.

"What?" Chris asked.

"That look you just gave me. That's the look you keep giving the camera. Like you're so sure of yourself, you're not even here. You're somewhere else, right? You're *there*. What's the deal, Holmes? They change your meds? Don't take this the wrong way, Holmes, but I always thought of you as the kind of guy who seemed happiest when you were lifting weights in front of a full-length mirror."

Chris felt it too. His face tugged into a smile. He wasn't who he said he was. He wasn't who he wanted to be. He was someone else.

"Whatever! I'm tired of looking at your perfect mug. Let's go smoke some cigars."

Chris shook his head. "You go ahead."

"Cubans, man, they're legal here!"

"No, really, I'm good."

"He doesn't want a cigar," Reed pondered aloud with furrowed forehead. "He's on the cover of *Cigar Aficionado*, but he doesn't want to smoke a cigar." Chris held his gaze until the older man shrugged. And with that, Reed walked away, leaving Chris to contemplate the restaurant's vanity bonfire, burning bushes on white walls, slippery memories infused with Technicolor.

Obviously, Holmes smoked cigars. Boxes of them, sausage stogies hand wrapped by an ancient coven of Havana *abuelas* barely visible as they sit working in their own private clouds of pungently sweet smoke. But not The Lost Expert. The Lost Expert didn't smoke cigars, or anything else for that matter. Was that who he was? Who he wanted to be? It was getting late. Laurie would be worried. He'd just give her a quick call. Reassure her. He didn't have to get into all the details. Anyway, she wouldn't believe it. Who would believe it? He wasn't the most exciting boyfriend, he wasn't overflowing his bank account or working on the cure for a deadly disease or dreaming up the next great Hollywood franchise; but he was present, always around. In the evenings, if Chris had successfully fended off Krunk's advances, they would sit on the couch chatting. Quite often, Laurie would bring up some self-improvement article she'd come across that had reminded her of something — say his difficulty saving, or his lack of concentration, or his inability to settle on a long-term career goal, etc. Chris would listen, nod. It would sink in, he figured. Eventually. They might watch a show on Laurie's laptop or read their books. Sometimes Laurie would ask for a shoulder rub, sometimes they'd play Scrabble. Chris always lost. By 10:30, Laurie was yawning, and they were off to bed.

He'd just give her a quick call before —

"Excuse me, are you ...?"

Chris turned, looked up. A blond woman in a stylish business suit that bared unseasonably tanned arms and long legs stared down at him.

"Yes," Chris said immediately.

"I love your movies," the woman said.

The way she said it, with just a faint tinge of irony. She knew better. She didn't love his movies.

"Thanks," Chris said.

A laugh, suppressed. They both looked over at the table the woman had come from. It was, in fact, the only table still occupied in the restaurant. The other two women at the table, also fashionably made up, gave drunkenly embarrassed thumbs up.

"Please," Chris said. "Sit down."

"Oh no, I don't mean to interrupt. You're with your friend."

"Oh, ah, yeah. He's, uh, not exactly my —"

"I know," the woman giggled. "He's Bryant Reed."

"You recognize him?"

"Oh, well, I'm a bit of a film geek." The woman laughed prettily. She was older than Chris by at least ten years.

"Sit down. He won't mind."

Out of nowhere, a glass appeared for the woman and both their flutes were filled.

"Oh!" the woman said, surprised and pleased.

"Would you like a drink?" Chris managed.

"I said to my friends, 'He looks a little lonely, doesn't he?' And they said, 'Go over, say hi.' So I thought — when else would I ever get the chance to —?"

"What's your name?" Chris asked.

"Daphne."

"Daphne."

Daphne sipped her drink and leaned in.

"Don't get me wrong, we're used to seeing all kinds of — you know, with the film festival and all — and, well, I guess it's, like a, a Toronto thing — I mean," Daphne giggled, "I hope I'm not — bothering you."

Chris shook his head and smiled, encouraging her. Daphne rambled on. Before Laurie, he'd always been fallback material, a second choice, end-of-the-night-you'll-do type. He was tall and skinny, and everyone had always told him he was good-looking, but somehow that had never translated into making him attractive. His mother always said he just needed a bit more in the confidence department — as if you could buy it at Hudson's Bay, save up for it, waft it on, the man perfume that vanished your problems.

Daphne laughed at something she said. She twirled a manicured finger into her long hair and considered him. Chris thought of Alison, her similar gesture; the way she'd looked at him when he'd asked her about his scene in the bedroom. Her smile, a shimmer on her lips. She believed in him. She wanted to believe in him.

The door to the restaurant opened. Chris looked up, relieved. Reed stepped toward the table. "I see you've got company," he said mockingly. "Don't stay up too late now. We've got the big Jew scene tomorrow. And don't even think about ..." He gestured at Chris abruptly, imprecisely, then turned away. Chris flushed. But the embarrassment he felt receded almost instantly as another emotion flooded over him. Relief. Reed was gone. It was over. All he had to do was walk out of the restaurant and into the dark, anonymous city. He'd go straight to Laurie's. He'd shake her awake and tell her everything.

"Wow! Bryant Reed!" Daphne breathlessly gulped at her champagne. Chris slumped. Daphne had perfect posture and beautiful brown-green eyes. In his new world, everything seemed to have a sexier, shinier, more exciting counterpart. Daphne replaced Laurie. Bryant Reed a more accomplished, but just as jaded, Krunk. Thomson Holmes as the new Chris? Sure, why not?

"I could use some fresh air," Chris said. He didn't know how to extricate himself. When he stood up, so did Daphne. The restaurant was empty now. A hostess appeared out of nowhere with the suit jacket Chris didn't remember taking off.

The next thing he knew, Daphne's enveloping perfume was heavy in his nostrils and throat. They were kissing, Chris realized with horror. Like her store-bought scent, Daphne was enthusiastic — her tongue writhed in his mouth. Chris was numb, his arms at his sides in the straitjacket of Daphne's embrace.

Daphne disengaged. Sighing theatrically, she laid her head on his shoulder.

A flash brightened the air. Chris squinted at the fading glare, confused and blinking.

Then he saw the photographer, a balding man leering at them through the long lens of a camera, his stare menacing and hateful. Jesus Christ! Paparazzi! The man, diminutive but with a wiry, muscular frame, clicked the shutter aggressively, catching Chris staring right into the lens. Point and shoot. Your prey frozen in place. Revealing light, surging then diminished.

Chris found himself being pulled into a black suv. The door slammed. Final flashes lit the sky, miniature implosions of time and space obscured by the tinted windows. The vehicle sped away, flattening Chris against the upholstery.

EXT. GHETTO — MID-MORNING
A neighbourhood of small, crowded streets.
There are six- and eight-storey tenement
buildings, their ground floors lined with
shops selling smoked fish, pickles, hardware,
and everything under the sun. THE LOST EXPERT
passes the meat market — live chickens
fluttering piteously in crowded cages. Women
argue with the butcher and his sons in Yiddish.
On the street, almost a dirt track, donkeys
and draft horses slowly drag wagons filled to
bulging. Their drivers, peddlers, shout out
their wares. There is a single car in the
procession, an open-topped Model T, its horn
honking incessantly. The Lost Expert comes
to a stop outside a small bakery. We see that
following respectfully behind him is a retinue
of ghetto Jews, poor but noble. The Jews are:
the imposing RABBI, his ruddy face obscured
by a giant grey beard, his black, ill-fitting
suit flapping in the wind; the rabbi's BEADLE,
a small nervous man, flitting about beside the

rabbi. Behind the rabbi and the beadle are
the TAILOR and his WIFE. The wife, hair in a
kerchief, sobs valiantly and heaves her bosom.
The tailor, gaunt and dressed like the beadle,
in a requisite faded, not quite tattered black
suit, prays to himself, his braided side curls
scraping the sides of his head as he fervently
recites incantations in muttered breaths.

RABBI

Here is where the boy was last seen,
Hashem's will that we will find him!

TAILOR
(half moaning)
Baruch Hashem.

TAILOR'S WIFE
My only son! I sent him for bagels! And a
babka! A chocolate babka!

THE LOST EXPERT
How long has it been?

RABBI
Two days.

TAILOR'S WIFE
(crying out in anguish)
He's a good boy! A good boy!
Never in trouble!

                    RABBI
        Our boys, they do not do that. They do
                not run away.

The Lost Expert nods. He notices, for the first
time, a TALL MAN standing across the street.
His trench coat flaps, but his dark grey fedora
and thin blond hair are seemingly glued to his
forehead, unmoved by the wind. The man's cold,
bloodless blue eyes methodically contemplate the
scene, sizing up guilt and innocence, life and
death. The man pulls the collar of his coat up.
His face disappears into shadow.

                    RABBI
        (following the Lost Expert's gaze)
        They do not help us. They only beat
        us and take our money. Protection! (He
        looks skyward.) There is only one who
                protects us!

                    TAILOR
                Baruch Hashem!

                TAILOR'S WIFE
                (near hysterical)
            My boy! My only boy!

The Lost Expert nods curtly, a gesture to nobody
indicating his solidarity of purpose. He mounts
the stairs to enter the bakery. The beadle makes

to assist the rabbi up the stairs, but the Lost Expert puts up a hand, signalling them to stop. He'll enter alone.

INT. THE BAKERY
The smell is sweet, yeast, cocoa. The BAKER'S WIFE, a wizened woman with a long face, her hair covered with a kerchief, watches him enter. The counter is piled high with braided challahs. The Sabbath is coming. Night will fall and the ghetto will pray for deliverance from their follies, from the follies of their ancestors, from the failings of Adam, of Abraham, of Moses — men, prophets, truthtellers, sinners.

> BAKER'S WIFE (Yiddish w/ subtitles)
> (yelling into the open door of
> the kitchen)
> It's the Goy, Shteymie.

The BAKER, Shteymie, comes through from the kitchen. His beard is matted with flour. He dusts off his hands and stares suspiciously at the Lost Expert.

> THE LOST EXPERT
> The boy was here?

> BAKER
> The boy was here.

THE LOST EXPERT
What did he buy?

BAKER
He bought, the boy, a dozen bagels. He
bought a babka, ehm, a chocolate roll.
He bought a bread wit da kimmel.

THE LOST EXPERT
Kimmel?

The baker gestures to a stack of breads.

THE LOST EXPERT
A rye?

BAKER
(nodding)
With seed.

THE LOST EXPERT
Did he say anything?

BAKER (Yiddish w/ subtitles)
Shlema, did the boy say anything?

BAKER'S WIFE (Yiddish w/ subtitles)
What do I know if he said anything? He
was just a boy buying bread!

The baker looks over at the Lost Expert and
shrugs, spreading his hands.

THE LOST EXPERT
Which way did he go when he left the
store?

The baker points. The Lost Expert walks to the
window, considers the grey street. The rabbi
and the beadle, the tailor and his wife stand
outside, shuffling and keening and praying.

BAKER
You will find him?

EXT. THE SHTETL STREETS
THE LOST EXPERT walks down the main street of
the shtetl, his entourage following behind,
others glancing curiously at the scene. Across
the street, the TALL MAN with the thinning blond
hair keeps pace on the periphery. We can't quite
make out his face. His hands are jammed deep
into the pockets of a long, thin trench coat.
The Lost Expert stops where the road meets a
dark alley and ponders its narrowing depth.
The Lost Expert bends down on one knee and
inspects the ground in front of him. We see a
small-sized shoe print in the scuffed dirt. The
Lost Expert steps carefully over the print and
leads them deeper down the alley of rubble and
cracked pavement. At the end of the alley sits
a decrepit, narrow two-storey house. Its front
window is covered with several layers of filthy
yellow lace curtain.

THE LOST EXPERT
Who lives here?

RABBI
(exasperatedly, to the beadle)
Answer him! Answer him!

BEADLE
It's the Widow Luba.

THE LOST EXPERT
Does she have children?

BEADLE
No. No. She could never bear them.
It killed her husband, to have a
barren wife.

TAILOR'S WIFE
(groaning)
The *alte makhsheyfe*!
(English subtitles: The old witch!)

TAILOR
(to his wife)
Quiet!

The Lost Expert knocks on the rickety wooden
door. The TAILOR'S WIFE cries out incoherently.
At the top of the alley, the tall man in the
trench coat stands motionless, barely visible
in the shadows. The Lost Expert knocks again,

harder. Finally, without a word, The Lost Expert puts his shoulder to the door, which gives way. The gathering gasps. The Lost Expert disappears into the dark of the crumbling house.

INT. THE WIDOW'S BEDROOM
It is dark, the curtains drawn. THE LOST EXPERT pauses in the cluttered room to get his bearings. Behind him, he can hear the RABBI struggling slowly up the rickety stairs, breathing heavily as he takes arthritic steps on swollen ankles. Eyes adjusting, the Lost Expert surveys the room. On the crumbling credenza sits a cheap bottle and two goblets showing the sticky remnants of red wine. Fruit flies scatter as the Lost Expert inspects them. Then he steps to the room's window, overlooking the street.

He sees a ledge covered in bird excrement mixed with caraway seeds. The Lost Expert wheels around, stops in front of the closet door. He pulls on the handle. The closet is locked. The rabbi, the BEADLE, the TAILOR, and the TAILOR'S WIFE arrive, all of them sweating heavily and breathing hard as they cram into the room. The Lost Expert uses his elbow to smash in the closet's thin wooden door. The tailor's wife screams. The Lost Expert wrenches the closet open. The closet is deep and messy, piled with trash bags of clothing, old pillows, and yellowed bedding. The Lost Expert peers in. He yanks away a stained, fringed tablecloth.

A BOY is revealed, peering up at them, eyes
wide, skin luminescent, his side curls swaying
gently. He clutches a half-eaten loaf of bread.
Then, revealing herself looming behind the boy,
is the WIDOW LUBA, a withered figure in black,
her grimace of gnarled contempt etched into the
lines of her shadowed face.

EXT. RIVER PARKLAND — PICNIC SPOT BY THE RIVER —
NOON (FLASHBACK — 1903)
BOY LOST EXPERT and his MOTHER sit, shoulders
touching, on the grass at the bank of the
river, watching the sluggish current. The sun
disappears behind a cloud, and the mother looks
over at the boy's impassive face.

                    MOTHER
              Eat your sandwich.

                BOY LOST EXPERT
        (looking down at the sandwich in his
           hands as if surprised to see it)
                I'm not hungry.

Mother takes a big bite of her half, chews
willfully.

                    MOTHER
                (still chewing)
           It's good. Just try a bite.

Boy Lost Expert shrugs, looks up at the sky.

BOY LOST EXPERT
It's going to rain.

MOTHER
(scrutinizing the sunny skies)
Why do you say that?

BOY LOST EXPERT
(jumping up, shouting)
It *is*! It *is* going to rain!

INT. SHTETL — THE WIDOW LUBA'S BEDROOM — LATE
MORNING (1928)
The WIDOW LUBA lunges, screaming and clawing at
THE LOST EXPERT.

WIDOW LUBA
The boy — he is mine! He will marry me!

The RABBI, suddenly powerful, pulls her off
the Lost Expert and slaps her across the face
angrily.

WIDOW LUBA
The devil to you! *Zol makekhs vaksen*
offen tsung!
(English subtitles: May pimples grow on
your tongue!)

The TAILOR falls to his knees, supplicating
God. The Lost Expert extends a hand to the BOY.
The Widow Luba mutters incomprehensible curses.

Outside, the TALL MAN takes his hands out of his trench coat pockets and walks on.

EXT. THE RIVER PARKLAND — PATH IN WOODED AREA — LATE AFTERNOON (FLASHBACK — 1903)
Thunder rumbles in the distance. BOY LOST EXPERT half-runs, half-trips down a small path, narrow and obstructed by tree roots and large rocks protruding out of the ground. A light rain has started, and the wind is picking up, swirling through trees and along the path, sending a kaleidoscope of leaves up into the air. The sky continues to darken. The boy hears a muted cry coming from just over the next hill. He runs faster. He reaches the top of the hill and sees his mother. Abruptly, he stops running. His mother is lying across the path, unmoving. There is a dark figure over her. The dark figure grabs his mother by the arms and starts to slowly tow her off the path and into the woods. He stands, frozen, watching his mother disappear. Then, finally, he runs down the path and picks up her straw spring hat from where it lies half crushed in the dirt, its peacock-blue bow sullied.

CHRIS BLINKED AND EMERGED. Crew members eddied around him in the small, hot room. A bright light switched off. He felt dizzy, nauseous, as if spinning worlds were colliding — the blinding flash from yesterday — empty air bursting — that strange woman's hot breath on his cheek. Shtetl slums, crazy Yiddish witch crones throwing themselves at him, angry men watching silently from a distance. His stomach tipped. He closed his eyes and shook his head. *Breathe. Just breathe.*

"Anywhere else and we'd be mobbed," Reed announced jovially, appearing at his side. "That's what I love about this place. The people do whatever we tell them! The streets look like whatever you want!"

Chris opened his eyes. The view from out the window. An alley crowded with their film equipment; purposeful people sporting walkie-talkies and baseball caps. Halfway down, he could see flimsy metal balustrades blocking off the curious onlookers being watched by several private security guards and a bored-looking policeman.

"Still," Alison said, "we should get him out of here."

"Right," said Reed. "Let's get him out of here."

Alison led them out of the house. There was a murmur from

the small crowd when they emerged. Alison quickly ushered them through a weedy, abandoned parking lot leading to another side street. A security guard followed them discreetly. To Chris, who had wandered through these streets countless times over the years, everything seemed different, foreign. He was a stranger.

"Nice escape route," Reed said. "You've got yourself a top-notch assistant there. Whaddya pay her? I'll double it." He seemed to be taking a new tone with Chris, chummier and more intimate. Like we're friends now, Chris thought.

"I'm not for sale," Alison said.

"They won't get the Jew stuff," Reed continued, ignoring her. "They'll hate it. But this is the heart. This is what it's all about, right?" Chris nodded, hoping Reed would keep talking. He didn't get it either. Why was the Lost Expert suddenly in a shtetl? Where was all of this supposed to be taking place? He'd kept his eyes open for a script he could read, but nobody seemed to have one, and he hadn't worked up the courage to ask. His only instructions came from Reed, who mysteriously appeared beside him before each scene, whispering murmured bits of dialogue, fragments of a whole that, so far, had completely eluded Chris.

"It's symbolism," Reed continued. "No, it's essentialism. Taking things right down to their essentials. The Jews. The chosen people. Chosen for what? Forever cursed. Fucking wanderers. That's what we are. No one wants us! No one wants to be us. They're lost in the desert, right? But he will. He'll help them. He's drawn to them. He doesn't want to be. But he is. He doesn't know why. Nobody ever knows why they help the Jews."

They were in the park now, Chris realized, nearing the trailers. His head hurt, a throbbing in the frontal lobe, like something was trying to push out. Reed kept talking. Dazed, Chris watched his footsteps, stepping carefully, not wanting to trip and fall in front of Alison, who was walking, tight-lipped, a few steps ahead. Another pulse pushed against his forehead. Chris grimaced. It was cloudy, but the sky seemed much too bright. Maybe Thomson Holmes owned sunglasses? He must own sunglasses. He'd quaffed a lot of champagne last night. At least a bottle. Maybe more. Then *Daphne*. And that photographer. Pointing his camera, like he was going to shoot. His chauffeur-bodyguard had grabbed him, taken him back to the hotel, marched him up to his suite. He'd fallen asleep on the luxurious couch facing Thomson Holmes's giant-screen tv. He hadn't even turned it on. And he'd never called Laurie.

Oh shit. What was the matter with him? Laurie!

"You can't escape who you are," Reed continued. "The Lost Expert tried. He didn't want to be set apart, to be different. But now he sees that he has no choice."

"Like all superheroes," Chris said, suddenly picking up on the thread of Reed's discourse. He was surprised at the definitive tone of his proclamation.

"Yeah," said Reed, stopping and grabbing Chris by the arm and turning him so they faced each other. "You're not as dumb as you look, are you, Holmes?" Reed waited, as if expecting an answer. Chris breathed, focused on breathing. "Just like all the rest of them," Reed went on. "Jew boys! Who do you think invented Superman? A couple of schleppy little Jews."

"He's got a special power," Chris said, getting into it now. "He's got responsibilities. They make him different from everyone else."

"It's a curse as much as anything else," Reed continued. "He'll have to decide. Does he want to fit in? Be accepted? Or be cast out? Which is harder, Holmes? Going along with the bullshit or trying to fight against it? Does it even matter what you decide? To the Jews it does! For the Jews, there's what you do in this world, and there's the world to come. The Messiah returns and raises the righteous! If you believe in all that religious shit." Reed laughed curtly, clearly amused at the idea that Thomson Holmes might have religious beliefs.

"Here we are," Alison said, interjecting. "You should probably rest up before the afternoon shoot, Thomson." She gave Chris an enigmatic yet somehow knowing look. Chris got it. She wasn't happy.

"The thing is, Holmes," Reed went on jovially, "the Jews aren't just symbolic. They're real. They really existed. They don't anymore. Now they're just history. You see me? I'm a goddamn ghost. That's what this is really about. Things get lost, and you can't find them anymore, no matter how hard you look." Reed scuffed at the trampled grass, his faced scrunched like he was about to cry.

"The only thing is —" Chris said.

"What?" Reed barked. "What?"

"When you think about it —"

"What? When you think about what?"

"That scene, finding the boy ..." Chris hesitated.

"Go on," Reed said.

He could feel Alison, next to him, listening quietly.

"Well, it's just — It changes who The Lost Expert is, doesn't it? There's a difference. A difference between being lost and being taken."

Nobody said anything. Wind blew through the trees, and a black squirrel scampered up a beech branch attired with brown, drooping leaves.

CHRIS WAS ALONE IN his trailer.

The cameras, the lights, the crew scurrying about while Reed whispered in his ear. Like a drug, it was all fake, totally pretend. But it was also real.

And last night. Had that been real too? Some sour, boozy tongue in his mouth. The way that Daphne had moved against him, her body pulsing.

Shakily, Chris pushed himself out of the armchair. He poured himself a generous helping of Thomson Holmes's best scotch. He took a mouthful, almost a gulp. Smokey with hints of vanilla and coffee. High-end hair of the dog.

What did he think he was doing? Acting? Krunk said celebrity was nothing more than a shell game. He said famous people were pretenders, human chameleons whose instinct to change colours was what allowed them to effortlessly stay on top of the electronic undercurrents. "Riding the waves," his friend said mockingly, "riding the waves right to the top."

Chris knocked back another dram. The liquid heat sloshed around his empty belly. He slumped back down in the armchair and closed his eyes.

He woke with a start. Alison was there. She leaned forward and put her hand on his forehead. He could see down her creamy top to the lace of her bra.

"Thomson? Wake up! You feel hot. Do you feel hot?"

"I'm fine, Mom," he said. "Really. I'm fine. Don't make me stay home from school. I have an algebra test today."

She tried to suppress it, but a faint smile played across her lips. "Are you always such a smart-ass?"

He shrugged. "Today, I guess. It's not me, anyway. It's the hangover." Chris made a face of regret and pressed his fingers to his throbbing temples.

"Right," Alison said, her voice somewhere between stern and noncommittal.

"Got a bit too —" Chris put on an embarrassed grin.

"It's none of my business, Thomson. What you and Reed get up to."

"Yeah, no. I mean, we didn't —"

"But when Maddy finds out."

"Maddy?"

Alison gave him that look again. Who are you?

"Right, right," Chris said loudly, forcing himself to smile. "Maddy." His skull tightened. His brain felt compressed. "Hey, uh, do you have any Tylenol or something?"

"Tylenol? But you don't —" She shot him another strange who-are-you look, then bustled off to get him the pills.

I don't what? Chris wanted to call after her. Maddy? Alison's smooth palm lingering on the damp of his forehead.

Alison returned with two orange pills and another bottle of water. He took the pills and washed them down.

"Thanks."

Alison nodded. Chris felt sweat on his upper lip. Reflexively, for something to do, he pulled out his phone and flipped it open.

"What is that?" Alison said.

"What?" Chris asked, confused.

"That."

She was pointing to his phone, the old Nokia he had inherited from Laurie when the bank gave the staff new iPhones last year.

"Oh, uh …"

Alison laughed. "Where did you find that thing? Put it away before anybody sees. You're exclusive to Samsung, remember?"

"Oh, yeah. Right."

"Where did you get that thing?"

"I'm not sure," he said lamely.

"God, Thomson." Alison stood, looking at him, hands on her hips. "I'll go check on your new phone. It should be here by now." She moved to the door of the trailer. "I'll be right back. Try and stay out of trouble, okay?"

INT. THE APARTMENT — EARLY EVENING
THE LOST EXPERT lies on his back on the bed in
his shirtsleeves. The usual clamour and bustle
through the open window — shouts, police sirens,
a homeless lady yelling the same obscenity over
and over again. The door opens. SARAH bursts
into the room, the baby on her shoulder. She
approaches the bed with heavy footsteps. She
stands over him, scrutinizing him.

                    SARAH
                  (suddenly)
          Do you think this is a joke?

The Lost Expert doesn't move. His chest rises
and falls, easily, calmly. His eyes stay fixed
on the ceiling.

                    SARAH
                  Do you?

The Lost Expert lies perfectly still. Outside,

another siren. Sarah walks over to the window,
slams it closed.

                    SARAH
                  Answer me!

                THE LOST EXPERT
            I was listening to that.

                    SARAH
             (suddenly uncertain)
              Listening to what?

                THE LOST EXPERT
                 (sitting up)
             The noises. The outside.

Sarah looks at him like she's pondering an alien
species. Finally, she takes the baby off her
shoulder and thrusts it at the Lost Expert.

                    SARAH
        Here. Look at him. You have a son now! Do
        you want to ruin his life? Do you? Look
          at him! What's the matter with you?

                THE LOST EXPERT
          (sitting up and taking the baby)
          They saw my classified, in the *Post*. A
        little boy was missing. They needed help.

                    SARAH
                 (near tears)
        What classified? What are you talking
                    about?

                 THE LOST EXPERT
          I've quit my job. And school.

                    SARAH
                  (stunned)
                    What?

        The Lost Expert gently takes her hand.

                 THE LOST EXPERT
       Sarah, they're people, like anyone else.

                    SARAH
          Have you gone completely mad?

                 THE LOST EXPERT
          He was barely more than a baby.

                    SARAH
                 (softening)
                How old was he?

                 THE LOST EXPERT
          He was five. He was the son of
                  the tailor.

                    SARAH
      But … how are we going to live? I don't
          suppose they paid you?

The Lost Expert swings himself off the bed. He
puts the baby in his bassinet then leads Sarah
to the kitchen. He opens the pantry. The shelves
are filled with breads, bagels, and cookies.
Sarah stares at the overflowing shelves.

                    SARAH
            You are. You are crazy.

The Lost Expert takes a bagel. He bites into it.
He chews methodically, slowly.

INT. RUNDOWN LUNCHEONETTE — AFTERNOON
THE LOST EXPERT opens the door to the diner.
He is carrying the newspapers under his arm,
along with his notebook and pen. The small
luncheonette is mostly empty, patronized only
by two elderly women who fall silent when he
enters and a homeless man pouring heaping spoons
of sugar into his cup of coffee. The Lost Expert
takes his usual seat at a back table. The women
whisper to each other, scowl at the Lost Expert,
and noisily pack up and leave. The waiter
watches them leave then reluctantly approaches
the Lost Expert.

                  THE LOST EXPERT
                Good afternoon.

WAITER
(grimacing)
If you say so.

THE LOST EXPERT
Coffee please. And something for my
friend over there. Whatever he wants.
And …

WAITER
Yeah?

THE LOST EXPERT
(hopefully)
Any messages?

WAITER
(shaking his head, disgusted)
Messages? Plenty a' messages. Threatening
you, calling you kike lover, threatening
me. Someone left a pig's head for ya by
the back door, I almost broke my neck on
that thing. One guy said he was going
to burn the place down. Look, don't take
this the wrong way. I think you're all
right, man. But we're barely making it
as it is. You know what I mean?

THE LOST EXPERT
(standing up and putting a dollar bill
on the table)

I understand. I'm sorry for the trouble
I've caused you.

The Lost Expert starts to walk toward the door.

WAITER
Hey! Wait!

THE LOST EXPERT
(turning)
Yes?

WAITER
Can you really? How did you find …?

EXT. RIVER PARKLAND — WOODED PATH — LATE
AFTERNOON (FLASHBACK — 1903)
BOY LOST EXPERT watches his MOTHER being slowly
dragged into the woods. He tries to yell, but
nothing comes out. There is the menacing rumble
of thunder. Lightning flashes overhead. The boy
looks up.

CUT TO

FATHER gets on a bus, an old, faded rucksack
slung over his shoulder.

CUT TO

Dark, ominous clouds; the sky opens up; rain
falls in dark, heavy sheets.

                                    CUT TO

A flash of lightning above the boy. Thunder
booms. Trees all around the boy ignite. More
lightning and thunder through the jutting
flames. The storm is just overhead.

                    BOY LOST EXPERT
                    Momma! Momma!

We see a slow reveal pull back gradually forming
into a bird's-eye view of the boy's immediate
surroundings; then the entire forested area;
then the region, the state, the country, and
beyond, all of it surging through the boy's
mind.

                                    CUT TO

His mother, dragged through a swampy area by her
arms. She wakes up, kicks her legs frantically,
and twists out of the hold of the dark figure.

                    BOY LOST EXPERT
            (quietly, in awe, now standing in a
                    circle of flame)
                    Momma ...

The fire abruptly extinguishes. The rain stops
as quickly as it started. The boy looks around
him, at first in wonder then with purposeful
determination. He plunges into the woods.

INT. DINER (1928)
THE LOST EXPERT staggers, almost falls.

                    WAITER
              Hey, you okay?

                THE LOST EXPERT
                   What?

                    WAITER
                 You okay?

The Lost Expert hurries out of the diner and
into the gloom of the street.

CHRIS WAS ALONE IN the wide back seat. The driver took a slow, gentle turn, and Chris felt the brand-new phone in his pocket push against his hip. Alison had given it to him at the end of the long day. They'd done three scenes. Reed had been ecstatic. He kept shouting expletives. He talked about the dailies and how terrific Chris looked in them. He hugged Chris and told him the dailies were amazing. Had he seen them? He had to see them!

Awkwardly, Reed's enthusiasm did not extend to other actors in the scenes. Darlia Cross, the actress playing Sarah, was ridiculously famous in her own right. But Reed said nothing about her. Chris was becoming increasingly conscious of his co-star's frosty silences before, during, and after shoots. Bizarrely, he found himself flashing her reassuring smiles whenever he caught her eye. Once, between takes, he even told her what a great job she was doing. She ignored him.

After each scene, even as Reed was still ranting and pronouncing, Darlia was enfolded by her entourage and swept away. It was unnerving: her icy green stare shifting from rage to compassion to, when the cameras were turned off, blank disinterest. They were shooting a movie together, playing husband and wife. But he hadn't yet had a single conversation with her.

Chris wanted to tell her not to worry. He wanted to tell her that there wasn't really a Lost Expert; there wasn't even a Thomson Holmes. He couldn't say that. Could he? Krunk's favourite Godard movie: "If there's nothing to say, let's have a minute of silence." "You can be so stupid sometimes," responds the Darlia-like love interest played by the gorgeous, mysterious Anna Karina, also Godard's young wife at the time. *Band of Outsiders*, Chris thought, remembering one of Krunk's lecture-rants. A movie about a trio of would-be robbers that's really about bank robber B-movies. Was Reed's movie also a movie about movies? Maybe that's why it refused to coalesce into any recognizable genre. Lulled by the smooth ride, Chris imagined The Lost Expert's bizarre, horrifying pastiche of an origin story — a weird aside channelling *Shazam!* and *Creature from the Black Lagoon.*

The town car braked, and Chris shifted awkwardly, feeling the new phone in his pocket, thinner yet heavier. He resisted the reflexive urge to consult it.

"Here," Alison had said. "Don't lose this one. And answer it, okay?"

"Okay, okay," Chris had said, pretending to be sheepish.

"They've transferred all your data over. You have a bunch of messages," Alison had noted. "Maddy called twice. She's on that spiritual retreat thing, so she must be pretty concerned."

"Maddy … right." He'd heard that name before.

"And your father called. And some other guy who didn't say much, but —"

Chris held up his hand.

"What?" Alison said.

"Maybe we'll talk about this later?"

"You don't want your messages?"

"I'm just — I'm really trying to stay in the moment. Is that okay?"

"Oh, okay." Confusion bordering on worry. Something else, though, too. Wonderment. Respect? Either way, Chris couldn't help it. He didn't want to know about Maddy's spiritual retreat and Thomson Holmes's father or anything else about Thomson Holmes's world. He was in too deep already. Was Holmes a good son? Chris doubted it. "Well, look at the dailies at least," Alison concluded warily. "Reed wants you to. They're on your phone."

He stepped out of the elevator and followed the porter to the — to his — room. The bellhop opened the door, turned on the lights, and asked him if there would be anything else. "No, no," Chris muttered. He didn't meet the young man's eye. He had nothing to tip him with. Just a last tattered five-dollar bill. He couldn't give the guy his last five. He needed it for the subway. Or else he'd be walking home. After a prolonged hesitation, the bellhop bid him a disappointed-sounding goodnight and softly slipped out of the penthouse suite, closing the door behind him.

Now Chris was alone. It felt like he hadn't been alone since he'd stumbled into the park after his shift. Which was when? A day ago? Two? He took off his light black coat, an Armani made of a shiny microfibre that slithered against him like it was alive. He held it. He wasn't staying. He couldn't stay. His stomach grumbled. He was hungry. Movie stars, it seemed, didn't really eat much. He sat on the couch. He needed to think. Or maybe it was the opposite: he needed to stop thinking altogether. He picked up the remote, turned on the TV, then muted it. He flipped blankly through the channels. His phone tremored briefly — the new Samsung. Incoming, Chris thought. A text or an email. He dropped the remote in his lap, pulled out the old Nokia, and called Krunk.

BY THE TIME THE suite's cordless rang, Chris was lying prone on the leather settee, his shoes off, his eyes closed. First, he fumbled for his old Nokia, then for the brand-new Samsung, and then, finally, he realized that it was the room phone and he reached over to the side table, nabbed the receiver, and delivered a curt hello.

"Yes, sorry to disturb you, Mr. Holmes, but your guest has arrived?" The way the concierge said it, oozing distaste for whatever was in front of him, Chris knew immediately who he was referring to. "A Mr. Tokes."

"Tokes?" Chris stifled a laugh. He'd told Krunk not to use his real name. "Uh, yes, thank you, please send him up."

Chris hung up, liking the way he'd responded to their bent-over-backward politeness with an affected air of patrician indifference. Then he thought of the young bellboy's disappointed look. They'd bring him up and want a tip. Maybe Krunk would have some cash? Yeah, right. From what Chris could tell from his extremely limited time in the celebrity stratosphere, Thomson Holmes was expected to tip everyone, all the time, compulsively. And not just a buck or two. Apparently the rich travelled in a flurry of twenties and fifties. The way the hotel staff looked, the obsequious shift of their eyes, the regretful stance of lingering hopefulness. It was painful. Whatever, Chris thought. Tomorrow was Monday. Back to the breakfast shift.

The bellhop knocked, and Chris opened the door. Krunk walked in, wearing a hoodie with a ripped pocket, a pair of tattered yellow corduroy trousers, and oversized mirrored sunglasses. He looked like a cross between a trucker hat hipster and an incel. That wasn't exactly the image they'd discussed over the phone. Chris had suggested sunglasses, but also told him to dress up a bit, to try to fit in.

Almost inevitably, Chris felt himself extending his last five to the bellhop, who slickly accepted the blue bill. The bellhop gave a slight bow of thanks and asked if they needed anything else before smoothly turning on his heels and exiting the room. The door clicked softly shut. Krunk pulled off his sunglasses. He blinked a few times, his yellow-brown pupils showing their permanent red tinge, the result of near-constant all-nighter screening sessions. He flipped the hood off his head and took in Chris's acid-washed jeans and Euro-cut dress shirt ensemble.

"Holy fucking mother of a rat's anus!"

"I know. I know. They think I'm —"

"Thomson goddamn Holmes!"

Chris couldn't help it. He started laughing. So did Krunk. Krunk laughed like a braying donkey. Chris felt tears rolling down his cheeks, spilling out. "Nice shirt," his friend said, and they both cracked up again. "Agggh!" Krunk screamed at the top of his lungs. "Give me a hug, you crazy fucker." They embraced tightly. The familiar odour of used fry oil, day-old coffee, and stale beer. Chris closed his eyes and breathed in deeply.

They toured the suite and then stepped out onto the balcony. It was a cool night, getting cooler. The city below felt far away, streetlights lit up like distant stars.

"Nice view," Krunk said.

Chris nodded. "I guess this is how the other half lives."

"More like the other half a percent," Krunk snapped.

Chris wrapped his fingers around the cold metal of the railing. He leaned out toward the point where the city met the lake and seemed to plunge into vast emptiness. "Take deep breaths," he heard Laurie say. Laurie had started going to yoga on Sunday afternoons. She was trying to get Chris to go with her. She would come home and say, "You're breathing all wrong. Here, like this. From the centre."

"So …" Chris said. He was waiting for his friend to take over, to explain to him what he'd been doing and what he should do next.

"Fuck." Krunk pronounced. "Fuuuuuuuuuuuuck."

"Yeah," Chris said.

The Nokia vibrated quietly in one of his pockets.

"That'll be Laurie," he said.

"You better answer it."

"I'll call her back."

"Dude, answer it! She's seriously freaking out. She's called me like ten times. I was like — he's your boyfriend. How the eff should I know where he is?"

Chris pulled out the phone. It stopped ringing.

"Answer your phone. She was really worried about you. Couldn't you have called her or something?"

Chris didn't reply. He tracked a plane descending. Krunk, the king of inconsideration, was trying to make him feel guilty? He was the one who was always teasing him about his short leash and even shorter cock.

His phone, vibrating again. Same caller.

"Just answer it," Krunk barked. He stomped inside.

"Laurie?"

"Chris, oh my god! Are you okay?"

"I'm fine. I'm fine."

"I've been calling for days."

"I know. I know. I'm really sorry."

"Where are you? I thought you were …" Laurie stops, a sob caught in her throat. "I called your mom, the restaurant. I was just about to call the police."

"No, no, I'm okay," Chris said.

"Where are you?"

"I got a new job," he said brightly.

"What? What are you talking about?"

"Out of the blue, I got this job. On a movie set."

"On a movie set?"

"Yeah, it's really cool."

"When did this happen?"

"Uh, Friday. After work. I was just walking home when all of a sudden I ran into this guy I knew. And he asked if I had a few hours to help out because they were super short-staffed, some kind of flu bug. So I said okay. And I ended up working, like, really, really late."

"But you never came home! I was up all night worried!"

"I know, I know. I'm so, so sorry. I just — I was working so hard I lost track of time."

Chris gulped for air. Krunk said all movies were fiction and all fictions were lies and that the best lies adhered so closely to the truth, they made a whole new reality. Whatever that meant.

"You couldn't have called me once? This whole time?"

Laurie was seriously pissed. This was not progress.

"I know, I know. I'm sorry. I screwed up. I was just working and working and working. It was really crazy. They hired me! I worked all day. And I'm working tonight."

"They hired you?"

"Yeah. And they pay really well! Like, unions and stuff."

"That's great! But, Chris, honestly, you're like a giant seven-year-old. You can't just disappear. You need to call, no matter how busy you are."

Chris felt relief blossom in his chest. She believed him. She was forgiving him. He also felt a twinge of annoyance. Krunk and her, lecturing him like he didn't have a clue. What if they hadn't hired him? Anyway, why had he said that? Now she was going to start asking about his new job.

"I know, I know, I'm sorry."

"I'm just glad you're okay. And you got a new job! That sounds like so much fun. Is Krunk working there, too?"

"No, no," Chris said jovially. "It's just me."

"Great!" Laurie said.

"Well, anyway, I have to get back to work."

"You do?" Laurie sounded both enthusiastic and disappointed.

"Yeah. I'm working all night."

"All night?"

"But I'll be back tomorrow afternoon. We'll have a nice dinner."

"Oh, well. Okay. I'll see you then, I guess. Just don't disappear. And answer your phone!"

Chris flipped the Nokia closed.

Through the glass doors, he watched Krunk inspecting the shimmering bar of high-end liquors. He was shaking his head. Chris couldn't tell if it was in response to the conversation he had just overheard or the abundance of untouched top-shelf booze the hotel provided. At any rate, he'd lied through his teeth. Laurie had barely put up a fight. She was so eager for him to do something with his life that she could just forgive his complete disappearance for two whole days. Or had it been three? Chris knew he should be relieved. Mad at himself, if anybody. Instead, he felt an anger welling inside him: a bitter oozing, compelling and familiar. The look on the face of the paparazzo who'd caught him making out with that woman. Daphne. He hated Thomson Holmes. He hated him more than anyone else in the entire world. And Daphne, draping herself over him like a fur. Her tongue wriggling in his mouth ...

What was wrong with him? What was he doing?

"What are we waiting for?" Chris said loudly as he came back inside. "Let's have a drink!"

"Are you crazy?" Krunk's reedy voice was higher than usual, almost cracking. "When we walk out of here, they're going to be scouring the place. It'll be CSI meets CSIS when they find out about this. They'll be like, who *was* that guy? Fingerprints, hair samples, DNA, everything, man. Everything."

Chris put his hands in the pockets of his acid-washed jeans. Just as quickly, he pulled his hands back out and ran his fingers through his hair.

"You don't seem to realize how messed up this is," Krunk said.

"Yeah, well," Chris said nonchalantly, "I already touched stuff." Seeing Krunk's scowl, he quickly went on. "You can take your glass with you. If you really think —"

He poured two glasses from a gold bottle labeled Hakushu 18 and handed one to Krunk, who took it reluctantly and didn't drink. Chris took a swig. The booze felt good on his scuffed throat.

"You don't even look like him," Krunk complained, watching angrily.

"C'mon, man," Chris said vaguely.

"Thomson goddamn Holmes."

"You want room service? We could get room service."

Krunk put his glass down hard.

"Don't you get it, man? This isn't a joke! For one thing, you are impersonating a guy worth millions. Hundreds of millions."

"Yeah." Chris scrunched up his face. "But it's not like I — I mean, I didn't touch his money. And, anyway, I didn't mean to."

"You didn't mean to?"

"It was an accident."

"Listen to yourself. You think you can just tell them, 'Well, you know, I didn't mean to impersonate one of the world's most famous and richest men. It was an accident.' You think anyone is going to believe you didn't stage the whole thing? Disappear Thomson Holmes, star in his movie, sleep in his suite!"

Chris drained his glass.

"I haven't done anything wrong," he snapped.

Krunk looked at him disbelievingly.

"But you're wearing his clothes! You're sleeping here, for fuck's sake!"

Chris didn't answer.

"So where is he? Where is he, then?"

Chris shrugged.

"You don't know? He could walk through the door right now!"

"He hasn't, though," Chris said weakly.

"Any second!"

"Bryant Reed said I was giving the best performance of my life."

"Of your life?" Krunk stepped close to Chris and leaned in, spitting a little as he declaimed, "You are not Thomson Holmes! This is not your life. Thomson Holmes is a world-famous celebrity asshole. And he's missing. What if he's dead? What if he's kidnapped? Who do you think's going to get the blame? Or what if he's alive, what if he's fine and downstairs in the lobby right now asking for the key to his fucking penthouse suite? Then what?"

As if on cue, a phone rang. Both of them startled. It was the other phone. The new phone. Chris looked at the display. It was Alison. Krunk stared at the gleaming gadget, his eyes bulging.

"They gave it to me. It's Alison. My assistant."

Krunk shook his head. He picked up his glass of scotch and

drank. He carefully wiped the surfaces of the glass with the sleeve of his hoodie. The phone stopped ringing.

Chris didn't know what to say. He'd never seen his friend so rattled before. "I know how crazy this looks. But I —" His anger was gone. He just wanted Krunk to realize, to understand, that what had happened wasn't — he wasn't impersonating anyone. Or if he was, it wasn't the person Krunk thought it was. "The movie. There's no script. Before each scene, Reed comes around and tells me what's going to happen. And then I just improvise."

"You improvise?"

"Yeah, like, the dialogue and stuff. I don't know how to explain it. It just takes over."

"It just takes over," mimicked Krunk, adding a high pitch to his tonal nasality. Something flashed in his eyes. Chris stepped back, surprised. The photographer. Krunk. Both of them. Jealous, Chris thought, though he knew that wasn't it. At least not exactly.

"We gotta get out of here," Krunk said. "Right now. How do we get out of here? Maybe there's a stairway, there must be, like, a fire exit? Do you know what they'd do to us if we got caught in here?"

Krunk snatched the empty glass out of Chris's hand and started wiping the sides clean with his hoodie sleeve. "Get your stuff or whatever," he said. He put the glass down and headed to the door of the suite.

Then he looked back at Chris, who shrugged again and said, almost sadly, "I don't have any stuff."

"Then let's go!" Krunk pulled the sleeve of his hoodie down over his hand and turned the knob of the door to the hallway. The Samsung rang again, loud in the sepulchral silence. "Turn that thing off, will you?" He led them past the elevator toward the dim glow of an end-of-corridor door barely lit by an emergency exit sign. Impatiently, Krunk pushed at the door, which groaned then reluctantly opened to reveal a bare concrete stairway. "C'mon," he said, looking back at Chris. "Hurry up."

"Dude," Chris said, "we're on the thirtieth floor. Let's take the elevator."

"Not safe," Krunk barked. "Cameras in the elevators. Cameras everywhere," Krunk muttered, jamming the cheap sunglasses back on his face 'and pulling his hoodie over his buzz cut. He moved into the stairway and began descending, one heavy booted footfall at a time.

"Okay," Chris said faintly. "Geez. Wait up."

"When we get out of here, we're gonna get rid of our clothes," Krunk said between heavy breaths. He was dripping sweat. Chris thought he looked ridiculous, in his sunglasses and hoodie, like one of those super fat guys at the beach who tries to cover up his grossness in a massive Hawaiian shirt and rustic straw hat. "Everything goes in the garbage bag. Mine too. They could match fibres."

Chris grunted. Twenty-plus floors still to go. His shins were starting to hurt. Fibres. Fuck you, fat-man-on-the-beach. Fuck you and your fibres. He picked up the pace, his Italian loafers slapping the metal stairs in flat counterpoint to the thump of Krunk's heavy boots.

After another ten floors, Krunk stopped. "I need a break." Breathing heavily, he pulled a smashed pack of cigarettes out of the pocket of his hoodie, but didn't tap one out. "Jesus," he gasped.

Thomson Holmes's phone rang again.

Chris pulled the phone out of his pocket. It was Alison for the fourth time.

Krunk looked at the phone like it was diseased. "Take the battery out of it. They've got GPS, they can track you with that."

"Nobody's tracking me," Chris said.

"How do you know?"

The phone stopped ringing, then rang again.

"Give it to me." Krunk yanked it out of Chris's hands. While Chris watched, he carefully wiped down its shiny surfaces with the sleeve of his hoodie. What about fibres? Chris wanted to blurt. Cradling it in his sleeve, Krunk bent down and gingerly slid the phone onto the landing.

Anger surged through Chris again.

"We're just going to leave it here?"

"Yeah. Let's go."

They scurried downwards, the abandoned phone bleating into empty space. Chris pictured Alison dialling, dialling, leaving messages in her soft, persistent voice, the phone, illumined by her presence, buzzing soulfully, pining for him.

Eventually, they reached bottom. They stood, panting and sweaty, in front of a thick metal fire door. Its high glass window was grey. Soft light filtered through. "This had better not be locked," Krunk said grimly. He pulled down the sleeve of his hoodie, then grasped the handle of the heavy door and pushed through. They stumbled into the gloom of an empty, unadorned back passageway. "Get outta here," Krunk was muttering. "Take the subway. Faster. More anonymous." He led them along the corridor, then through a door. The door turned them out into a carpeted hallway near the main-floor elevator area just off to the side of the check-in. Krunk, moving quickly now, shoved his sunglasses back up the bridge of his nose, tugged his hoodie into place, and plunged into the main lobby. Chris followed but was almost immediately intercepted by the hotel concierge on duty, who cut him off from Krunk, his arms waving like the wings of a disturbed peafowl.

"Sir, sir! Sorry to disturb you! There is an urgent message from —"

"Thomson!" Alison called, jumping up from a chair and rushing over. "There you are. Where have you been? Why aren't you answering your cell?" Alison's soft brown hair glimmered in the soft lobby lights as she shook her head indignantly. Chris felt suddenly relieved. Here was Alison. Looking for him. "You're late! They're waiting for us on set!" Realizing that people in the lobby were listening, Alison lowered her voice. "We'll discuss it on the way." She took Chris's arm, felt the shirt, hot and wet. With a quick glance, she saw that Chris was drenched in sweat. "What have you been doing this time?" Not waiting for an answer, Alison started to pull him through the lobby. Chris resisted for a moment, then let himself be led. They moved past Krunk, some guy in a weird get-up Alison didn't even notice.

A car idled out front. The driver closed the door after them. Chris caught a last quick glimpse of his friend, slouched low, hoodie pulled down past his forehead. Chris raised a hand, pushed his palm against the cold window. Krunk scowled and shook his head. The limo lurched into traffic.

INT. STREETCAR — MID-MORNING

THE LOST EXPERT, pale and weary, rides the
streetcar, which is full but not crowded, the
bulk of the crush having already exited near the
centre of the city. Outside, the intersection
is a sea of women clutching parcels to their
chests, hawkers and newspaper boys, panhandlers
and heckling drunks diving to avoid sharply
dressed men in Model Ts. The seat next to the
Lost Expert is taken up by a MAN IN A PINSTRIPED
SUIT. He holds the *Daily News* tabloid up in
front of his face. We see headlines: "Lindbergh
Prepares for Next Adventure"; "Germany
Protests Restrictions"; "Allan Proposes Cut to
Immigration". The Lost Expert looks out the
window. There are campaign posters plastered to
every utility poll: *Join Allan's Army*, *We Are
Stronger Than We Know*. The streetcar clears the
crowded intersection and lurches ahead. The man
lowers the paper.

JOEL MCCANN
What a display! We gotta get this city
cleaned up!

THE LOST EXPERT
(wary)
It could certainly benefit from some
improvements.

JOEL MCCANN
(pointing at a passing Allan's Army sign)
He's the man to do it, I'd say.

THE LOST EXPERT
I try to stay out of politics.

JOEL MCCANN
You're a smarter man than me! Hey, you
look familiar. Have we met?

The Lost Expert considers the man, who has pale,
watery blue eyes and a soft, forgettable, not
quite pudgy face.

THE LOST EXPERT
I don't think so.

JOEL MCCANN
Say, didn't I see you in the paper?
Aren't you that guy, the guy who found
that kid?

THE LOST EXPERT
Yes, that's me.

JOEL MCCANN
Well, I'll be. And you really found that
Jew boy?

THE LOST EXPERT
I just try to help.

JOEL MCCANN
Modest too!

The streetcar slows.

CONDUCTOR
Beltfield. Beltfield next.

JOEL MCCANN
Is this your stop?

LOST EXPERT
No, I'm on until Westdale.

JOEL MCCANN
(jovially)
Back to the Jews, huh?

The Lost Expert looks out the window.

JOEL MCCANN (CONT'D)
Hey no offence! No offence, bud! Here,

let me properly introduce myself.

Joel McCann extracts a business card from a
silver case and passes it over to the Lost
Expert. *Joel McCann, Senior Advisor, Allan for
President.*

                    THE LOST EXPERT
          (glancing at the card then immediately
                    passing it back)
            Like I said, I'm not interested in
                        politics.

                    JOEL MCCANN
          Now, I respect that, I really do. But
          this is an awfully important election.
          Look around you. Look at all this mess!
          Our cities are crumbling. Families are
          going hungry. We've got a chance here for
          real change for the first time in a long
          time. And we sure could use a man like
                    you in our corner.

                    THE LOST EXPERT
              You don't need my help.

                    JOEL MCCANN
            We all need help! This country needs
                        help!

The red brick walls of the increasingly packed
tenements hurtle by.

JOEL MCCANN

Mr. Allan, I know, would love to have you
with us. A man with your unique abilities
with the leader of the country behind
him. Just imagine the possibilities!
The way I see it, Mr. Allan could be an
exceptionally good friend to someone
like yourself. Just look at Lindbergh.
With the right friends and the right
direction, well! A man can really
get ahead!

THE LOST EXPERT

I appreciate that, Mr. McCann. But as
I said, I really prefer to stay out of
politics.

CONDUCTOR

Union, Union next.

JOEL MCCANN
(unfazed)

Of course, of course … the little
Jewish boy. We get it, really, we do.
Look, just between you and me,
Mr. Allan is actually very sympathetic
to their situation. That aspect of
the campaign has been overblown.
There's a certain working man's part
of the voting public that responds
to that kind of a tone. Well, you
understand, I'm sure! It's unfortunate.

But you'd be surprised at how open
Mr. Allan is.

THE LOST EXPERT
Is that true? Allan isn't against
the Jews?

JOEL MCCANN
I'm sure he'd like to hear your views on
the matter.

THE LOST EXPERT
Me? Why?

JOEL MCCANN
These are unusual times. And you're an
unusual person.

CONDUCTOR
Parkville. Parkville next.

JOEL MCCANN
(getting up)
This is my stop. It was nice talking
to you. Here. Keep my card. You never
know.

Accepting the card, the Lost Expert watches
through the window as Joel McCann steps off the
streetcar, letting the day's newspaper fall from
his hands onto the dirty street. The newspaper
swirls in the wake of the departing streetcar.

INT. JEWISH BAKERY — MID-MORNING
The bakery is full of PALE, BEARDED MEN with
dark side curls hanging out of battered black
hats. They sip watery coffee while talking
worriedly to one another in Yiddish.

                    ESTHER
          (gruffly, putting down a plate of
              Mandelbrot cookies)
                    Here.

                  THE LOST EXPERT
                  What's this?

                    ESTHER
          Eat a little something.

                  THE LOST EXPERT
                  Thank you.

                    ESTHER
                   (kindly)
          Esther. My name is Esther.

                  THE LOST EXPERT
               Thank you, Esther.

                    ESTHER
      Things will be hard for you now. Because
                  you helped us.

THE LOST EXPERT
I did what anyone would do.

ESTHER
(pushing the plate closer)
Even a big hero has to eat.

INT. JEWISH BAKERY — LATE AFTERNOON
The RABBI comes into the bakery. A few slumber-
ing old men raise their heads, mutter blessings
and greetings, and go back to sleep. The rabbi
takes the seat across from THE LOST EXPERT.

RABBI
(in accented English)
A blessing on you and on all the
righteous amongst the gentiles!

THE LOST EXPERT
Thank you, Rabbi.

RABBI
I'm glad to see you again.

They are interrupted by ESTHER'S MOTHER, who
bustles over with tea.

RABBI
(Pouring tea, casting a disapproving
glance at Esther's mother as she leaves)
Nuh, she forgot the sugar. (whispering)
She does it on purpose.

THE LOST EXPERT
(taking a sip)
It's already sweet.

The Rabbi drinks then makes a face.

RABBI
She does it on purpose!

The Rabbi puts his tea down.

RABBI
This man, Allan. He says he will build a
wall, wall in the Jews. Once they wall us
in, they will starve us. They will deny
us medicine. Disease will spread. We will
die in the streets like dogs.

THE LOST EXPERT
Rabbi, it's just the promises they make
to get people to vote for them. Maybe
things won't be so bad.

RABBI
(resigned)
From your lips to God's ears! But in the
meantime, what will be will be. *Hashem*'s
way or man's way. Each of us decides.

THE LOST EXPERT
What do you mean, Rabbi?

RABBI
(suddenly excited)

We decide! We choose! There is no all
of a sudden, no bad luck, no *Dybukks* and
the eye and tying seven knots in the
payots to ward off the widow's curse!
Those men, like Allan, they look at the
Jews and think, "They somehow keep on
living and existing; some of them even
get rich! They must sneak out at night
and drain the blood of our children to
mix into their *matzahs*. How else? How
else could they succeed? They must be
evil. They must be stealing from us
somehow!" But they are wrong, of course.
Not wrong to hate the Jews. Everyone
hates the Jews! But wrong because there
isn't any evil! There is just what
Hashem made. There is us. There are our
choices, and how we are judged for those
choices. There is the covenant. Now is
an illusion. There is only the eternal.

THE LOST EXPERT
I don't understand, Rabbi. Isn't
there evil?

RABBI
When a Jewish boy is born, there is
joy, yes, but also there is sadness.
The baby sees his poppa and his momma,
but he is sad. Why? Because in the

place before, the angels taught him to
chant the Torah. But as soon as he is
born, he forgets. He forgets! Because
he must choose. He must decide. Will he
remember? Does he want to go with *Hashem*
and remember? Or does he want to forget?

The rabbi stares angrily at The Lost Expert,
his long beard grazing the wood of the table in
front of him.

INT. APARTMENT — EVENING
THE LOST EXPERT eats stew served to him by SARAH.

> SARAH
> (pointedly)
> It's mostly potatoes.

> THE LOST EXPERT
> It's fine. It's good.

> SARAH
> The price of meat has gone up again.
> Everything keeps getting more and more
> expensive. How do they expect us to live?

> THE LOST EXPERT
> (chewing)
> Sarah, don't worry so much.

They sit in silence. The Lost Expert
methodically eats his meal.

THE LOST EXPERT
(looking over at Sarah's plate)
You're not eating?

SARAH
(shrugging)
I'm eating.

THE LOST EXPERT
Try and eat something. For the baby.

Sarah picks up her fork and pushes her food
around.

SARAH
You really spent all day there?

The Lost Expert takes a big swig from his glass
of water.

SARAH
You could be working. What are we going
to live on?

THE LOST EXPERT
Things will turn around.

SARAH
What are you expecting to happen,
exactly? More missing Jews?

The Lost Expert gets up. He collects the dishes
on the table. He starts washing the dishes.

Sighing, Sarah walks ponderously to the couch.
She switches on the radio.

                    NEWSCASTER
        Reclusive millionaire Harold Allan
          continues his strong bid for the
          Presidency. Today, Allan, who rarely
         appears in public and keeps his face
        hidden when he does, claiming he wants
        policy not personality to be the core
           of his campaign, held a rally in the
          Southeast. Over five thousand men and
           women attended, most of them hoping
          to catch a glimpse of the reclusive
           candidate. However, Allan didn't
         speak; the enigmatic businessman stood
        alongside his vice-presidential running
          mate and main spokesperson, Florida
        Senator Hatcher Huckabee, who delivered
                this message:

                    HUCKABEE
        People say, "It's hopeless." People say,
         "There's nothing we can do." But Harold
         Allan says, "We've got an army of people
           out of work, out of hope, people who
           can't feed their families, people whose
          hands are lying idle." Harold Allan says,

"So let's take back the country. Let's
form an army, a people's army." Harold
Allan says, "We need an army! We need
an army because we're at war! We're at
war against outsiders who come into our
country and weaken it! Outsiders who
don't share our values. Outsiders who
only care about getting rich, no matter
what. Outsiders who don't believe in
this country, who want to degrade it, who
want to see it fail." Harold Allan says,
"There are too many outsiders in our
country! And because of them, there are
too many people who are desperate, who
have been corrupted, who are hurt by the
greed, by the lawlessness!"

The Lost Expert listens to the radio as the
bubbles of a soapy plate slowly slide off and
onto the linoleum floor. The hot water runs,
filling up the sink with steam.

"CUT!" REED YELLED.

"Okay, people," Tina bellowed, clapping her hands loudly. "Get some rest! Lots to do tomorrow. Time is money! Let's pack up the set."

The crew, their faces becoming more familiar to Chris with each shoot, lurched into action, coiling cables and dismantling light stands. Alison appeared at his side. She handed him his bottle of water. The clean-up went on around him as if he weren't there. Chris felt the water slide through him. He was empty. He couldn't remember the last time he'd eaten. That strange restaurant with Reed. He could still taste the gamey tray of slippery mini-burgers. And Daphne, her tongue, metallic and insistent, like a probe. Then that paparazzo, watching him, stalking him.

Yesterday, maybe? He felt thin, tight, his collarbones protruding. And yet he also felt bigger, taller — expansive in that way that people feel when they have no choice but to take up space.

All eyes on him, all the time. Time again. Time flies. Only time will tell. He had utterly and completely lost track of it. Or it of him. Was it possible to slip out of normal time? That sense again, that he was the looming giant. He turned and saw the girl who played the waitress at the Jewish café — "Esther." She was standing in the back of the set, by the coffee urn, trying not to stare at him. Their eyes met. The girl raised her eyebrows. Chris stared back curiously. He felt like he knew her.

Rachel, he almost said out loud. How was it possible he was only now recognizing her? But it was her! Of course, it was her. A faint sheen of sweat broke out on his forehead. She was coming over. Would she —

"I'm really sorry," she said, timidly approaching.

"What for?" Chris managed.

"I was terrible. Really terrible. I was so nervous! And I almost spilled coffee on you!"

"No, no, you were great!"

She looked at him strangely, nervously, struggling to smile.

"Thomson Holmes," Chris said, extending his hand.

"Oh, I'm, I'm Rachel. Rachel Small."

"Nice to meet you."

Rachel giggled. "Sorry," she said. "You must think I'm such a —"

"No, no —"

"It's just — it's funny. The way you introduced yourself. Like I wouldn't know who you were."

"Right, yeah."

"So, uh, Thomson Holmes. Would you like a real cup of coffee?"

All around them, the crew was working furiously to pack up. Alison, who had faded into the background, suddenly returned. "Thomson has to go," she said evenly.

Chris gave Rachel a pained grin. "Don't we — I'm sure I have five minutes. For a quick coffee."

Alison consulted her phone. "All right. Five minutes."

They moved to the side, careful to stay out of the way of the crew.

"You remind me of someone," Rachel said as she poured him a coffee. "Which is weird, right? Because usually it's the other way around."

"How do you mean?"

"Well, like, usually you say so-and-so looks like that guy in that movie or whatever. But in this case, you look like this guy I know. I work with him, actually."

"Really?" Chris was trying to keep his voice steady. He felt his smile, his cheeks tightly bunched.

Rachel considered him curiously, her slightly buck teeth, crowded together and pushing out, offset by the perfection of her lightly freckled, arching cheeks.

"So," Chris said, desperate to change the subject. "Are you in other parts of the movie?"

"Maybe," she said. "I'm not sure. I hope so! They said it'll depend on the story, on how things go."

"Well, here's hoping then." Chris toasted with his paper cup.

Rachel flushed. "Thanks. My agent was freaking out. I mean, mostly I've just done music videos and commercials. I was the exasperated teenage daughter in a dog food commercial last month."

"And now you're here! That's amazing!"

"Excuse me," Alison said forcefully. "I hate to interrupt, but, Thomson, we've really got to go."

"Oh, yeah, right. Sorry." He made a face for Rachel's benefit. He put his coffee down and stuck his hand out. "Well, it was nice meeting you, Rachel Small."

"You, too. You're different than …" Rachel flushed. "I mean," she hurried on, her hand lingering in his. "You read all these things — you know."

Alison next to him, watching.

"Anyway," he said. "I've got to go."

"Oh, wait! Here!" She fumbled in her purse, spilled a vintage silver card holder onto the floor, which popped open and spewed lavender business cards.

Chris crouched down, helped her gather the cards up.

Alison exhaled warningly.

"Oh my god, I'm so — Here," Rachel said. "I mean, take one. I mean, that's what I was trying to do in the first place. Give you my card."

"Thanks."

"In case you ever …"

They straightened up. Alison took his arm, applied gentle pressure.

"Well, bye."

They stepped away, then Chris turned back.

"Hey," he said. "What about the guy? The guy who you work with who reminds you of me?"

"It's so weird! You really remind me of him!" She frowned, tossing her mane of hair.

HE WOKE UP WITH a start. Where was he? He'd been dreaming. He and Laurie on a trip to an island, somewhere sunny and hot, but people were chasing him, shouting his name — Chris! Chris! — and trying to get his autograph. He kept explaining to Laurie that on this island he was incredibly famous, but Laurie just laughed and laughed. In the dream, he'd started off annoyed at the way she wouldn't listen to him and ended up furious with her, his heart beating so hard he could feel his blood starting to boil. He was just about to do something — scream at her, shake her, hit her — anything to get her to stop laughing and listen to him.

Then he woke up.

He was sprawled on the vast sectional in the living room of the Thomson Holmes hotel suite. On the glass coffee table, the old Nokia — *What is that?* — and next to it, the new phone — *You're exclusive to Samsung, remember?*

Remember? Chris stared down at the new phone. They'd left it on the stairs. Hadn't they? And now? The cat came back, Chris thought frantically.

Jesus, man, get a grip.

Someone must have found it. Tracked it. Krunk was right. Were they actually tracking him?

He picked up the Samsung, felt its slim, humming heat in his palm. It was there. It was real.

Chris dropped the phone with a thump.

He hurried to the liquor cabinet and poured himself a golden double. He held the tumbler for a moment before drinking. It was sturdy but also felt delicate; the new, improved Chris could crush it easily between his fingers. Fingers, Chris thought. Fingers and *fingerprints*. The nooks and crannies of singular identity etched ever so delicately in grooved skin. "We're all special," Krunk liked to mockingly intone. "Oh, Hollywood, bring me your weak and huddled masses so I can change them all into Spiderman the Karate Kid!"

For fuck's sake! Chris threw the gold at the back of his throat.

PARTIALLY NUMBED BY DRINK, Chris staggered through the streets. It was a long walk home.

Home. He had a hard time picturing it.

Laurie. Laurie was home. Apparently, the film shoot was moving up north the next morning. They'd be shooting there for a week. Reed kept talking about getting lost, lost in the woods. The director had been vague. His usual modus operandi, from what Chris could tell. Vague yet somehow convincing. Like a dream, Chris thought. The phone, the creepy photographer, Alison, Esther/Rachel — what else was it if it wasn't a dream? A movie, of course. Chaplin in *The Idle Class* or *The Great Dictator:* the Tramp, confused, mistaken for someone of means and import for the umpteenth time. "Look up, Hannah, look up!" Poor Chaplin. By then it was too late, though he didn't know it. It wasn't a dream. It wasn't some rainbow in the sky. It was the opposite. It was reality.

A dizzy spell washed over Chris, and he closed his eyes for a moment. It passed. He opened his eyes to see that he had arrived at familiar stomping grounds: Ossington and Bloor. The McDonalds and its McCafé. A favourite haunt of Krunk's — cheap coffee, open twenty-four hours, he could even sleep there for an hour or two, no questions asked. Across from it was the Ali Baba shawarma and falafel. Then the unassuming, low-slung Ossington Baptist Church. A CIBC bank branch, where Chris kept his meagre savings of a few hundred dollars on a good week. Reality. Back to reality. The Jewish bakeries had been boarded up. The lost cats had all been found. At home, Laurie would give him the cold shoulder and eventually a sternly worded lecture. At some point, makeup sex. Makeup sex would be good, Chris thought. Makeup sex would be great. Up north, there would just be bare trees and Reed and the cold, harsh glare of Darlia as she swept them all away like a winter wind.

His phone bleeped. *Alison*, Chris thought eagerly. Too late, he realized he still had it — the Samsung. The latest texts jumped up on the screen, pressing forward like desperate fans seeking an autograph.

Today. 2:04 a.m.

> Bit old for you, isn't she?

> What about the agreement?

> The agreement, Thomson!

Then: blurred photos capturing the torrid conclusion to his night out with Reed. The photos had been taken from too far or too close. Their grain and tone felt like they were from some other time, the Jazz Age, an air of mysterious impropriety hanging over the improbable riot of quotidian post-war life.

> *We'll release the video.*

> What about the agreement?

> The agreement, Thomson!

> You have two days to get us the rest of the money.

Chris felt his mouth fill with the taste of flat wine: alcohol and rotting fruit. The bald paparazzo with the expression of mournful, muscular disgust plastered on his face as he aimed the camera at Chris's bull's-eye forehead. Chris tried to swallow. But his mouth was dry, empty of anything but that horrible, bilious flavour. Daphne's tongue, Reed's champagne. *What video? What agreement?*

"Hey, man, got some change for a coffee?" Homeless dude gesturing at the McCafé. Chris jammed the phone in his pocket. Bloor and Ossington at two in the morning. He shook his head and picked up his pace.

AT LAURIE'S PLACE, HE fumbled with the lock, dropped his keys, swore, picked them up, and finally let himself into the familiarly gloomy front foyer. Chris knelt down to take off his shoes. Laurie did not allow shoes in the apartment. He froze when he realized the kitchen light was on. There was someone sitting there, at the small second-hand Formica table. Him, Chris thought. Paparazzi man. Another dizzy spell rushed over him, followed by a surge of nausea. Chris staggered to the sink.

"Chris? What the hell! Are you okay?"

He heaved a few times, but didn't throw up.

"Here, drink this."

Laurie with a glass of water.

He took a tentative sip, then chugged the rest. He closed his eyes and ran a dirty palm over his face as the water settled into his tight, empty stomach.

"Chris? What's going on? Are you okay?"

Feeling like he might fall over, Chris summoned the will to drop into one of the three kitchen chairs set around the chipped table.

"No, yeah, I'm fine. I just …"

He smiled up at her weakly. Her expression had set into a frown.

"What have you been doing? I've been calling you! You said you were coming home tonight. For dinner!"

Laurie wasn't quite yelling. She was pale, her face slacker than Chris remembered.

"Yeah, I —"

"You what? You *what*, Chris?"

How could he explain it to her? It was all so stupid. Their tiny kitchen. The tap dripping, something the landlord had promised to deal with more than a month ago.

"Chris! What is going on?" Now she was yelling. Her cheeks had gone blotchy, and she looked like she was going to cry.

He couldn't. He couldn't explain it to her.

"Laurie, god, I'm such an idiot! This new job has been crazy! I just keep losing track of time! I'm so, so sorry."

"What are you wearing?"

A Thomson Holmes outfit involving a slinky black button-down short-sleeved shirt and strange orangey-white pants with elaborate pockets.

"They lent me some clothes. Since I've been sleeping on the set."

Laurie wrinkled up her nose as if Chris had brought with him some terrible new smell that she couldn't identify. Chris went on, unable or unwilling to stop himself.

He couldn't meet her for dinner after all. Tomorrow they were heading up north. He had to help pack everything up. He would have called, but his phone was dead. It was an all-nighter type situation. An entire movie shoot heading into the woods. It was an enormous undertaking. All hands on deck. He couldn't say no, they were counting on him. When he got back, he promised, things would settle down, go back to normal. That was the movie biz, apparently. He shrugged and flashed her a gee-whiz smile.

"So you're going with them?"

"Yeah. Just for a few days."

"*Days?*"

"It's just a week. I know it's last-minute. It's really good money, Laurie. As soon as I'm home, I'm going to make it up to you."

At this point, Chris was in the bedroom. He'd grabbed a tote bag and was randomly stuffing socks and underwear into it. Laurie's expression had set into something he hadn't seen before — a kind of bewildered desperation.

"Chris. Hold on. Are you …?"

"They're expecting me. I'll call tomorrow."

He pecked her on the check and hurried out of the apartment.

DURING KRUNK'S 9/11 OBSESSION, they'd watched all the related dramas, documentaries, and dark web conspiracy videos. But mostly he had forced them to watch the amply available cell phone footage. The disaster happening in real time. Krunk went on and on about jet fuel capacity, U.S. air defence protocols, and the melting point of high-rise-grade steel. Meanwhile, Chris watched the people — specks picking up size and speed as they fell.

What would he have done?

Several streets away, Chris stopped in front of a dumpster occupying the small front lawn of a half-demolished row house. One hundred, fifty, even twenty years ago, these were undesirable dwellings stuffed to the gills by waves of poor immigrants — Jewish, Portuguese, Chinese, Italian. Now, one by one, the houses were being bought at a premium and redone in accordance with the needs of childless professional couples whose priorities were eight-burner stovetops and airy, light-in-fused, Peloton-equipped workout rooms. Things can change without evolving or improving. They can be the same, only totally different. If they'd known, maybe they wouldn't have done it, wouldn't have sold low in the early nineties, abandoning their once tightknit communities for the spacious anonymity of the suburbs. If they'd known. In a single motion, Chris sailed his randomly stuffed tote of saggy underwear and faded T-shirts into the dumpster. Briskly, he set off through the city, darkness punctuated by streetlamp coronas and the blur of flickering shapes keeping company with the last of the late-night Netflix insomniacs.

INT. STREETCAR — MORNING RUSH HOUR
The bulb in the front of the streetcar flickers,
creating an eerie, strobe-like sense of displaced
motion. THE LOST EXPERT stands in the middle
of the crowded car amongst the other passengers
who can't find a seat, holding on to a strap,
his long arm extended, his body swaying back and
forth with the erratic motions of the train. A
MAN comes through the car with a sign: *Looking
for work*. *Hard worker*, underlined in red. Someone guffaws. The car jerks to the right as it
takes a bend just a touch too fast. The man with
the sign loses his balance, jostles another man.

                    OTHER MAN
              Hey! Get offa me.

                    HARD WORKER
              Take it easy there, bud.

                    OTHER MAN
              I'm not your bud!

HARD WORKER
(shouting now)
You think you're better than me?

The Lost Expert looks up at the sound of the
yelling. He catches sight of the tall, faceless
TRENCH-COAT-WEARING MAN he first saw in the
Jewish quarter. Trench Coat Man walks through
the disturbance and on toward the back doors of
the car.

THE LOST EXPERT
(trying to get through the crowd in
the car)
Excuse me! Out of the way, please!

OTHER RIDER
(pushing at Hard Worker)
Step outta my face!

THE LOST EXPERT
Let me through!

Hard Worker pushes hard and swings his fists at
everyone around him.

HARD WORKER
Don't put your hands on me! Don't you
ever put your hands on me!

The car lurches to a stop. The lights flicker on
and off. The two men collide again, then start

yelling and punching. The Lost Expert, behind
them, is knocked backwards into a crowd of
people. The lights go off, bathing the crowd in
the shadowy gloom. There is a collective groan.
The Lost Expert scrambles back to his feet.
Trench Coat Man is gone.

EXT. LEAFY NEIGHBOURHOOD NORTH OF THE CITY —
LATE MORNING
Houses overlook a steep gorge tightly filled
with vegetation. Down in the gorge, THE LOST
EXPERT slips through bare trees hung with brown
vines. He follows a muddy trickle of water
through waist-high brambles, thorn bushes
snapping and tearing at his thick pants. He
pushes through, then stops in a small clearing
and comes upon an ELDERLY WOMAN in a nightgown.
She is crouching in a murky pond. The woman's
white hair is tangled, her pink robe smeared
with mud, her bare feet blackened. The woman
sways unsteadily as she peers at the ripples
on the brackish surface of the water. The Lost
Expert watches her eyes trail past, skimming
clusters of water bugs with interest and almost
delight. Although she is elderly and gaunt,
there is a glow to her. She is in the liminal
space between life and death, swaying between
the two, momentum carrying her farther and
farther into the place from which no one comes
back. The Lost Expert continues to watch her,
almost in a trance.

EXT. POND — AFTERNOON (FLASHBACK — 1903)
BOY LOST EXPERT crouches by the bank of a swamp.
There is smeared mud and matted long grass.
Dazedly, he stares at the spot where his mother
was dragged into the water.

EXT. GORGE — MORNING (1928)
THE LOST EXPERT kneels by the small swamp, next
to MARTHA, the lost elderly woman.

                    THE LOST EXPERT
                    Martha?

                    MARTHA
          Albert? Is that you, Albert?

                    THE LOST EXPERT
                    (reassuringly)
          Yes, Martha. It's me. It's Albert.

The old woman smiles lovingly and collapses in
the Lost Expert's arms.

INT. LIVING ROOM OF SUBURBAN HOUSE

                    MARTHA'S DAUGHTER
          Thank god, you found her.

                    HUSBAND
          I should never have left her.

MARTHA'S DAUGHTER
Honey, you can't blame yourself. It was
just for a minute.

HUSBAND
I thought she was resting.

THE LOST EXPERT
Who is Albert?

HUSBAND
Albert?

DAUGHTER
Albert is her brother. He died in the
war. Why?

THE LOST EXPERT
She called me Albert. When I found her.
She told me she'd been waiting for me.

The daughter puts her hands over her face and
starts crying.

THE LOST EXPERT
It's almost her time.

Daughter sobs.

HUSBAND
(holding out a wad of crumpled bills)
Here, please. For your trouble.

THE LOST EXPERT 139

THE LOST EXPERT   139

                    DAUGHTER
          Thank you, thank you so much.

                  THE LOST EXPERT
               (accepting the money)
            Take care of her. Take care of
                    your mother.

INT. APARTMENT — EVENING
THE LOST EXPERT sits at the kitchen table
across from Sarah. He watches expressionlessly
as she slowly and deliberately counts out the
crumpled bills in front of him. There are
seven one-dollar bills.

                      SARAH
                 (expressionless)
                 Seven dollars.

                  THE LOST EXPERT
                 It's something.

She gets up and goes to the bedroom, closing the
door behind her. The Lost Expert sits there for
a long time, just staring at the bills. Outside,
there is the sound of yelling, then a scuffle,
and the familiar sound of a bottle breaking.

INT. APARTMENT KITCHEN — MORNING
THE LOST EXPERT, still his pajamas, enters
the kitchen, pauses, and looks around. The
apartment is dark and quiet.

THE LOST EXPERT
Sarah?

The Lost Expert switches on the light,
illuminating the kitchen. There is a note on the
empty kitchen table next to the still crumpled
bills. The Lost Expert reads it: *I've taken the
baby to my mother's.*

He stares at the note. Eventually, the noise of
horses' hooves, a car's trilling horn, and angry
shouting breaks him out of his thoughts. He
grabs up the small pile of crumpled bills in his
fist and runs to the window. He leans outside
and throws the crumpled bills out.

THE LOST EXPERT
(yelling)
Shut up! Shut *the hell* up!

There are enraged responses from the street,
which the Lost Expert muffles by abruptly
yanking the window closed. He sits back down
at the kitchen table, his head in his hands.
Finally, he gets up and goes to the side table
by the front door. On the table is a crumpled
business card, which he picks up: *Joel McCann,
Senior Advisor, Allan for President.*

PART TWO

THEY TOOK OVER A summer camp closed for the season. The crew spread out to the different cabins, occupied creaky bottom bunks, watched the butts of their flicked cigarettes trail red into the dark, encroaching forest. It was late afternoon. A gloomy chill, spread by the wind off the lake, swept through the camp, a harbinger of coming winter.

Chris, feeling as if he were under some strange spell of shape-shifting, quietly toured the campsite with Alison. She had reluctantly acceded to his request that they stay with the crew in the camp rather than in the luxury country inn an hour or so up a small country highway, which was instead left entirely to Darlia and her entourage.

They climbed a steep path to reach the camp director's cabin, newly outfitted with two space heaters and heavy flannel sheets. The shack sat on the flat of a small hill with its back to dense woods. It overlooked the camp and the open expanse of the lake. Inside there was a cot, a scarred wooden desk, and a rack of splintering plywood shelves.

"Is it okay?" Alison said worryingly.

"It's fine," Chris said. He turned back to the lake. "It's got a great view."

"It is pretty," Alison said.

He looked at her and smiled. Alison wore sky-blue corduroy trousers and a fashion designer's take on a lumberjack jacket. Her milky cheeks were tinged pink from the cold air.

"What about you? Are you going to be all right?"

"Sure," she said brightly.

"It's not exactly your element."

"And what exactly do you know about my element?" Alison teased. She shifted toward him. Or else he wished she did. A gust sent a kaleidoscope of furled leaves swelling. Chris took a deep breath, relishing the rich air.

"Well, well, well," boomed Bryant Reed, stomping up the hill, huffing and puffing and swinging his mud-spattered hiking boots. "How are my two lovelies today!" He hooked an arm around each of them, pulling them into his burly chest in a bear hug. Reed smelled of tobacco, clover, and swamp. Chris had a sudden memory: kissing his grandfather on the cheek a week or so before he died. The white stubble bristling against his lips. And the sadness: a terrible feeling rushing through him that had no outlet, nowhere to go. Sour breath hissed from his grandpop's lips as he tried to speak before finally leaving off in favour of resting his paper-thin fingers on Chris's open palm.

Chris shivered.

Reed released them. "What is it, Holmes? What's up?" The director's voice, suddenly intimate and low.

"What? No. Nothing. Just …"

Reed and Alison looked at him expectantly.

"It's just — I was thinking — We don't really process things when they're happening. We don't get it. Only after."

He felt free in the dilapidated camp. He was someone, somewhere, else. He could say anything.

"That's why we need movies. They're as close as we can get to it. To going back to what happened."

"What happened?" Reed blinked owlishly at him.

"Everything. Nothing. We're never sure."

"We're just animals," Reed said.

"Animals who keep wanting to remember."

"Animals with history," Reed said, liking the idea.

"Animals trying to understand how we became human. Where we came from, where we've been."

"Stories," Reed said.

Chris nodded. The sky settled low on the horizon.

"I have no idea what you guys are going on about," Alison said primly.

"Sure ya do, sweetheart," Reed boomed.

They wandered over to the dining hall for dinner. Chris was aware of his breathing, the deep, unruly air in his lungs. Around them, the camp was descending into shrouded darkness, a self-contained universe swinging the gates closed. Falling leaves, still supple, blanketed the pathways. Reed whistled. The tune was melancholy, but he seemed relaxed in a way that Chris hadn't encountered before.

"You know what the best thing is about this place?" Reed said, stopping at the foot of the stairs heading up to the ramshackle dining hall. Dramatically, he pulled out his cell phone. It gleamed in the settling dark. "No signal," he said. He had the phone by the tops of his fingers like it was something with a disease. "Dead as a doorknob," he said happily.

According to Krunk, Reed had made his best films in the late eighties. Before cellphones, Chris thought. Before the internet. *The Lost Expert* was before all that too.

"Dead," Chris repeated approvingly.

Inside the dining hall, the crew was already settling into
heaping piles of food and loud conversations punctuated by
obscenities and laughs degenerating into smoker's hacks. There
was a hint of a lull when they walked in. Eyes turned — fearfully,
Chris thought — to Reed, ballcap pushed halfway up his forehead, his usual half-grin half-grimace on his face.

Alison offered to get him a plate, but Chris insisted on helping himself. He lined up with the others and heaped on beef stew
and mashed potatoes. His mouth watered. Honestly, he couldn't
remember the last time he'd eaten an actual meal. He sat down
on a bench between two grips and stuffed his face.

IT WAS A CLEAR, starry night. The crew built a bonfire on the beach
by the lake. The flames clawed jealously at the moon, full and
bright against layers of enshrouding greys. The crew cackled
merrily. They cheered when one of them fed the blaze with another
of the hunks of soggy wood they'd dragged from the low-lying
patches of forest on the far side of the beach. If a piece was too
big and wet, they helped the wet wood along with liberal shots
of barbecue starter, each squirt instantly producing a bright red
blaze yielding to oily green flames and smudged, brackish smoke.
They passed around forties of Canadian Club and cheered when
another dead solider was tossed into the lake, left to glint and
burble, a bottle with no message.

Chris sat overlooking it all on the teetering picnic table posi-
tioned just outside his cabin. He nursed a can of beer, surveying
the goings-on down below. He was thinking about Krunk's
uncle. What ever happened to that guy? Before Chris's parents
split, but after his grandpop became too old and frail to spend
as much time with him, there had been a string of summers
spent at Krunk's Uncle Luke's place. The boys had been ten,

eleven, twelve. "Uncle Luke's" was a constantly mutating plywood shack stuck in a buggy deciduous forest adorned with frequent swamps, deep glacial lakes, and dark cliffs jutting out of the wet earth, abruptly blocking the false paths and fake trails the boys followed like they were heading somewhere.

Uncle Luke oversaw the boys with a madman's whims. Some days, he exploded into rage and barred them from the "cottage" till late at night while he went about the perpetual process of expanding the dwelling using scrap heaps of plywood, greyed-out two-by-fours, and rusted sheets of aluminum. Other times, he insisted on joining the boys in their games, taking on the role of soldier or hunter or tracker with a zeal as assiduous as it was discomfiting. Chris remembered — could this really have happened? — Uncle Luke outfitting them with armaments. Chris with an air pistol, Krunk with a rifle-looking thing, and Uncle Luke with a handgun. They crept through the woods to the edge of the swamp and at Uncle Luke's whispered directive opened fire at a giant bullfrog. He thought of the way the frog had exploded. "Nothing left but the liquids!" Uncle Luke had extolled. Chris put his beer down. He remembered it so clearly. Uncle Luke's round, red face.

What about the agreement? Chris thought. Sour, half-digested stew rose up, burning his throat. That short guy, the bald photographer. The grey under his eyes, the dark gap between his thin, sullen lips.

How was it possible that they'd never talked about Krunk's lunatic uncle? The summers they'd spent, eyeing him warily as they sat outside the shack eating cold Chef Boyardee with their fingers, tossing the empty cans over their shoulders into the pressing forest. Summers like open secrets, things everyone knows but can't bring themselves to say out loud. Those distant summers smelling of pine and puberty, their hair knotted with resin from the gnarled trees they challenged themselves to climb. A million years ago. Yesterday.

A large flame suddenly shot up, followed by whooping cheers and a bottle hitting water with a thud. Chris drank from his beer, forcing himself to swallow. The moon lit the camp, and Chris thought of the lights they used to illuminate film sets, fulgent and all-encompassing. Uncle Luke howling at the night, blasting off rounds with his .45 Colt, the sound echoing in Chris's ears. *That was the beginning*, Chris thought. *The beginning of what?* Chris folded his arms against his chest. Nightfall, settling like a fog. First frost. Begin at the beginning. Drop out of college. Watch your former peers scuttle past, on their way, in a hurry. Chris wasn't like them. He wasn't on his way. Loneliness spreading in a slick. Krunk had everything. Parents to hate. A vision of himself. A career — better than a career. An anti-career. What did Chris have? Abruptly, Chris stood up. He drained his beer and stepped on the can, crushing it.

At the fire they fell quiet, nodding at him and quickly looking away, shuffling closer to one another as if for protection and comfort. Chris surveyed the group. Five guys and one burly lady, all of them dressed in jeans and sweatshirts emblazoned with the logos of TV shows — some new, some very, very old — shot decades ago on the cheap at Toronto soundstages. *Starcraft, The Boys, Amazon, La Femme Nikita, Titans.* They sported rough beards and wraparound shades, either pushed up into scraggly salt-and-pepper hair or dangling around their red, wattled necks. Their cellphones and pagers hung silently off their belts. They were drunk and melancholy, in the throes of the exhaustion of working people who'd known feast and famine and were solemnly working their way through a long, but ephemeral, banquet.

Chris rubbed his hands and leaned in, wanting the heat on his face. Nobody spoke for a few minutes. Then a man with a tattered Winnipeg Jets cap and a face like a dropped tomato spat at the coals.

"Helluva night," the man, Frankie, said in Chris's direction.

"Look at that moon!" Chris said agreeably. Obligingly the group raised their collective gaze. "You could get lost in there." The group nodded, as if they all knew what he meant. One of them handed him the bottle of rye. Chris drank and passed it along.

The murmured conversations resumed. Frankie, the set builder, began talking about his winters, spent on a Hawaiian island camping on the beach. "It's a whole community there, man," Frankie told him. "We look out for each other. This one time ..." Chris listened to the man talk, pictured their ramshackle, ephemeral village of tents and tarps. The wind and the surf and the campfire smoke. He'd never been to the ocean.

A hand on his shoulder. Chris looked up. It was Reed, face a furrowed shadow under his trademark Penguins cap.

"Mind if I borrow him?"

"Take him away, *Capitan*," Frankie the set builder slurred.

THEY WALKED ALONG THE water, following a path that bordered the woods.

"What are you doing up?" Reed demanded. "You're in wardrobe at six." His voice, throaty and resigned, implied an artist's weary burden: the long journey to first light.

"Wardrobe," Chis said, yawning. "I don't like that lady."

"Eloise? What's wrong with Eloise?"

"Ah, nothing," Chris muttered. He kept forgetting the way Reed leapt on every offhand remark and comment.

"He doesn't like Eloise," Reed said to himself.

"She yelled at me."

"She yelled at you?" Reed sounded amused. "What did she say?"

"She said that I was a 'naughty boy' for wearing my own stuff in a scene. She said it was against the rules. Unions and all that."

"She said that to you?" Reed blew air through pursed lips. "Good old Eloise," he said affectionately. Reed clapped Chris on the back. "But, seriously. Long day tomorrow."

"What are you doing up?" Chris replied, grinning cheekily.

"Don't sleep much," Reed grunted. "The doctor gave me these pills."

"You don't take them?"

"Ah, shit, Holmes. I'm an old man. What do I want with fucking sleep?"

How old are you? Chris wanted to ask. But he stopped himself. Reed pulled a cigar out of his pocket and paused to light it. They stood next to shallow water propping up browning lily pads. A bridge of grey logs and yellowed rope continued the path.

"Leads to an island," Reed said exhaling.

"Shall we?" Chris stepped onto the bridge. Wood cracked, and the rope strained. Reed put a heavy hand on his arm, stopping him.

"Hey, Holmes."

He looked back. Reed's thick eyebrows reduced his eyes to shadow.

"Be careful. You're the star of the show, remember."

Snake's Island was a jumbled peninsula of rocks and boulders, the cracks between them presumably home to any number of black, sinewy water snakes invisible in their dark, wet crevices.

Chris and Reed found perches on the rocks and looked out over the lake at the moon's rippling reflection.

"This place reminds me of the camp I went to when I was a kid," Reed said, puffing meditatively on his cigar. "Jew camp. Camp Gesher. Means 'bridge' in Hebrew. We were supposed to be sharing everything. You got a candy bar in the mail from your mom, you had to break it into ten pieces. It was supposed to be like a kibbutz. We chopped vegetables, collected trash, cleaned the toilets. In return they taught us Israeli dancing, knot tying, and bonfire building. We soaked thick ropes in gas and spelled *Am Yisreal Chai* out in the water then lit the ropes on fire. The Land of Israel Lives! Saturday night everyone stood on the beach with their arms around one another's shoulders watching the burn and singing '*Hatikva*' at the top of their lungs."

Reed glanced over at Chris.

"You with me here, Holmes?"

"Not really," Chris admitted. "Hatik-wa?"

Reed chuckled and pulled on his cigar.

"Fuckin' *Hatikva*," he said, exhaling sweet smoke.

They sat in silence.

"So," Reed said, stabbing into the night with the red, glowing tip of his stogie. "When did you quit?"

"Ahh." Reed kept doing this to him. Catching him off guard. "A while ago?"

A frog bleated from the nearby underbrush.

"Haven't heard that song in a long time," Reed said.

"Bullfrog," Chris said guiltily.

"Reading the *Times*, you'd think that there wasn't one left in all eternity."

Chris leaned down, picked up a pebble, and threw it in the water.

Reed puffed on his cigar.

At the bonfire, someone laughed then started into a hacking cough.

"Roadies," Reed said. Chris didn't say anything. He could feel Reed's eyes on him, examining him. "Goddamn!" Reed said. "You're like a sphinx these days. Almost makes me miss the other Holmes. Remember him?"

Chris froze.

Reed didn't wait for an answer.

"The one who sat in my office flexing his biceps and telling me about the vintage DeLorean he'd just bought for three point two million dollars. *Back to the Future*, eh, Holmes? That's what I said. Remember that? You seemed confused, and I thought, 'Well, he's not the sharpest blade in the block.' But I guess I was wrong."

They listened for the frog. It had gone silent.

"I guess."

"You guess." Reed sucked on his cigar and exhaled dramatically.

"You think he watches his movies?" Chris said.

"Who?"

"You know. *Back to the Future*."

Reed's tone softened. "Poor fucker. He's a good guy. For a Canadian." He opened his arms to encompass the tree-lined lake. "Canada. Look at this shit. Wasted on these dopes. We should just invade. Call it, like, Michigan North. Eh, Holmes?"

"Yeah. I think I saw that movie."

Reed made a pained face. "*That* was not a movie."

Chris giggled, let himself relax.

"You still got it?" Reed demanded.

"What?"

"The car."

Chris shrugged. "I guess."

"*I guess*. Used to be you wouldn't shut up. Especially about your toys. Now when you talk it's like you're on some different plane of existence. You're like some kind of antimatter philosopher or something. It's like you should be in the crazy house, but, somehow, you pass. You're like — what's-his-name? Chauncey! You're like fucking Chauncey!"

Chris grinned, his stomach gurgling nervously. "It doesn't matter," he said.

"What doesn't?"

Chris didn't answer.

"So, what *does* matter?"

Chris hesitated. "This. What we're doing. *The Lost Expert*."

Reed took one last furious puff on his cigar then tossed it into the water.

They walked back the way they came. The air was still, and Chris felt the energy draining from him, his feet stumbling on shadowed roots and rocks.

Then, out of nowhere, Reed stopped and held up a wavering finger. "You feel that?" He didn't wait for Chris to answer. "Getting cooler. Well, fuck. That sucks."

INT. BAKERY — MORNING
THE LOST EXPERT sits at his table with his mug
of coffee and a plate of Mandelbrot. Outside,
the day darkens and it begins to drizzle. The
door to the bakery opens. Enter a MAN IN HIS
FIFTIES. He wears a tweed overcoat over a
tailored suit and a felt homburg with black
band. A hush falls in the café as people stop
talking to stare fearfully at the man. The man
approaches ESTHER.

                    J.P. BARTNER
        I'm looking for someone. I don't know
            his name. He, ah, helps people —
                    find things.

The man stares into the eyes of the waitress as
if refusing to acknowledge his own hesitation.

                    ESTHER
                  (frowning)
        There is no man like that here.

J.P. BARTNER
I was told he comes here.

ESTHER
(shrugging)
I don't know such a man.

THE LOST EXPERT
(calling from his table)
It's all right, Esther.

The man strides impatiently to the Lost Expert's
table. He stands over him imperiously.

J.P. BARTNER
You helped my granddaughter?

THE LOST EXPERT
Your granddaughter?

J.P. BARTNER
(impatiently)
You found her cat.

THE LOST EXPERT
(smiling faintly)
Missy.

J.P. BARTNER
(already sitting down)
May I join you?

THE LOST EXPERT
Please do.

J.P. BARTNER
And you found that (lowering his voice,
looking around) Jew kid?

THE LOST EXPERT
Yes, I found him. I work with anyone,
regardless of —

J.P. BARTNER
Never mind that.

The Lost Expert falls silent and stares at the
man.

J.P. BARTNER
(suddenly extending a hand)
J.P. Bartner.

THE LOST EXPERT
Bartner's? As in, "Pile 'em high, sell
'em low?"

J.P. BARTNER
(grimacing)
We offer value and satisfaction.

THE LOST EXPERT
My wife shops there.

                    J.P. BARTNER
          A smart woman, I'm sure.

                      ESTHER
        (appearing over Bartner's shoulder with
             her mother watching anxiously
                from behind the counter)
        Can I get you somethin', mister?

                    J.P. BARTNER
          Coffee, strong. And hot.

                 THE LOST EXPERT
                (smiling faintly)
        I should warn you. The coffee here is
               neither strong nor hot.

J.P. Bartner considers his surroundings
dubiously.

                    J.P. BARTNER
        This is the first time I've been to the
                  Jewish quarter.

                 THE LOST EXPERT
        I quite like it here. But then again,
           there don't seem to be many other
        establishments where I'm welcome. Since
         you're here, you should try the cookie
        they make, it's called the man-del-brat.
         They're excellent. Here. (pushing the
             plate toward Bartner) Try one.

J.P. BARTNER
(dismissing the suggestion with
the wave of a hand)
My granddaughter said you were a waiter
at the Sutton.

THE LOST EXPERT
I used to work there.

ESTHER
Here's your coffee.

Esther drops the coffee on to the table. The
thin liquid spills over into the saucer.

J.P. BARTNER
(ignoring her)
So, what? You're some kinda psychic? You
do tricks, like Houdini?

THE LOST EXPERT
I'm afraid you've been misinformed.

J.P. BARTNER
How's that?

THE LOST EXPERT
I'm not a spiritualist. I don't have
any psychic "powers." I just try and
help people.

J.P. BARTNER
So, like a P.I.?

THE LOST EXPERT
I'm not a detective. I don't sneak
around.

J.P. BARTNER
Just as well. I've gone through three
already.

THE LOST EXPERT
You're looking for someone.

J.P. BARTNER
(sighing, pained)
Nothing. No trace of him. Nobody knows a
darn thing.

THE LOST EXPERT
There are always traces.

J.P. BARTNER
What's that supposed to mean?

The Lost Expert is silent, expressionless.

J.P. BARTNER
Look, you come recommended. And not just
from my granddaughter, if you catch my
drift. People in high places think you

can help me, and for some reason they
seem to want to help you. I don't get
it, but, okay, I've got nothing left
to lose. But I need to know that you
won't — Can I trust you? How do I know
I can trust you?

The Lost Expert opens his large hands and puts
them face up on the table. The Lost Expert's
weathered hands are worn, creased with deep
lines. He stares into Bartner's eyes.

                    J.P. BARTNER
                 (sighing, resigned)
     It's my brother. He's missing. Lost.
     He wandered off. (lowering his voice)
     He has problems. He was in a place.
     Very well appointed. The best care.
           They're supposed to watch him
     twenty-four hours a day. Somehow, he
     ran off. Been six months with no trace
           of him. He's clever, my brother.
     Disturbed, but clever. My mother is
           very upset. She's elderly, in her
     eighties. I hate to see her like this.
     He's probably dead, I know. But if he's
           dead, then where's the body?

                    THE LOST EXPERT
                    He's not dead.

                 J.P. BARTNER
     He's not dead. You would say that,
   wouldn't you? You want the job, right?

             THE LOST EXPERT
   You only have to pay me what you think
               I deserve.

J.P. Bartner gulps at his coffee and makes a
disapproving face.

             THE LOST EXPERT
    It's not something I can explain.
    But I know it. He's out there.

               J.P. BARTNER
      How much to get started?

Bartner extracts an envelope from his coat
pocket and slides it across the table. The Lost
Expert stares at the envelope but doesn't touch
it. Bartner lurches up. He throws a dollar bill
and a card on the table.

               J.P. BARTNER
   Here's my assistant's calling card. All
      further communication will be
          through him.

The Lost Expert watches Bartner. He stops at the
door to the bakery, then, looking suddenly small
and stricken, he turns back to the Lost Expert.

J.P. BARTNER
He's my only brother.

The Lost Expert nods, his face set.

EXT. LARGE MANSION CONVERTED INTO A MENTAL
HEALTH CARE FACILITY — LATE MORNING
THE LOST EXPERT arrives in the back of a Packard
limousine. The uniformed driver opens the door
for him. An imposing Victorian building looms
over a groomed front lawn glistening with flower
beds and shining green grass. The Lost Expert
shields his eyes from the sun and directs his
gaze past the building's daunting entranceway
and up at the windows of the building.

The Lost Expert slowly mounts the front steps.
Dragonflies zigzag overhead, and a squirrel with
an acorn in his mouth rushes up a drainpipe. A
single cloud moves across the blue sky. A flock
of birds, rising from the trees, disturbed,
settles back down again. A plaque beside the
door: Waverly House. Please Ring for Entry.

INT. A LONG HALLWAY
THE LOST EXPERT and DR. WONG, a thin, slightly
stooped man in his sixties with receding grey
hair, proceed down the hall. Light slides
through ornate glass windows and catches on
hardwood floors polished to a shine. Dr.
Wong, elegantly dressed in vest and bow tie
draped by a starched white doctor's jacket,

walks deliberately and slowly. Wong and the
Lost Expert proceed through the corridor,
their footsteps the only sound disturbing the
sepulchral silence.

                    WONG
        (stopping in front of an imposing wooden
        door and unlocking the door with a key)
                This was his room.

INT. BEDROOM IN THE INSTITUTION
The room is large, painted a soft sky blue.
There is a plush bed, a desk, and a leather
armchair next to a fireplace. One wall features
a bookshelf lined with titles. Sunlight flows
through the large window. The Lost Expert looks
out the window. It is a long way down to the
grounds.

                    WONG
                (grimacing)
        That's the window, yes. Staff were
        instructed to monitor him frequently.
        But there was no way to know that he
        would risk his life in this manner.
        The grounds are monitored at all times
        by our guards, but somehow he evaded
        them, and the dogs as well. We engaged
        the Pinkertons. Several of their best
        attempted to track his whereabouts, but
                they failed.

THE LOST EXPERT
(interrupting)
I'm not here to review your security
procedures.

Dr. Wong falls silent. The Lost Expert prowls
the room. He stops in front of an imposing
gramophone embedded in an oak stand.

THE LOST EXPERT
Did he enjoy listening to gramophone
recordings?

WONG
He did. He enjoyed a wide range of
recordings. It was the only thing that
seemed to calm him. But more recently he
began listening to one recording over
and over again.

THE LOST EXPERT
What recording was that?

WONG
It did not appear to have a name,
exactly. It was a sort of spiritual
recording. It appeared to have been
recorded in the south. A folklore
compilation. A "race recording,"
I believe.

                    THE LOST EXPERT
            I would like to hear the recording
                      in question.

                          WONG
            I'll have it brought up from the
                        basement.

The Lost Expert opens the drawers of the desk.
He finds sheets of paper. He flips through them.
Nearly every page has a detailed pencil sketch
of a desolate cabin in a woods.

                          WONG
            In the last few weeks, he drew that
                image repeatedly. He would not
            discuss its significance. We encourage
                self-expression in our patients,
            but unfortunately, after an incident in
                which one of the staff members
                was threatened, we were forced to
                      remove his pencils.

                    THE LOST EXPERT
            I'd like to take a drawing with me.

                          WONG
                        (nodding)
                        Very well.

The two men are enveloped by the near-total
silence of the room.

EXT. THE REAR GROUNDS OF WAVERLY HOUSE
DR. WONG and THE LOST EXPERT walk through
the lush grounds, occasionally passing staff
accompanying shuffling patients wrapped in
pajamas, robes, and slippers.

                    THE LOST EXPERT
             (gazing around the lush gardens)
                 And he had no visitors?

                         WONG
                       Very few.

                    THE LOST EXPERT
                 He did have visitors?

                         WONG
             His brother would visit briefly once a
             year. More recently, a cousin came to
                   see him several times.

                    THE LOST EXPERT
                       (sharply)
                 When did this start?

                         WONG
             About ten months ago, I believe.

                    THE LOST EXPERT
             Was that around the time he became
                   more unresponsive?

                    WONG
                  (rattled)
              Yes. I suppose.

               THE LOST EXPERT
      What was the cousin's name? Do you know
                what he wanted?

                    WONG
      Visits with family are not monitored.
           May I ask why the concern?

               THE LOST EXPERT
        Michael's parents were both only
       children. He did not have any cousins.

INT. DR. WONG'S OFFICE — LATE AFTERNOON
A large, prominent oak desk faces a couch and
two leather armchairs. Shelves are lined with
books about psychiatry and psychology.

                    WONG
            (seated at his desk)
       Michael went through an abrupt change in
              the last few months before he
          left us. In our sessions he would
      refuse to respond, just stared at a point
                  over my head.

THE LOST EXPERT leans back in the armchair facing Dr. Wong's wide, burnished desk.

The stiff leather creaks. Looming above the
doctor's chair, a painting. A thick forest at
dusk. The muted purples, blues, and browns. A
rippling creek.

                    THE LOST EXPERT
                Is this where he sat?

                        WONG
                        Yes.

                    THE LOST EXPERT
                (pointing to the painting)
                That is what he stared at.

                        WONG
            (turning, considering the painting,
                        surprised)
                    This painting?

                    THE LOST EXPERT
            What does this represent? Where was
                        it done?

                        WONG
            It's a scene from the Tanoquin Forest
                Reserve. It's one of the largest
            untampered boreal forests in our
            hemisphere. It begins about two hours
            southeast of here. Most of our patients
                find the image quite tranquil.

There is a knock on the door.

                    WONG
          Excuse me for a moment.

Wong gets up and opens the door. A
BURLY, RED-FACED MAN in a white orderly's
uniform says something quietly to
Dr. Wong, and they both step out into the
hall. The Lost Expert gets up and moves behind
Dr. Wong's desk to inspect the painting. The
luminescent dusk suggests something foreboding.
A swamp occupies the foreground, its waters
still and heavy. From the hall come smatterings
of a hushed, intense conversation.
Dr. Wong returns to the office. He closes
the door and leans against it, as if slightly
shaken.

                    THE LOST EXPERT
               Dr. Wong?

                    WONG
          The record could not be located.
               It is missing.

THEY MOVED SLOWLY THROUGH the woods, Reed at the head of their snaking line. *Snakes*, Chris thought as he followed the director's steps. The tightly packed grey-green firs were readying for hibernation, their needles prickly and unforgiving in the almost-frosty morning. For as long as Chris had known him, Krunk had harboured a snake obsession. It culminated in his organizing a sparsely but virulently attended Bad Snakes film festival held at an underground cinema accessed through an alley off Spadina. Chris, of course, had been pressed into the role of ticket-taker, concession stand operator — no-name beers and smokes, grocery store popcorn in paper bags — and crowd wrangler as the all-day, all-night event sluggishly scrolled through a slate of B-movies — *Anaconda*, *King Cobra*, *Python*, *Piranhaconda* — culminating in a midnight double feature showing both *Snakes on a Plane* and its straight-to-video rip-off *Snakes on a Train*, these final movies screened, bizarrely, with the audio turned off, alternative soundtrack provided by an experimental jazz band called FUGH whose members played atonal horns through three hours of serpents versus humans trapped on moving vehicles. Krunk, high on speed he'd upbraided Chris for declining, took the stage both before and after the films to rant about how snakes were biblically miscast creatures, innocent victims of the myth of evolution. They were beautiful, he insisted, portals to a time before there was a world, when snakes — the primordial not-yet of slithering, interwoven, scaly bodies — were all that was or would ever be.

Chris dragged his feet, kicked up shallow puddles of pine needles. They were moving slowly but surely toward a spot in the deep woods only Reed could identify. Chris didn't mind the hike, though of course he and Reed were the only ones without gear; the ten ragged and hungover crew were hampered by tripods, lights, batteries, booms. Chris could hear them breathing heavily from their beer bellies, stumbling and cursing as sharp boughs slapped faces their hands were too full to protect. It was a nice change, not having to do the grunt work. They were, he was sure, not enjoying this outing nearly as much as he was. Reed paused to consult his topographical map. Chris took the opportunity to suck in an extra-large gulp of the fresh air. Reed had been right. A cold front had come in. The cold made deep breaths almost painful, like those polar bear swims, Chris thought, Speedo-clad urban warriors running into winter Great Lakes, their friends cheering them on, filling their pledge forms, $10 or $20 for Haiti, for prostate cancer, for manatees and dolphins and red-tailed newts. Nobody raised money for the snake. Never for the snake. Maybe Krunk was onto something. The snake as a symbol of how humanity had cleaved itself from the natural world right from the beginning.

In those summers with Uncle Luke, Krunk's obsession had guided their days. Chris often thought of the hot, dry final summer they spent up north, an entire summer devoted to the hunt for the Massasauga rattler, Ontario's only poisonous snake, whose territory theoretically included the forests and Precambrian rock slabs framing ice-age lakes they spent their days exploring, unmolested by any civilizing force. They were twelve years old with time on their hands. They found plenty of snakes that summer, black and coiled in the cracks of the rocks, yellow and serpentine in the murky olive water lapping the shoreline, emerald and wriggling in the makeshift paths the boys formed as they tramped through the woods on their way to various hideouts and hidden waterways. But they never saw the rattler. As the summer went on and their search remained fruitless, their outings became increasingly ritualistic, with Krunk setting the agenda. Everywhere they went, they hunted snakes, chased them, flushed them out, grabbed them by their necks, their bodies writhing, twisting, turning, their eyes bulging, their angry tongues darting in and out of their oblong mouths. Krunk led them on increasingly ardent marches that didn't end until past dusk, any snakes long since retreated into their lairs.

Chris picked up his pace as Reed made a sudden turn and disappeared into a thicket. Krunk, Laurie, Reed. He'd always been a follower. Was it so bad? To be pulled in the wake of someone else's obsession? That's what he was doing now, wasn't he? Following a man who wasn't even there. Reed popped back into view. He had stopped in front of a rocky outcropping that all but blanked out the clear blue sky somewhere way above.

"Up there," Reed half-gasped, the air catching in his throat and wheezing out.

"Up there?"

Reed had replaced his Penguins ball cap with a battered lime green toque sporting an orange and white pompom. He was wearing a lined corduroy jacket, his usual dirty jeans, and a pair of expensive hiking boots that gave him the air of an eccentric mountaineer.

"Goddamn cigars," Reed barked.

Then he laughed, which turned into a cough that continued until he managed to expectorate a large blob of yellow phlegm onto a lichen-covered boulder that Chris had just been about to take a seat on.

By now the rest of the crew had struggled over. They heaved down their equipment, drained bottles of water, unzipped ski jackets, and gazed warily at the cliff that blocked their path.

"Oh yeah, we're going up," Reed yelled gleefully at them. "That's the shot we want! Panoramic vistas, people! Vistas!"

The crew groaned. "That's what helicopters are for, asshole," one of them muttered.

To which Reed replied without taking his eyes off the cliff, "No copters. I'm a nervous flier," which generated chuckles. Everyone knew Reed was a notorious flier, famous for backing out of flights minutes before takeoff, his sudden premonitions of doom sabotaging meticulously planned agendas and schedules.

"Take five," Reed yelled, "then we're going up." He pushed past Chris and hefted himself onto the lichen rock seat, a manoeuvre Chris watched with a straight face he attributed to his recent crash course in method acting.

"You know," Reed said, oblivious, his low grumble-whisper beckoning Chris closer. "Most of my family died in a forest like this."

"They did?" Chris didn't get it. Reed had told him several times about his two ex-wives, both of whom he claimed to still love madly, and three estranged children, no mention of ongoing love, but as far as he could remember they were all fine; even his parents were alive and kicking, living out their nineties in some middle American suburb somewhere.

"My grandparents' brothers and sisters, their children, dogs,

cats, the town goat. All of 'em, dragged out into the cold Lithu-
anian woods and shot dead." Reed gestured to the bowl of the
forest floor where his crew had taken up various positions of
repose, as if this had been the exact spot where it happened.
"Well," he said thoughtfully. "Maybe not the goat."

"Why?" Chris said, only somewhat less confused than before.

"Why not the goat?"

"Why were they killed?"

"What's the difference," Reed asked sardonically, "between
a pizza and a Jew?"

"Huh?"

"The pizza doesn't scream when you put it in the oven."

"That's ... that's not funny, man."

"Yeah, well, neither was *Schindler's List*, ya know? Or that
other one with that mincing Italian."

"*Life Is Beautiful*," Chris said dutifully, finally understanding.
Krunk had gone through a thankfully brief concentration camp
movie phase.

"Yeah," Reed said.

A gust of wind pushed through, rattling the trees.

"This is my Holocaust movie," Reed announced.

"This is a Holocaust movie?"

"Don't tell New Line," he mock-whispered. "They think
it's an action flick." Reed swiped at his sweaty brow with the
heavy fabric of his jacket. "Anyway, when all is said and done,
this one is for the Razakovskys of Lithuania, aka the Reeds
of Pittsburgh, god only knows how we ended up there." Reed
looked skyward. "Of course," he went on, "it won't matter to
my mother. As far as she's concerned, it's all over, baby blue."

"What is?"

"The line," Reed said jovially. "The Raza-Reeds. Barring

extremely unlikely unforeseen circumstances, especially since the vasectomy, the line dies with me."

"But don't you have —?"

"The kids don't count, I'm sorry to say. Beth was Jewish and we had Bobby, but he's a boy, and he's gay, so that's no good. Then I married Zara the Ethiopian supermodel princess, but she was the wrong kind of Ethiopian, no airlift to the holy land for her; we had us a couple of girls, but, well, as far as my mother is concerned, black Princess Zara couldn't make Jews no matter what, so that's it," Reed announced glumly.

In the sky above, a lone plane propelled past, rumbling low over the trees as if pulled down by the lakes it was designed to land on.

"Ugh," Reed said. "I hate flying in those. Don't you hate those?"

"Dunno," Chris said breezily. "Haven't tried it."

Reed looked at him strangely.

"I mean, uh ..." Chris felt acid surge in his stomach. He shrugged, trying to affect nonchalance.

"Well," Reed boomed suddenly. "What are we waiting for, people?" He clapped his meaty hands.

THEY REACHED THE TOP an hour later, the crew gasping then groaning upon seeing that the plateau of the cliff Reed had forced them to climb flattened out into a forest floor dominated by tall, thick-limbed trees. The dense forest guarded another hillside, this one sweeping up into a ridge standing between them and anything that might be considered even remotely panoramic.

"All right," Reed said, "no need to panic." He consulted his map with furrowed brow. Chris scanned the forest, not particularly concerned about the fate of the excursion. Reed had invited him on it while making it clear that the journey was entirely optional — for the star. Curious, and with nothing else to do, Chris had tagged along, though he probably shouldn't have. He had to stop talking to Reed. To anyone. They knew more about Thomson than he did. Thomson Holmes probably owned a float plane. He was probably in the goddamn thing right now.

"Lookee here," said Reed, his thick finger trailing off the map and pointing into a slight opening in the forest wall. "That's an old logging road. Goes right to the top, I think." Map dangling from his thick hand, Reed stepped to the gap in the trees and squinted.

"Yup," Reed boomed. "This is it! Let's saddle up."

The going was easier on what had, indeed, been a rough road, though it hadn't been used for at least ten years. The tracks, pushed into the hard dirt by who knows how many successive waves of thick truck tires, overflowed with sharp weeds. The flat part of the road had sprouted everything from sickly saplings to creeping raspberry and blackberry vines to feral thigh-high grass gone dry and yellow, thick straw clinging at them as they pushed through. They were moving faster now, steadily ascending despite the crew's curses and gasps. Reed, who seemed to have given himself over to wherever the track lay, had gone voluble, waving his arms as he monologued.

"People think film is about bringing things to life, bringing things into the light. But it's exactly the opposite, you know, Holmes?" Reed, swinging his arms and marching belly first, didn't wait for a reply. "It's about capturing life, using it, sucking up life and processing it. We have more in common with whoever made this road, with the loggers and poachers and zookeepers, than we do with the great artists of our time. No offence there, Holmes, but it's true. We put people in cages and we aim our cameras at them and we take what we want, or at least what we can get from them. We don't bring things to light; we use up all the light there is, all the light people have."

Reed uttered his trademark guffaw, which promptly turned into his trademark dry cough punctuated by muttered expletives. Still coughing and clearing his throat, he suddenly shot forward, turned a corner, and disappeared. Way ahead of the rest of the crew, Chris quickly followed, thinking that enough world-famous Hollywood types had already disappeared on his watch. He found himself striding up the last particularly steep patch of obsolescent road before lurching to a halt to avoid bumping into Reed, who was standing guard at the abrupt conclusion of their journey. Chris pushed in beside Reed, and the two of them stood, silent, transfixed, momentarily dumbstruck.

THE CREW SET UP to film. Reed oversaw the process, whispering and plotting with his director of photography, a dour, almost-mute German fellow who had resolutely marched in the rear, all but buried in a tangle of devices. The German was rumoured to vastly prefer collaborating with his fellow countrymen, having worked with all the greats from Wim Wenders to Rainer Werner Fassbinder, his name regularly associated with the films of Krunk's all-time hero, Werner Herzog, who was — Reed had jealously told Chris as an aside a few days ago — almost done raising money for a feature filmed exclusively inside an active volcano. With nothing to do, Chris reflexively felt for his phone to text Krunk, then remembered where he was. Or maybe who he was. Self-consciously, he slowly took his hands out of his coat pockets then slid them back in. As he fidgeted, he pondered the weird detail that in cold weather, Krunk always wore gloves with no fingers, ready at any moment to roll a joint or grab cellphone footage for his experimental collage project featuring nothing but stripped abandoned bicycles and ripped billowing plastic bags caught in the limbs of the city's sickliest trees. It was cold, getting colder, and Chris wasn't wearing his gloves. He shivered in a spasm that knocked his knees together and almost knocked him down. Reed steadied him with a hand on his shoulder.

"I know it," he muttered, believing that Chris had been shaken by the view splayed before them.

Hadn't he?

Ahead was an eerie, vast clear-cut. The slope down, the long valley, and the next gentle cresting hill over — all stripped down, nothing but scrub and dirt for miles in either direction: the panorama Reed was looking for — or, at least, Chris thought, the one he'd found. Behind them, the thick woods — oaks, tall, thin birches, copses of firs and pines — closed ranks in mute judgment. In front, there was nothing left, no judge, no jury, no witnesses. Extending up and down the hills, bordered by a lake on one side and vast empty horizon to the north and east, was nothing but stumps, thousands upon thousands of stumps dotting the landscape, a world remade by some mad pointillist. Only the desolate vastness formed no image, assumed no gradual reveal of purpose or pattern. There was the barren earth, windswept and dry without the protection of the trees. And there were the stumps, not yet decaying or decomposing, simply there, under a sallow sun and blue sky, the whole scene a cipher, raw material, an absent purpose. Reed was right, Chris thought. It wasn't about life at all. How could it be? Death provides. Where had he heard that before? Something Krunk had said? The title of a Communist-era underground film they'd shown at a screening of celluloid *samizdat*. No, he remembered now. It was the Lost Expert who'd said it. Wasn't it?

Chris shivered again, realized he'd been shivering all along. Sharp wind from the exposed lake sweeping through the denuded valley, buffeting them. Reed would want him to go down there, go into the wasteland, pick his way through what had once been a world. He'd do it, why not? What Reed had said: An entire village marched into the forest and shot. An emptiness and nothingness that festers and rots. Wasn't that what the Lost Expert was all about? He wasn't acting, exactly, just letting something he'd long shut out back in. But once the river flowed, what next? Chris turned to Reed. The director was gazing over the desolation with unencumbered lust. What did he see? Only its devastating beauty.

EXT. TANOQUIN FOREST RESERVE — MORNING
THE LOST EXPERT drives along a rutted track in
a black, battered Ford pickup. Densely packed
trees push against one another, their limbs
encroaching onto the muddy road. The Lost
Expert guns the loud engine up a crumbly hill
and abruptly jams on the brakes at the top. He
surveys the track in front of him, blocked by a
fallen tree and a spreading swamp. He puts the
truck into park. Still in the driver's seat, he
closes his eyes.

                                        CUT TO

A TALL BLOND MAN in a trench coat ascends the
stairs of Waverly House. There's something in
the way he holds his head: you can't quite make
out his features. He seems to be smiling, or
grinning, or else his expression is perfectly
empty.

                                        CUT TO

MICHAEL listens to a record, his expression
beatific.

                                        CUT TO

The Lost Expert in the vehicle. He jerks out of
his trance, clearly troubled.

                        MUSIC
                (crackling gospel blues)
        Oh Lord … Oh Lord … Oh Lord, bring her
                    back to me!

EXT. THICK FOREST — AFTERNOON
THE LOST EXPERT works through tightly packed,
diminutive trees, their bare branches twisted
into one another, struggling for space. He
pushes through a grove of stunted cedars and
stops abruptly, teetering on a rock jutting out
over a dark lake. The lake is small, the forest
on the other side clearly visible. The sun
emerges from under a cloud, and the Lost Expert
squints. He hears something in the underbrush
and pulls out a small pair of binoculars. He
scans the opposite bank. A moose breaks through
and plunges into the water. The Lost Expert
watches the moose swim to a marshy area and
clamber up a steep bank before disappearing
into the backwoods.

EXT. CLEARING IN THE WOODS — DUSK
THE LOST EXPERT stands over a SCRAWNY MAN who
lies twitching in restless sleep next to the
embers of a fire burning under a flapping
canvas. Up close, it is abundantly clear that
the man is not in good shape. His lips are
cracked, and his face is sallow. The Lost Expert
crouches next to the man, who blinks awake. He
jerks, startled, and tries to get up. The Lost
Expert restrains him with a broad, dirt-stained
hand on his chest.

                    THE LOST EXPERT
                      Michael.

Michael groans and struggles, shaking his head
back and forth.

                 THE LOST EXPERT (CONT'D)
            It's all right. You're all right now.

Michael calms. The Lost Expert helps him to sit
up. He takes out a canteen, gives him a sip of
water. Michael coughs, sputters, then drinks
hugely.

EXT. CLEARING — EVENING
MICHAEL and THE LOST EXPERT are eating beans
from cans warmed up on the fire. The fire is
built up high, and the two men sit as close to

it as they can. A misty rain falls. The fire
crackles, and occasionally a bird squawks.

                    THE LOST EXPERT
            Did someone tell you to come here?

Michael doesn't answer. He finishes his beans
and digs into the empty can for any remains,
licking the sauce on the spoon.

                    THE LOST EXPERT
            (removing the sketch drawn by Michael
              that he took from Waverly House)

        Do you know the man in this picture? Did
                  he come to see you?

                      MICHAEL
              (furiously shaking his head)
                        Him!

                    THE LOST EXPERT
        Who is he? You wrote under the picture,
        "Beaoman." Is that his name, Michael?
                      Beaoman?

                      MICHAEL
            (whisper-singing to a blues tune)
            God isn't true / that's nothing new /
            going deep underground / going to buy
            that promised land / all gonna come /

before we even know / all gonna come / I
think you know / how to / be a man / be a
man /be a man.

THE LOST EXPERT
He gave you a record, didn't he? Is that
from the record he gave you, Michael?

Michael leans into the fire, whispering and
raving.

MICHAEL
Be a man! Be a man …

THEY HURRIED THROUGH THE dark, their feet crunching leaves stiff with early frost, the hum of a portable generator getting louder as they approached Reed's cabin. It was almost midnight. Alison had knocked on the door of Chris's shack on the hill, summoning him to an urgent meeting.

Reed's domain was a gutted cabin, its interior now dominated by a long, battered wooden desk atop which perched several elongated computer screens angled together and attached by thick cables to a humming black box lodged down below. Surrounding the screens, and spilling onto the wall behind them, were an array of sticky notes, some crammed with tiny scribbles of writing, others sporting just one or two words written hurriedly in illegible, indelible Sharpie. The sticky notes formed an elaborate traffic pattern, a chronicle of potential intersections — to Chris they looked like an inverted map, roads to nowhere, accidents and dead ends. Bryant Reed sat at the desk, staring into nothing, dwarfed by his role as the cartographer. His face, shrouded by lamplight and computer screen, showed dark bags under his eyes.

"What took you so long?" he asked, swivelling in a battered office chair and addressing nobody in particular. There was an open bottle of scotch on the desk next to a half-full glass. "Boy oh boy." Reed rubbed his hands together in mock excitement, then clapped them hard on his own cheeks. "We're in for it now!" Chris followed Alison into the cabin. "Sit down." Reed swung out of the way to reveal a love seat jammed against the back wall. "Yeah, yeah, sit down."

Alison slipped by, twisting sideways to avoid touching Reed. Chris followed, brushing past the sour-smelling director and lowering himself down beside his assistant. The proximity was a shock. Alison felt it too, Chris was sure; the spots where their bodies touched, the gaps where they didn't. "Have a drink." Reed sloppily poured amber liquid into several smeared glasses before wheeling himself forward and proffering the scotch. "L'chaim," Reed announced, sloshing his newly topped-up glass as they toasted. Chris sipped. He'd been worried on the way over — had he finally been discovered? But sitting next to Alison, immersed in the madness of this make-believe world, he was unbothered. *I'm not here*, he thought, stealing a glance at Alison's perfectly angled cheek.

The lamps flickered. Outside, crickets chirruped the end of summer. Alison turned her glass around in her hand, the golden brown liquid gently undulating. Nobody spoke.

"So," Chris finally felt compelled to say. "What's going on?"

"What's *going on*?" Reed repeated dramatically. "Oh, nothing. Nothing at all. Just a little bit of *mutiny* is all, Holmes, nothing for you to worry your pretty little head about." Chris blinked at the venom in Reed's voice. Reed was pissed. At him? He looked for a sign. Reed's glower was directionless, seemingly aimed at everything.

"Darlia," Alison said evenly, "has threatened to leave the production."

"Threatened?!" Reed jolted back to life. "She's packing her bags. She's booking a flight."

"Why?" Chris said.

"Why?" Reed gesticulated, spilling drink. "Because this isn't the romantic bullshit she's used to, with a script full of canned one-liners and a leading man with as much chest hair as brains. That's why!"

"She's expressed concerns about the direction of the story," said Alison.

"It's not working," Reed said in a nasal imitation of a starlet falsetto. "It's too hard." Reed made a face like he was going to spit. "If she walks off, she'll never work again. She'll be sorry. It'll be like she just disappeared." Reed snapped his fingers. Chris felt the sound travel up his spine.

"I'm sure it won't come to that," Alison said primly.

"Why is she blaming me?" Chris said. "I'm too what, exactly?"

Alison turned toward him, her knees brushing his legs, a subtle shift.

"She says she isn't connecting with you," Alison explained. "She says your energy is disturbing."

"Your *energy*!" Reed scoffed.

"She's really leaving?" Chris ran his fingers through his hair.

"You know what she said?" Reed locked eyes with Chris, dropped his voice to a whisper. Alison gestured vaguely at Reed, a signal of censure he ignored.

"She said you were like a different person."

Chris twitched out a smile.

"She said you were a *totally different person*. And I said, 'That's called acting! That's what he gets *paid* to do.' She should try it sometime."

Chris felt Alison's hand on his knee, gently squeezing. "You're not responsible, Thomson. It's just not what she was expecting."

Reed was getting loud again. "She has to work with an actual actor for a fucking change and it's freaking her out."

Alison took a small sip of her scotch, an inscrutable expression on her face.

"You've got to deal with this," Reed said. "Lay on the old Thomson Holmes charm. Tell her how great she's doing. Tell her she's heading straight to the Oscars, for Christ's sake. Bat those baby blues of yours and convince her to stay."

The tone was commanding. Reed pulled off his Penguins cap and mopped at his forehead with the sleeve of his flannel shirt. *He needs me*, Chris realized. What would happen if she really did leave? Would the studio pull the plug? Reed would go insane. The man was possessed. *The Lost Expert* was everything to him.

"She's in her hotel suite," Alison explained. "She said she would at least sit down with you before she made any final decision. But, Bryant, I'm really not sure if this is the best way to —"

Reed interrupted. "You'll talk some sense into her, right Holmes?"

"Me? What am I supposed to do?"

"Holmes! You're all I've got."

Alison leaned in and whispered a single word in his ear: "Hawaii." Chris heard it as a sensation, lava flowing through him.

"All right!" Reed shouted manically into his walkie-talkie. "He's ready! Bring the car!"

"HELLO? ANYONE HOME? DARLIA?"

Darlia emerged, padding in petite bare feet across interlocking rugs.

"Thomson," she said with just a hint of a smile.

Chris blinked, his eyes adjusting to this most recent gloomy interior. The suite had been custom decorated — throw rugs, framed paintings, chrome lamps exuding fuzzy non-directional light. Long, silkily diffuse curtains separated the front sitting room from the mysterious bulk of the space. Chris ran his fingers nervously through his hair. He'd seen her movies. Everyone had. A few of them were classics. *The Boxer's Daughter*. Krunk had taken him to see it several years back, late-night double feature with *Raging Bull* at the rep cinema. Chris had liked it a lot. Afterwards Krunk had raved about it. He said it was a noir masterpiece, a reinvention of the character study that didn't so much study as penetrate, strip away, relentlessly reveal.

She'd been twenty-two when she'd made that movie. And right after it, the other big one she'd made, in which she affected a very Southern accent that made her seem both vulnerable and vengeful, deserving of what she got. Ten years ago. Another time. Today, people talked about her with a reverence reserved for the truly iconic. Even Krunk. Of course, he larded any compliment with a vitriolic rant against every movie she'd made since, including the handful that, as far as Chris could tell, had been pretty okay — at least by Hollywood standards.

Hawaii, Chris repeated to himself in a mantra. Darlia wore black yoga pants and a yellow tank. She was fresh faced, like a college student off to Pilates. Her pouted mouth flickered with potential expressions she couldn't decide to put on. Her green eyes were spiral orbits that would suck him in if he got too close. She looked like what she was: a star.

"What are you staring at?" Darlia asked playfully, a coy grin on her face.

"Oh — uh —" a nonplussed Chris muttered awkwardly. "Just, you know —"

"Thomson!" She threw her arms around him. He stood, stiff, awkwardly holding her. She smelled of lemon and vanilla. "It's all a big mess, isn't it?" Then, lowering her head to his shoulder, she started to slowly cry.

"Shush," he said, patting her back as her small form trembled against him.

"I'm sorry," she said miserably.

"It's okay. Really."

She pushed away. Desperate to avoid her gaze, Chris looked down. Her bare feet were tiny, as if just born. Darlia giggled nervously. She wiggled her toes. "They centre me."

Chris nodded, not getting it, smiling vaguely. *Hawaii.*

"That's it? Nothing to say?"

He stopped smiling. What was he supposed to say?

"It's freaking me out. It's like you're him."

"Him?"

"That stupid Lost Expert."

Chris looked down at her, suddenly aware of his abruptly over-large body.

"Let's sit," Darlia said. She gestured to the short couch and the club chair.

He sat down on the couch. "Can I get you something? I've got tea. Just herbal, though."

"I'm good, thanks." Chris swallowed hard. Darlia pulled the club chair close, so close that when she sat down, her bare knees brushed against his legs. She leaned forward expectantly.

"So," Chris said cautiously. "You don't like the movie."

"No, no, it's not that." It struck Chris that she was the sort of person who couldn't stand to be objectionable while objecting. "I love the movie concept. And Reed, Reed is really a genius, isn't he? He's just … it's just …"

"You don't know what it's about," Chris said with sudden inspiration. His voice was loud in the deep quiet of Darlia's New Age country retreat.

Darlia nodded. She closed her eyes. She sighed deeply. Chris felt her breath on his face, warm and tinged sweet.

"Do you know?" she asked. "Do you know what it's about?"

Chris shook his head. He proceeded haltingly, unsure of what she wanted to hear. "I think that's the point, though. It's like we're all in the dark, groping around trying to find it. We know it's there; we can feel that it's there. It's about trying to find that thing we've all lost, even though we haven't really lost it, because it's been there all along. It's just that we've lost sight of it."

"That's really beautiful, Thomson." She opened her eyes. "Who are you again?" She didn't wait for an answer. "Look, don't take this the wrong way, but you really are like a different person. I don't know if it's the movie or what, but you're so much more … Everything about you is different."

Darlia seemed tired now, tiny cracks fissuring from the corners of her eyes, her glow fading ever so slightly.

"I don't know," she said. "My agent told me it was going to be an action picture, a cerebral action picture. Bryant Reed's big comeback. And then he said you were attached. And I thought maybe if we worked together again, I could … And then I see that you're so different now."

"Hawaii," Chris said, almost without thinking. The word, stuck in his head since that moment in Reed's cabin.

Darlia jerked back as if hit. Then she laughed darkly. "A long time ago, right?"

Chris nodded. He had no idea what they were talking about. But he felt it, in the pit of his stomach, a troubled history between them, an inevitable truth he didn't want to know.

Darlia stared darkly down at the ornate patterns beautifully stitched into the small Persian rug that adorned the seating area.

"It's you," she finally said, the misery in her voice terrible and palatable. "I took the part because of you. I wanted to try and understand ... what happened. What happened to me. Then. What you did. It wasn't right, Thomson. I was just a kid. *Night Lighting*," she said sarcastically.

Night Lighting. Hawaii. For once Krunk's endless rants and lectures were coming in handy. Action flick. Surfing. A volcano explosion. Holmes is the star. Darlia is the co-star and love interest. It's her first big break. She gets trapped. Earthquakes. Floods. Volcanoes. Lava approaches. The Holmes character. He has to rescue her.

"And, honestly, it makes me sick, Thomson. You make me sick. I thought maybe if I worked with you again. After all this time. If I told you to your face what you did. What you did to me. My therapist — don't you dare laugh! — she says I have to face up to my past, accept it, not bury it. Do you understand what I'm saying, Thomson?"

"Darlia, I'm —"

"And I know there was that agreement. But that was — Jesus, I was so stupid! I signed. I took the money. I kept my mouth shut. And for years I was afraid, Thomson. You know what? I was terrified."

Darlia was weeping now. "I thought I could ... move on. But it makes me sick, Thomson. It makes me sick to look at you." She put her face in her hands.

The agreement. The agreements. The same weird cover-up? How many agreements were there? Thomson Holmes! What had he done? Chris felt it tangled up in him, a thick fabric of regret. Why? He hadn't done anything. This had nothing to do with him. But there it was anyway, a knotted ball of wool, stuck in his stomach, slowly unravelling.

"I'm sorry, Darlia. I'm really sorry."

Darlia looked at him, her eyes searching and open, tears running down her cheeks.

"Who the hell are you? Even your face. Around your eyes. It's softer. It's like you're — I don't know. Like you're not you. Okay, it's a role. But right now. Even right now. You're so …."

"Darlia."

"And you're listening!" Darlia said, almost spitting the words. "Thomson Holmes is actually listening."

"Darlia! I'm not that person anymore. That was so long ago, and I'm so sorry about what happened. But, for what it's worth, I'm different now. I am a different person."

Darlia sobbed, and Chris felt the tears hitting him like a heavy rain. "On set," she said through great gasps, "when we're doing a scene, it's like you're in a trance. It's like you don't even see me."

"I see you. I do. It's not me." Chris was thinking aloud now, following his own train of thought. "It's the Lost Expert. The character. Right now, I don't think he can see you. I mean — his wife. He can't see her. He's too focused."

"And you?"

"Me?"

She leaned in close. "Do you see me? Do you see me now?"

"I see you," he said quietly. "Of course, I see you."

She looked at him, eyes streaming tears, regret and rage and embarrassment moving across her face.

"It's not what happened," Darlia said. "It's what you did. *You* happened."

Not sure what to say, Chris stayed quiet.

"For fuck's sake, Thomson!" Darlia slapped him, hard, on the face. He felt it and didn't feel it. "Get out. Just get the hell out of here!"

Chris stood up. Darlia, her face in her hands, her blond hair shielding her.

Had he made things worse or better? Thomson Holmes, predator, pig, problem solver.

How long? How long had this been going on?

"Darlia," Chris finally managed. "I'm so sorry. You don't have to accept that. You shouldn't accept that. But it's all I have. What else is there? What I'm hoping is you'll stay. You'll stay, and we'll make something else. Something beautiful."

Darlia raised her head. Tears glazed her cheeks. She wasn't crying anymore. She stared at him, her expression empty but not blank.

EXT. TANOQUIN FOREST RESERVE — NIGHT
A light rain falls outside. THE LOST EXPERT and
MICHAEL sit under the crooked canvas tarp. Water
drips through.

                    MICHAEL
              (jerking spasmodically)
              How did you find me?

                    THE LOST EXPERT
          A lot of people are looking for you,
                    Michael.

                    MICHAEL
          (shaking his shaggy head, laughing
                    crazily)
                Looking!

                    THE LOST EXPERT
          It's time to come home, Michael.

                         MICHAEL
                 (increasing his agitation)
                No, no, no, no, no, no.

                      THE LOST EXPERT
             I can't leave you here, Michael.

                         MICHAEL
                 No, no, no, no, *no*.

                      THE LOST EXPERT
           You'll die here, Michael. Let me help
                          you.

                         MICHAEL
                          No.

        Michael scrambles to his knees and pulls a knife
        out from beneath a tattered blanket.

                      THE LOST EXPERT
              That's not who you are, Michael.

        Michael slashes at the air with the knife and
        begins to gently sob.

                         MICHAEL
                          No.

                      THE LOST EXPERT
             Who's talking to you, Michael? Who's in
                      your head?

The Lost Expert closes his eyes and hums a bit.
He sings under his breath.

>   THE LOST EXPERT
>   The devil's gone lost / God's no better. /
>   heads are rolling down / down underwater.

>   MICHAEL
>   (eyes lighting up, singing in a
>   harsh whisper)
>   Think I'll fall my way / think I'll fall
>   away / think I'll fall / think I'll fall …

>   MICHAEL AND THE LOST EXPERT
>   (howling together)
>   Aaaaaaa … waaaaaaay.

The sounds of their singing trail off and the
distant but present noises of the woods reassert
themselves.

>   THE LOST EXPERT
>   Put the knife down.

Michael lets the knife fall. He covers his face
with his hands, weeping.

>   THE LOST EXPERT
>   Let me help you.

Michael falls onto his side in the fetal
position.

MICHAEL

No, no.

ALISON WOKE CHRIS AT 6:00 a.m. She knocked softly, then opened the cabin door and stepped in. Chris was already awake, but he pretended to be sleeping, luring Alison closer until she was leaning over him, her hair smelling of woodsmoke and strawberry, her breath a waft of pine. "Thom-son. Wakey-wakey, Thomson."

It was their last day up north. Tomorrow they would head back to the city. Darlia had flown out early but promised to return to the movie after completing an elaborate session of personalized yoga, aromatherapy, and isolation baths. "She's going to do a 'speed round recalibration,'" Reed had told Chris, his complaints about the forthcoming bill his way of complimenting Chris for his efforts.

Chris made his own more modest ablutions in the large, empty communal camp bathroom. Graffiti was scrawled on the walls: *Debbie Does Doofus. Camp Shab Forever! Mitch W. Was Here!* Studying his face in a dirty mirror with a crack running down the side, he looked lean, angular, and unfamiliar. His blond-brown hair, slick from his shower, sat flatly on his head, emphasizing his jutting forehead and sharp eyes. Outside, he could hear the crew muttering, swearing, trudging through the campsite, hauling

gear, getting ready to follow the Lost Expert wherever he had
to go.

Where would they go that day? Reed kept pushing the crew
deeper and deeper into the forest. What were they looking for?
Reed had shown him rushes: billowing white clouds moving
ponderously across skeletal vistas of bare branches, waves
splashing over the deep centre of the silent and mysterious lake,
at its depths still a million-year-old glacier, eternally melting.
They were beautiful images, alive and true, but Reed sat watching them with his Penguins cap pulled so low it almost covered
his dissatisfied smirk.

Alison was elusive, disappearing then reappearing just when
he was wondering what could possibly have happened to her,
popping up out of nowhere with piping hot cups of coffee from
the camp cafeteria. She was an absent presence — where was
she when she wasn't leading him to the next place he needed to
be? He found that he couldn't function on the set without her.
The rhythms of shooting eluded him. He didn't know where
to go, what he should be doing next. And the way she looked
at him as she led him to and fro. Her liquid brown eyes, pools
of inscrutable insight. No, he told himself. She didn't know.
Nobody knew.

Chris's stomach rumbled, and he came back to himself. What
now? Adrift without further instruction, he climbed back up
his hill and planted himself on the picnic table like a king on his
throne. The weather, consistently bright and cool since they'd
arrived, had gone mercurial. It was warmer, and the sky seemed
to be settling, a barely lit gloom pushing black-grey clouds.
There was no sign of the sun, and Chris had no idea what
time it was. A warmish wind picked up. All he knew was that
he was hungry. Lately, he was always hungry. Hoping it was

at least nearly breakfast time, he made his way down the hill toward the dining hall, the last of the fallen leaves spinning in gritty mini tornadoes.

Inside he was surprised to find Alison sitting alone on a bench nursing a cup of tea. She wore a white ski hat with a pink bow. "Hey." She waved to him. Chris waved back. Had he missed breakfast? No, he realized, it was too early for breakfast. He filled up a mug of coffee from the giant percolator and sat on the bench across from his assistant. Empty tables and benches splayed out all around them. From the kitchen they could hear the cooks preparing the morning meal.

"I saw you up there, on your hill," Alison said teasingly. "Meditating, maybe?"

Instead of answering, Chris took a sip of his coffee. The wind gusted, sending forest detritus bouncing against the thin wooden walls of the dining hall. Alison shivered.

"Are you cold?" Chris asked.

"I'm all right," Alison said. She gave him a pale smile. "I don't like storms."

"I think it's going to blow over," Chris said, intending his pronouncement to comfort.

"I hope so."

They listened to the gathering gale outside.

"Are you hungry? Would you like something?"

"Some cereal would be great. Rice Krispies? And a banana?"

Alison disappeared into the kitchen and returned with a tray. Thomson peeled his banana and cut it into his cereal.

"Any milk?" he asked her.

"I thought you hated milk. Aren't you lactose intolerant?" Alison looked at him curiously.

"Right. I'm off dairy." There was an open strawberry yogurt

next to Alison. "Can I have this?" Chris was already dumping the small container into this bowl and stirring.

Alison watched expressionlessly as Chris attacked his cereal. Her big eyes and small hands wrapped around her mug made her seem at once girlish and worldly, like a high-schooler coughing on a cigarette.

Bit old for you, isn't she?

Grabbing his mug, Chris moved to the front to get a better look at the camp through the larger window. The looming black slab of sky was now pressing so low Chris felt he could reach out and touch it. There was action down by the beach, Reed and Clipboard Tina urgently conferring, the German gesticulating at an increasingly feral-looking grouping of techies and crew. Alison joined him by the window. The water of the lake surged in angry chops.

"They're up to something," Chris said.

Alison shrugged, smiling weakly. "Storm chasing."

That was it, Chris realized. That was what Reed had been waiting for. "Thanks!" he yelled at a surprised Alison as he hurried out the front door of the dining hall. Fighting the wind, Chris pushed down to the lakefront.

By the time he got there, the discussion was over.

"Sorry, bud," Reed muttered, looking past him.

"What? What is it?" Chris asked.

"She won't let ya."

Tina looked over them both imperiously. "You can do what you want," she said to Reed. "But Mr. Holmes will be waiting this one out safely inside. We can get another director, but there's only one star of the show."

"Gee, thanks," Reed grumbled. He looked at Chris forlornly. Thunder sounded from a distance. Reed perked up. "Is the crew ready?" he yelled. And then, frantically looking around: "Where's the German? What's the twenty on the German?"

"You're with me, Mr. Holmes," Tina said politely, firmly taking his arm.

Tina installed him back in his cabin. "Don't move," she told him before hurrying out. "Don't move a muscle."

Chris stepped briskly to the window, watching intently as the storm took possession of their little enclave, powerful gusts ripping at the newly naked trees. It hadn't occurred to him that he'd be banned from this culminating journey to the heart of the maelstrom. It was too dangerous. There was insurance. There was liability. He should sneak out, he thought. Krunk style, before Krunk went weak. Reed would want him to. Forget Reed! What would Thomson Holmes do? Chase the storm like a superstar! *So where was he, then?* Whitecaps surged, and the glass in the window rattled. Startled, Chris jerked back from the window.

Anyway, there was that guy. The stunt double. He'd kept away from Chris and Chris from him. Was it on purpose, an unspoken movie set superstition? You never met your double. You never watched the dailies on a Wednesday. The irony of being a movie star. You were eternal, yet perpetually on the brink of obsolescence. You had to keep upping the ante, Chris thought. What Alison had said: "I don't like storms." Who did? Reed, crazy Reed. Chris had never thought of himself as a risk taker. But now he felt a surge of energy inside him. Reed and the crew pushing triumphantly through the slashing winds. The lake writhed in anticipation. Orange buoys marking the swimming area jerked crazily from side to side.

The rain came, dull thuds against the walls and roof of the cabin like open-handed slaps from some impertinent god. Chris felt the whirl of the storm in the pit of his belly. He stood by the window, riveted, undecided, imagining he could still go, still find Reed and the crew, still make the bold, brave decision. The door to the cabin blew open. Cold rain lashed the side of Chris's face. Numbly, he moved to close the door. But there was a visitor hovering at the doorstep. She was familiar to Chris, though he couldn't quite place her. She was pale and plain, her doughy face scrubbed of any adornment. She looked rough, and Chris wondered if she'd been drinking. But no, there was something ghostly about her. Like she'd risen from the dead. Behind her, black sheets of rain spilled from the sky's torrent. Wet leaves and broken branches whipped. The woman made a face, her mouth contorting like she'd lost language.

"What?" Chris yelled. "What is it?"

The woman leaned in, and they were nose to nose.

"I have a son," she screamed furiously. Fat drops of rain clung to her cheeks. "A fifteen-year-old son."

"What? What happened?" The grey horizon pressed lower. Thunder boomed.

"He fired me!" she snapped.

Wardrobe lady, Chris finally realized. It was Eloise. The wardrobe lady.

"What? I didn't —"

"Shut up," Eloise screamed, grabbing the front of Chris's shirt. Lightning flashed, and Chris looked down to see the fabric bunched up in the white blob of her fist.

"But I didn't tell him to —"

"Shut the *fuck up*!" Eloise's angry eyes bulged, then brimmed. Chris, his face inches from hers, felt claustrophobic.

"Look," he said, begging her. "Look. It'll be okay. Just, let's get you out of the rain. I'll talk to him, I'll —" He took her arm, trying to pull her into the cabin and out of the storm.

"Don't touch me!" Eloise screamed. "Don't touch me, you fucking pervert!"

Startled, Chris lurched back, slipping on the worn wood of the cabin, now wet and slick. He went down hard, slamming his head. Lightning flashed twice. Chris felt suddenly heavy, as if he were thrashing in thick, brackish water. It was a memory. Somewhere terrible he'd been and had never planned to go back to. He spluttered, coughing. He flailed, failing to get up. The rain came down harder, on him, on everything.

LATER, IN BED, NAKED, the comforter damp. He felt clammy all over, as if wrapped in a bubble of weirdly warm, swampy water. He heard the door to his cabin creaking open. He tensed. Eloise, coming back. The photographer. Was this part of it? Was this his payback? He'd ended it, he thought. He'd broken it. The agreement. Night wind whipped past, circling then whirling back out again.

Light steps on the rough, complaining floorboards.

"Thomson?"

It was Alison.

"Are you asleep?"

A shuffling of wet synthetics — a coat coming off. Then more sounds: clothes dropping.

"Thomson? The power is out. There's no light. Can I ...?"

Shivering, she climbed in next to him.

EXT. PARKING LOT OUTSIDE A MOTEL OFF THE HIGHWAY
— LATE AFTERNOON
MICHAEL sits submissively in the back seat
of a limousine with open driver's cabin. A
newsboy's flat cap is pulled down almost to
his eyes. He sways rhythmically to music only
he can hear. The DRIVER, a disconcertingly
large fellow, stands with his arms
folded next to the vehicle. THE LOST EXPERT
stands a few paces away with BARTNER'S
ASSISTANT.

                    ASSISTANT
        I assume this will cover your fee and
                    any expenses.

The Lost Expert takes the envelope without
looking inside it.

                  THE LOST EXPERT
         Has the family ever had any contact
         with a man who calls himself Beaoman?

                    ASSISTANT
        I've never heard of anybody by that
                     name.

                  THE LOST EXPERT
          Are you familiar with the man in
                 this picture?

The assistant glances grimly down at the Lost
Expert's sketch.

                    ASSISTANT
                      No.

The Lost Expert looks over at Michael.
He is rocking violently in the back of the car.

                  THE LOST EXPERT
              What will happen to him?

                    ASSISTANT
        We've arranged to have him transferred to
              a more secure facility.

                  THE LOST EXPERT
              What kind of facility?

The assistant shrugs.

                  THE LOST EXPERT
          A man will come see him. He mustn't be
          allowed to see him. Tell Mr. Bartner

what I said. Beaoman. Or whatever he'll
call himself. Maybe he will claim to
be someone else. Maybe he will be in
disguise. Look again at his picture.
This man here. He'll come to see
Michael. Don't let him. You mustn't
let him.

ASSISTANT
I'll let him know. Now, if you'll excuse
us, it's a long drive.

The impeccably dressed assistant gets into the
enclosed part of the limousine next to MICHAEL,
who shrinks away from him. The driver pulls on
a pair of bulbous goggles. With a great gust of
exhaust, the limousine pulls away.

PART THREE

HIS FORMER LIFE: MAKING lattes for the morning regulars; lounging on Laurie's sagging second-hand couch, rubbing her feet and listening to classical music on the radio; drinking cheap syrupy port out of jam jars while watching the shadowy Dr. Caligari roam around the imaginary German village Holstenwall, local town turned monochrome nightmare. *The Cabinet of Dr. Caligari*, Krunk's favourite movie. They must have watched it at least thirty times. At first, Chris had thought it was terrible.

"Ha!" his friend responded triumphantly. "They booed it in New York and Berlin!" Chris wasn't surprised. The relentless shadowing and deliberately tormented angles failed to hide the fact that the set didn't just look like it was made of paper, it literally was made from paper. Even its faux spooky intertitles felt paper thin: *Spirits surround us on every side*.

But for Krunk, all of that only added to the greatness. *Caligari* was not just an improbably successful homemade independent, a pre-digital *Blair Witch*. It was the bible of the psychological thriller — the urtext from which entire genres, entire eddies of the subconscious imagination, had sprung. Its hokeyness was its holiness. And the set — especially the depictions of the town fair — were brilliantly evocative of the flimsy nature of modern civilization, its predilection to papering over everything that lurked under order and civility. As Krunk put it: "One spark and it's up in flames!" Most importantly, Krunk fervently dis-agreed with the film theorists and semiotics PHDS — who else cared? — passionately arguing that the film's beginning and ending flashbacks undermined the message of the world's first horror movie and first post–World War I international hit. Instead, Krunk pontificated to anyone who would listen — usually just Chris — that adding an *it-was-just-a-dream* framing to the tale of the ringmaster who turns a sleepwalker into a killer was a brilliant move. Making it all the fantasy of a park-bench-bound deranged lunatic served to create yet another layer of messaging. The classic directorial escape hatch — it was all just a dream, wasn't it? — underscoring the growing power of popular culture to manipulate weak-willed populations. The ultimate expressionist nightmare-fantasy: no past, no present, no future, only a series of moments — dreams, really — open to endless interpretation. "And so," Krunk enthused, chest puffed up and voice near cracking, "we come to the present day, in which Caligari's legacy reaches its final solution: total immer-sion! There is no authority, no reason, no science, no progress! There is only what you want to believe! Everyone else is crazy! Now back to the real world!"

The real world.

In this case, a hotel room. Much to Chris's surprise, they had gone straight from the closed-up summer camp to Pearson Airport. The flight had been long, notable primarily for the fact that Chris, who had never flown before and had always imagined it as a cramped, unpleasant process better avoided, seemed to have an entire section of the plane to himself. He quickly and easily fell asleep in a seat that stretched out to become a bed with the push of a few buttons. Now, awake and rested, Chris inspected his surroundings. Even with the blinds pulled closed, he could see that the room was bright and solid, the opposite of Caligari's distorted, stretched-out nightmare. Up north, it had all been dreams and shadows, fallen heaps of leaves and sudden skitterings in the still woods. Following Reed through the bush, he had wondered if he himself wasn't a somnambulist upon whom a spell had been cast. Couldn't it just be a dream? Wasn't it?

Wrapped in a plush hotel robe, he warily pushed aside a curtain as if it might reveal his worst fears. His room overlooked a lake swathed in bright sunshine. The lake, a rich, deep blue, filled the bottom half of his view. Long and thin, with no start or end, the length he could see was bordered to the north by low-lying hills. This was a radically unfamiliar landscape. Chris, who'd never left Ontario, had never seen a sky quite so expansive. Its beauty was disconcerting. He didn't know what to look at or how to look at it. The postcard-perfect view felt wrong to him. Up north, he'd been at home in the claustrophobic press of heavy bush, half-buried boulders, and interminable swamps. That was what he knew — the urban east, even its wilderness pressed in, enclosed. He was not supposed to be here. He was supposed to be back home, apologizing to Laurie, ruefully reporting his misadventures to Krunk, impressing himself by making a list of the colleges he might attend, the programs he might pursue.

Up north, he'd kept telling himself that when he got back to the city, that was it. He'd be out. He'd be done.

Instead, he'd arrived somewhere else. Somewhere solid and real, the complete opposite of the claustrophobic, phantasmagoric bush with its sudden storms and tangled hummocks. What had happened there — his long walks with Reed, the vast empty madness of the clear-cut valley, the wardrobe lady's sudden rageful appearance — those could all be discounted. They had happened. But maybe they hadn't happened. And Alison. What had happened with Alison.

Chris squinted up at the blue of the clouds. Even the sun's clear yellow rays seemed different. He was in a small Canadian town on the western side of the country. British Columbia. They were here, he knew, to shoot the casino scenes and film in an area that was somehow going to pass for the Nevada desert. That was all Chris knew.

Breakfast arrived on a tray, grapefruit and lightly buttered toast and black coffee. Chris ate absent-mindedly, sitting in bed and watching a show on the History Channel about the search for the Sasquatch. Just when it was getting good — they were closing in on a bigfoot just a few miles south of the British Columbia border in a rangy zone of Washington State — there was a knock on his door. It was time for his workout. Rather than argue, Chris threw longing sidelong glances at the TV as he got ready. Up north, he'd learned to grimly succumb to the machinations of an interchangeable array of ponytailed, blond-streaked brunettes. Women named Barbara, Betty, or Babs, impossibly fit Lycra-clad forty-somethings who put him through his paces as if he were a prize pony.

After his workout, it was back to his room. Lunch appeared. Or maybe, Chris wondered hopefully, the sliced melon, cottage cheese, and kale smoothie were just a snack? Then another woman arrived to ask him, somewhat warily it seemed to Chris, if he'd like to take a Jacuzzi. Chris looked at her blankly, and she indicated the massive sunken tub in the bathroom he hadn't even noticed.

"Oh, yeah, sure," Chris said. She drew the bath, adding powders and liquids that burbled and released pleasantly pungent aromatics. She turned on the jets, then seemed to linger around the edges of the tub, as if unsure of how best to next proceed.

"Excuse me," she said. "Your bath is ready."

"Okay. Thanks." Chris wished, once again, that he had something in his wallet to tip with. His wallet, as empty as it was threadbare.

The woman left.

Chris dropped his robe and got in, currents of hot water shooting into his back. His muscles were tight on him, not unfamiliar but increasingly prominent. Chris slid down until the scented, fizzy water blotted out the light. In the throbbing dark, Krunk was there, still pontificating: "The nerve of that small-town bureaucrat! Two million dead, four million wounded in a pointless global conflict fought trench by trench in honour of the *Vaterland*, but Caligari's somnambulist exhibit is too profane for the town fair? The good doctor wouldn't stand for it. Why should he? They want to banish the darkness? They were the ones who unleashed it!" Chris surfaced, breathing hard.

Hurrying over to the closet, Chris fumbled into the least obnoxious uniform he could find, a slim-cut sports jacket over a sheer designer T-shirt. He accented himself with the partial disguise of sunglasses and baseball cap — he was, he reasoned, a movie star after all — and turned to the full-length mirror mounted on the closet door. Beneath the slim lines of his jacket, his stomach grumbled. He was hungry. He was tired of salads and small portions of grilled or poached fish or chicken. He missed eggs sunny side up, yolks running into side bacon. Pizza slices dotted with green olives and closing time-congealed pepperoni. Late-night fries smothered in diner gravy. In the mirror, he saw a man's face, light tan splayed over a square jaw and tight, high cheekbones. The man grinned, showing dimpled blond stubble and long white incisors.

He took the elevator to the lobby, stepping into an empty vestibule. Chris surveyed the small hallway cautiously then proceeded into another wide hall, one of those strange liminal spaces found only in hotels. This long corridor had a large two-sided fireplace in its middle. On both sides of the burning fire — first reminder to Chris that there was, apparently, a fall here too — stiff-looking, high-backed, red-upholstered velvet chairs were arranged. Rustic tree stump coffee tables sat in between the chairs, providing, if nothing else, the illusion of the possibility of leisurely fireside chats. The grey walls were adorned with oil paintings — landscapes of the same natural world Chris had contemplated through his room's window. The idea, obviously, was to make displacement and anonymity pleasant and comfortable — even desirable. But where was everybody? Where was Alison?

Passing the fireplace, he heard his name.

"Thomson. Thomson Holmes."

His new name.

Chris turned. A short man, barely visible in one of the high-backed, deeply plush armchairs. Chris felt a shock of recognition: the shaved head, protruding brow, and squashed nose belonged to his mystery texter, holder of the agreement, the photographer. Close up, there were new details. A permanent expression of disgust bordering on disdain. A short scimitar-shaped scar running down one cheek. Scarface, Chris thought. A little Scarface.

The man, the Little Scarface, leaned forward languorously.

"Do you have a minute, Mr. Holmes?" he half-whispered, half-ordered.

"Actually," Chris managed, "I'm —"

"It'll just be a minute," Little Scarface said, his words pleasantly unctuous. "I've come all this way, after all. All this way just to see you, Mr. Holmes. Thomson. Can I call you Thomson?"

"I have to go."

"So soon? I was told you had the day off. Speaking of which, how is the movie going? How's old Bryant doing? And I suppose they got the usual waiting for you up there? Up there in the penthouse, Thomson, they got the usual? They got all that arranged? They taking good care of you?"

Chris didn't know what he was talking about. *The usual?* Little Scarface shot out a snake-like arm. His fingers wrapped around Chris's wrist.

"Sit with me for just a minute, Mr. Holmes."

Haplessly, Chris let himself be pulled into the adjacent chair.

"We made an agreement, Mr. Holmes," Little Scarface said quietly, leaning in with confidential intimacy. His languid, crooked smile never shifting, Little Scarface continued. "But you're not keeping up your end."

"I'm shooting a movie," Chris said, resisting the urge to jump up, to run away.

"Up here in Canada. Shooting a movie. That's not what we agreed to. That's not part of the agreement."

"But ..." Chris continued weakly. "We can — When it's over —"

"When it's over," Little Scarface repeated glumly. He let go of Chris's wrist and held up his hands in a kind of mock surrender. To Chris, the empty palms seemed at once supplicating and menacing. "That's not what we agreed to, Mr. Holmes. Shooting a movie is not what we agreed to."

It wasn't clear to Chris if he was asking a question or reiterating a fact. *The agreement? The usual?* Little Scarface leaned in. He seemed genuinely pained.

"When we talked in Toronto, Mr. Holmes. And I showed you the video. Remember the video, Mr. Holmes? We agreed that the movie business wasn't going to be a priority for you anymore. Didn't we agree on that? I thought we were on the same page. But then you disappeared, Mr. Holmes. You dropped off the map. Where did you go, Mr. Holmes?"

Chris jumped up. He ran down the barren corridor, through double doors, down another hall, and through another set of doors. He stopped in a vacant ballroom. Tables draped with white tablecloths looked like rows of coffins covered with the flag. At the far end were floor-to-ceiling windows that showed the lake, its waters glittering in the sun. Chris heard a noise from the corridor. Someone was coming. He threw himself under one of the tables.

Catching his breath, he peered through the inch or so gap between the tablecloth and the floor. The scene was more *Shining* than *Caligari*. Empty expanses versus claustrophobic folds. He could hear Little Scarface now, walking through the ballroom, each footfall punctuated by a click. *Heels?* Chris thought absently. He was eerily calm, contemplating his pursuer's sartorial choices. Then they came into view. Cowboy boots. Well-worn, but an affectation nonetheless — reddish tan with alligator tail–like ridges running from the tongue to the toe box.

Chris held his breath as the boots circled.

"Well fuck," Little Scarface said, his voice higher and wheezier than it had been when he'd been talking to Chris in the lobby. He seemed at a loss, almost disconsolate. Chris supressed a hysterical giggle. He should crawl out. Show himself. He stayed where he was.

HE FOUND HIMSELF WANDERING along a waterfront path, lake to his left, perfectly groomed grass to his right. He was right to have hidden. What good could come of listening to that creepy little man and his threats? Had he been threatening him? *Not me*, Chris told himself. Thomson Holmes. There was a video. The word made Chris's stomach sink. Video. Those grainy photos of him kissing that random woman. Her lipstick-smeared face, mascaraed eyes dull and glossy. He looked like he was propping her up. Like he was pulling her in. He felt the panic again, the heat spreading. Where was Alison? He had to find her. He had to find her and explain to her. What had happened. To him. To them. What had happened? Day off, he thought randomly.

It occurred to him that out in the open like this he was visible from just about anywhere — the rooms of the many hotels and condos overlooking the water, the higher points of the park's grassy knoll. Little Scarface could still be looking for him. Chris picked up his pace. His throat was dry, and his leg muscles felt oddly twisted. Up ahead was a path away from the water that seemed to loop back to the small downtown and the hotel complex. He hurried toward it.

"MR. HOLMES. OVER HERE!"

The low summons issued from under a filthy Winnipeg Jets cap. It was Frankie the set builder. Frankie wore the baseball cap on stringy, greasy hair draped over the shoulders of a faded jean jacket. He was with three other similarly dressed-down people, members of the *Lost Expert* crew.

"How ya doin', Mr. H.?" Frankie asked.

"I'm good, thanks," Chris answered warily. "How are you all doing?" He kept his voice and his gaze low.

"We're great," Frankie said so loudly that Chris felt compelled to take a step back. "Day off, so here wese all are out on the town. Not really my scene, but ya know what they say — when in Rome. It was Jen here's idea to come over here, she's got a buncha coupons, eh? For the buffet and free drinks."

"Frankie," Jen said warningly. "Mr. Holmes doesn't want to hear about our coupons."

Not exactly sure what they were talking about, Chris looked around. Next block over was the complex where he was staying. On the broad sidewalk in front of him were small groups of people who looked quite different from the crew — business-people released from their conferences and younger tourist couples sporting halter tops, short skirts, chinos, and polos. The building they were entering and exiting was as unprepossessing as the resort where they were staying and might even have been part of it. *Lakeview Casino*, Chris read.

"Jen, Mr. H is cool, he knows the score, dontcha, Mr. H?"

Jen cast Frankie a murderous glance. The rest of the group were silent, following the proceedings, clearly uneasy to be in quite such proximity to the star of the show.

"Cool it, Frankie," Jen said warningly. "Sorry, Mr. Holmes," she said, darting him an apologetic look.

"Say, Mr. H.," Frankie continued. "You heading in? You wanna join up for a drink?"

"Frankie —" Jen hissed.

"Oh, come on, Jennifer! That old busybody had it coming! 'Con-ti-nuuuu-ity,'" Frankie mimicked.

Frankie's eyes were bloodshot and wet, giving him the look of a decrepit dog, wounded yet insolent. A ripple of tension moved through the group. Was Frankie right? Did she have it coming?

Before Chris could make up his mind to stay or flee, two people approached from the other direction: a middle-aged couple, the woman, heavyset and heavily made-up, already pulling out her phone.

"Are you Thomson Holmes?" she yelled. Chris didn't respond. "Oh, my goodness, Charles, it is, it is Thomson Holmes! Can we get a picture? Thomson, can we get a picture?"

Suddenly, the woman was knocked aside. A tall, bearded man with an impressive gut and a headset smiled at Chris. "Mr. Holmes," he said. "I'm sorry about that. This way, sir." The man made a right-this-way gesture, and Chris gratefully stepped forward. Somewhere behind him, he heard the click of a camera. He quickened his pace. "Thomson! Thomson!"

INT. MEETING ROOM IN THE PALM RESORT HOTEL AND
CASINO — AFTERNOON
The room is long and thin, dominated by a
cherrywood table polished to a high shine. The
table is topped by leather blotters, each one
flanked by a fountain pen and writing pad. Six
people, FOUR MEN and TWO WOMEN, all dressed in
formal business attire, are clustered around one
end of the table, gazing intently at THE LOST
EXPERT, who sits uncomfortably in a stiff chair,
his dirty boots planted on the art deco black-
and-white-patterned ceramic floor. At the far
end of the table is a large topographical map of
Sand City and the surrounding desert plains.

                    JEFF MARSHALL,
               ASSISTANT TO THE PRESIDENT
          Great, we're all here now. Let me make
          the introductions. Over here is Vince
            Callagio, president of Security and
                    Customer Safety.

He gestures to a burly man in his fifties,
dressed in a suit, vest, and bow tie. Then to
a DARK-HAIRED WOMAN in her early forties in a
red dress.

                    JEFF MARSHALL (CONT'D)
          This is Evelyn Munroe, ladies' hotel
          detective. This is Lester Sullivan and
          David Amber, who also help out around
          here. Of course, you've already met our
             president, Mackenzie McDonald.

                    MACKENZIE MCDONALD
                       Call me Mac!
          (Appreciative chuckles from everyone at
                      the table.)

                     VINCE CALLAGIO
          My team has prepared a complete report
          on the incident. Now, on the night in
             question Duchess Laura was —

                     THE LOST EXPERT
             I'll need to see her room.

Evelyn and Vince glance at each other.

                     EVELYN MUNROE
                 That's not a problem.

                    LESTER SULLIVAN
          Of course, you'll understand that the

duchess sometimes engaged in certain
activities that, while not necessarily
condoned by the hotel, but within the
privacy of her suite, you see —

MACKENZIE MCDONALD
(sharply)
I've been assured he understands that.

The Lost Expert stands up and walks to the map.
He stares at the map while the others watch him
silently. With one long finger he traces a path
only he can see.

THE LOST EXPERT
After I see her room, I'll be leaving
immediately.

JEFF MARSHALL
Leaving?

THE LOST EXPERT
(stabbing a point in the map)
Here. She's somewhere here.

VINCE CALLAGIO
(incredulous)
In the Dead Heights Basin?
How can you know that?

                    THE LOST EXPERT
        As I said, before I go, I'll need to see
          her room. As well as the hotel ledgers
                     for the last week.

                  MACKENZIE MCDONALD
                     (standing up)
             Whatever he needs, people!

INT. ELEVATOR
EVELYN MUNROE, hotel detective, appraises
THE LOST EXPERT thoughtfully. We can see that
despite her youthful appearance and voluptuous
beauty, her eyes hold a sharp wariness. She nods
to the young man in the bellhop uniform working
the levers of the glass elevator.

                    EVELYN MUNROE
        The duchess was staying in our penthouse
           apartment on the fifteenth floor.
          We'll arrange a suite for you on the
                     same floor.

                    THE LOST EXPERT
        That won't be necessary. I'll be leaving
                 as soon as possible.

                    EVELYN MUNROE
         Are you sure that's wise? It's after
        three. It will be getting dark in a few
                        hours.

                    THE LOST EXPERT
             (stepping out of the elevator)
              It's always getting dark.

INT. DUCHESS LAURA'S SUITE
THE LOST EXPERT stands in the middle of the
suite, his eyes closed. EVELYN MUNROE eyes him
warily, shifting on her high heels.

                    THE LOST EXPERT
                    Tell me again.

                    EVELYN MUNROE
             (trying not to show her impatience)
          As I've said, since arriving, the duchess
           mainly spent her time in the suite. She
            made several calls for lemons and ice.
          She and the duke are currently estranged.
          They've only been married sixteen months.
          They have an infant daughter. The duchess
          was drinking gin. We also found evidence
               of non-prescribed stimulants.

The Lost Expert scans the room, eyes falling on
the leather blotter of the desk, which is dusted
with white powder.

                    THE LOST EXPERT
                    Cocaine.

                    EVELYN MUNROE
          We found a considerable supply. Just

after 1:00 a.m. she proceeded to the
casino floor. After around forty-five
minutes she requested a bottle of
champagne. She drank several glasses.
Her mood, which was tense at first,
gradually became gayer. At the lobby
bar, the duchess ordered another glass
of champagne. She walked to the terrace
area, drained her drink, then proceeded
through the gate into the cactus garden.
The cactus garden borders the desert
and is normally locked from sunset to
sunrise. We don't permit guests in the
garden after dark. However, in this
instance, the gate was open. We are
looking into the matter of how the
gate could have been unsecured at that
time. The Duchess entered the cactus
garden unimpeded. The cactus garden
borders several hundred miles of desert
landscape. There are two short trails
one can follow from the garden. They are
marked, but not for night hiking since
the garden is locked and secured at
sunset as part of our regular protocol.
We found her shoes — bespoke Italian
leather high heels — at the start of the
western trail, which is 2.2 miles long.
There are tracks from her bare feet at
the beginning of the trail, but the wind
erases them about one quarter of a mile
in. She hasn't been seen since she left

>   the cactus garden at roughly 2:45 a.m.
>   the night before last.

>   THE LOST EXPERT
>   (opening his eyes)
>   Thank you.

The Lost Expert surveys the messy room, taking
in the brassiere thrown over the back of a
chair, dirty glasses and room service dishes,
a shimmering dress dumped in a corner. There
are books and pamphlets heaped up on the coffee
table in front of the couch. Titles include:
Laugh and Live by Douglas Fairbanks, *The
Richest Man in Babylon* by George S. Clason,
and *The Rising Tide of Color Against White
World-Supremacy* by Lothrop Stoddard.

>   THE LOST EXPERT
>   How many days in advance did the duchess
>   make her reservations?

>   EVELYN MUNROE
>   The duchess arrived with no reservation.

>   THE LOST EXPERT
>   (nodding as if he expected that answer)
>   I'll look at the ledgers now.

Evelyn Munroe nods, prepares to leave.

                    THE LOST EXPERT
          Oh, one more thing if you will.

The Lost Expert brings out the drawing of
Beaoman.

                    THE LOST EXPERT
          Have you ever seen a man who looks
                    like this?

                    EVELYN MUNROE
          (seeming flustered for the first time)
          Why, yes, I believe he's been a
          regular over the last month or so.
                 What about him?

EXT. THE DESERT — NIGHT
Sand City glows in the near distance, a giant
orb of pulsing light. THE LOST EXPERT wears a
small rucksack. He walks slowly away from the
glowing star of the city, moving toward the dark
hills and dunes in the distance. The moon hangs
over him. The sands are deep and soft, sifted
by the relentless winds. The Lost Expert plods
forward, slowly and steadily. The clouds shift
and shadows lengthen. Suddenly, the Lost Expert
stops. He stoops, picks something up, brushes
sand off the object. It is a gold two-hundred-
dollar chip.

"RIGHT THIS WAY, SIR."

The bouncer led Chris through a large, somewhat tired room about a quarter full of people feeding coins into slot machines. Only a few glanced up from their relentless pursuit. Chris had never been in a casino. He looked around curiously, not paying attention to where they were headed.

At the far end of the room, they came to an elevator marked private, which the bouncer accessed by flashing a key card.

"After you, sir."

The elevator opened to a small foyer lit in blue. A heavily made-up woman in a tight black dress rushed up to Chris and, smile shining, effusively welcomed him. He wasn't sure what he was being welcomed to, but she didn't seem bothered by his hesitating silence. "Right this way, Mr. Holmes," she said knowingly. He followed her through another opening framed by dim blueish light then down a dark hallway and into a quiet lounge, thick with cigar smoke. There, four people, three men and a woman, their faces mostly in shadow, were playing cards, chips piled up by their elbows. An unsmiling middle-aged lady wearing a paisley vest and a green visor spoke softly. "Place your bets, please." There was a bar, staffed by another young woman in a tight black dress, and there was another bouncer here too, dressed in a suit and tie and earpiece, standing silently in a corner with his arms crossed.

Did they think he was here to play?

He went to speak but stopped himself. Thomson Holmes probably did. He was a probably an aficionado. Cigars, poker, cars, *women*.

Thankfully, they led him past the game and into an alcove leading to another door.

"Mr. Berinstain is already waiting for you, Mr. Holmes," the hostess said happily. "He arrived early."

The hostess opened the door. Reflexively, Chris stepped in.

The room overlooked the water. He found himself momentarily blinded by its pretty brightness. Chris blinked a few times and then saw that, as promised, a man — a Mr. Berinstain — was there, sitting calmly with his hands folded on the pale, gleaming wooden conference table. He had a flat face with acne scarring on the cheeks, a weak chin that stretched into a thin neck, and a sunken chest ending in a belly bulge barely camouflaged by a golf shirt.

"Have a seat, Thomson."

He knows. Chris felt the heat on his face. His whole body was suddenly heavy. He dropped into a waiting chair. *Berinstain*. A name he'd heard, or seen, a few times. Maybe Alison had mentioned him? Someone important. His lawyer? His manager? The door to the room had closed behind him. They were alone.

Berinstain considered him with a watery, inscrutable gaze. "Sorry for all the cloak-and-dagger stuff. I just wanted to make sure that we could talk." He slid an envelope over the smooth table toward Chris. "Here," he said. Puzzled, barely suppressing the urge to bolt, Chris peeked into the envelope. It was full of American hundred-dollar bills.

"Spending money," Berinstain said. Then, clearing his throat, he opened the dossier in front of him. "Two and a half million dollars in cash and assets have been transferred from Holmes's holdings and other elements of the estate over the last month," he drily informed Chris. "Within hours of the transfer," Berinstain continued, "the accounts disappeared, their contents most likely liquefied into cash at considerable loss to their owner. This transfer represented the bulk of Thomson Holmes's liquidity. This means," Berinstain continued with all the inflection of a bored algebra teacher, "that for all intents and purposes, Thomson Holmes's accessible accounts are empty. In fact, Thomson Holmes is actually four million dollars in the hole." Berinstain closed the folder and crossed his arms over it.

Chris was trying to process this information. Did Berinstain think he'd taken the money?

"Take a moment," Berinstain said. "Have a drink of water."

He watched, expressionless, as Chris gulped from the glass in front of him.

"Thomson? Do you wish to notify the police of the unusual transfer of assets?"

The way Berinstain stared at Chris reminded him of the eyes in the buck head Krunk's uncle had mounted on the wall of his cabin. "Won it in a bet," he'd muttered, refusing to elaborate. The boys had imagined those blank eyes, always open, were spying on them, watching them as they slept huddled together on the floor in their tangle of sleeping bags. Resisting the resurgent urge to make a run for it, Chris willed himself to stare back at Berinstain. *He knows. Clearly, he knows. But he doesn't care.*

"I don't think that would be a very good idea," Chris heard himself say.

Berinstain nodded in agreement. "Please don't misunderstand me," he continued, the faintest hint of a smile now playing on his thin lips. "I am not altogether hostile to the opportunities this unique situation suggests. As such, I agree that we should keep the involvement of outside parties to a minimum."

"To a minimum," Chris heard himself repeat. His voice was level, responding to Berinstain's quiet monotone. But suddenly he wanted to punch him, this grey-faced money man. *He doesn't even care.*

"Do we agree, then, that for all intents and purposes of our business arrangement," Berinstain said pointedly, "the man sitting in front of me is Thomson Holmes?"

Chris jumped to his feet. Berinstain didn't flinch. Feeling ridiculous, Chris made a show of striding to the window and looking out over the river and up to the hills. Where was he? Out there. Out there somewhere.

"How did you know?"

"The DeLorean," Berinstain said. "Reed told me you were so into your role that you could not even remember whether or not you still owned the DeLorean."

"The DeLorean."

"Other assets," Berinstain said, reopening his manila file, "including the Hollywood Hills home, the vacation property, and the yacht, have been put up for sale at below market prices. The sales were initiated from a numbered corporation that led to a bank operating on charter issued by the Cayman Islands." Several vehicle sales had already gone through. "However," Berinstain droned, "it would be possible to stop the bulk of these sales or allow them to proceed in a more conventional manner to ensure that the proceeds remain in your legitimate, accessible accounts. Either way, it would be advisable to reset all security protocols including completely disabling all online access, changing all credit cards and bank account numbers, and requiring double signatures for all significant transactions. Do you agree to this?" Berinstain swept his gaze from the papers to Chris.

"The house," Chris said. "I want to keep it."

Berinstain raised his thin, grey eyebrows. He made a faint, dismissive gesture. "We'll see what can be arranged."

Chris picked up his water glass and brought it to his lips. It was empty. His hand was shaking.

He knows! He knows I'm a fake! But he doesn't care!

Berinstain extracted a large sheaf of documents. Sign here, Chris thought, feeling as if he were sinking. Harry Houdini, the Hungarian rabbi's son, wrapped in chains and manacles and dropped mercilessly into murky water, only to emerge as a free man. The Lost Expert, pulling the smoky, murky casino air into his lungs, struggling to breathe. And here. Chris sucking at the perfectly tempered air through his big white teeth. And here. And here. And here. His heart pumped, but his chest smouldered.

"And just this last one, here, please."

Berinstain gathered the papers and secured them in an attaché case.

"Very good," he said. "Do you have any further questions, Thomson?"

EXT. THE DESERT — DAY
The late afternoon sun is intense.
THE LOST EXPERT arrives at the partial shade
created by the cresting dune. He lowers
himself to the shadowed sand. A vulture circles
overhead, dark against the burning orb in the
sky, its shadow tracing the Lost Expert's supine
body before moving slowly on across the vast
empty skies. The Lost Expert's eyes flicker, and
we can see he's somewhere else.

INT. HOTEL (montage)
The DUCHESS in the elevator. In a tight dress,
cloche hat pulled tight over her brown curls,
she is the flapper ingenue, her hazel eyes
wide and innocent, open to every possibility.
But her jaw is set, her expression wary and
weary, her face a makeup mask.

                              CUT TO

The duchess making her way to the casino floor.

                                        CUT TO

A crowd of revelers, a stag party, twenty drunk
men chanting someone's name. They move past
the duchess, and she is lost in the crowd. In
slow motion, the faintest glimpse of half a
man's face in the group of chanting men. He is
tall, blond, his expression vacant, hidden. He
leans in, stopping the duchess as she passes,
whispering something in her ear.

                                        CUT TO

Her heavily mascaraed eyes widen.

                                        CUT TO

The man disappears into the crowd.

EXT. DESERT
THE LOST EXPERT opens his eyes suddenly, looks
around as if seeing the surroundings for the
first time.

              BOY LOST EXPERT'S MOTHER (V.O.)
          Where are you? Where'd you go? Mommy's
                  looking for you …

INT. HOTEL (montage)
Slow motion: the same again, the key second

prolonged, the scene dissolving into grainy
inscrutability.

EXT. DESERT — SUNSET
The red desert sun sinks beneath the endless
sand.

INT. HOTEL
Paused still image: The face of the man,
shadowed, blurred, his lips barely open.

EXT. DESERT — SUNSET

                    THE LOST EXPERT
            (voice cracking, barely audible)
                      Beaoman

                  THE DUCHESS (V.O.)
                  (mocking laughter)
            Well! And did you ever find her?

EXT. THE DESERT — NIGHT
A gusting wind blows. THE LOST EXPERT pushes
through the swirling sand and dust in a stagger.
Silt sticks to his eyes and crusts the tight
press of his lips. The sky coruscates, cloud and
moon intersecting to make chiaroscuro patterns
of shadow on shadow, an ominous painting on the
low-pressing sky. The Lost Expert stops, sways
in the wind under the muted light show. Hands
shaking, he brings his canteen to his lips. A
few remaining drops decrescendo into his mouth.

He lets the canteen slip from his hands. It
immediately disappears under blowing sand. The
Lost Expert takes a few more steps, then falls
to his knees. He struggles, seems unable to
get up.

                    .THE DUCHESS (V.O.)
              (laughing drunkenly with feigned
                         bravado)
           Choose a number! Choose a number!

The Lost Expert manages to rise. He squints
through the blowing sand. He appears to see
something up ahead, a glimmer of white against
the impenetrable black. He staggers forward
into the howling wind of the maelstrom.

               BOY LOST EXPERT'S MOTHER (V.O.)
            It's just you and me now, baby. That's
               all right. Isn't that all right?

EXT. THE DESERT — NIGHT
THE LOST EXPERT laboriously trudges up a large
sand slope, slipping and falling, clawing
forward and upward on his hands and knees. His
face is blistered, his eyes almost completely
crusted shut. He crawls with excruciating
slowness. At a cautious distance a coyote keeps
pace, shuffling and keening through the night.
The Lost Expert crawls.

                    BOY LOST EXPERT'S MOTHER (V.O.)
                              (desperate)
              Hey! Come out! I give up, okay?
                              I give up!

                              MAN (V.O.)
                             (despairing)
              I can work. I'm strong. I wanna work!
                     If someone would just …

The Lost Expert crests the hill and manages
to get to his feet. He sees the duchess in
her white, flouncy dress. She is face down,
unconscious, several coyotes warily eyeing her.
He steps quickly toward her, and the animals
slink away. He rolls the duchess over. Her eyes
flutter.

                                        CUT TO

Beaoman's hovering, shadowed face.

                                        CUT TO

The pale, delicate fist of the duchess,
clutching a single black chip.

                                        CUT TO

The Lost Expert pulls something out of his
rucksack. He fumbles, his hands shaking.

>   CROUPIER (V.O.)
>   (expressionless)
>   Red seventeen. Red seventeen.

>   THE DUCHESS
>   (coughing, spitting sand)
>   Did he …? Did he win?

The duchess faints. A bright red flare ignites
in the dark sky high over the desert, the Lost
Expert's face bathed in the bloody glow.

CHRIS WAITED IN A brand-new double-wide. The trailer was almost empty, save a lavishly soft leather La-Z-Boy. Chris pulled the lever and the chair reclined gently, footrest extending. He closed his eyes. *That's not what we agreed to. Liquidity zero. Sign here. And here.* The length and emptiness of this mobile home on the edge of the faux mini-desert was disconcerting. Why was it here? Why was it so empty? It's a reality check, Laurie liked to say, discussing her response to the outsized retirement plans of her clients — cruises, European villas, Freedom 55. A white scar cut into a taut cheek. Sunken lips and uncashed cheques. Inside was new car smell and stretched-out emptiness, like a cube had been dragged into a new shape — had that been a Max Ernst hanging on the wall of the recreated 1920s casino boardroom? "Oh, you're so surreal!" Krunk had shouted drunkenly to an empty street. "You're like the matrix without the ones and zeros!" Inside was the air-conditioned hum-whine. Outside, the distant crackle of walkie-talkies, murmuring voices getting louder.

"Use John!"

Alison, Chris realized, suddenly attentive to the contours, if not the substance, of the conversation.

Reed, dismissive. "He's tougher than he looks, your little man."

That set her off. They went back and forth. Alison was worried. The role was getting to him. He'd been overworked up north. She wanted Reed to use John instead. The stunt guy / body double. John was the stunt guy. Alison. He'd slept with her. He'd gone too far. Or not far enough.

Anyway, the show would go on. Reed didn't care about people, even himself. That's what made him what he was. Total focus. A will to move mountains. *Fitzcarraldo*, moving a 320-ton steamship up and over the Andes to the Amazon on the other side, and if the occasional extra ended up with one less leg, well, that's what insurance was for. "What do you want to do?" Reed yelled at Alison. "Sit around here for a month waiting for him to *feel better*? We don't exactly have forever, you know!"

Two people fighting over him. The last time that happened was back in the divorce days. Fourteen-year-old Chris, quiet, unassuming; Krunk, his only pal, advising him — how to shave, how to catch your cum in a wad of Kleenex, how to skip school and spend a day at the movies.

In the year that followed, his father checked out, moved almost two hours down the highway for an insurance job in Waterloo and a new life. He remarried and lived childless with his perfectly acceptable second wife. The few times Chris had visited, they'd spent the evenings sitting primly in a room they called the parlour. His dad's new wife sipped white wine over ice cubes. Some kind of classic lite played on the radio. Despite the soporific music, it was the familiar silence trapped in his dad's tight grin that stayed with Chris. He took the early bus home.

The argument had faded out of earshot. The trailer was huge, flimsy, the La-Z-Boy a ridiculous island. Eyes still closed, Chris tried to envision the upcoming scenes. The desert. Lost in the desert. But his thoughts went in another direction. Berinstain. The new Thomson Holmes. Alison. The surrounding Mojave moving in, piling up, spilling through the high-set slat windows. The burning sand surging through the trailer, consuming the floor, the chair's legs, the footrest, until he was in sand up to his neck, up to his chin — his mouth crusting over; all that was left were his lips — a white scar.

Chris jerked up, a surge of something like electricity shooting through him.

THE SUN BLAZED, AND the members of the crew were almost unrecognizable, shrouded in baseball cap-kaffiyeh get-ups that protected the lower halves of their faces from the blowing sand. Reed barked orders, the German quietly but furiously conveyed his own plans, and the components of the shoot gradually assembled into a complex orchestral arrangement. Under the artificial shade of an erected canopy protecting them from a not-particularly-hot sun, Chris stared out into the desert, trying to focus on the mountains in the near distance. The landscape was at once sparse and luxuriant. His gaze wavered between the parallel lines of sky and sand before settling on the optical illusion of their meeting at the base of the hills. It was beautiful and disruptive, before and after. What came next? Everything he'd known and been. Alison fidgeted and paced next to him, unable to stay still, her breaths in short, anxious bursts, mini exhalations of heated indignation. Chris tried to catch her eye, wanting to reassure her. *Really, it's okay. I'm fine.* She was avoiding him. His sense of exhaustion and anticipation had diminished to a dull, somehow comforting haze. *Guess what,* he wanted to tell her. *I'm selling it. The DeLorean. It's fine,* he'd assure

her. *I don't need it anymore.* He could see through the haze that
what had seemed so terrible and real was something else entirely.
It was the Just Beyond, the cinematic totality awaiting capture.
The desert — a British Columbian oasis standing in for the
Nevadan real deal — was nothing, could be anything: some
shimmering mirage softening into cerulean sky.

It was time. At Reed's signal, Chris tromped forward, nose
low, sniffing for a scent. That's what Reed had told him to do.
Plunge ahead with abandon; go on the hunt the way only the
Lost Expert could. "This is what he lives for," Reed had hissed
to him. "This is *who* he is." There would be someone else in the
scene, someone he was looking for. Chris had nodded, not really
listening as Reed went on: a hotel detective, a faceless man, a
missing princess. "In a way it works. This fake desert. It's not
perfect, but nothing is!" Chris strode through the arid emptiness.
Specks of sand blasted his cheeks, carried by an incongruously
cold wind. He kept his head on a swivel, his posture stiff, trying
to convey a Lost Expert aura of meticulous, yet somehow confused, persistence.

Reed barked orders, gesticulated, pointed. Hearing and not
hearing, Chris experimented with a ponderous gaze, peered over
his shoulder at the director and his array of cameras and mics.
Reed shook his head in something that looked like disgust. Chris
felt himself flush. He had a headache. It was the same one he'd
had after waking up in the camp director's cabin in a puddle
on the splintering floor. It had returned. It was making a kind of
whooshing sound in his ears. Or it might have been the natural
sound of the desert, the empty quiet of a place as loud and all-
encompassing as a Hollywood sound effect.

He jogged down the bowl of a long valley. The sand sucked
at him as he piled into its soft middle. For a time, he didn't seem

to be moving at all, everything around him growing larger without getting any nearer. He looked back only once. Reed's mouth, an empty oval. No sound reached him. That was fine. Chris didn't need direction; his limbs, unleashed, struck out on their own.

His legs churned, and he sank into a slow memory. Saturday morning cartoons: alone in front of the basement television picking sodden Froot Loops from a plastic cereal bowl. On the small, fuzzy screen, Wile E. Coyote's purgatorial antics stretching the hours through a generic background of box canyons and washed-out gorges — a world Chris had never imagined might actually exist somewhere. Déjà vu. Here he was. Haunting himself. The farther you get, the closer you are.

Shadows crossing his path snapped him back to awareness. Chris skidded to a stop, barely avoiding crashing into three scraggly, overlapping trees. Joshua trees, Chris thought or imagined. Could they be? Here? Or were they trucked in from California? He'd done a report on desert habitats in eleventh grade. How different those low, bare trees were from the hearty forest denizens he and Krunk had grown up wandering under. In the pictures on the library computer, the Joshua trees seemed more like beasts than anything that grew, desert gargoyles waiting for the sun to go down and the moon to disappear behind sudden clouds. In real life they looked stunted and mistreated. Branches, twisted in defiance, reached toward the unforgiving sun. The malnourished Y-shaped limbs seemed weighed down by the greyish fluff wrapped haphazardly around them. Upon closer inspection, the soft-looking fuzz was made up of sharp clusters of needles, the desert tree's harsher version of leaves.

The wind blew, stirring up sand. Chris squinted, wiped at his face with the shoulder of his shirt. He was losing it. Losing himself. So what? Let it happen. Thomson Holmes. Lost Expert.

. The sand slowly resettled around him. It was bright. Too bright. Then: a near-distant rock formation, emerging from the distance. The cliffs jutted out of the desert at sharpened angles. Chris imagined cairns lurching together to form a surreal obstacle course. He raised his gaze from the bottom of the cliff to where its flat pinnacle pushed into the blue sky.

From behind, he heard Reed. The crew. Alison, he thought. Or said. He never should have —

It was what Thomson Holmes might have done. But not him. Not him? Déjà vu redux. The sequel always rings twice. He plunged ahead, swelled with determination. To reach his destination. To somehow cleanse himself, wash away the stink of that perverted oasis, stardom. "Stop!" Reed yelled. "Cut!"

The wind again. A surge from the west, the whoosh inside his skull crashing into the gale bellowing around his ears. Chris shook his head like a horse trying to free himself of the bridle. *Don't think*. Closer to the rocky tower, the terrain was haphazard with boulders. He leapt from rock to rock, propelling his imbalance into the next wild bounce.

And then he was there, face-to-face with the high, red tower. He panted, air, sulphur, and dried sage filling his lungs.

Noises behind him. He stretched his neck to gaze at the top of the wavering cliff. Where was he? Wile E., setting a dynamite trap. Had he always been like that? Alone and sad? He shook his head, trying to banish the image.

He began the ascent. Porous, craggy rocks offered grips and holds but ripped at his fingertips and palms. Grit collected in his wind-tousled hair, sliding down his neck and back. Despite the air's chill, he was perspiring. Good. Verisimilitude. The higher he got, the more he felt his pale skin glowing. Before the shoot, Alison had offered to put sunscreen on him. He'd declined.

He rose, proceeding mainly by feel, grabbing with his hands, scrabbling with his authentically worked-in moccasin toe work boots. At times, he felt his grip loosening, his body in danger of slipping to the rock beds that were six, then ten, then twenty feet below. So what? What did it matter? When he slipped, he let himself go slack, willed himself to fall even as he regained position and pulled himself upward, urged on by the shouts and yells from below.

Thirty-five feet up, he half-crawled over the crumbling lip of the clifftop. He lay on the flat, weathered, rock, desperately catching his breath. His skin cooled then peeled off like eggshell. Raw now, flesh exposed to the world, he forced himself to his feet. On rubber legs stretched ten times their size, he stood towering over the edge of the world. The blazing sun hung in the ceiling of the sky, so big he felt like he could almost touch it. Sure, why not? He could do that. He could do anything. He revolved slowly, his own mini-planetoid, billionth rock from the sun. A great emptiness, filled only by the sound of his own beating brain.

Down below, small and faceless, the crew were scarab-like, scurrying to and fro, yelling things, their distant voices indecipherable. Chris flared his nostrils and let out twin blasts of sour air that he pictured as shooting flames.

INT. HOSPITAL — DAY

THE LOST EXPERT blinks awake. He sees Esther
sitting in a chair next to his bed. She is
looking at him, eyes large with concern.

                    THE LOST EXPERT
          (surprised, clearly trying to suppress
                        his pain)
          Esther! What are you doing here?

                    ESTHER
                    (icily)
          You have a visitor.

We see that JOEL MCCANN is in the
room, standing near the door. Esther
gets up.

                    ESTHER (CONT'D)
          I'll leave you two alone.

Esther leaves the room.

> JOEL MCCANN
> Friendly girl.

> THE LOST EXPERT
> She's protective.

Joel McCann drops a newspaper on the Lost
Expert's chest.

> JOEL MCCANN
> This ought to cheer her up.

He taps the headline. The Lost Expert grimaces
in pain.

> JOEL MCCANN (CONT'D)
> (reading)
> "On the Rugged Margins: The Lost Expert,
> Harold Allan's Mystical Man in the
> Mountains."

McCann reaches into his coat pocket and puts a
thick envelope on the tray near the bed.

> JOEL MCCANN (CONT'D)
> Mr. Allan sends his hearty
> congratulations.

> THE LOST EXPERT
> I've already been paid. I can't accept
> that.

                    JOEL MCCANN
        The duchess's family is exceedingly
        grateful. They've thrown their heartfelt
          support behind the Allan campaign.

Joel McCann pushes the envelope of money closer
to the Lost Expert.

                JOEL MCCANN (CONT'D)
          Consider the money an investment.
          In your operation. Rent an office.
        Get an assistant, maybe this dame? You
        can't keep doing everything out of that
        bakery. This is your moment! Mr. Allan
                  just wants to help.

                  THE LOST EXPERT
                How is the duchess?

                    JOEL MCCANN
                    (sighing)
        Poor girl. She's a bit of a lost soul.
        By now she should be on a boat back
                    to Europe.

                  THE LOST EXPERT
          Has she said anything? About what
                happened to her?

McCann shrugs. From beneath the sheets, the Lost
Expert pulls out the crumpled sketch of Beaoman.
He puts it on the tray in front of McCann.

                    THE LOST EXPERT
                  Do you know this man?

Joel McCann smiles indulgently. He puts on a
pair of reading glasses.

                    JOEL MCCANN
            Eyes aren't what they used to be, I'm
                      afraid.

                    THE LOST EXPERT
              Does he work for you? Have you seen
            him around, as part of your larger
                    organization?

                    JOEL MCCANN
              He doesn't look familiar.

                    THE LOST EXPERT
              Look again, please, Mr. McCann.
                  It's important.

                    JOEL MCCANN
              (squinting at the picture)
                I can't place him.

                    THE LOST EXPERT
            He goes by Beaoman. He was involved in
            the disappearance of the duchess. He was
            also involved in that other case, the
            Bartner brother. I know how that sounds.
            But I believe it to be true. Have you

seen him? Is he connected in anyway to
the Allan organization?

                    JOEL MCCANN
                (smiling indulgently)
I assure you, all of Mr. Allan's advisors
are handpicked and completely trusted.

                    THE LOST EXPERT
This man, he operates under the surface.
He may have different identities.
He may be using a different name.
He might be altering his appearance.
He's more than just dangerous.

                    JOEL MCCANN
                    (frowning)
What do you mean? Like he's some kind of
shape-shifter? You serious about this?

                    THE LOST EXPERT
Do you believe in pure evil, Mr. McCann?

                    JOEL MCCANN
Listen. You're tired. You need to rest.
I'll ask around. See what I can find out.
In the meantime, rest up. We need you
focused on growing your organization.
                    On this.

McCann taps on the headline.

> JOEL MCCANN (CONT'D)
> This is what you should be focusing
> on. And of course (glancing toward the
> hallway and the waiting Esther) on your
> lovely wife and son.

McCann leaves. The Lost Expert, wincing, closes
his eyes. Pink message slips rain down on him
from above. The Lost Expert jerks back into
awareness.

> ESTHER
> (dropping the last of the message slips)
> I'm not your secretary, Mr. Lost Expert.

Esther spins away.

> THE LOST EXPERT
> Esther!

Esther turns back, her face angry.

> THE LOST EXPERT
> Thank you.

Esther's face softens.

> ESTHER
> (stepping toward the Lost Expert's bed)
> Is it true?

THE LOST EXPERT
Is what true?

ESTHER
(pointing to a newspaper picture of
Allan, her voice tinged with bitterness)
Are you really on his side?

THE LOST EXPERT
Esther, he's not what he seems.

ESTHER
But he hates us.

THE LOST EXPERT
He's just saying things to get elected.
They all do it.

ESTHER
But he says he's going to make all Jews
sign a register? And close up the shtetl?
No one in and no one out?

THE LOST EXPERT
He won't do those things.

ESTHER
How do you know?

THE LOST EXPERT
I won't let him.

ESTHER
You better not.

CHRIS FELT THE SHEET on top of him, light and cool against his hot skin. He opened his eyes. He saw black-on-grey shapes, a drifting surface skein of purple nothingness. Dark, he thought. Or perhaps his eyes were covered. Bandaged? A possibility that should have filled with him anxiety. He thought to wave a hand in front of his face.

WAKING UP AGAIN.

Quiet and dark; he held his body still. He heard his own breathing. It was slow and steady. *I flew*, he remembered. He felt only a little exultant. *I flew*. Lying there, trying to form another coherent thought, he gradually detected the scent of a separate body. There was someone else in the room with him. Chris breathed in through his nose: cigar, leather, sweat, a hint of decay.

Reed.

Reed was there, by his bedside. Reed was talking — had been all along, Chris realized, his growled voice moving in and out, over and under, like a radio station slipping through signal.

"... Great stuff by the way, Holmes. You shoulda seen Ally's face! Jesus Christ, when you wake up you're going to be sorry!

Anyway, we got it. Got it all! Wait till they get a load of this. Press is going to have a field day. I swear, Holmes, for a second you just hung there, up in the sky, like a fucking phoenix. In the future — god, I hate that word almost as much as I hate those cunty air quotes people are always using — you can jump all you want, it won't matter. Nothing will matter, Holmes. We won't die or be born. We won't even be human. When I was pitching this, one of the producer a-holes asked, 'Is this science fiction?' I was like, 'Fuck no this isn't science fiction!' Who the fuck do they think I am? James fucking Cameron? No offence, Holmes, unless you're secretly a *Titanic* fan, in which case fuck you …"

CHRIS OPENED HIS EYES. Alison was looking down at him. Reed was gone, a fever dream.

"Thomson. How are you feeling?"

The sun shimmered through the lightly covered window, casting a halo over Alison's light brown hair. Chris blinked and squinted, trying to adjust to the brightness. Was it morning? Early afternoon?

"Do you want some water?" Alison leaned over him. "Are you hungry? Do you want me to —"

He kissed her, sitting up suddenly, opening his arms, and pulling her in. She stiffened, surprised, then kissed him back. Her mouth tasted like blueberries and honey. His mouth was raw, salt and iron, blood and heat. They rolled together. He was on top, then she was on top. She pulled off her polo shirt, revealing a sheer bra, dark nipples against pale pink fabric. Then her small breasts against his bare chest.

ALISON DOZED. CHRIS LAY awake, smelling her silky hair splayed out next to him, soft and scented with lilac. Climb, Reed had told him, talking through an endless night that Chris felt sure had been several nights, days and days of nights. Climb. He could feel it receding, like a distant lightning storm, its thunder still echoing. Were they together? Were they a couple? What had happened? Had he fallen? Jumped? *Flew?*

"Thomson?" Alison stirred, waking.

"Yeah?"

"Are you okay?"

Chris squinted at the high ceiling, painted a sky blue and softly lit by a small, simple chandelier. The light starred into blurry, overlapping pattern. His stomach was long and taut, strained, empty.

"Yeah. I'm okay."

"Good. I'm … I was worried about you."

"I'm okay. Really. I feel fine."

"Are you hungry?" Alison asked.

"No. I'm not hungry. I feel empty," Chris said dreamily. "Like him. Like The Lost Expert."

"Empty?"

"Empty. If you lose everything. When you lose everything. Then you're just empty."

Alison propped herself on an elbow. "Thomson. It's too much. You aren't the Lost Expert. You have to eat. You have to take care of yourself." Seeing his cocked grin: "What are you smiling about? You and Reed. You're a couple of pigs in shit, aren't you?"

Alison rolled out of the bed, out of his reach. She stalked angrily across the carpet, paused abruptly at the door to the ensuite bathroom: "I'm not going to save you, Thomson. If that's what you think. That's not how this is going to go."

PART FOUR

CHRIS OPENED THE WINDOW and breathed in. The air drifting up from the Great Lake at the bottom of the city was cool and damp, familiarly tinged with hints of seaweed, car exhaust, and the coming winter. Home. He could keep his head down here. Stay out of trouble. Acid surged through his empty stomach. Up north, he'd been ravenous, but ever since the desert, he'd lost his appetite. He couldn't remember the last time he'd eaten. He felt light all the time, lighter than air, ready to float away. They were on Queen Street West now, Toronto's beating heart. Chris watched his driver try to pass a slowly accelerating streetcar. His driver braked abruptly and curse-muttered as his attempt was cut off by the streetcar's warning clang and a fast-arriving lane of parked cars. They fell into place behind the other vehicles inching forward only slightly faster than the perambulators window-shopping on the sidewalk.

Suddenly feeling eyes on him from the street, Chris retreated inside and raised the tinted window. He contemplated the intimately familiar panorama from his new, protected vantage. The store specializing in Asian papercraft; the boutique bookstore selling what Krunk liked to call "hipster porn"; Manila, a new "it spot" of "reinvented" upscale Filipino cuisine; a pop-up ice cream

shop, summer tenure almost done as reflected by waning lines
for the latest food craze of charcoal-infused black sundaes served
in kale-cone bowls dyed an alarming mahogany.

Eventually, they passed the café. Chris imagined the cook, Syed,
sweating over the béchamel sauce, a Syrian with an engineering
degree concocting the special of the day — croque monsieur
with side salad. Did Syed have an engineering degree? Everyone
joked about it, but nobody really knew. They called him Sid the
Kid, though Syed was a grizzled man anywhere between forty
and sixty. They preferred to think of him as one of them, young,
feckless, different only in ways that enhanced, rather than diminished, possibilities. Chris craned his neck to catch a glimpse of the
girl behind the register. Was it Rachel, working the breakfast shift?
Who else could be sporting such an unruly mane of blond hair?
She'd texted him — Thomson Holmes. She had a new agent. After
the movie finished shooting, she was thinking of moving to L.A.
He'd promised to call her.

"Here we are, Mr. Holmes."

"Thanks."

Trained now, he waited for the driver to open his door. He felt
the bulge of cash Berinstain had given him. He'd taken it. But
hadn't spent any. Before the desert, he'd stopped trying to tip the
functionaries. For one thing, he'd had no idea how to access any
of Thomson Holmes's money even if he wanted to. For another
thing, whenever he'd tried to go off the script already written for
him, he'd ended up setting in motion whole chains of unfortunate
events — rewrites, wardrobe crises, cracks in the thin veneer of
filmic continuity, Reed freaking out, people losing their jobs.

Keep calm and, as his pal would say when confronted with
the sight of fawning celebrities going through the motions on the
red carpet, be a good little movie star. It's not like he was asking

them to open the car door, work the buttons of the elevator, appear next to him with a giant umbrella if there was even a hint of a rain cloud in the sky. They just did it and they expected him to expect it. Trying to stray from all of that was a surprising amount of work. It sounded ridiculous. But it was true. Being served and waited on and letting other people do every little thing for him — it wasn't fun, it took a kind of steely effort. Even not tipping took something out of him.

The players and their set had moved to the small park only a few blocks away from his and Laurie's apartment. *Laurie*, he suddenly thought. He hadn't spoken to her in days. Possibly weeks. He owed her for this month's rent. Guilt flamed on his cheeks.

There were fewer trailers on this more compact set, though they'd still managed to take over the entire side of a park and a block and a half of prime parking. Tina met him, sporting her ubiquitous clipboard and headset. She crackled a message, received a reply. Tina said something to him about his trailer. Chris ignored her. He looked around for Alison. Tina went on, loudly apologizing about something, an inconvenience, nothing concerning, they had a guy, he was dealing with it. When they got near Holmes's deluxe portable, it became clear what she was talking about. The smooth white siding sported an eye-catching extra.

Day-Glo graffiti.

Chris froze. the sprayed-on words, each line written in a different fluorescent hue.

Clipboard Tina was still talking. A V of geese moved high overhead, beginning their habitual journey south. A passing car honked repeatedly as it cruised by — protesting the movie set's appropriation of most of the park and all the parking in the neighbourhood.

A power tool kicked into action. Chris felt a physical jolt. A man in coveralls was aiming a serious-looking nozzle at the graffiti words. Water shot out in a thin, painful-looking jet. Spray bounced off the trailer's thin side. Immediately, 'The' and 'Girl' began to dissolve into angry orange streaks.

Then Reed was beside him, red-faced and breathing heavily.

"What in the hell is this? If this is who I think it is, then let's just say there are worse things than being blackballed."

"She didn't have anything to do with it," Chris said slowly.

"Oh yeah?" Reed's normal angry squint turned confused under his ball cap.

"It's a message."

"A message?"

"Yeah."

"What do you mean? A message from who? About what?"

Chris didn't answer. Dripping streaks, the remains of the half-blurred words formed orange-tinged mutant tears dropping on the closely cropped grass. Reed looked around desperately. He spied Tina waiting at a discreet distance. "Alison," he barked at her. "What's the twenty on Alison?" He steered Chris toward the trailer. "You have a bit of a rest, and we'll pick this up later, okay, Holmes?" Looking back at Tina desperately. "Alison? Where's Alison?"

Chris let Reed usher him into the trailer. Reed set him in a leather armchair, opened his bottle of water, and handed it to him. Chris drank from it automatically.

"Now, you just take it easy. Alison will be by. Any minute. You'll have some lunch. We'll get to the bottom of this!" Reed backed out.

The door to the trailer clanged shut. *Ask him about the girl.* The girl, Chris thought. The girl, the girl, the girl. What had Thomson Holmes done? And to whom? Was that why he'd disappeared? *What do they want from me? What am I supposed to do?* His phone buzzed. *Alison*, he thought, grabbing it up.

Welcome home, Thomson.

Did they ask you? Did they ask you yet?

INT. KITCHEN, THE LOST EXPERT'S APARTMENT — DUSK
THE LOST EXPERT sits at the kitchen table.
The kitchen slowly darkens with the fading
light of day. SARAH sits across from him. She
picks up an overstuffed envelope and takes out a
thick stack of hundred-dollar bills. She starts
counting them.

                    SARAH
          (looking up in mid-count)
          All this from one job?

The Lost Expert nods gravely.

                    SARAH
          That's amazing.

               THE LOST EXPERT
               (expressionless)
          The client was very generous.

                    SARAH
              (smiling teasingly)
        You didn't even talk about money,
                  did you?

                THE LOST EXPERT
                    No.

                    SARAH
         But you found him? Whoever they were
                looking for?

                THE LOST EXPERT
                   Yes. -

                    SARAH
               (wonderingly)
          And then they just paid you all
                 of this?

The Lost Expert sighs. Sarah gets up and walks
over to where he sits stiffly in his chair,
staring at a patch of fading, peeling paint
above the kitchen counter. She puts her arms
around him, leaning into his neck.

                    SARAH
        I'm so proud of you. And I'm glad we're
        back. But you have to promise. No more
        of that other stuff. With those people.
        Okay? Do you promise? We have to start

looking out for ourselves, for the baby.
             Okay? Do you promise?

The Lost Expert, his gaze on the money on the
table, nods curtly.

INT. BEDROOM, THE LOST EXPERT'S APARTMENT — NIGHT
SARAH, in a white camisole, is on top of THE
LOST EXPERT. Her eyes are shut. The camera
gradually moves to the Lost Expert's face.
His eyes are open, staring up at the stained
ceiling.

EXT. THE POOR SOUTHWEST END OF THE CITY —
MID-MORNING
THE LOST EXPERT walks past crumbling three-
storey walkups with bars on shaded windows and
grills blocking the bottoms of circular wrought
iron fire escapes. On the next block there are
shabby storefronts, many of them empty, their
windows adorned with faded For Rent signs and
bright orange signs blaring the Maverick Party
campaign slogan: Join the Army. Some windows
also display blue Jewish stars with an orange
circle and slash over them. A GIRL on a wooden
scooter goes by.

                     GIRL
                Hey! Mister!

The Lost Expert looks. She gestures crudely.
The Lost Expert trudges along in the thin fall

sunshine. He turns a corner and comes adjacent
to a crowd of people waiting in front of the
Mother of Mercy soup kitchen. Some seem at
ease, smoking bent cigarettes, laughing with
one another, passing around a bottle. But there
are also young and elderly couples, their
arms tight around their bodies, trying to make
themselves small. Babies squall, and children
protest and are immediately shushed. Two smiling
young women in bright yellow dresses circulate
amongst the crowd, handing out something that
the Lost Expert can't quite see. On the steps
leading up to the door of the building stand
several burly crewcut types wearing short black
jackets sporting large Allan's Army buttons. The
Lost Expert stands on the edge of the crowd and
watches the scene.

                 CLEAN-SHAVEN SQUARE-JAWED MAN
                 (speaking loudly to the people
                          around him)
          I can't get any work. Nobody's hiring.
                 Everyone's laying off.

                      HOMELESS MAN
          It's them Jews and them others comin'
          over here from them stinkin' countries!

                     HOMELESS WOMAN
          Jews, Jews, Jews, I'm sick to goddamn
                  death hearing about 'em.

                    NEW DAD
          (indicating a woman with a baby in
                    a stroller)
          Please! There are families here.

The Lost Expert watches a blond woman moving
through the crowd, whispering, smiling, pressing
something into people's hands. When she passes,
he approaches the drunk HOMELESS COUPLE on the
edge of the ragged lineup.

                  THE LOST EXPERT
                  Excuse me?

                  HOMELESS WOMAN
                  Whaddya want?

                  THE LOST EXPERT
          That woman, what did she give you?
                What is she handing out?

                  HOMELESS WOMAN
          Go ask her, you so interested.

The Lost Expert extracts a bill from his
billfold.

                  THE LOST EXPERT
                  I'm asking you.

The woman grabs the money.

                    HOMELESS WOMAN
              Now we're talking. But what
                    about Paulie?

Paulie leans into the conversation, grabbing the
Lost Expert's arm and breathing boozy spit on
his face.

                      HOMELESS MAN
                  Yeah, what about me?

The Lost Expert withdraws another dollar.

                    THE LOST EXPERT
                Show me what she gave you.

The homeless woman and man both open their fists
to reveal bright white buttons: Allan's Army;
Jobs for Life; Join Now.

                      HOMELESS MAN
                     (enthusiastic)
                    Jobs for life!

                    HOMELESS WOMAN
                (sarcastic and leering)
            You never even had a job for a day!

                    THE LOST EXPERT
            (pulling out the sketch of Beaoman)
              Have you ever seen this man?

The woman casts a nervous glance around to see
if anyone is observing them.

                    HOMELESS WOMAN
          C'mon, Paulie, let's go get a bottle.

                    HOMELESS MAN
          (eyes moving shiftily, muttering)
             I mighta seen him around …

                    HOMELESS WOMAN
               Let's go, Paulie.

The woman pulls the man through the crowd. They
disappear. The Lost Expert pockets the picture
and the button. The doors to the building open,
and the crowd surges forward.

EXT. SW PART OF THE CITY, A FEW BLOCKS AWAY,
DOWN TOWARD THE WATERFRONT — NOON
In a rough-and-tumble dockland area with
processing plants, small factories, and
ramshackle offices, THE LOST EXPERT stops to
examine a scuffed metal plaque affixed to the
door of a crumbling three-storey Victorian house
wedged between similar dwellings: Black Birds
Records. He looks for a knocker or doorbell, but
there is nothing. The Lost Expert pulls at the
battered wooden door. It's unlocked. Surprised,
he lets the door fall closed again. He pauses
and glances around warily. The Lost Expert

bangs on the door with a gloved hand, producing
a muffled, hollow knocking. Finally, the Lost
Expert yanks the door open again and hurries
inside.

INT. BLACK BIRDS RECORDS RECEPTION
THE LOST EXPERT stands inside a dingy reception
area with a few torn leather armchairs and
a battered desk strewn with records barely
illuminated by a lamp shaded in green glass.
The dusty telephone on the desk rings shrilly.
After five rings, the phone goes silent. There
is a door on the other side of the room. The
Lost Expert makes his way over to it and passes
through.

INT. NARROW HALLWAY
The hall, dimly lit with a single bulb, is lined
with framed records. THE LOST EXPERT ponders
them. The black discs are elaborately labelled
with an angry-looking bird spreading its wings
over the title and artist. On either side of
the player hole is the phrase "Electronically
Recorded."

The titles speak for themselves: "Black
Horse Blues"; "Boar Hog Blues"; "Waitin' for
the Sunrise"; "Just a Little Longer to Go";
"Trixie's Blues"; "Cross Road Blues"; "Looking
to My Prayer". Titles of longing and seeking.
Titles of need deferred, of salvation and sin.

The Lost Expert stares at each one in turn and, at the last one, he gently drags a long finger down the glass, clearing off the dust.

The Lost Expert walks down the hallway. He opens the first door, which leads into a recording studio. Peering in, he sees an empty room filled with unfamiliar, neglected equipment: microphones on stands, large box speakers, an array of turntables, tangled heaps of wires, all of it covered in a thick layer of neglect and dust.

INT. NARROW STAIRCASE
THE LOST EXPERT ascends a narrow stairway. Faintly, we hear music that grows louder as he makes his way up. A guitar repeats the same sad blues lick over and over. Then there is rhythm: drums and a plaintive horn. A woman sings, hoarse voice low and pleading. The Lost Expert arrives at the top of the stairs. The music is very loud now, and the singing descends into a keening moan as one guitar repeats the melodic core and another guitar rips into a ferocious blues solo.

INT. A LARGE OFFICE
THE LOST EXPERT squints as he enters the room, which is flooded with greyish light from the long windows overlooking the street below. There is an elaborate white wooden desk, a meticulously carved white sofa with maple

trim, and matching armchairs. On the walls are
more records in white frames. The Lost Expert
inspects the framed record titled "(Good) God
Gonna Come" by Bessie Styles and the Beehives.
Electronically recorded, of course. GEORGE
JASON PAULSON, a man in his early sixties with
long white hair and a white beard, sits behind
the ornate white wooden desk. Behind him on a
matching white credenza is an all-white record
player and a full bar. A record made of white
vinyl embedded with swirls of crimson revolves
on the record player. The man, in a crumpled
white suit, waistcoat, and bow tie, intently
reads an official-looking letter. When the song
ends, the needle scratches slightly and remains
in the final groove. The white-suited man looks
up, annoyed. He sees the Lost Expert and takes
the needle off the record. The room plunges into
silence. The man in the white suit stands up and
extends his hand. The men shake.

GEORGE JASON PAULSON
(in an affected, guttural cockney accent)
Well, hello there! George Jason Paulson,
at your service!

THE LOST EXPERT
Fine to meet you.

GEORGE JASON PAULSON
(motioning to the bar)
Can I offer you something?

> THE LOST EXPERT
> No, thank you.

Paulson pours himself a healthy portion of
bourbon.

> GEORGE JASON PAULSON
> Foul stuff you Yanks drink, but I'm
> afraid I've become somewhat partial
> to it.

The phone rings downstairs, and George Jason
Paulson shakes his head apologetically. He
smiles impishly, and in that smile we can see
that he is older and more exhausted than he
makes himself out to be.

> GEORGE JASON PAULSON (CONT'D)
> Girl's quit again. Well, we're a bit late
> on her pay, to be honest. That's the
> business for yah. Now then, how can I be
> of assistance?

> THE LOST EXPERT
> I'm interested in a record your label
> released.

> GEORGE JASON PAULSON
> Label's released a lot of records.

> THE LOST EXPERT
> That record there, as a matter of fact.

The Lost Expert points to the wall and "(Good)
God Gonna Come".

>   GEORGE JASON PAULSON
>   Yeah, I'm familiar with the album, mate.
>   What do you want to know? You lot have
>   been coming around quite a bit lately.

George Jason Paulson looks curiously at the Lost
Expert.

>   GEORGE JASON PAULSON (CONT'D)
>   Mind, you don't look like a newsie.

>   THE LOST EXPERT
>   I'm not a reporter.

>   GEORGE JASON PAULSON
>   Not a reporter. But still 'ere asking
>   questions.

>   THE LOST EXPERT
>   I have a friend. That record. It
>   helped him.

>   GEORGE JASON PAULSON
>   (softening)
>   Is that right?

>   THE LOST EXPERT
>   (taking out his billfold)
>   I can pay you for your time.

                    GEORGE JASON PAULSON
                  No, no, not necessary.

George Jason Paulson sits down in one of the
chairs in front of his desk and gestures for the
Lost Expert to do the same.

                    THE LOST EXPERT
              You mentioned there had been other
                inquiries regarding that record?

                    GEORGE JASON PAULSON
            Steady stream, guv, a steady stream.

                    THE LOST EXPERT
                   Why the interest?

                    GEORGE JASON PAULSON
              (looking oddly at the Lost Expert)
                   The Ashberry Three?

                    THE LOST EXPERT
                  (shaking his head)
                     Another act?

                    GEORGE JASON PAULSON
            Where you been, mate? It's been in all
              the rags. The Ashberry Three? Ashberry,
                   North Carolina?

The Lost Expert shakes his head again,
perplexed.

GEORGE JASON PAULSON (CONT'D)
Three fourteen-year-old girls sneak off
in the middle of the night into the
woods? Southern town, Ashberry, real
small place with a river running into
a whole lotta swampy woods. Gators and
all that. Only here's the thing: them
birds are never seen again. Only thing
they find is some weird-looking shrine,
deep in the swamp, buncha animals ripped
apart, cats and dogs and opossums, all
arranged inside a pentagram, as if we
didn't get the general idea. And right
in the middle of it all, good old Bessie
Styles and the Beehives. It's playing
on a record player. Just spinning and
spinning round and round in the middle of
those dark, empty woods. Now, how does
that happen, guv'nor?

THE LOST EXPERT
What song?

GEORGE JASON PAULSON
What song?

THE LOST EXPERT
Yes. What song?

GEORGE JASON PAULSON
Track thirteen, 'course! The secret
track.

                    THE LOST EXPERT
              "Disappeared By Blues".

                  GEORGE JASON PAULSON
                    That's the one.

                    THE LOST EXPERT
                      (monotone)
            "Devil's disappeared me / took me to
        his place / dark coven underneath / gone
                    without a trace."

                  GEORGE JASON PAULSON
                        (sadly)
                  Yeah, that's the one.

                    THE LOST EXPERT
                    And the girls?

                  GEORGE JASON PAULSON
            Not a sniff of them. Said it yourself,
              didntcha? *Gone without a trace.*

                    THE LOST EXPERT
                    Did they run away?

                  GEORGE JASON PAULSON
              Could be, could be. Nobody's seen
            them. They had five hundred volunteers
              searching the swamp! Course they're
            blaming it on us. Devil music, Satan's

blues, Black voodoo. They don't always
put it in the politest of terms.

THE LOST EXPERT
And the act?

GEORGE JASON PAULSON
Bessie Styles and the Beehives? Weren't
a real band, not a proper act at all.
Found Bessie in Littleton, years back.
Not far from Ashberry, come to think of
it. That would have been the summer of
1919. Terrible heat that summer. You
wouldn't believe the heat. But Bessie was
cool as a cucumber. She was just a slip
of a thing. Heard her singing as she was
sweeping her mammy's porch. What a voice!
I rounded up a band to record her the
very next day. Paid her fifty dollars on
the spot. Most money she'd ever seen! I
had no idea what she was singing about.
Old folk songs, call and response, stuff
from the sugarcane fields, bits and
pieces she'd picked up, I suppose. I'll
never know. Never saw her again. Not even
sure if that was her real name.

THE LOST EXPERT
You never saw her again?

Paulson doesn't answer. He stares intently at

the Lost Expert as if seeing him for the first
time.

                    GEORGE JASON PAULSON
        Listen, I don't want trouble. Especially
            these days. Just between you and me,
        we're shutting down the enterprise. I got
        a ticket booked, passage back to England.
        Go back home for a while. Change in the
        weather, right? Winds is shifting, mate.

                    THE LOST EXPERT
            I think I know what you mean.

The phone rings again.

                    THE LOST EXPERT
            (pulling out the drawing)
            Have you ever seen this man?

Paulson peers down at the picture then puts on a
fake smile showing yellow, crooked teeth.

                    GEORGE JASON PAULSON
        Never seen the bloke. Listen, I don't
        know what I can do for you. It's like I
        said. I don't want trouble. Closing shop
        for a while. Heading home. If I were you,
            guv'nor, I'd forget about whatever
                        this is.

CHRIS STOOD BEHIND THE screen in the back of the trailer in a pair of grey, tight-fitting silk boxers. Groggily, he looked down at his bare feet. The Lost Expert outfit lay crumpled on the buffed floor. The hiking pants were worn, and the tweed jacket was splattered with mud and had a rip in the shoulder Chris hadn't noticed before. He hooked his finger through the rip and slowly raised the Lost Expert's crumpled garment to his nose, inhaling deeply. The jacket smelled familiar: sweat and smoke, soggy boy armpits, wet woods, soaking feet. Where had he been?

"Yoo-hoo? Thomson?" A woman's voice followed by light knocks on the trailer's already opened door.

Chris rubbed the thick, sturdy fabric of the Lost Expert's trousers between a flat thumb and forefinger.

"Thomson? Anyone home?"

On hangers was the ubiquitous outfit: Thomson Holmes's tight jeans, a purple v-neck sweater, a mauve t-shirt that felt like it was bonding with his skin as he pulled it on.

The door to his trailer squeaked closed.

"Alison?" He hurriedly fumbled with the buttons of his fly. No one else had permission to come into his trailer. No one else would dare.

"Thomson? Are you in there?"

It was starting to gloom over, the light through the trailer's high, narrow windows casting long shadows. Almost evening, Chris thought. The realization did nothing to pull him out of his muddy sense of being in between. When he was acting, he disappeared. There was just the Lost Expert. But when it was over, it was almost like what he figured jet lag might be like — a groggy, confused dis-awareness separated from the temporal by a thick haze sticking to everything. Tough terrain to slog through. *Do they know? Have you told them yet? What about the agreement?*

"Thomson?" The voice, high and gentle, with just a hint of steel, like a wire bridge swaying resolutely in a storm.

Darlia, he realized with a mixture of fascination and dread. Outside of their scenes, Chris had barely seen her since their strange encounter.

"Yoo-hoo?"

He poked his head out from behind the screen.

"Oh, *there* you are. What are you doing back *there*?" She wrinkled her nose curiously. Chris grabbed the sweater and quickly pulled it over his head. Darlia followed his movements with predatory alertness.

"Do you mind if I ...?"

She crossed the trailer and, moving to the minibar, poured them both two fingers of vodka. "Don't you have any ice? Oh, well, never mind."

Darlia handed him a glass, then gracefully settled on the settee, patting the space beside her. She was dressed in a green velvet outfit that made her look like a cross between a punk park ranger and a pixie huntress. Her hair was up in a casual yet expensive-looking braided bun. She had her own stylist on set. She was smiling implacably.

Darlia patted the small space next to her again.

"Sit down with me." She pouted.

Chris hesitated. The sun was setting.

"C'mon, I won't bite." Darlia's giggle was like crystal champagne flutes clinking. Chris considered her again. Her smile was small and pointed and perfect. She probably would bite. But he was pulled in by her pulsing shimmer, that undercurrent of potential implosion — no wonder they called them stars.

Darlia's perfectly manicured hands were folded over something that sat on the small space created by her crossed legs. It was a document of some sort, bound with a plastic spiral. Chris felt a surge of excitement. Was that it? Surely Darlia, of all people, would have it: the script, master plan to Reed's giant mess of a movie.

He wedged in next to her, instantly enveloped in her intricate, expensive scent of lemon, almonds, and pine.

"You were fantastic today, Tommy," Darlia purred.

"You too," Chris murmured.

"You're really helping me, you know," Darlia continued. "Really grounding me. You're so different now. So intense and focused. It's amazing."

She put her small head on his shoulder. He felt her needy languor spreading through him.

Darlia spoke, and Chris listened. She talked about Reed's vision, about how her character was developing into something far more interesting than she'd originally thought. Chris nodded along, occasionally glancing down at her lap, hoping to see the cover page, but her fingers covered the upper half.

"I just wanted to thank you. For what you said last time we …
talked. You were right about this movie. It's going to be something special. There's something that happens between us when
we're on set. It's you, really. I'm just following your lead. We
barely need to speak. It's amazing. I mean, she loves him, doesn't
she? And she wants him to succeed. Desperately. More than
anything else in the world."

"She does," Chris heard himself say. His words were husky
and weighed down. "She loves him."

"That's the tragedy, isn't it?" Darlia sighed.

Chris grimaced, like he'd tasted something sour.

Darlia snuggled closer to him. They sat there, neither one of
them speaking. It was surprisingly easy to be with Darlia, exis-
tentially calming, like resigning yourself to being toyed with by
a lioness. Chris felt her heat next to him.

"And," Darlia continued, "I just wanted to say that I would
never — I mean, all of that — It was so long ago. And I was —
well … We were young, right? Anyway, when I was — you acted
like a complete gentleman." She trilled a laugh. "Imagine that!
Thomson Holmes, gentleman." She laughed again, her citrus
scent now tinged bitter.

"People can change," Chris said. "They can be better."

Darlia raised her head from his shoulder and kissed him on
the cheek.

"You're sweet."

Chris flushed from head to toe.

"Thomson," Darlia said, her tone subtly toughening. "I wanted
to ask you. I've been working on a project." Again Darlia trilled,
this time nervously. "A script, actually." Darlia's hands suddenly fluttered in the air, finally unveiling the bound mound
of paper. "I've been working on it on and off for years. Bill, my

agent, he didn't think it was a good idea. If it's not broken, don't fix it, right? But after what you said to me, and seeing how you've changed, I decided to polish it up and move ahead. I don't care what Bill says. I'm going to direct, too."

"Oh yeah?" Chris murmured. He tried to stay impassive. She didn't have the key to unlock *The Lost Expert*. Time was passing. *Did you tell them yet?* Chris rubbed his temples and pictured it: His best pal frying convenience store bacon for his breakfast while bad-mouthing the host of the drive-home radio show on the CBC. After the surprise return, they'd do the usual, head out to any number of possible destinations: a full night at the multiplex moving from theatre to theatre on a single ticket; an obscure basement screening of found seventies Super 8 footage; a projection of Yiddish silent movies in a North York synagogue; an evening of Indigenous queer experimental sci-fi at a sleek gallery. After that, there'd be bars that looked like diners and diners that looked like bars, there'd be alleys and dumpsters, his friend insisting on crouching in rotting muck with his Leica to get just the right shot of an abandoned bicycle stripped of everything but rusting gears decorated with two used condoms.

"They're in their early thirties," Darlia was saying now, talking slowly, articulating each word with her perfect diction. "And they come back to their old suburb, where they grew up. At first, I was thinking maybe Boston, because Bill says it's a bigger market, but I decided to stay authentic and go with where I grew up, in the Seattle suburbs. So everyone is going to be very conservative, stay-at-home moms, dads working in insurance and tech. Anyway, they meet again after not seeing each other for ten years, brought back to town when their third best friend from high school, Bethany, tries to kill herself. They come back to visit her in the hospital. I'll play her, of course. While helping her recover, that's when they realize that they've always, secretly, loved each other. Like, literally, loved each other. So it's a gay love story, but there's also a lot of other stuff going on. Like, it's the eighties and everything, and everyone's doing drugs and going crazy even though it's supposed to be all buttoned-up and conservative. It's *Brokeback Mountain* meets *The Ice Storm* meets *The Big Chill*."

Krunk, Chris thought. Krunk would love this.

"Of course, I'm no Ang Lee," Darlia said.

"And I'm no Jeff Goldblum," Chris heard himself saying in a high-pitched voice, still desperately trying to quell a hysterical giggle.

Darlia twitched her perfect, freckled nose. "You're *much* better looking," she assured him. She put a hand on his knee.

He knew and didn't know what was coming. Her hand, just above his knee now, hot through his jeans.

"Tommy, it'll really help me if I can say that you're attached to the project. You don't have to commit right now. I *want* you to, but you should read it first. I know you'll love it. Anyway, before this shoot I wouldn't have ever imagined … But you've changed so much. More and more I'm seeing you as one of the friends. Bruce, probably."

"Bruce?" Chris sputtered. It was all he could do now to contain himself. A hiccup squeezed past his constricted throat. The muscles in his thighs twitched. He shot up out of the love seat and busied himself pouring more vodka.

"He's one of the friends," Darlia went on, unperturbed. "His backstory is that he's super-repressed, in the closet, engaged to be married. He works on Wall Street and considers himself a macho trader, but …"

Chris felt her sweet breath in his ear and startled, almost spilling. Darlia was suddenly beside him, talking intently in a near whisper.

"I don't want to pressure you, especially now, in the middle of a shoot, believe me, I know it's the last thing you need. But, well, I have a meeting next week with a producer, I'll leave his name out of it for now, you know him, anyway, he's coming into town for another meeting and I set something up with him, and I think it would really help if I could tell him that you were at least seriously considering it."

"Sure," Chris said, handing Darlia her refilled glass. She smiled a Cheshire cat grin. He'd do anything for her, get nothing back in return, and not care at all. And anyway, it was time. Time to go.

"Really?"

"Sure. Of course."

"Oh, Thomson." Darlia exhaled his name like Marilyn Monroe singing happy birthday to JFK. "Thank you. It means so much to me."

"To Bruce." Chris saluted, somehow staying straight-faced.

Beaming, Darlia clinked his glass. They both swallowed their drinks. Darlia put her glass down and took a step back as if to consider the totality of Chris's oversized persona.

"Are you taller now, Holmes?" she teased. She crinkled her pixie smile. "There's just something so *changed* about you."

"Knock knock, coming in," a voice called, opening the door and stepping into the dimly lit trailer. This time, it really was Alison. "Oh! Sorry! I didn't know you had company."

Chris blushed, heat spreading over his face. Darlia stepped away from him.

"Darlia came over to tell me about a new project she's —"

"Still in development, dear," Darlia cut in. "Very much under wraps. Hush-hush. Anyway, I was just leaving."

"Well, really sorry to interrupt that then!" Alison said vigorously. "But Thomson has an appointment with Reed in his trailer. He wants to go over tomorrow's shoot with you and show you some footage, remember?"

"Right, yes, yes. I was just on my way." Avoiding Alison's gaze, Chris wiped at the beads of sweat on his upper lip. Darlia shifted closer to him. He felt her small, perfect hand curl around his forearm.

"This sounds interesting," Darlia said, flashing her dangerous smile. "I think I'll join you. I'm sure Reed won't mind."

"DARLIA," REED BOOMED AS soon as the group stepped up into his beat-up makeshift office. He flashed a confused look at Alison. She shrugged. "What a wonderful surprise! Have a seat. Here. Just, let me … just move these … papers over here … And a drink! Let's get you a drink." He looked around the trailer for someone or something. "Can someone get Darlia a drink! A drink for Darlia!" Reed carried on, shouting and fawning over Chris's co-star. Finally, they all settled — glasses in hand — around Reed's long desk.

Alison got the lights. The trailer fell into the semi-dark of night-time screen time. Chris, suddenly realizing what was about to happen, grabbed the arms of his chair tightly. Each night, he'd gotten into the habit of deleting the link leading to that day's rushes. Just in case, he told himself. Just in case he woke up out of restless sleep and felt tempted.

If anyone asked what he thought so far, he'd just nod and smile vaguely. Up till now, it had worked. Somehow, it had worked.

It was the same with the acting he kept getting praised for. His "method" was to say as little as possible while staying as still as possible. *Less is more*, Chris repeated. His new mantra. The less he knew — the less he saw — the better.

"Here we go!" Reed yelled, clapping his meaty hands together expectantly.

His giant centre monitor unhurriedly drifted through a series of scene-setting tableaus: grey skies; foreground factories bellowing smoke; a flock of harried seagulls gaining altitude. A panning shot: the sallow, hungry faces of the extras; the women in worn, loose dresses; the men in fraying shirtsleeves. Then back to the low sky hanging over the wharf's industrial district.

Chris, entranced, forgot to be afraid.

A sudden change — the frame narrowing, the camera conveying singular purpose, near-manic urgency. Chris reacted with a muscular startle that almost tipped him out of his cheap office chair. He felt Alison and Darlia both casting sharp looks his way. Reed, talking, narrating, didn't notice. Chris kept his eyes on the screen.

A man was walking urgently down the sidewalk past boarded-up tenements festooned with signs. Despite the swing of his arms and heavy, frantic steps, the man's pace appeared to be deteriorating, as if muffled by the worn but not ragged working clothes he was wearing like a heavy blanket. Then, with the air of someone dazed by extra hours of preemptive, abrupt unemployment, the man — the Lost Expert, Chris finally allowed himself to think — stopped. He contemplated a particularly dense cluster of overlapping signs and posters for Allan's Army, for crackdowns on foreigners and Jews, for the rebuilding of America. As the man stared, the camera slowly climbed up his chest. Chris steeled himself for the shock. *It'll be me*, he thought.

But the cheeks were hollower. And the forehead appeared dramatically protruding, the eyes cast in permanent shadow. Had they altered his appearance somehow? Figured out some filter that somehow converted him into this long, lean loner?

The panic left Chris like a rush of air surging out of a punctured balloon. He deflated, slumping in his chair. It wasn't him. It didn't even look like him. It was some other Chris. Thomson Holmes Chris. The Lost Expert Chris. Thomson Holmes Lost Expert Chris. This man in dark Depression-era work clothes, this man squaring a broad jaw dotted with five o'clock shadow, this man darting his haunted gaze from poster to poster as if resolving to try and lose and try and lose and try and lose over and over again.

Reed was still talking, narrating the action or making notes for further edits, Chris couldn't tell.

"If we could — Beautiful — Yes — Hold that — That stare! — A little longer — Wait for it — *Wait for it* ... Now! Yes!"

Then he stopped talking.

"But Tommy," Darlia said into the sudden, buzzing silence. She grabbed Chris's hand in both of her smaller ones. "Just look at you. Look how sad they made you."

INT. — LOST EXPERT'S INNER OFFICE —
MID-MORNING

THE LOST EXPERT unlocks the door to a threadbare
office. On an empty, battered desk sits a flat,
square package wrapped in plain brown paper. The
phone rings, but the Lost Expert ignores it. He
picks up the package and examines it curiously,
then finally strips the paper off. He sees a
record, white with swirls of red mixed into the
vinyl like spilled blood: "(Good) God Gonna
Come", by Bessie Styles and the Beehives.

A note falls out of the package onto the battered
wooden desk. The Lost Expert picks it up.

Scrawled in barely legible handwriting: "Secret
Track — Ashberry — 1749 Gorham Crescent,
apartment 543."

The phone stops ringing. The silence, like the
wake of a passing train, momentarily startles.

INT. LOST EXPERT'S INNER OFFICE, LATE MORNING
THE LOST EXPERT lies on his back listening to
the record. His eyes are closed.

                    WOMAN (V.O.)
                 (singing-wailing)
      It's so delightful / this hunger I'm
     living / I'm hungry for living / fill me
      up if you can / here on my knees / lean
       in to the Lord / oh Lord fill me up /
        fill me up if you can / no one can!

                                        CUT TO

The record, blood-red vinyl, spinning on the
record player.

                                        CUT TO

BEAOMAN in the desert, draining the water from
the Lost Expert's canteen onto the contorted
face of the kohl-eyed duchess.

                                        CUT TO

The Lost Expert's MOTHER, face down in the
swamp.

                                        CUT TO

The RABBI, dressed as the devil.

                                            CUT TO

JOEL MCCANN, riding the streetcar, grinning
piggily.

                                            CUT TO

Blood-red vinyl spinning.

                                            CUT TO

The Lost Expert's baby, red-faced and crying.

                                            CUT TO

The disc spinning. Music (dissolving into
moans, frenetic guitar, bass, horns, and drums,
then incoherent screams).

                         WOMAN
              No one can! If you can. Empty man!
                      Be a man!

                                            CUT TO

The Lost Expert abruptly shoots up to a
sitting position. The song ends, but the record
continues to spin, emitting a faint background
hum. The phone rings in the outer room. Suddenly,
there is the scratchy sound of an old woman
crooning.

                    WOMAN (V.O.)
        (singing, scratchy, as if recorded
              outside a long time ago)
    Finder man, come and help / finder man,
    we're-a-goin' lost / find her man, if you
                    think you can.

                 WOMAN (V.O.) (CONT'D)
                      (talking)
       We all called him Meyer. Keep outta
        them woods, my mammy used to say.
        Meyer'll get you. He'll get yous
                     for sure.

                 INTERVIEWER (V.O.)
              (a question, inaudible)

                    WOMAN (V.O.)
    Ain't no Meyer, that's what we said. Wese
            ain't afraid of no Meyer.

                 INTERVIEWER (V.O.)
              (statement, inaudible)

                    WOMAN (V.O.)
            We used to [inaudible].

                 WOMAN (V.O.) (CONT'D)
        (singing in her low, gravelly voice)
    Finder man, where you at? / finder man,
    we're-a-goin' lost / finder man, you ever
                    coming back?

                    WOMAN (V.O.) (CONT'D)
                        (talking)
        But we ain't never seen no finder man.
      (chuckling ruefully) Meyer, though, yeah,
      we seen him. Kids going missing. That's
                  the way it's always been.
                 Folks just going missing.

                    WOMAN (V.O.) (CONT'D)
                        (singing)
        Finder man, we calling for you / finder
        man, we're-a-goin' lost / finder man,
                  when you coming back?

EXT. A DECREPIT EIGHT-STOREY BROWNSTONE — EARLY
EVENING
A sign out front: Broadview Manor. Vacancies.
Scrawled hastily underneath: No Jews.
A GROUP OF MEN in their twenties are clustered
outside; they wear dark suits and bowler hats,
laughing loudly and drinking from their flasks.
Some of them wear Allan's Army buttons. They
stop talking when THE LOST EXPERT approaches,
tracking him menacingly with dead eyes. He
moves through them without slowing his stride.
Reflexively, they part and let him by.

INT. WILLA'S APARTMENT
THE LOST EXPERT is in the living room of a small
apartment. The windows are covered by yellowed
lace curtains. There is a single lamp with a
red velvet shade barely illuminating WILLA,

a tiny figure sitting in the centre of an old
couch, also upholstered in red velvet. A partial
patchwork of indeterminate knitting sits in the
old woman's lap along with needles and wool.
The Lost Expert perches in a straight-backed
chair facing the shrivelled figure. When Willa
speaks, he immediately recognizes the scratched,
gravelly voice from the "(Good) God Gonna Come"
record.

                    WILLA
       Finder man. Been waiting for you. Been
              waiting a long time.

The Lost Expert leans forward in his chair and
stares intently at Willa.

                 THE LOST EXPERT
       Tell me about him. Tell me about Meyer.

                    WILLA
                 (as if far away)
                  He took us.

                 THE LOST EXPERT
       He took you? Where did he take you?

Willa abruptly picks up the knitting on her lap
and starts to knit. The Lost Expert leans back
into his chair and hooks a single large finger
into the handle of the small mug on the card
table beside him.

THE LOST EXPERT
(sipping)
This is good coffee.

WILLA
(as if to herself)
When he came, you could feel it. Here.
(tapping her chest) Like a cold rain.
Like a deee-luge.

THE LOST EXPERT
You saw him?

WILLA
(working her needles)
I ran. Lord almighty, how I ran.

THE LOST EXPERT
(pulling out the sketch of Beaoman)
This man? Is this who you saw?

Willa's face remains impassive, but her tiny,
wizened hands show her agitation as the needles
click feverishly.

WILLA
(singing woefully)
Find the girls, finder man. Find the
girls, if you think you can.

WILLA (CONT'D)
(speaking)
Wasn't no finder, though. Only all us
kids, gone lost.

THE LOST EXPERT
Was it this man? Was this the man who
took them?

WILLA
(looking up into the Lost Expert's eyes)
Nobody took 'em. They got lost, is all.
All by themselves, they gone lost.

THE LOST EXPERT
I —

WILLA
(dismissing him with a wave of
her needles)
Been waiting, finder man. Been waiting
a long time.

THE LOST EXPERT
How do I find him? Where do I look?

WILLA
Follow the Brown.

THE LOST EXPERT
The Brown?

WILLA
(impatient)
The Brown! Past Broken Creek. He'll be
there. He's always there.

INT. LOBBY OF APARTMENT BUILDING
The GROUP OF YOUNG MEN he saw earlier are just
outside. They are wearing white hoods now, their
eyes and lips shadowed. THE LOST EXPERT freezes,
waiting without panic, as if already knowing
what is going to happen. They see him and pile
into the lobby.

PACK LEADER
Well, lookee who's back! We recollect his
face now, don't we, boys? If it isn't
that Jew-lover!

The leader punches the Lost Expert in the
stomach. He doubles over. The gang beats him.
The Lost Expert is silent as the blows rain down.

IT WAS DARK WHEN Chris was finally alone, finally able to slip out of his trailer. No one seemed to be around, but just in case Chris scuttled quickly from under the slide to behind the climbing wall. Streetlamp glare muted by the large maples and lindens cast nighttime shadow over the well-worn playground equipment. Chris edged along until he was a few feet from the chain-link fence that separated the park from the playing field of the Catholic primary school. Well, it had been a Catholic school until last year when changing demographics and declining religious affiliation finally caught up to the enrollment levels, resulting in the school's closure, the students amalgamated with two other schools to achieve efficiencies of scale the church once enjoyed through sheer ubiquity. Despite his name, neither of his parents had ever been religious. Thinking about it, Chris realized that he didn't even know if they believed in God. Did they? Could they have once? *But, Tommy, look how sad they made you …*

Chris leapt the waist-high fence and began trotting through the field, aware that in the dim streetlight he was in danger of falling into one of the holes dug by the small, yappy dogs that infested the fenced-in area on weekends and after work. As he ran, he felt the envelope of money Berinstain had given him pressing against his thigh. Two thousand dollars. Just like that. Spending money. Pocket change, for a guy like Thomson Holmes.

Having effected his escape, unseen and, more remarkably, uncontaminated by mini designer dog turds, Chris felt himself gain confidence in his planned defection. He was out. He had some money. He hadn't done anything that — horrible. He was done. Done with all of it. Done with that man on the screen, that sad, horrible reflection. He'd drunk another three fingers of vodka back in his trailer while waiting for the coast to clear. He was done, he'd kept telling himself. It was over.

Once upon a time, a movie star disappeared. His parents got divorced. His dad remarried. He moved out on his own, went to college, dropped out of college. Chris had always thought he'd eventually outrun it, that sense that he'd failed something — though he wasn't sure what. Put enough distance between yourself and the past and it should eventually just fade away, shouldn't it? But now, now that he was a big success, a movie star, he saw how it really was. It was always there, whispering to him, stalking him. *Did you tell them? Do they know? How sad you are?*

Where'd you go, Little Scarface? Where was Thomson Holmes? And Alison? Shouldn't he at least say goodbye? Goodbye to Alison?

KRUNK'S BASEMENT BACHELOR PAD was accessed through the back alley that ran parallel to the restaurants and shops fronting Spadina between Dundas and College. This was Toronto's Chinatown: cheap restaurants with faded placards in their grimy windows promising a Three Course Lunch Special, the price crossed out and raised a dollar a time over the years. Chris and Krunk were regulars for the $4.99, the $5.99, and, more recently, the $6.99. Hot and sour soup, spring roll, General Tso's chicken.

He tried picturing it: Darlia raising a deep-fried chunk of battered chicken coated in thick red sweet and sour mystery sauce to her perfect pursed lips.

Chris veered into the alleyway, ill lit, trash strewn, just barely wide enough to admit a delivery van. He stepped quickly, familiar with the uniquely greasy cracked pavement. He and Krunk had a running joke about it, alternated between calling it "the tunnel of love," "the fecund funnel," or, most insensibly, "the Last Little Alley in Texas." His loafers raised a slapping sound out of the porous concrete, the only thing out of place in this familiar scene until the Holmes Samsung startled him by vibrating in his pocket. Ignoring it, Chris quickened his pace.

The Krunk lair sat underneath Kwai-Soo Very Gourmet BBQ, whose trademark dish was barbecue pork on rice; according to Krunk, they went through fifteen pigs a night, last orders placed at 3:30 a.m., the restaurant finally closing at 4:00, around the same time his best friend usually stumbled home.

Chris slipped into the back door of the restaurant and was blasted, as usual, by greasy, steamy fumes laden with intermingled sauces — garlic, ginger, fermented black bean. Without pausing, he headed down the rear stairs. He'd made the same journey thousands of times before, could probably do it blindfolded, practically had done it blindfolded — the dim light bulb burnt out, the two of them drunkenly clutching at the banister as they half slid, half fell down the slippery flight of stairs, landing in a pile of cursing, sweaty joviality in front of the door to Krunk's basement hideout.

He hesitated at the door. It wouldn't be locked. It never was. Krunk claimed the restaurant and all within were protected by the North American tongs and a lock would be superfluous. In truth, Krunk had gotten tired of constantly misplacing his keys. Chris felt a surge of nervous anticipation. He'd tell him everything. Then he'd call Laurie. Make amends. Tell her everything — almost everything. He'd go see his mom. Stay for the weekend. Compliment her pot roast.

Hearing clattering dishes and muted voices, he pushed on through. Krunk in his basement burrow conducting his standard one-way conversation with his much-reviled CBC radio while microwaving some pre-departure repast.

"Hey?" Chris tried to call. "Krunkie! You home?" But his words had barely escaped from his tight throat before they were throttled by the familiar narrowing of the already narrow hallway. Chris stopped on the threshold, disoriented. The radio was on, but it was playing what sounded like big band, exuberant trumpets and trombones. And the smell wasn't irradiated bacon. Something more refined was in the air, like the cooking of actual food, which his friend never did. The light flickered gently, dim and incandescent instead of the harsh bare fluorescent that usually illuminated Krunk's setup. And the voices weren't just Krunk talking to the radio. Two actual voices, Chris realized. A high laugh followed by a lower chuckle. Then it hit him. Krunk was with someone. He'd finally done it. Gotten a girl down to his crypt.

Chris tried to stop himself. But it was too late. He was already breaching the darkness, moving into the field of soft light — candles! — enveloping the couple on the couch. There were glasses of red wine and the remains of a spaghetti dinner on the sheet-covered milk crate coffee table. Chris, feeling his full height, the ceiling just about brushing the top of his increasingly Holmesian brush cut, looked down at the two people on the couch. Canoodling. A word his mother sometimes used, half-kidding, half-serious, as if any other term was too painful for her to muster. Noticing him, unlikely paramour Krunk jerked away from his companion.

Then the woman stood, her bare knees knocking the milk crate table and rattling the plates.

"Chris?"

It was Laurie. Red splotches bloomed on her pale, lightly freckled checks. She looked at him wide-eyed, then looked back at Krunk, who was white and slack-jawed on the couch.

"Chris ..." Laurie said again.

A wave of repulsion crashed through him. He opened his mouth. To yell or laugh or throw up. Nothing came out.

"Chris? Are you okay?"

"Bud ..." Krunk finally managed, his folksy voice as fake as the dust-covered plastic rubber tree next to the sofa, stolen from some movie set or other. Krunk wasn't even looking at him, was, instead, stupidly pondering the sauce-spattered plates in front of him. Chris leaned in, off balance, thinking to slap the dunce off his best friend's face.

"Chris?" Laurie pleaded.

The candles flickered, as if stirred by a sudden draft.

Chris whirled and ran.

"Chris!" Laurie cried.

He stumbled on the dark stairs, his hands catching his fall, palms smeared with decades of greasy filth.

HE DIDN'T STOP UNTIL he'd reached the literal bottom of the city. His soles ached. His thighs pulsed with heat. Breathing heavily, he climbed the rubble of rocks between the path and the water. He thought of the desert, the cliff he'd ascended and, apparently, dramatically descended.

Chris gazed out over the Great Lake. The dark water slapped restlessly at the concrete breaker wall as if mocking this human attempt at containment. Sweat, trapped between his T-shirt and

the increasingly ragged purple sweater, made him feel soupy
and ridiculous. Angrily, he wrestled with the clinging cashmere,
teetering on the boulders as he pulled the sweater off. Clutching
it in a fist, Chris ducked under the rusting guardrail. The moon
came out, revealing brown, burbling, oil-streaked spume foaming
against the break wall. Then clouds rolled in again, and everything returned to muted metal hues of grey. Without the faint
moonlight, it felt like there was nothing between himself and the
Great Lake. He could barely tell where the crumbling concrete
of the container wall ended and the murky vastness of the water
began. Leaning over, hanging on to the rusted railing with one
hand, Chris flung the sweater skyward. He peered through the
gloom. He couldn't see past the end of his extended arm. It was
as if the sweater just disappeared.

The Holmes phone rang. Then, right on cue, the flip phone.

One buzzed and vibrated, one let out a muted, sad bleat.

Cold wind swept up from the restless water, pushing through
him and rapidly cooling him down.

Buzz buzz buzz. Bring bring bring.

A splash a few feet out. Chris squinted into the mist. What was
there? Nothing you could see. Cold, dark water, ice-age deep;
barnacled shipwrecks, remnants of the great era of schooners
and steamers; drums of industrial waste, their rusted barrels
slowly leaking centuries of progress across the lakebed; bodies,
Chris suddenly thought — bodies drifting along the bottom,
mouths agape, eyes pecked out, mouths stuffed with stones. *Did
you tell them? Do they know?*

Buzz buzz buzz. Bring bring bring.

The phones began anew. Which one held the answer? One.
One quest, one ring, one villain, one girl. One right decision.
One hero. One last chance.

Bring bring bring. Buzz buzz buzz.

"Hello?"

"Is that you, son?"

A tinny voice sounding farther away than the caller really was.

"Chris, are you there? Son?"

Not who he'd expected — Laurie or Krunk, the two of them feigning worry and taking turns frantically dialling and redialling.

"Yeah, Dad, I'm here."

The last time he'd spoken to his father had been a perfunctory call after his birthday to thank him for the generic holiday card stuffed with a single red fifty, five months ago.

"Dad? I'm here. Hold on a second."

He sat down on the thin strip of concrete, dangling his hot, quivering legs over the restless lake.

"Can you hear me, Chris? It's a bit noisy. Where are you?"

"I'm in the city."

"Oh. You're okay, then?"

"Sure, Dad."

"Your mother is worried about you."

"Mom?"

"She asked me to call you. Said she hadn't been able to get hold of you. And that you'd broken up with your girlfriend?"

"Mom asked you to call?"

"She says you haven't been answering your phone."

"I've just been really busy, Dad."

"Your mother mentioned something about a new job? In film?"

"Yes. I've been working really long hours."

"Good. Good. What's the gig? I suppose you're just doing the grunt work? Any chance of upward mobility?"

Upward mobility?

"Uh, yeah, Dad. Lots. Loads."

"That's good to hear, son."

There was a pause. The wind picked up. Chris realized he was cold now, pockmarked with goosebumps.

"And your girlfriend, what was her name again?"

"Laurie."

"Right. Yes. Laurie. Are you guys —?"

He'd never meet her, Chris thought.

"Chris, you still there?"

"Dad?"

"Yes?"

"I have a few days off. I was thinking maybe I could come visit?"

"Sure. Sure thing, son. When were you thinking of coming?"

"Tomorrow? I could catch the Greyhound in the morning."

"Tomorrow? I'll have to just … Let me just check with Susan, get back to you on that."

"Okay."

"It's just, you know how Susan his." His dad laughed nervously. "You know how Susan is about surprises."

"You know what? Forget it. It's okay. Don't worry about it. It's too short notice."

"Why don't you go see your mother? She's worried about you. And then we'll schedule a proper time for a visit. Next month? We could take a drive, see the fall colours?"

"Okay, Dad. That sounds good."

The fall colours, Chris thought. In November.

Another awkward pause. Chris swung his feet. His loafers dangled from his toes.

"Well, it's getting late. You sure you're all right?"

"Talk to you later, Dad."

"Sounds good."

Chris swallowed heavily. He hadn't cried since his grand-father's death. That's how it was, he thought. It wasn't anything new. That's how it had always been. Christopher Hutchins had been replaced a long time ago. His father, packing his bags in the middle of the night. His mother, pill vials spilling out of her handbag. Or else, like Thomson Holmes, he'd been just plain disappeared.

But he was still here. Still here, starring in a movie. A *Bryant Reed* movie, Krunk. Remember him? Pioneering filmmaker who shattered the Hollywood studio system?

You get something too, Chris told himself. *You get more than something. You get more than they can ever imagine.*

Buzz buzz buzz.

Phone number two.

It was Alison.

"Thomson! What's going on? Where are you?"

INT. THE LOST EXPERT'S OFFICE — MIDNIGHT
THE LOST EXPERT sits on the faded couch. ESTHER
dabs at a cut on his cheek.

                    ESTHER
               Does that hurt?

                    THE LOST EXPERT
                         No.

                    ESTHER
               It's very deep.

                    THE LOST EXPERT
                    I'll be fine.

                    ESTHER
               You need a doctor.

The Lost Expert twists away from Esther's
ministrations.

THE LOST EXPERT
Esther, what are you doing here?

ESTHER
The rabbi sent me.

THE LOST EXPERT
Why?

ESTHER
(sarcastic)
Why?

THE LOST EXPERT
You shouldn't be here. You
should go.

ESTHER
Go? Where should I go?

THE LOST EXPERT
(exasperated)
Home! It isn't safe!

ESTHER
Yes, it's safe at home.

The phone starts to ring. Esther answers it.

ESTHER
The Lost Expert's office. How may
I help you?

Esther takes notes.

                    ESTHER (CONT'D)
                     (reassuring)
        Yes, that's right. We'll be back in touch
           shortly. And don't worry. I'm sure we
                        can help.

Esther hangs up the phone.

                   THE LOST EXPERT
                    (not unkindly)
              You shouldn't say that.

                       ESTHER
                     Say what?

                   THE LOST EXPERT
                That we can help them.

                       ESTHER
          A missing couple. Young. Just married.

                   THE LOST EXPERT
        I'm not a miracle worker, Esther. I'm not
         one of your angels. I can't always make
                    things better.

                       ESTHER
        The rabbi says nobody should do anything.
          We should all just be. Be with *Hashem*.

The Lost Expert climbs to his feet with a
grimace.

                    THE LOST EXPERT
              He's an old man, Esther.

                       ESTHER
              You think I don't know that?

                    THE LOST EXPERT
          Esther. You don't know what it's like out
                        there.

                       ESTHER
          (extending the message slip to him)
                    So show me.

INT. SMALL, RAMSHACKLE HOUSE ON THE EDGE OF THE
CITY — LATE NIGHT
ESTHER and THE LOST EXPERT are in an uninviting,
unfinished basement room entirely dominated
by a large, ornate four-poster bed. They are
accompanied by a grim-looking couple, the woman,
PATRICIA, frail-looking, older than her years,
the man, MARTIN, muscular, sturdy, his face
lined with deep grooves.

                      PATRICIA
          We're doing our best for them. They just
          got married last year. But things aren't

so good right now. Emma was in secretary
school till Ricky got laid off. He was
working as a cleaner downtown. Martin.
(looking at her husband) They cut his pay
at the factory.

Martin nods and looks away, embarrassed.

                    PATRICIA (CONT'D)
We said we would fix up the basement for
them. At least until they could get back
on their feet.

The Lost Expert contemplates the bed, which is
mussed, a heavy comforter tossed aside, exposing
the stains of a bare mattress.

                    THE LOST EXPERT
What happened to the sheets?

                    PATRICIA
(abruptly bursting into tears)
I don't know! They're good children!
Always clean! Always neat!

INT. SMALL SITTING ROOM IN BACK OF THE HOUSE

                    THE LOST EXPERT
Is there anywhere they might have gone?
Friends they could be staying with?

                        PATRICIA
        I don't know. They've been so strange
        lately! They don't tell me nothin'!

                         ESTHER
                 (handing her a tissue)
        Don't worry, Mama. We'll find them.

THE LOST EXPERT gives Esther a warning glance,
which she ignores.

                         MARTIN
        (stoic, wiping at his eyes with a sleeve)
                 Thank you. Thank you.

The Lost Expert gets up, pulls aside the
tattered curtain, and looks out into the bleak
night. There is a small area of paving stones,
their backyard, and behind that, a rickety fence
sealing off the dark space beyond.

                     THE LOST EXPERT
                 What's behind there?

                         MARTIN
        Old railroad tracks. They don't use 'em
        anymore. Nothin' there but rag pickers
                     and hobos.

EXT. CUL-DE-SAC SIDE STREET ENDING AT A
PARTIALLY COLLAPSED FENCE — LATE NIGHT
A patch of trampled grass and weed separates

the end of the street from the fence and the
dark area beyond. The grass is littered with
cigarette butts and other random urban detritus.
The wooden fencing has all but collapsed,
providing easy access to the zone beyond. It
is dark, the final streetlamp of the cul-de-sac
just barely reaching them. THE LOST EXPERT
shines a dim flashlight, following a tunnelled
path of trampled crabgrass and shattered glass
into the deep shadows of the space past the
rusted rail tracks. In the permeated darkness,
figures shift, and noises — shouts, moans —
occasionally reach them.

                    THE LOST EXPERT
          Esther, you should wait back at the
                        house.

                        ESTHER
             I'm coming with you.

                    THE LOST EXPERT
          Esther. This isn't what you think it is.

                        ESTHER
                 What is it, then?

The Lost Expert navigates through the collapsed
fence. Esther follows him.

EXT. THE DUMP
THE LOST EXPERT and ESTHER follow a narrow

path into the gloomy space. They move past
huddled shapes sleeping on discarded mattresses.
There are piles of trash in heaps all around
and underfoot. The Lost Expert and Esther
pass makeshift shelters made out of scrap
wood and rusted metal. Esther steps on the
remains of a glass syringe. They pass a WOMAN
sitting by herself, her mostly bald head in
her hands. Esther's eyes are half closed, her
lips moving in silent prayer. They come to a
GROUP OF BEDRAGGLED MEN standing around a fire
they've built in a metal drum. The Lost Expert
approaches, indicating to Esther to wait in
the shadows. He shows the men a formal portrait
photograph of the young couple dressed in their
wedding attire.

                    THE LOST EXPERT
                Have you seen these two?

The men shrug and shake their heads. Then one of
them takes a second look at the picture. Hand
trembling, he points to a stilted structure,
once a water tower or grain elevator, the
abandoned structure now a makeshift multilevel
shanty apartment block haphazardly augmented
with foraged and found materials. The entire
shaky complex is a maze of protruding pieces of
old lumber and reclaimed railroad track walled
by sheets of rusty, jagged metal.

INT. LABYRINTH
They pick their way through the interior of
the structure, ducking through low passages
half filled with silt and dust. Paths veer
in different directions. After some time, the
labyrinth opens into a larger chamber. The smell
is decay and rot, sweat and fear, feces and
the forsaken. The Lost Expert scans the dark,
claustrophobic space with his dim flashlight.
ESTHER stands close, holding her kerchief over
her mouth and nose. Suddenly, the Lost Expert's
flashlight catches a tall man, well dressed in a
suit topped by a trench coat, his face obscured
as he stoops low to enter a tunnel on the other
end of the chamber.

                    THE LOST EXPERT
                  Stay here, Esther.

The Lost Expert sprints across, his flashlight
beam swinging wildly. He runs through the narrow
passages on the other side, the man just out of
view. The Lost Expert turns the corner, crashes
into someone who swears and pushes at him.
The Lost Expert shoves the man into a wall of
trash and runs forward. A piercing scream. It
is Esther. The Lost Expert scrabbles to a stop.
He stares into the murk of the passage ahead.
Esther screams again.

INT. CENTRE OF THE LABYRINTH
ESTHER holds a filthy, stained bedsheet and

is staring in horror at what she's found
underneath.

THE LOST EXPERT runs over. Lying on overlapping
flattened pieces of cardboard is the YOUNG
COUPLE, crumpled over each other. Their wrists
are slashed, and they are both covered in each
other's clotted, still drying blood. An old
kitchen knife lies on the ground between them.
The knife's blade glistens wetly in the Lost
Expert's flashlight.

                    THE LOST EXPERT
                      Esther …

Esther buries her face in the Lost Expert's
shoulder and sobs.

                    THE LOST EXPERT
                     (disengaging)
         Esther, we have to go. I shouldn't have
         brought you here. It isn't safe. We have
                    to go, Esther.

INT. THE LOST EXPERT'S OFFICE — EARLY MORNING
THE LOST EXPERT gently pulls a tattered blanket
over ESTHER, who lies curled up in the fetal
position on the battered couch.

BACK IN THE TOWN car, heading up Avenue Road to Eglinton. The more things change, Chris thought randomly — Krunk's standard pronouncement on sequels, remakes, and just about anything Hollywood. He had his own version: The more time and space he put between himself and his erstwhile best friend, the more Krunk's spiels and catchphrases popped into his head. Staring out the window, he wondered about it. Was it an unconscious process? His brain trying to remind him of his natural place in the pecking order? Or was he trying to do the exact opposite? Rid himself of it all, a massive emesis to make space for something new? The landscape passed with unassuming familiarity, the anonymous buildings on the periphery an afterimage blur. He couldn't focus. Krunk and Laurie. Sure, why not? Let them have each other. He needed to keep reminding himself to keep it together. He could have more. More than anyone could ever imagine. Acid coursed through his stomach.

Beside him, Alison sighed restlessly, as if Chris's unease had woken something in her as well.

"I talked to that actor," she suddenly blurted. "The young woman they hired local playing the girl who works in the bakery."

"Rachel?"

"Yes, Rachel. I wanted to warn her."

"Warn her?"

He didn't understand, and then, suddenly, he did.

"Oh."

"She said you were a total gentleman. You hadn't even asked her out."

Chris felt himself blush.

Alison continued, speaking to herself, her long, pale fingers fanning the faintly illuminated interior of the car. "Everyone says you're just so different. Since you came back from wherever it is you disappeared to. But I don't know. I don't know, Thomson. I mean, you and me. What are we doing here? It's … it's a bad idea."

"Alison, I really like you. I mean, I really, really like you. We don't know each other that well. But I want to get to know you better. And Rachel — she reminds me of someone — like a sister."

"It's true, isn't it?" Alison said, almost wonderingly, as if she'd seen a unicorn.

They were both blushing now, facing each other. Had they kissed that night, in the camp cot together, holding each other as the rain pounded and the wind howled? Chris remembered their naked bodies against each other. Her sweet, soft breath on his ear.

"Thomson," Alison said quietly, "where were you?"

THEY PASSED A CLUSTER of pylons and yellow tape. Half-completed roadwork now abandoned until spring. A sign of the change of season, along with the arrival of nights conjuring up the magic glitter of frost. The light ahead changed to green before they had to slow down. The driver accelerated into a road cleared so suddenly that it seemed like they were the only car plowing its way through the middle of the huge city.

"Good," Alison said. "No traffic. We're late."

Chris looked at her, his eyebrows raised in a question: Late for what?

"It's that interview with the *Esquire* guy," Alison said peevishly. "Read your calendar, okay?"

"The interview?"

"Yes, Thomson, the interview."

On cue, the car pulled up to the curb outside a formal-looking restaurant. It was tucked away amid a complex of older condo buildings.

"Scaramouche," he said out loud, feeling more and more adrift from himself. He heard Krunk mocking: "Billionaires mix with celebrities and oddities at this inconspicuous locale featuring fresh pasta hand-pulled by authentic little old Italian ladies flown in from Puglia."

"Hello? Thomson? You okay? Can we go in now?"

An interview.

"Thomson?"

He was lightheaded, floating away. He couldn't breathe. He saw himself from up above, writhing on the sidewalk.

Alison's hand, far away from him, then somehow lightly on his shoulder. "Are you okay?" He'd gone pale and weak-kneed. A kid, standing before the judge at the custody hearing. Being interviewed. *Who would you like to live with, son?* He'd just stood there, sniveling, a thin line of clear snot running from his left nostril.

"Thomson?"

"I can't," he managed.

"Why? What's wrong?"

Chris shook his head.

"Of course, you can," Alison said reassuringly.

The thickset driver stood by the door, waiting with his arms folded.

"Thomson, let's just …"

She managed to pull him out of the car and into the dark foyer of the restaurant.

"What's the problem here, Thomson?" Alison said softly and ferociously.

She was standing very close to Chris. In the muted light of the foyer, they were like lovers in a quiet but furious state.

"Thomson," Alison hissed.

"I can't."

"It's been on your schedule for months. It's a very big story. The cover of *Esquire*. You and Reed and Darlia all working together. We talked about this, Thomson. You wanted to do this."

"Not anymore," Chris said sharply.

Alison stiffened.

"I'm sorry," Chris said quickly. "I didn't mean to …" He took a deep breath, filling his lungs, then slowly exhaling. "Alison," he said. "I'm really sorry. It's just that I really need to focus. No calendar. No calls. No interviews."

Alison looked at him searchingly. Outside, the clouds were clearing. The foyer brightened momentarily, revealing tiny particles of dust drifting through the small cloister. The space between them, infinitesimal, yet bracketed by millions and billions of microorganisms so tiny they didn't even register. What if he told her the truth? What then?

"Alison."

"It's all right, Thomson," Alison said, her small hand on his bare forearm. "I get it. Focus. Right. No problem. No more interviews. But this one is very important. It's for Reed, really. His big comeback, the two of you working together. If you don't do it, he's going to freak. And Maddy — Maddy's going to really freak. Listen, it's prearranged. There's an agreement. They aren't going to ask you about any of that other stuff."

Alison took his arm firmly. Chris stepped forward heavily, dread lurching through him. She guided him to a table at the back of the room. There, a lanky, slightly rumpled man sporting a fuzzy floating afro, five o'clock shadow, and a creased light blue linen blazer was waiting. He stood as they drew near.

"Thomson," Alison said, her voice bright and airy. "Meet Jonah Jackson from *Esquire* magazine."

"Nice to meet you," Chris mumbled. He stared down at the blank, blue-lined notebook sitting between the silverware in place of a plate. *I'm lunch*, Chris thought. His stomach tilted. *Walk away*, he told himself. *Pretend you have to throw up.* He couldn't. Not with Alison standing beside him, gently squeezing his shoulder.

"Okay, then, I'll leave you two gentlemen to it. Let me know if you need anything."

And she was gone.

They stood for a moment, eying each other. "Well," Jonah said. "Shall we?"

"Yeah."

They sat. Chris cleared his throat as if to make some declara- tive statement, then abruptly cast his gaze down, inspecting the table's gleaming flatware and glasses. His stomach felt tight, a rubber ball. A waiter came and filled up the water glasses and gave them menus, which they both immediately put aside. Jonah Jackson of *Esquire* magazine sipped from his glass of water and said, "So, how is the movie going?"

Chris felt air in his open mouth. Jackson's digital recorder blinking red. The reporter poised over the blank page with an expensive-looking pen. Chris grabbed his glass, chilly against his hot, sweaty palm. The room swayed. He hadn't said anything. Nothing he couldn't take back. Chris thought, suddenly, of a book Laurie had been keeping on her nightstand the last few months. *Awaken Your Inner Path.* One of those self-help guru-lite books Krunk put in the same category as vegans, yoga, and movies about divorcees discovering their G-spots in dusty foreign climes. Chris had flipped through it. It was written in aphorisms. Something about unravelling the knot. Following the thread to see where it goes. It had sounded lame at the time. But the image came back to him now. A life, all knotted up or all splayed out, unravelled. It's the same life, but in one you can't tell where you're going or even what path you've been on. And in the other, well, it's all just a big, useless mess, isn't it? He looked at his big hands, fingers tangled around the water glass, his wet palms magnified.

"Mr. Holmes? Are you okay?" Jonah Jackson, *Esquire* magazine reporter. He sounded bewildered but also, somehow, amused. Chris blinked open his brilliant blue eyes.

"I love this city," Chris announced.

"You do?" Jonah Jackson seemed surprised.

"Sure, I do!"

"You don't hate the East Coast? Didn't you once say that you had a thing against weather?"

"Oh, yeah, sure, but … the Lost Expert loves it, right? Weather!" He smiled, feeling suddenly charming. "You know, I've been thinking that this could be a great place to settle down."

"Here? Like, *Canada*?" Jonah Jackson couldn't hide his astonishment.

"Sure! Why not?"

"And is there anyone in particular you'd like to settle down with?"

Chris smiled again, showing teeth. "I used to not really

understand it," he said. "The whole acting thing. But now —
lately, I think I'm starting to get it. I mean, is it that different
from what we do every day? Most of the time we're just trying
to be somebody that somebody else wants us to be anyway.
Aren't we?"

Jonah Jackson nodded and scribbled in his pad.

EXT. SIDE OF A TWO-LANE RURAL HIGHWAY — MORNING
A Greyhound bus pulls off the shoulder of a
narrow road, revealing THE LOST EXPERT. He
stands in the dust as the hot, dead air stirs
then slowly settles. Behind him, a faded gas
station and general store — Cullin's Gas & Get.
Facing him, across the road, a thin river, the
desultory brown flow following the roadway.

EXT. WOODEN PHONE BOOTH BESIDE THE GAS STATION

                    SARAH
                    Hello?

                  THE LOST EXPERT
                    It's me.

                    SARAH
        Where are you? A man came looking for
                  you. He said —

THE LOST EXPERT
A man? What man?

SARAH
I don't know. A man! Mac-something.
McCall? He wanted to know where you were.
He said that you were doing something you
shouldn't be doing.

THE LOST EXPERT
He said that? Sarah, what did he say?
Exactly.

SARAH
I don't know! The baby was crying!
Where are you?

THE LOST EXPERT
What did he say, Sarah?

SARAH
(incredulous)
Just come home! This is about — them,
isn't it? You're not some big hero!
Please! Stop what you're doing and
come home!

THE LOST EXPERT
Sarah, I can't. If he comes again, Sarah,
don't let him in. Don't let anyone in.

                        SARAH
What are you talking about? We have a son
  now! Please! I'm frightened! Why are you
                    doing this?

                  THE LOST EXPERT
    I'll be home soon, Sarah. But I have to
    go now. I love you. I love you both.

The Lost Expert hangs up the phone. He stands in
the booth, his face impassive, his eyes hooded.
With one finger, he traces the crossed-out
Jewish star someone has scratched into the
wooden wall.

EXT. EDGE OF THE SWAMPLANDS BY THE SIDE OF THE
BROWN RIVER — LATE MORNING
THE LOST EXPERT stands on a rickety old wooden
dock. The rough planks, cracked in places,
creak as he shields his eyes from the sun and
contemplates the slow-moving, silty water. The
river cuts through yellow sawgrass, runs past
and under a sprawling willow tree, then narrows,
curves, and disappears into a walled tangle of
mangroves. Occasional oblong bubbles break to
the surface, stirring the clots of rotting swamp
grass. An abandoned dugout thumps gently against
the dock. The Lost Expert closes his eyes. He
sees Beaoman slowly dragging his mother into the
woods.

                    RABBI (V.O.)
                     (praying)
              Baruch Attah Adonai …

                    WILLA (V.O.)
                     (singing)
          … where you been, finder man …

                  GANG LEADER (V.O.)
                    (chanting)
               Sacrifice! Sacrifice!

                    SARAH (V.O.)
         (murmuring over the baby's cries)
        Hush now, baby, don't you cry, Momma's
                      gonna …

                    RABBI (V.O.)
        Where to go? There is nowhere. Why would
        we go? There is nowhere! Nowhere to go!

The Lost Expert is in the dugout. He stands,
using a long branch as a pole. Slowly, he floats
through and under the willow. The swamp closes
in around him.

EXT. BROWN RIVER AS IT FLOWS INTO THE BOTTOM OF
BROKEN CREEK — AFTERNOON
THE LOST EXPERT emerges from the narrow river
into the wider Broken Creek. He pushes through
the increasingly shallow creek until the dugout

runs aground on a puzzle of cracked mud pieces.
He stands in the craft as it slowly tips to one
side, at which point he jumps out. A shrill cry.
The Lost Expert scans the sky. Turkey vultures
circle high above him, barely visible. The
sun is red and small and angry like a swollen
pimple. The Lost Expert struggles forward now,
using the crooked branch as leverage to help
wrest himself out of the enclosing bog. His
boots disappear into the muck, then laboriously
re-emerge with squelching reluctance.

FLORIDA. ALL HIS CHILDHOOD, he remembered hearing other kids talking about it — Florida for the holidays; Florida for March Break. His family never went to Florida. But now, here he was. In Florida — in Reed's version, anyway, relentlessly poling through a swamp tributary pursued by tangles of cameras and lights he was supposed to be ignoring.

"Cut, cut!"

Chris cast an irritated look behind him. Reed wasn't happy with something — the timbre of the light, the resonance of the audio, the grain of the view through the wide-angle lens. The production ground to a halt for what seemed like the hundredth time that morning. Or maybe it was afternoon already. Film shoots were all about time, Chris was learning. Break time, over-time, setup time, blocked-out time for each step in the action of a scene. The crew assembled booms, rearranged tripods, then abruptly reached for their cracked iPhones while the seconds on their breaks ticked past and Reed cursed unions and mosquitoes.

What mosquitoes? They were inside, as hard as that might be to believe. "Eighteen thousand square feet, baby," Reed had enthused mournfully. "Bean counters say it's cheaper than an actual swamp, *if you can believe that*. Only reason I went with it was 'cause this way you can be the one in the boat. Otherwise, it'd have to be John again. Fucking John! So don't screw it up, Holmes!"

Apparently, Chris was supposed to act as if there were all kinds of miniature winged menaces. At random intervals, he'd see the signal that meant he was supposed to fan at the clouds of nonexistent gnats dive-bombing his face or slap at the minuscule illusionary daggers probing his exposed flesh. *Proboscis*, Chris thought. *Bite me*. He wished there were actual biting bugs. Their presence might speed things up. Instead, he was stuck in a cramped, unsteady boat floating in all of two feet of water, awaiting instructions to proceed with the next scene. His first vacation to the sunshine state was not at all how he'd imagined it. Chris closed his eyes, willing himself back into it. They were in the swamp. Things happened slowly here. The Lost Expert poling sloppily through the waterway's thin tributaries, where dense thickets of mangrove elided time and denied the set's routine. "Feel it," Reed had ordered him. "The quagmire's primeval stew swirling and bubbling its foundational microorganisms, billions of years old, born and dead in a day, endlessly reincarnated!" Instead, Chris pictured the real Thomson Holmes rearing up from the depths, sinewy arms draped with swamp weeds, naked torso smeared with mud. Uneasily, he stretched his cramped legs and arched his back. The craft wobbled. Grabbing for the sides, he almost dropped the long pole, his sole navigation tool.

"Holmes!" Reed bellowed from somewhere behind. "Watch what you're doing! No sudden moves!"

No sudden moves basically meant no moves. The slightest twitch set the craft teetering in its two feet of water. His legs ached, his back ached, his arms ached. His boat was a hollowed-out log, a rudimentary canoe, if you could even call it that. It was like something from an old-timey pioneer museum dedicated to the hardships of the newly arrived Europeans, boldly setting out to clear the swamp of the alligators and panthers and primitives who'd ruled before the movies and theme parks took over. Chris had no idea why the Lost Expert couldn't have at least come across a rusted-out fishing dinghy or something. Reed kept calling it the dugout: "Now get in the dugout, Holmes, and push yourself around the corner there." The dugout teetered and spun and seemed perpetually to be on the cusp of overturning.

THEY'D BEEN AT IT since daybreak, the fake swamp feeling more and more real to Chris as shooting proceeded. It was hot — sweat running down his face hot. The water was dark; he couldn't see the bottom. Whatever they'd used to create the mangroves was really working. They were astonishingly imposing — a thick wall on both sides of the waterway. The more time Chris spent floating and free associating, the more aware he was of the massive movie-set-cum-swamp. Inhospitable, impossible, its meaning and true purpose hidden, it nevertheless pulled him in. He waited for his prompt, then leaned in with his pole, probing the manufactured murk for a bottom he was beginning to doubt. The dugout wobbled forward, barely pushing through the brownish-yellow sediment coating the darker green water.

Coming up, a penultimate scene. The swamp would widen to something like a shallow lake. Reed had told him to paddle resolutely through the middle until he reached the central island heap of mud and roots and guano. At which point he'd somehow exit the dugout and scrabble up the muck, thereby surveying his surroundings with Lost Expert equanimity — the inescapable certainty of absence, a shrouded dread clinging to everything. To what end, Chris wasn't sure. The movie, like the swamp, was in its own time zone. Maybe these scenes in the swamp were the finale, but it was also possible they were in the middle, or even the beginning. Film scenes weren't shot in script sequence. Reed had been vague. Just: "He's sinking now, Holmes. He's really sinking." Chris pictured the great Thomson Holmes sucked deeper and deeper into something he did not know how to get out of. Alison, trying to assuage Chris's obvious nerves, had assured him that the water would never be any higher than his knees. He could do that, he told himself. He could sink.

Chris poled forward. He saw the signal and channelled a cloud of gnats — orbiting his head, dispersing and regrouping, divebombing his lips and nose, kamikaze crazy. Chris shook his head as if slapping performatively. They'd even put bug spray on him, which reminded him of his days in the woods with Krunk when they were kids. The smell of deet permeating everything — skin, clothes, food. And he was hot, the heat way up, sweat pouring off him, soaking through his Lost Expert outdoor adventure outfit of stained fleece and thick hiking pants. They wanted him this way — hot, bothered, swarmed. It was like when he was a kid: bugs in his ears, bugs in his nose, biting flies crawling along his hairline and into the garden of scalp barely shaded by his short blond hair. *Bite me*, Chris thought again, this time angrily. He gave Reed the finger but did not dare a peek over his shoulder to see Reed and the German, both laughing flatly. Chris jammed his pole through the clinging surface sheen. Sweat dripped down his face, off his nose. The tough fabrics trapped the heat and perspiration to his skin. The longer the day went on, the more he felt uncomfortably swaddled, like a giant baby.

Doing his best to ignore his surroundings, he leaned his weight on the pole and pulled. When he next looked up, he saw he'd arrived at the widened area, the river now some ten feet across. The water here was barely moving, if at all, a thin veneer of brown hiding an oleaginous black bottom.

Chris stabbed at whatever was·supposedly crawling into his ear, then plunged the pole into the expanding channel. The dugout teetered, and he froze, looking down at his mud-stained knees, waiting for the lopsided craft to settle. Krunk said nature was the only thing worth fetishizing, whatever that meant. Reed said movies were antithetical to nature, that even movies set in natural environments were at best awkward, papered-over negations, like kids' shows about putting down the remote and going outside to play. Krunk and Reed. What had Alison said? Pigs. Pigs in shit.

Alison, who trusted him now? Who loved him? He hadn't meant to lie to her. Or with her. Laurie sitting on Krunk's lap, kissing his spaghetti-sauce-stained chin. Ugh.

Did you tell them?

Did you tell them yet?

Chris jabbed at the swamp, but the pole slipped in his sweaty hands, skimming ineffectually along the plastic bottom. The dugout slid sideways into the bank.

"Holmes! What are you doing, Holmes?"

Dangling mangrove pushed into Chris's face, and he found himself suddenly off-balance, trying to get his head and upper body out of the slimy, rubbery overgrowth.

"The fuck, Holmes?"

Chris shoved the pole into the bushes along the bank, trying to push off. He hit something too soft and dropped the pole with a surprised yelp. A man jumped up from the tangled foliage, cursing and flapping around as if in parody of some disturbed shore bird. Chris reared back, the dugout tipping as he flailed. Water rushed in. Chris tipped too, slow enough to see that the man — entangled with camera gear, a member of the crew — was now falling face first into the water.

"Holmes!" Reed bellowed gloriously. "Holmes!"

Under, it was quiet. He drifted, his heavy boots gyrating mud, the oscillations pulling him into the swamp's soft underbelly. Instead of panicking, he felt himself calming at the warm water's viscid embrace. The water was deep enough here that he could almost wade in it. It felt good, wet and warm, like a drink from a hose on a hot summer's day.

Chris bumped against something and realized it was the camera guy. He was floating face first in the water, a stream of red unfurling from his forehead. For a moment, Chris didn't react. He merely watched the surreal spectacle of the unconscious body sinking under the weight of interlocking straps dangling cameras and battery packs. Chris counted five bubbles escaping from the man's lips and drifting up out of the murk. *He's drowning*, he thought dispassionately. *I will save him.*

REED ISSUED MUTED INSTRUCTIONS and occasionally cast a glimpse back at Chris, who sat watching tea-coloured water run from his hair, down his forehead, and onto the rubber floor of the massive film set.

Chris was empty, unnerved by his unexpected actions and exhausted by the surprising difficulty of pulling the man's dead weight out of the fake silty, clinging darkness.

Who had he been as a calm determination came over him and he surfaced, holding the camera guy's head and shoulders above the water, waiting for help? Chris thought of a movie his alter ego had made: Holmes playing a soldier abandoned in the jungle. The big actor, shirtless, clutching a machete, waiting upriver to exact his revenge on a slow, puttering boat full of the enemies of true American manhood.

A heavy bulk settled next to him.

"How ya doing there, Holmes?"

The crew kept a respectful distance, vaping and texting and muttering imprecations in barely audible voices.

"You see the darndest things in this business." Reed sighed. "Most of it awful. But then, every once in a while —". He grabbed Chris's hands in his own. "He could have drowned you both, you crazy fucker." Reed exhaled, shaking his head in rueful admiration. He let go and fumbled in his shirt pocket for a pill vial. "Here, put these under your tongue and let 'em dissolve."

"What are they?"

"Beta-blockers. They calm everything down."

"I don't need them. I'm fine."

"You sure? I'm fucking frazzled. Holmes, you saved Skinny Al. We didn't even know he was in trouble." Reed paused. "Here. Take 'em."

Chris shook his head. His mouth was dry. All this water. Nothing to drink.

"Take the pills, Holmes. You'll be fine. I should have told you we were putting Al in the mangroves. That's my bad. That one's on me." Reed chortled like the whole thing was one big joke. Then, seeing the look on his star's face, he softened his tone again.

"Take the pills. Everyone takes the pills."

"They do?"

Reed shifted uncomfortably.

"Look, I get it," he said. "What you're feeling. You're the hero! You're the Lost Expert! He's going to find them. He's going to confront whatever took his mother away from him. He's going to do all that! But look, he's not going to flail around and slap at the bugs and look like some snotty little runaway kid. He's going to keep calm, right, Holmes? The calmer he seems, the more the audience will know, will understand, how afraid he is. You've got to take all that extra energy and push it down, real deep down."

The swamp gurgled. A small red fish jumped out of the water then disappeared back under its own ripple. Chris might have imagined that. There was a sudden buzzing from an electric box somewhere behind them. The crew shifted restlessly in place, sipping their coffees, fanning their faded ball caps at the heat and nonexistent bugs.

"Do you?"

"Do I what?"

"Do you take the pills?"

Reed pulled his lips in, baring his big yellow teeth.

"Course I do. Everyone takes the pills."

Chris ducked his head between his knees. He put the pills in his mouth and poked them under his tongue as instructed. His finger tasted of the surrounding muddy alluvium. Head down, he contemplated the smeared tops of his wet hiking boots.

Reed patted him on the shoulder, his hand lingering.

Chris thought of his mother. Ever since the divorce, she'd been taking them too. Her mood pills. When he'd told her that he was dropping out of university, she'd only smiled vaguely. "Oh, well, you can always go back, dear." She'd patted him on the hand and offered him another cookie.

EXT. MANGROVE SWAMP, THE BROWN RIVER AFTER IT
HAS RE-FORMED AT THE TOP OF THE CREEK — LATE
AFTERNOON

The river, a gash of chocolate mud, pulls at THE
LOST EXPERT's calves as if yearning to suck him
down. The banks on both sides are consumed by
mangroves with mottled black-grey branches and
dark green leaves. The Lost Expert struggles
forward, and the river gradually deepens. The
water is almost to his waist, purling around
him. Half walking, half swimming, he suddenly
disappears with a muffled shout. In his place,
a tornado of thrashing water and churning mud.
An eternity. A minute. The Lost Expert struggles
to his feet, gasping. He holds something long
and limp in his arms. It is a young alligator,
its short legs slowly clawing and pawing the
open air, protesting The Lost Expert's tight
grip. The alligator piteously tosses its diamond
reptilian head side to side. In its closed mouth

is a white purse, once bordered by rhinestones,
now stained by green algae and torn almost in
half. Abruptly, the alligator hinges open its
long snout. The purse falls into the water and
disappears. The alligator shows rows of teeth
like sharp, dirty rocks. Twisting out The Lost
Expert's arms, the reptile launches at his neck.
The Lost Expert and the alligator tussle, again
disappearing underwater. We see a smoky haze
rolling over the water, the sun streaking the
air red and orange and purple. A granular murk,
a thickness settling, the heat gone corporeal.
The Lost Expert re-emerges, the gator in his
arms bucking spasmodically, the creature's neck
unnaturally twisted. The alligator goes still.
The Lost Expert gently places its body into the
river. Its remains bob, then settle. The dead
alligator floats just under the waterline. A
vulture screeches in the sky. The Lost Expert
looks up; several of the birds are circling a
plume of smoke in the distance. Blood from a
deep bite on his shoulder drips into the water.

EXT. FOLLOWING THE RIVER — SUNSET
THE LOST EXPERT wades slowly through ankle-deep
water. Visibly exhausted, he occasionally trips
and staggers before regaining himself. The
river has narrowed again, mangroves branching
and twining into one another and forming an
arch over the strangled waterway. The setting
sun casts shadows, deepening pockmarks on the
surface of the swamp. The smoke in the air is

more obvious now, drifting in opaque clouds
through the occasional angled beam of dappled
sunlight, then disappearing into the extending
gloom. The Lost Expert coughs into a swollen
fist. Small black crabs creep out of the water
and onto the trunks and protruding branches of
the mangroves.

EXT. PARKLAND — EVENING (FLASHBACK — 1903)
BOY LOST EXPERT stands, dirty and wet, in
the middle of a trail, eyes wide, countenance
confused. A PARK RANGER kneels in front of him.

                    RANGER
              Are you lost, son?

Boy Lost Expert looks down at his battered,
muddy sneakers.

                    RANGER
            Where are your folks, son?

EXT. DENSE FOREST BEYOND THE BROWN — TWILIGHT
(1928)
THE LOST EXPERT trudges through a thick forest
of small conifers punctuated by the occasional
stand of palms. The forest has been burning,
and parts of it continue to smoke and smoulder.
The smoulder intensifies the deeper in he goes.
He passes pines, small and grey, their needles
burnt off. Then on through a grove of palms
billowing thick, blinding smoke. The burnt

and burning trees occasionally open to small
pools, their surfaces crusted with skittering
black water bugs cutting panicked paths through
wet grey ash. The smoke thickens until it is a
dense but ghostly fog floating two feet above
the surface. The Lost Expert coughs. Tears
pour from his eyes. He stumbles into a puddle,
falls. He proceeds on hands and knees, heading
for a small hillock supporting an unscathed,
full-grown royal palm. Coughing and retching,
he crawls to the top of the hill. Laboriously,
he pulls himself to his feet. He is just high
enough to rise above the smoke blanketing the
woods. Holding the tree for support, he coughs
until he can breathe again. The moon appears,
eerily bright for a moment. An owl, sharp talons
dangling, wide eyes aggrieved, floats past.
Then the cloud and soot close in, and the sky
disappears.

                    NEWSCASTER (V.O.)
          And it's official, reclusive millionaire
             Harold Allan and his Maverick Party
          have won the election. The country has
          given him the mandate for change that
             he's been asking for. The eccentric,
          reclusive businessman who has kept his
          face shrouded throughout the campaign and
          whom many considered too divisive to win
          a general election has been elected the
          next president. The people have spoken.

                        WILLA (V.O.)
                 Where ya been, finder man?

The Lost Expert sways on his feet.

                        RABBI (V.O.)
                 There is no evil! There is only God!

                                        CUT TO

The thugs beating him, the only sound their
grunts and the rhythmic thud of their boots
against his ribs.

                                        CUT TO

His mother, face down in the water, slowly being
dragged out of the swamp.

                                        CUT TO

A purse sinking.

                                        CUT TO

A baby gazing straight ahead, wide-eyed and
passive. A shrill scream.

                                        CUT TO

The Lost Expert's eyes shoot open.

EXT. A SHACK ON THE EDGE OF THE WOODS — NIGHT
THE LOST EXPERT stands at the edge of the woods,
considering an old cabin of weathered grey wood
sitting in front of a dark tributary. Creeper
vines climb the walls. Moss and fungi grow out
of its flat roof. Behind the shack flows the
slow-moving river.

                    NEWSCASTER (V.O.)
        Thousands have gathered here, outside the
                ghetto gates, to celebrate
                    Allan's victory.

                    CROWD (V.O.)
            Build the wall! Build the wall!

The Lost Expert, on the edge of the clearing,
breathes through a hand loosely pressed to his
mouth and nose as the hazy smoke swirls around
the shack then consumes it.

INT. SWAMPLAND SHACK — NIGHT
The door creaks loudly. Something small and
black runs across the mottled floor and
disappears. The Lost Expert steps in. The
floorboards groan. In the centre of the shack's
single room is a charred, broken stool that
someone used to build a fire. Three crushed tins
of beer lie in a corner along with the shattered
glass of a smashed bottle of bourbon. A ladder
missing several rungs leads up to a dark loft.

EXT. HIGHWAY — NIGHT (FLASHBACK — 1903)
BOY LOST EXPERT, alone in the back of a police
car, driving along the highway.

INT. SWAMPLAND SHACK — NIGHT (1928)
A wet groan from the dark loft. THE LOST EXPERT
staggers against the wall and catches himself.

                                        CUT TO

A baby.

                                        CUT TO

A white purse, slowly sinking.

                        RABBI (V.O.)
                  (laughing uproariously)
                  He's an orphan!

                                        CUT TO

The Lost Expert climbs the ladder, his muddy
boots bending the warped rungs.

INT. SWAMPLAND SHACK LOFT — DEAD OF NIGHT
In the granular dark of the loft, THE LOST
EXPERT can just make out the shape of a person
lying on his side on a dirty mattress. The Lost
Expert drops to his knees beside the mattress.
He rolls the figure onto his back.

THE LOST EXPERT
You!

GEORGE JASON PAULSON, eyes fluttering, blood
crusted in the corners of his mouth, tries to
speak. His words are indecipherable, a sinkhole
gurgle.

THE LOST EXPERT
Where is he? Tell me! Tell me where
he is!

George Jason Paulson mouths sounds. Pink foam
burbles from his nostrils. He groans piteously,
and one hand flutters to his belly before
dropping back down to the dirty mattress. George
Jason Paulson has a knife protruding from his
stomach.

THE LOST EXPERT
Did he do this? Where is he? Where are
the girls?

GEORGE JASON PAULSON
Urgggulls …

THE LOST EXPERT
Tell me! Tell me, goddamn it!

GEORGE JASON PAULSON
(laughs)
Grrrllllssss!

The laugh turns into a sunken rattle. George
Jason Paulson dies. The Lost Expert backs
shakily away from the mattress. He trips over
something behind him and falls. Scrambling to
his knees, he comes face to face with WILLA. Her
withered throat is slashed, her dead eyes open
in recrimination. Outside: the flash of fresh
fire followed by thick new smoke.

THE WAVES WERE SMALL and persistent, churning against the wide beach and retreating in a foamy surf of sand. Chris stood close enough to feel the frigid spray on his bare feet. He looked down and saw that the cuffs of his designer trousers were getting wet. He took another step toward the Great Lake. The cold didn't bother him. He was drawn to it. It was a clear start to the evening. Chris imagined it as something he might see down south, dusk in the Keys, the low sun a hanging orange fruit against a wide sky, shaded streaks of light blue. His mind, too, was clear. He didn't need pills.

He thought of his mother. He'd talked to her a few days ago. He'd told her that the shoot was moving to Florida. She'd been so excited for him, he'd thought it was true. One day, he'd said to her, they would go together. He imagined them, reclining on lounge chairs, sipping drinks festooned with umbrellas and pineapple chunks.

A sea of sand away, Alison stood, first toying with a lock of her long hair, then fingering the single strand of pearls that lay against her soft throat.

If he could just tell her. The lies scrubbed off by the choppy green waves of Lake Ontario, tenacious like teeth and just as terrible. Sean Penn in *Sweet and Lowdown*, begging for a forgiveness he could never allow himself. *"I made a mistake! I made a mistake!"*

Alison put a hand on his arm, surprising him. "Thomson. We should go."

The ocean. He'd never seen it. He couldn't tell her that. He took her hand and stepped forward, pulling her to the edge of the surf.

"Who knew?" he said. "Who knew Toronto had beaches?" He knew, of course.

"Thomson." She gently extracted herself. "Come on — you're getting all wet."

He was up to his ankles now. The sun hung in pregnant pause at the exact point where the lake reached the horizon. *You can really see it*, Chris thought. The curve of the earth, the way everything goes around and around and around.

In past his belt, the water cold and wonderful against his crotch and his belly. The waves kept coming, though smaller now, surprisingly gentle. How far could he go? A large bird crossed the sky in front of him, then turned and crossed back again. It flew low, heavy and awkward — a pelican. A seagull, actually, a sky rat on patrol for a floating French fry. The ugly grey-white bird cast him a scornful glance. Chris thought of Little Scarface, his bright, sunken eyes. Where was he? Nearby, Chris was sure. Here. There. He could be anywhere.

Did you tell them?

"Thomson? Come out now!"

Another step forward. The bird ascended, flapping out of sight. Alison's voice was distant, barely audible over the sound of the water and the wind. Once upon a time, Chris had been afraid — afraid of going under, of not being able to see what lurked on the bottom. Now he knew. Underwater, everything was calm. Surprisingly, he'd liked the feeling, liked the strange way the movie set's tap-water swamp had clung to his skin, so different from the glacier lakes he and Krunk had swum in up north, those deep, freezing ice-age reservoirs, the water slicking off him, the sky shifting from sunny clear to grey cold in the time it took him to clamber in and out.

Chris breathed deeply, his shirt pillowing. He'd call his mom more. He'd call her every day. He was someone else now. *We've all lost people*, Chris thought. *It's what happens*. The Lost Expert. He'd lost his mother. He kept trying to get her back. But he couldn't, really. That's the thing. Even if he somehow found her, or whoever killed her, he wouldn't get her back.

"Thomson!"

He turned to the beach and waved at Alison to reassure her. Alison had put on mirrored sunglasses, one-way windows reflecting Lake Ontario's expanse. She folded her arms against her torso. It was cold, getting colder. Another of those crazy-eyed seagulls pecking at something bundled up in a wad of rotting kelp. "Woo!" Chris yelled, falling backward into the cold froth. "My own private Idaho!"

THEY SAT TOGETHER ON the beach, a blanket from the trunk of the town car draped around his shoulders. The day was ending. The sun had dropped below the surface of the lake, and grey sky tinged with the city's waking glow loomed behind them. Nighttime, Chris thought uneasily. He resisted the persistent urge to turn away from the water and inspect the quickly shrouding darkness beyond the boardwalk path. What did Laurie always say? "Stay in the moment. Try to relax."

"This is so great. It's like the ocean! I love the ocean! What about you?" Chris asked emphatically, turning to Alison. "Do you like it?"

"Me?" Alison seemed surprised he'd asked. "It scares me, I guess. I mean, I grew up in Vermont, so I never really — Snow was more our thing. Me and my brother, we spent all our time building snow forts in the woods near our house."

"That must have been fun."

"It was."

"And your brother? Is he still —"

"Yup, still there. He and his partner, they have three kids and the farm, they make cheese and maple syrup and keep bees."

"That sounds great."

"It's a lot of work, but he loves it."

"Do you visit?"

"I do, when I have the chance."

"Do you think you'll move back one day?"

"Oh, definitely. I never thought I'd end up in L.A." Alison laughed in that way people do when they're looking at the choices they've made with a kind of rueful amazement.

"Yeah," he said. "I know what you mean."

Alison's tone changed. "Thomson." She took a deep breath. "I need to tell you something."

Instinctively, he avoided her big brown scrutinizing eyes. He looked over her, distracted, scanning the boardwalk and the road beyond. Where was he? *When will you tell them?*

Alison continued. "Whatever happens with — all this, I don't want there to be any more secrets between us."

At the word *secrets*, Chris's heart started pounding. He gathered a handful of wet sand in his fist and squeezed, grains grinding under his fingernails.

"Alison —"

"Thomson. I know what you've been doing. Look."

She dug into her handbag and pulled it out. His battered old leather wallet, peeling at the edges and swollen in the middle as if waterlogged then dried: a birthday gift from his mom when he'd turned twenty-two.

He took the wallet from her and held it in his hands. The old wallet, much heavier than it should have been, a fossil turned to rock. Sweat broke out on his upper lip. Once upon a time, it had been a game. *Catch Me If You Can*, DiCaprio dapper in a pilot's cap. He wiped at his face with his bare arm.

Alison, half smiling at him, the cat who ate the canary.

"Look inside, Thomson."

Reluctantly, he flipped it open. His driver's licence. His Revue Cinema loyalty card. His ScotiaBank entry-level Visa.

Alison took the wallet back and slipped out his green Ontario health card. "You even have one of these," she said wonderingly. "One of these health thingies."

They both pondered the extracted card as if beguiled. Chris suppressed a Krunk rant: Good for free medical anywhere in the true north strong and free! Comes complete with passport-style picture for identification by the petty bourgeois bureaucracy! Bonus points: a rare middle finger to Canada's southern neighbour's preference for leaving the poor with few if any defences against state-enabled corporate predation!

"Christopher Hutchins. Nice name. It suits you. Oh, and look, I see you made yourself … younger."

Her tone was playful, affectionate.

"Alison. I can — let me —"

"It's okay." She leaned in close, scrutinizing him. He felt her breath on his cheek. "I won't tell anyone."

"You won't?"

"I get it. The pressure and everything. The need to escape."

He found himself nodding, too relieved to speak.

She kissed him, gently at first, then with increasing passion. He kissed her back.

"I should have told you."

"Yes, you should have. *Christopher*."

A light behind them. Chris stiffened. A car passing, its headlights just visible.

Alison didn't notice. She laid her head on his shoulder and sighed.

PART FIVE

STUMBLING INTO THE SPARE, gleaming kitchen, he discovered it was just after 6:30 a.m. California time, which, he ponderously calculated, made it around 9:30 a.m. in Toronto. It was a veritable sleep-in for the former breakfast waiter Chris. Still, he felt heavy and exhausted. They had landed at LAX late the previous night. "Welcome home," the flight attendants had chorused as he disembarked. *Home*, he kept thinking. It had all been so simple. Just like jovially telling Alison he'd "misplaced" his passport. Within hours he'd been at the U.S. consulate. He'd signed some documents and autographed whatever anyone asked him to autograph. He had no idea what Thomson Holmes's signature looked like. Apparently, no one else did, either. Finally, after a series of poses — Thomson Holmes shaking hands with the Consul General, her assistant, her assistant's assistant, and so on and so forth — they'd issued him a temporary passport. Handshakes all around. A few more pictures. Alison, standing to the side observing the proceedings through tired eyes and a tight, worried smile, touching his arm. He knew the drill. It was time to go. Time to go home.

Home. He hadn't even been sure how he'd get into it. His house. Was he supposed to have a key? But his usual driver,

whom Chris had been surprised to find welcoming him at
arrivals, punched in a security code that opened a gate, then
did the same to the front door. He'd stumbled into unfamiliar
sheets, beaten down by what he didn't know.

Chris opened a chrome refrigerator built into a tiled wall. It
was empty. No neighbour entrusted with a spare key had popped
by to stock it up with milk and fruit and juice after his long
absence. Did he even have neighbours? He shivered, exposed in
the refrigerator's pale light. He looked down past his Thomson
Holmes paisley boxers to his thighs, pale and goose-bumped;
still visibly his despite the best efforts of his brassy trainers.
But he was home. Or, at least, he'd arrived at what passed for
home to one of the most recognizable celebrities in the world.
It was a home devoid of the characteristics the word typically
evoked: no family snapshots, framed treasures, tchotchkes on
the mantel, ugly ties shoved into the back of a drawer. Here,
the slate walls were empty. Did Holmes take it all with him? Or
was he just like this? A bizarre inversion, the superstar black
hole, the man himself not particularly notable, slightly above
average height, sporting a physique one step below aggressively
muscled, intellect average, little to no evidence of a complex
interior life. But that was the mystery, wasn't it? This blank slate,
this dwarfed star, capable of lighting up screens with a boyish
energy that never seemed to dissipate no matter how many times
it was diluted.

Chris padded down the hall, heading to the bedroom. He felt
stodgy, drugged. Maybe he'd sleep for a few more hours. But
the brightness of the living room caught his eye. Still on auto-
pilot, he entered the room and stopped, stunned. The room
was dominated by a floor-to-ceiling window framing a slow
decline saturated in sunshine. The view was of a long slope of

rocky outcroppings swathed in straw-like grass. Here and there, scrappy beige bushes pushed spiked leaves out of clustered mounds of sandy soil. And amidst it all, barely visible through stunted trees with green leaves tinged rust, were the bits and backs of other houses, cubist designs made to look like they were clinging to the rocky embankment for dear life.

Standing there, Chris thought about Krunk again, how he talked about it, how he centred his life around it. Hollywood, L.A., the movies. "It was in Hollywood," he'd begin with a snarled erasure of the perennial once upon a time. "Hollywood." Krunk's voice in Chris's head like a never-ending book on tape.

Hollywood, where set builder Marion Morrison got his big break, the mongrel Irish-American director Raoul Walsh spying him manfully dragging a couch across a soundstage. Krunk, lecturing his sparse late-night audience, urging them to picture it: the long, stretched face and dark, foreboding stare of actor-turned-director Walsh — the quintessential assassin, Chris remembered Krunk calling him. He played John Wilkes Booth not once but twice. Then a shift to directing, an insatiable hunger turned to the nascent craft of filmmaking. Eagerly, some might even say desperately, he set upon the young, strapping stage-hand. "And who might you be," he demanded, not even trying to hide his vampiric need.

"Marion Morrison," the wide-eyed country boy answered, his naked ambition as plainly visible as the empty, sprawling plains whence he hailed.

Walsh hurriedly rebranded him. "John Wayne," he pronounced, trying it out. "Introducing John Wayne."

Wayne was to star in *The Big Trail*, Walsh's directorial debut, a film, as Krunk enthused sardonically, "dedicated to the brave men and women who planted civilization in the wilderness and courage in the blood of their children." It was an epic, an odyssey of wagon trains and manifest destiny. "The first wide-screen movie ever shot," Krunk proudly announced, as if he'd had a hand in its monumental, if ultimately ill-fated, creation.

Chris looked over the views his domain commanded. In truth, he didn't remember much of the actual movie, only Krunk's pre- and post-screening lectures. The film had been a flop. He remembered Krunk's analysis of why, which was more histor-ical than cinematic. An epic portrayal of American expansiveness at a time when America was contracting, turning inwards in a 1920s spasm of dust bowl depression, bread lines, kidnappings — an America flirting not with freedom but with fascism.

Bad timing, Chris thought, considering the cloudless blue morn-ing. The sky was a startling azure, noticeably different from the grey of Toronto in October. The brightness made everything seem less temporal, more paradoxical — the Lost Expert in La-La Land, the illuminated possible, the perpetual here and now. A pale yellow sun bathed even the most recalcitrant corners of the descending hills; every particle of fine-grained sand was illuminated. Nowhere to hide, not that you would want to.

Origin stories. Chris's mind churned as he stood in the almost empty white room and tracked a clump of puffy clouds high in the bright sky. All this time, he'd believed: believed in Krunk, believed in his phlegmy negation of manufactured possibility as incompatible with the search for the truer eternal of Great Art. But now he saw, he felt, something different. The very hills underneath him were a part of it, the great story, a breezy promise stirring the silty topsoil, sharp-leaved bushes rustling defiantly, clinging to their rootless perches. Here was the centre of no-where from which everything radiated. Here, the schemers and plotters were revealed, exposed not as con artists, benders of words and peddlers of pyramid schemes, but as dreamers and diviners and believers. Is it so bad to be bright-eyed and muscle-bound and magnificently ambitious? To dream of being the first, the first to truly capture it? That version of America, that wide-open possibility of endless, bountiful land and light. It could be you. Why not? Why couldn't it be you?

Chris threw himself onto one of the room's creamy, austere couches, about as comfortable as they looked — not very. He'd replace them. He'd redecorate. That's what they did, the rich and famous. He was Thomson goddamn Holmes. He'd call Berinstain. He'd find out how much money Thomson Holmes had and how to spend it. He'd spend it. He'd spend it all. And then make more. Alison. He'd buy her things. Cars, dinners, clothes, jewels. Alison. He got a hard-on. He considering doing something about it, but instead rearranged himself so he could gently hump against the slick fabric of the sofa in relative comfort. Gradually, his motions slowed. He fell asleep.

INT. GREYHOUND BUS, ANONYMOUS COUNTRYSIDE
BLURRING PAST — DAY
THE LOST EXPERT sits in the back of the bus.
His breathing is ragged. He is unshaven, soot-
covered, mud-spattered, and bleeding heavily
from the alligator bite in his shoulder. He has
a half-empty bottle of whisky between his legs.
He mutters and slurs, occasionally waking up and
looking around in momentary panic.

                    BUS DRIVER
                    (yelling)
          New Paltz. This is New Paltz. We'll take
                 a ten-minute break.

The BUS DRIVER pulls into a gas station/diner.
The Lost Expert staggers off the bus.

EXT. PHONE BOOTH — ROADWAY GAS STATION/DINER
The Lost Expert listens to the phone ringing
and ringing. He hangs up and tries again.

THE LOST EXPERT
(muttering)
Sarah, pick up. Pick up.

INT. BUS — NIGHT
The Lost Expert twists and turns, his sleep
tormented. He wakes up and is surprised to see
that the RABBI is sitting in the seat next to
him.

RABBI
(kindly)
First, there's the — how you say?
The skin of the — The cut, when you are
a baby.

THE LOST EXPERT
The foreskin.

RABBI
Yes! Then you are committed to *Hashem*
and living a Jewish life. You are a Jew!
Whether you like it or not, you are a
Jew! And then you learn. You learn until
the Bar Mitzvah, the call to the Torah.
You read from the holy scroll. You finish
reading. *Yasher Koach!* You're a man!

THE LOST EXPERT
Just like that?

                    RABBI
     So, what's the problem? Who has a
     better way? One day you're a boy,
      the next day it's different. You
                 have new —

               THE LOST EXPERT
          — responsibilities.

                    RABBI
     Yes! It's up to you now — fulfill them or
        don't fulfill them. Nobody can
                   tell you.

               THE LOST EXPERT
     What about God, doesn't he tell you what
                  to do?

                    RABBI
            (ignoring the question)
     Jew or not, there is that day, when you
       become what you are going to become —
        there's the cut. The cut! Or stay a
                child forever.

The Lost Expert turns from the gaze of the
rabbi. He sees an OLD FARMER in the seat across
the aisle, his head bobbing as the tight,
weathered folds of his neck seem to resist
slumber.

                    RABBI
You're looking for something? What are
   you looking for? *Nuh*? Of course! The
 big *macher* who finds people! So, you're
        looking, always looking!

               THE LOST EXPERT
             (suddenly embarrassed)
               No, Rabbi. I —

                    RABBI
             (gesturing for silence)
 Listen! Let me finish. How do you call
it? "Destiny." You don't have a destiny.
There is *Hashem*, yes, but there is also
 freedom. You decide, not *Hashem*. Joseph
   sent for the Jews, he promised them
  a better life in the land of the many
  idols, away from famine and oppression.
 "Come to Egypt", he said. "I am a rich
 man here, respected and beloved." And so
 they came. *Hashem* said to Abraham, "Take
 Yitzhak to the top of the mountain. Take
 him there and make of him a sacrifice."
He told him, "Kill your firstborn son for
  me, because I want to see how much you
 love me." And Abraham took Yitzhak to the
  top of the mountain and raised a heavy
   rock over the head of his son. And his
 son said, "Abba. Wait. Abba." But Abraham
     did not wait. He did not hesitate.

THE LOST EXPERT
(spellbound)
He didn't hesitate?

RABBI
Well, maybe a little.

The bus winds on along the empty country roads.

CHRIS SLEPT LATE, TOOK long naps, ate sparingly from the mostly organic, entirely-too-healthful groceries that occasionally, mysteriously, showed up at this door. He swam in the immaculate outdoor pool every day, doing lazy laps under the red orb of a late-afternoon sun. In the pool house — a cross, he discovered, between a workout room and a man cave — he absently did barbell curls and watched old sitcoms on the only TV on the premises: *Hogan's Heroes*, *The Brady Bunch*, *The Beverly Hillbillies* — prehistoric daytime programming festooned with an endless parade of ads for pharmaceuticals aimed at the incontinent, impotent, and peri-menstrual.

The phone rang and buzzed and beeped. Chris dutifully kept it on and charged, listened to his messages, read his texts. The same names over and over again: Reed, Berinstain, and of course Maddy, his increasingly more frantic publicist. Every morning he rose early, promising to plunge himself into the dominion of one Thomson Holmes, worldwide star. Reed. Maddy. Berinstain. *Call them.* But the days slipped by. One evening, he worked up the nerve to text Alison and ask her to come over. Her answer was sparse and heartrending: *Yes. We need to talk. When's good?* Was she breaking up with him? Were they ever even going out? Chris couldn't bring himself to reply. *When's good?*

He spent hours in the living room, standing at the glass wall, pondering that magnificent view. It was his now. He thought of the Lost Expert, of the desert, of the great immensity — sky over sand. He'd stepped over the edge, stepped right into the sky, hung there — not falling — the long sweep of the world under him. There was the same thing here, that same something, a quality in the air, in the sky. *Isn't that what you saw, Reed, isn't that what you were trying to capture through the German's lens?*

He didn't just talk to Reed. He talked to all the people in his head — Krunk, his father, Laurie, Alison. He told them the truth, but they only ever responded with pat recitations.

"Well that just sounds like a fantastic opportunity," his father replied, unperturbed by his impersonation of an international celebrity.

"You're so weird," Alison said, pursing her pink lips into a quizzical frown.

"Oh, Christopher Robin," Laurie sighed despondently.

HE SWAM A METHODICAL front crawl. Mid-stroke, Chris dived deep. Water swamped his ears.

Reluctantly, he surfaced. With his eyes closed, the autumnal California sun was a light orange smear against blotchy-lidded darkness.

"I'll do it, you know."

Startled, Chris blinked open his eyes.

Little Scarface, instantly recognizable, even in Ray-Bans, a polo shirt, and a pair of Bermuda shorts.

"You think I won't? You think you can just ignore our agreement?"

The veins in his corded neck pulsed under a thick gold chain necklace. It looked fake. Like a cartoon or something green-screened. *Did you tell them?*

Chris cupped pool water in a palm. He watched it run through his fingers.

Little Scarface shot up from the plastic deck chair he was sitting on. He paced the pool deck agitatedly. Chris, still standing in waist-deep water, watched him through narrowed eyes.

"Once I do it, it'll be like sharks in chum. They'll all be coming for you. Coming out of the woodwork. How many others are there, Mr. Movie Star? 'Wait until the movie ends,' you said. But that was never the bargain. You're still in the goddamn movies."

Little Scarface was yelling. He picked up the deck chair and whipped it against the deck's adobe tiles. Plastic shattered. A jagged leg spun into the pool.

"Obviously, Mr. Holmes, you are not capable of keeping your word. Which makes me sad. Sad, but not surprised. Why would you give all this up just because you messed around with some girl? How old did she say she was again, Mr. Holmes? Twenty? Eighteen? Did you enjoy it? Was it good? Was it worth it?

I want to keep it, Chris had told Berinstain. *The house, I want to keep it.*

"My client was reluctant to accept the original arrangement. I managed to convince him that it was beneficial for all parties, particularly the young lady. You quitting the movies. You disappearing. You providing appropriate compensation. It was fitting. It was poetic, even. But now I'm coming to see it his way."

Chris pulled himself out of the water. He stood, dripping, on the pool deck.

"Who was that again?" he asked loudly. "Your client?"

Scarface, eyes blacked out, turned his gaze back to the pool.

The tell, Chris thought suddenly. Go ahead. Do it. Do what you're going to do. Krunk's uncle shooting into the lake, whooping and yelling and insisting he'd hit a huge fish. *Bang bang bang. Fresh fish for dinner!* The report of the rifle and the near-instantaneous splash of water. The hooting and hollering. The crazed look in his eyes. *There! Didja see that, boys? Got another one!*

"I think you should go now," Chris said loudly. Calmly, he ran a hand through his short blond hair then flicked the water on his hand in the direction of the intruder.

Scarface stepped back as if slapped. Then, collecting himself, he aimed at Chris with index finger and thumb outstretched in an inverted L.

"It's coming," Scarface said in a seething whisper. "Don't you get that? An accident. A suicide. Something."

Chris stared at the finger gun, pointing, wavering.

"Yeah. You can go now."

AFTER DIRECTING A REMARKABLE seven feature films in the two years of 1917 and 1918, Raoul Walsh made only one movie in 1919. It was *Evangeline*, star-crossed tale of Acadian peasants separated by their British overlords. The film, like the Canadian version shot six years earlier and purported to be the first feature made in that country, was based on the Henry Longfellow poem of the same name, which Krunk had dubbed "interminable" and set about attempting to memorize as his next art project/work of biting social commentary. "This is the forest primeval!" he'd proclaimed as they wandered past the seedy Parkdale flora and fauna of idlers, panhandlers, and Chinese grandmothers collecting empties. "The murmuring pines and the hemlocks! Bearded with moss! Garments green! Indistinct in the twilight!"

Walsh, recently wed to the ethereally expressive actress Miriam

Cooper, proclaimed that his new wife would play Evangeline. Miriam was appalled. She was a married woman now. She wanted to return to the respectability wrenched from her when her well-to-do father abruptly abandoned the family, leaving his eldest daughter to seek her fortunes in the unscrupulous world of film.

Origin story, Chris thought, sprawled on the uncomfortable living room couch, his mind plunging ahead like a runaway train. Miriam Cooper stumbling into a role as an extra, attracting the eye of the pre-eminent director of the time, D.W. Griffith, but departing before he could get her coordinates; reconnecting with him a few years later when, after several other failed attempts to get on screen, the stalwart waif spent a week staking out his New York production office. Then, a bolt of lightning: a Griffith associate recognizes her as the young woman they'd been looking for all along.

Cooper quickly became a Griffith favourite, one of the few leading ladies he relied on. Griffith's habit, Chris remembered Krunk explaining, was to shift his actresses from bit roles to leads and back again to keep their egos and remuneration in check. But Miriam Cooper played only big parts for Griffith, including a primary role in the director's infamous box office hit *The Birth of a Nation*. Griffith, feeling that Cooper could take her character's despair over news from the charnel house of the Civil War to another level, pulled her aside in the middle of shooting: "I'm sorry to say that I just got word that your mother has died. We'll finish the scene then get you back home."

"Kidding," he said afterwards. "Ha. Ha." Hollywood: cruelties and coincidences. On the set of that bizarre rerun of the Civil War and its aftermath, Miriam Cooper met one Raoul Walsh, playing the role of Lincoln's assassin for the second time.

"Lincoln is dead, Dixieland spins off its axis, but," Krunk announced sardonically, "the good whites of the South must not give up."

And so the film arrives at its heroic denouement, summed up by what Krunk described as the most chilling conclusion of all time, the film's final intertitle: "The former enemies of North and South are united again in defence of their Aryan birthright."

Krunk went on: "Love triumphs over politics, blood is thicker than geography, and the KKK is reborn!" An audience of three confused undergraduates — attracted by the promise of a free screening and ruinously unaware that the film spanned three long hours — squirmed in their folding seats. The impresario was just getting started. It was a particularly "on" night, Chris recalled. Krunk proceeded to rant, enthuse, and deliver such factoids as he deemed necessary for their true education for another hour and forty-five minutes. Chris had bet himself that the undergrads would try to make a break for it, but they didn't. By the time the college kids were released it was, in fact, the middle of the night.

The middle of the night. Chris got up from the couch and stalked through the house. All this ancient film history roiling through his brain. To what end? It was just after two. When was the last time he'd actually spoken to somebody? To a human being? Little Scarface didn't count. "Get some rest," Reed had said to him at LAX. "I'll be in touch soon." Chris was confused. Was the movie over? Was The Lost Expert done? How did it end? He lay in his Hollywood Hills hideaway, waiting for word. Walsh, Griffith, Reed, Krunk. Marion Cooper, Darlia Cross. The Lost Expert's signs and portents were everywhere: in the patterns of the leaves, in the movement of the clouds, in the quiet ripples of the pool stirring in the night.

Griffith couldn't deny the moon-eyed Miriam. Formerly a bit actor and on-set jack of all trades, Walsh now directed several films for Griffith. Then, in one fell swoop, he married Miriam Cooper, Griffith's muse, spiriting her away to a rival production company. Griffith stood frozen. He didn't know it yet, but his long downward spiral had already begun. *The Birth of a Nation* — a triumph and a curse. He would be hapless and bankrupt while the upstart Raoul Walsh made movie after movie, mostly forgettable, all profitable. Walsh and Cooper would part, reunite, part, reconcile. Griffith would never see her again, except on the big screen.

Alison! Chris thought with a kind of horror. He closed his eyes against the pressure building in his head. The darkness was grainy, deep with shadow and layer — as if he were watching a deliberately shrouded scene, everything muffled, barely enough light to show the outline of a lost soul feeling his way through a shadowy passage.

He hadn't seen *Evangeline.* Neither had Krunk. No one had for a hundred years. Along with its Canadian predecessor, the film was one of the thousands of movies that never made it out of the silent movie era. The accounts from the day suggested that it wasn't particularly memorable. A moderate success at the box office. Long since forgotten by anyone but academics and obsessives like his erstwhile best bud. The lectures, the rants, the books he'd ordered Chris to read, the innumerable obscure films he'd forced him to sit through. Sick, maddening preparation. For what? Tomorrow, the next day, the rest of his life. He'd play Thomson Holmes. He had to think of it like that. He had to find the calm he'd felt while the Lost Expert slogged through a murky, bottomless swamp. On to a new role: Thomson Holmes. Alpha male. Top Hollywood brand.

Origin story: Thomson Holmes, raised by his grandparents on their failing farm. Discovered on YouTube, a shy, good-looking, but clueless and desperately lonely sixteen-year-old dressed up in bizarre outfits and reciting dialogue from famous seventies movies that he punctuated with fragments of Shakespearean soliloquies. Today, they were perennial internet favourites, perpetually cropping up on all-time top ten viral video lists and can-do high school self-esteem assemblies dedicated to the power of the possible. Had Chris seen them? Of course he had. Everyone had seen them; their sheer ubiquity made them unremarkable, forgettable. He'd seem them and, like everyone else, transferred them into that part of the brain that neither remembers nor forgets, only shuffles through the slides, occasionally flashing a pertinent image. Laurie, pulling one up on her phone: "Oh my god, I loved these in high school. I used to watch them all the time."

On screen, a close-up of a bizarrely outfitted baby-faced Thomson contorted in adolescent agony: "Tomorrow, and tomorrow, and tomorrow — the last syllable of recorded time — Hey! I'm waalkin' here! — Creeps in this petty pace — from day to day — Up yours, ya son-of-a-bitch! — And all our yesterdays — That actually ain't a bad way to pick up insurance, ya know — have lighted fools — You talkin' to me? — to dusty death."

All paths, Chris thought, all paths to the same place. Hey! I'm *waalkin'* here! For Krunk, movies were life. But Chris knew better. He'd seen the close-up: the German's appraising eye narrowing. Reed's needy drive, the way the conjured swamp pulsed around you — subaquatic mud tide, thick ooze slowly pulling you down. It wasn't life. It was just another take.

Returning to the living room, Chris stood over the darkness of the hills, deep and wide, stretching on forever, barely molested by the lights below. There's a world out there, he told himself. The thought was at least comforting: a night world that had nothing to do with him, with any of this — chirruping black crickets, felted field mice, stealthy, brown-plumed owls. In the morning, he'd call Berinstain. Little fucking Scarface! How had he gotten in? He'd fire the driver. He'd hire a new driver. He'd hire ten drivers. They'd never get him. How could they get him?

He went back to the bedroom. He threw himself on the bed and surveyed the square space. Like the entire house, it lacked distraction. No TV, no video games, no books. Not even a freaking deck of cards.

There had to be something. Something he could hold on to, something that would make it all real.

Getting up, he walked to the large, deep wardrobe. Shoving shirts and jackets aside, he leaned into its interior, redolent of lemon cleaning oil. He pushed his head and shoulders in as far as they could go, pressing his palms against the dark wood of the wardrobe's back panel. He moved across, searching by touch. The wood creaked. His heart quickened. There, ever so faintly, an outlined gap under his smooth fingertips.

A hidden compartment. The raised wood slid to the side. Clumsily, Chris reached in, scraping his wrists. His fingers hit metal. Inside the compartment: a box. He yanked with all his strength, as if it might be bolted down. Encountering no resistance, he tumbled backward, ending up on his back on the cream beechwood floor, the box held above him in both hands, as if in triumph.

Eagerly, he brought the box over to the bed. It was shoe-box-sized, fashioned of steel. It had a keyhole. Chris's heart sank. Where was the key? The box was heavy, austere, and serious.

He tried the lid anyway. It popped open noiselessly.

Chris stared down, amazed. The only thing in the box was a single flat, cylindrical object. It fit neatly in Chris's palm. He examined it. Both sides were silver. One side featured an adornment, the initials T.H. Chris brought the object close. He saw a slightly raised spot, like a button. He pressed it with his thumb. Nothing happened. He pressed again, pushing down harder with his index finger. A blade shot out. Chris yelped and dropped the whole contrivance on the bed. He laughed at himself nervously. Gingerly, he picked it up again. The blade was black as coal. He ran a cautious finger against its edge. The knife was razor sharp. A switchblade. He'd been hoping for something else entirely: postcards, crumpled receipts, snapshots, foreign change, wine corks, scribbled ideas. Who was Thomson Holmes?

Did you tell them? Did you tell them yet?

Little Scarface, pacing the pool deck.

This wasn't what we agreed to.

The movies: an absence of people, the ghostly presence of their lingering. Reed and his one last great one, the Holocaust picture show. You can't take it with you, Chris thought, near hysterical as he popped the blade of the knife out of its holder over and over again.

EXT. THE CITY — AN AREA OF MODEST LOW-RISE
APARTMENTS — EVENING TURNING TO NIGHT

THE LOST EXPERT limps through the city. His
breathing is laboured. The gash on his shoulder
is open, and blood oozes through the torn,
stained shirt. He turns the corner of a darkened
side street and staggers onto a main boulevard.
YOUNG MEN wearing Allan's Army shirts and
buttons are everywhere, smashing storefront
windows and spray-painting "AA" and Jewish stars
on the doors of some of the businesses. A group
of these men thud past The Lost Expert and run
up the stairs of a three-storey walk-up. Limping
and breathing hard, the Lost Expert follows the
men up the stairs.

INT. BUILDING HALL AND NICELY APPOINTED
APARTMENT
THUGS pound on an apartment door until it's
finally opened by a WOMAN IN HER FIFTIES in a
bathrobe. The men push into the apartment, and

the woman screams. They begin breaking dishes
and knickknacks, yelling about dirty Jews living
where they don't belong. The HUSBAND runs in and
tries to intervene. They push him around.

                         WOMAN
        Leave him alone, leave him alone! We
               haven't done anything.

                         THUGS
           Go to the ghetto. All Jews in
           the ghetto. Do you understand?

                         WOMAN
        No, no, we aren't Jews, you're making a
             mistake, please leave us alone!

                         THUGS
          (pushing and punching the man)
            Jews get out! Jews get out!

                          MAN
              (gasping from blows)
              Stop. Stop. Please!

                    THE LOST EXPERT
                        Enough!

The thugs whirl around, surprised. THE LOST
EXPERT looms in the doorway. Blood drips on the
carpet. Several of the thugs lurch forward to

attack, but their LEADER holds up his hand, and
they stop.

                    THUG LEADER
                 C'mon, lets go.

THUG 1 helps himself to an apple out of a
glass bowl, then sweeps the glass bowl to the
floor, where it smashes. Thug 1 throws the
apple to THUG 2, who catches it and bites
into it greedily. Juice runs down his stubbled
chin. Staring at the Lost Expert, he draws his
finger across his throat. He spits apple in the
direction of the couple.

                    THUG 2
               Fucking Jew apple!

The thugs push past the Lost Expert and leave
the apartment.

EXT. THE CITY — NIGHT
THE LOST EXPERT staggers through the city. He
can hear shrieks and cries, shouts punctuated
by the sound of breaking glass. As he works his
way west, he passes GROUPS OF FRIGHTENED PEOPLE
being herded east toward the ghetto. The Lost
Expert mumbles to himself, looks away from the
piteous shuffling steps. Gradually, he moves
farther out of the city core. Here, the carnage
dissipates, and the city quiets. By now, the

Lost Expert can barely stay on his feet. He
staggers onward.

INT. THE LOST EXPERT'S APARTMENT — NEAR DAWN
THE LOST EXPERT stands in the kitchen, where the
food in the refrigerator has been thrown on the
floor and all the jars of dry goods have been
smashed. He walks into the living room, where
his records are shattered and upholstered chairs
have been slashed with a knife. He gets to the
baby's room, where he staggers to a stop. He
eyes the empty crib, the sheets and blankets
thrown to the floor, the mattress turned over.
In the dark corner, the rocking chair creaks,
and the Lost Expert spins around.

> SARAH
> (crying)
> They took him.

> THE LOST EXPERT
> Who took him?

> SARAH
> (breaking down)
> They took our baby!

> THE LOST EXPERT
> Sarah! Who? Who took him?

> SARAH
> Where were you?

THE LOST EXPERT
What happened? Sarah! Tell me
what happened!

Sarah jumps up and rushes at him, drumming
ineffectually at his chest.

SARAH
Damn you. Goddamn you!

INT. THE LOST EXPERT'S OFFICE — EARLY MORNING
THE LOST EXPERT stands, staring at the front
desk. It's littered with messages in Esther's
handwriting. He picks several up, looks at them
blankly, and lets them fall to the floor. The
phone rings loudly. He lets the phone ring, then
changes his mind and answers it.

THE LOST EXPERT
Hello?

MAN
Yes, hello? Are you the guy from
the paper? They came and got my cousin.
They said they were from the government.
They said he was collaborating. I said,
"Collaborating with who? Where are
you taking him?" They said I better shut
up or I was going to be next. What's
going on in this country? They can't
just take people away, can they? I
don't know where he is!

THE LOST EXPERT
I can't help you.

MAN
Please! Please! I read about you! You can
find him! I know you can!

THE LOST EXPERT
(hanging up)
I'm sorry.

RACHEL ARRIVED ONE EVENING, out of the blue, texting that she was at the front gate and hoping to see him. Gorgeous, newly lean and tall — half a foot taller since finally taking the plunge and moving to L.A. They'd been texting on and off since the film shoot at the café, but hadn't seen each other until now.

"Crikey!" Rachel said, opening and closing his cupboards. "Don't you ever eat?"

"Are you hungry? We could order in," Chris suggested.

"Nah, I'm okay."

But to Chris, she looked starved. Her face, now divested of its previous baby fat vestiges, had gone angular. Cheekbones protruded from under the mane of her curly dirty-blond hair. Rachel opened a few more cupboards before finally finding the wine glasses. Chris popped the cork on a bottle of red and poured. In the pool house he'd found one of those temperature-controlled wine refrigerators. It was full of what looked to be wines of extremely expensive vintage. He'd been hesitant to touch them, but finally pulled out two bottles at random to mark Rachel's visit.

With their wine, they adjourned to the living room.

"Nice place you've got here," Rachel quipped. She leaned toward him as she spoke, presenting him with a view down her loose top: black bra over a small chest.

"You're my first visitor," Chris replied.

"Really? I thought you'd lived here a long time."

"Since I got back."

Rachel laughed loudly.

"Anyway," Chris said. "Here's to L.A."

They clinked glasses.

Rachel gulped, draining most of her wine. Chris refilled her glass. She drank again, then launched into a frenetic explanation of what she'd been up to since he'd met her at the movie shoot.

Her new Hollywood-based agent had encouraged her to move. She'd left Toronto. She was living with two other girls in Los Feliz. She'd already auditioned for three movies — two indies and one studio gross-out comedy — and a superhero TV show in which she was supposed to play the best friend of a young family doctor who used her telekinetic powers for good. Her agent said she was going to get a callback and was in consideration to play the lead in one of the indies.

"Exciting," Chris interjected.

"You're making fun of me," Rachel pouted.

"No. I mean it."

She was off again, expounding on the difference between Toronto and L.A. and how everyone here was taking her much more seriously. In Toronto, they thought the idea of trying to become a starring actress was weird, suspicious, somehow silly.

Chris nodded. He'd heard all this before, with far more force, Krunk's malevolence for the Canadian film industry reaching its apotheosis when he'd proposed to create a short film consisting of scenes from every film Ryan Gosling had ever made, but with an animated Canadian flag plastered over his mouth. Armed with the concept, he'd applied for and received a five-thousand-dollar development grant. The money long since gone, he'd been claiming the project was in production ever since.

Rachel gulped her wine. She was on her third. Chris refilled. "Hey," she said. "You trying to get me drunk?"

"No!" he protested, feeling his cheeks turn red.

Rachel giggled. She had a familiar air about her — she was nervous and confident at the same time in a way that Chris now recognized and understood — it was the way of beautiful people.

"It's okay," Rachel said, looking him in the eye. "It's okay if you are."

"So, uh," Chris blurted, "what ever happened to that guy, the one you worked with? Who looked like me?"

"Oh, you mean Chris." Rachel frowned, annoyed. "I don't know. I guess he quit the café or something. I sent him a text telling him to come to this party I had, like kind of a goodbye party, but not really because that's lame. Anyway, he didn't come. He didn't look that much like you. I mean, not really. Why are you asking about him?"

The sun had dropped behind the distant city now. The light in the room was an afterglow of encroaching shadow. The wine sat in their glasses, a heavy red, like mansion drapes.

"You know," Rachel said, "Alison warned me about you."

"I know. She told me."

Rachel sipped, girding herself for something. "She was just looking out for me," she went on hurriedly. "But she didn't have to, right? I mean, you're not like that." Rachel wasn't looking at him. Chris followed her gaze. The long slope down, a settling velvet gloaming. "You're not," she said, turning back to him but speaking so quietly he could barely hear her. "You're not …" Her brown-green pupils, glowing and earnest.

Chris stood up and moved to the translucent wall looking over the Hollywood hills. Where was Thomson Holmes? Still out there? Doing it — the usual? He was. Chris felt it in the pit of his stomach. Little Scarface and Thomson Holmes. Twin dark moons circling his star. How could he explain it? To Rachel? To anyone? In the depth of the elongated gloom, it was hard to tell exactly where the glass wall ended and the long descent began.

He felt Rachel appear beside him. She took his hand.

"It's true what they're saying, right? That it wasn't you? That it was doctored?"

I'll release it. The video.

"You've seen it? The video?"

"Thomson, it's all over the news. Everyone's seen it."

Chris managed a breath.

"Is it true? That it's a fake?"

The usual? They set you up with the usual?

"Thomson?"

He didn't answer.

"Jesus, Thomson." Rachel let go of his hand.

"What? No! Rachel! Of course, it's true! I had nothing to do with it!" Looking at her, he took her hand and held it to his chest. They both felt it, a beating heart.

Rachel exhaled audibly.

"I keep telling people. It's not you. You're not like that!" She pressed in against him. Her body was hot like a fever. She shivered dramatically. "Got a chill," she said coquettishly, drunkenly. "Warm me up?"

"Rachel, no. You're my friend."

"I have friends." She stepped back, playing with the bottom of her shirt, pulling it up, exposing her midriff, posing for him.

An erotic memory Chris felt would be burnt into the matter of his brain for all time.

"Can't we just do it?" she asked hungrily.

"I don't," he croaked.

"You don't?"

"I don't have friends."

Rachel considered him, her expression wavering. "Talk about ironic. The first straight guy who's ever —" Rachel smiled wryly. "Fine, Mr. Thomson Holmes. I'll be your fucking friend."

INT. BLACK BIRDS RECORDS — AFTERNOON
THE LOST EXPERT runs through the dark corridor
and up the stairs. He barrels through the door
into George Jason Paulson's office. Reclined in
the white leather office chair, his legs propped
up on the cluttered desk, is JOEL MCCANN, belly
protruding from his pants, scuffed leather shoes
half off his feet. McCann is asleep, snoring
sonorously, his face peaceful. There is a radio
on the desk broadcasting news of cheering crowds
and the rising wave of confidence spreading
across the nation like a new dawn. The Lost
Expert stares at McCann with disgust, then
sweeps the sleeping man's legs and the bulk of
the mess off the desk. McCann blinks awake.

                    JOEL MCCANN
                   (unsurprised)
                      You.

                  THE LOST EXPERT
                  Where is he?

                    JOEL MCCANN
                     (smirking)
          What are you going to do?

                   THE LOST EXPERT
         (leaning into the desk and grabbing
         McCann by the lapels of his jacket)
             You think this is a joke?

                    JOEL MCCANN
          I'd be careful, if I were you.

                   THE LOST EXPERT
               (letting go of McCann)
             What do you want from me?

                    JOEL MCCANN
           You still don't get it, do you?
          Beaoman, Meyer, Satan, the devil,
          all that nonsense. It's not real.
                It doesn't exist.

                   THE LOST EXPERT
           What are you saying? What are you
          talking about? Where is he? What have
                you done with my son?

McCann leans over and turns up the radio. He
motions for the Lost Expert to listen.

                   NEWSCASTER (V.O.)
          In his first public appearance after

winning the election, Allan announced he
would immediately assume power, forgoing
   the customary transition leading up
to inauguration in six months. He also
ceremoniously removed the scarf he's been
using to obscure his face throughout the
   campaign. The audience gasped as his
square jaw, crooked nose, blond hair, and
    steel blue eyes came into view.

                  THE LOST EXPERT
                  Beaoman.

                  JOEL MCCANN
                  Keep listening.

              HAROLD ALLAN (V.O.)
   It's time for Allan's Army to *rise up*!
They are taking our jobs. They are taking
    our dignity. They don't belong here!
   It's time! Allan's Army is here. We are
   rising up! We are rising up! There will
be a new dawn in America! America first!
   America always! (wild cheering) Thank
you, thank you. (crowd quiets) But we are
   a compassionate country! We are a God-
loving country! Recently, my wife and I,
we adopted a baby. A poor baby orphaned
in the Jewish quarter. We love this baby!
   We will raise him as our own! We will
     raise him to be a great American!

The Lost Expert reaches over and turns off the radio.

                    JOEL MCCANN
          I'm not saying it's right. I'm not
                  saying that.

The Lost Expert stares through McCann.

                JOEL MCCANN (CONT'D)
                    (sighing)
          Jesus, what's this world coming to?

INT. THE LOST EXPERT'S APARTMENT — LATE AFTERNOON
THE LOST EXPERT walks through the destroyed kitchen.

                  THE LOST EXPERT
                  Sarah? Sarah?

The Lost Expert walks down the hall into the baby's room.

                  THE LOST EXPERT
                     Sarah?

He stands in the overturned baby's room. The rocking chair is empty.

                    THE LOST EXPERT
                    (unsure now)
                       Sarah?

The Lost Expert walks over to the small window
in the baby's room and looks out. The garbage-
strewn street is empty, eerily silent. In the
quiet apartment, he picks up, now, on the faint
sound of running water. The Lost Expert hurries
down the hall to the bathroom. The sound of
running water gets louder. He tries the door.
It is locked.

                    THE LOST EXPERT
      Sarah, it's me! Open up! Please, Sarah. I
             know where he is. He's okay.
               Please, Sarah! Sarah!

Water begins to flow out from under the locked
door. It swirls around the Lost Expert's boots.
Surprised, the Lost Expert looks down. The water
is streaked with pink.

                    THE LOST EXPERT
             Sarah! No! Please, no! Sarah!

FIVE LANES OF HIGHWAY in either direction. The occasional bleat of a horn. Through the tinted windows, the desert hills in the distance rose like a dream. Up ahead, a red mountain shimmered, burned bright, then hazed out. Everything loomed — far in the distance or way off in the past. It had been ten days since he'd come to L.A., and six days since Alison's text: *We need to talk*.

This time she'd called him. She'd asked how he was in the cautious, caring voice used around someone who's probably dying. Preliminaries over, she got quickly to the point. A breakfast meeting had been scheduled. He had to show up. If he did, they could talk after. But first, he had to show up. "Thomson," she'd said earnestly. "It's really important."

Suiting up for the outing, he considered himself in the full-length bathroom mirror. Ten days on his own. He'd already lost weight and body mass. Even his newly ordered one-size-down Thomson Holmes outfits were loose. He looked like a character from the eighties, a boyish Tom Cruise dressing up for *Risky Business*. This boy in a man's clothing — he didn't recognize him. His gaze was shrouded and secretive. He brushed his teeth, smoothed his hair with water from the tap. The man in the mirror. The man in the high castle. He tried out a confident, Holmesian smile. It didn't look right. It just didn't. Alison. When he saw her, he would tell her. He had to. What other choice did he have?

The traffic was endless. Chris tapped his foot, waggled his right leg, cracked his knuckles. He had no idea when they might arrive, because he had no idea where they were or where they were going. Was helplessness always the default setting for celebrity? He got into cars. He went where they took him.

His phone rang. He didn't recognize the number; it wasn't one of the usual roster of callers. He answered it anyway. What if it was Alison?

"Son! Finally! I've been trying you for days!"

Son? The word circled around his brain, a tiny spark looking to ignite.

"Oh, uh."

"Don't worry about it! Look, Thomson, it doesn't matter to me. What they're saying. I know it's not true. People will believe anything these days! I just want to know: What can I do? How can I help?"

"Oh — thanks. Thanks — Dad. I'm okay. Really."

"You're okay?" The old man, Thomson Holmes's father, apparently, sounded disappointed.

"No, I mean, not okay."

"So what can I do?"

They entered a short tunnel, overpass darkening the already tinted windows. Traffic at a standstill. A bang on Chris's window. He panicked, ducked.

The car lurched forward.

"Sorry about that, Mr. Holmes." His driver from the front seat. "Some homeless guy looking for a handout."

"Son, you still there?"

"Yeah, Dad. I'm here. But I'm — I'm on my way to a meeting. Maybe I can call you later?"

"Sure, sure, no problem."

"Okay, I'll call you back."

"Son. Before you go. I was thinking you might come for a visit? Lunch, maybe? We could spend a little time together? Would that be okay?"

"A visit?"

"Sure. It's not far, right?"

"I have to go. Let me call you back."

Chris tossed the phone onto the seat beside him. Unusually, it was hot in the car. He was sweating. He reached for his water. Weirdly, it wasn't in its usual spot. The phone slid back to him, bumped into his hip. They were winding down an exit ramp. He had forgotten that Thomson Holmes had a father. A father who, apparently, cared about him. Chris saw a speck high in the sky. A bird of prey. He watched the hawk seem to trail the progress of the interminable traffic, then abruptly set course for the hills.

THE MEETING WAS IN the downtown Los Angeles offices of Berinstain, Elfy & Wolfowitz. Alphabetical order, Chris thought as he was ushered into the wood-panelled boardroom.

Two more people arrived. The first was his publicist, Maddy. She was large, tanned, resplendent in an orange muumuu. Kissing both his cheeks, she stepped back to take him in. "Look at you!" she yelped in an overdone New York accent. "Oh, my *gawd*. You're practically a *scarecrow*. Who's taking care of this boychik?"

Reed showed up, unshaven and grizzled. He wrapped Chris in a hug that smelled like wet, dirty sweater.

"What are you doing here?" Chris asked. "Where's Alison?"

"Alison," Reed scoffed, avoiding Chris's eyes. He surveyed the table, picked up a Danish, and bit into it, sending flakes and crumbs spewing.

Berinstain cleared his throat, and everyone became sombre. They sat. The three of them proceeded to discuss the situation, only occasionally pausing to acknowledge that the subject of their conversation was there in the room with them.

"Nothing to worry about," Maddy said, as much to herself as to him, it seemed to Chris.

They discussed various ways to ameliorate the allegations.

Chris sat quietly as they agreed on a plan. A *Lost Expert* wrap party — surprise guests in attendance to show support for their good friend and colleague. And a major announcement to the press: He would be starring in Darlia's movie, the gay *Big Chill*.

"*Seriously*?" Reed moaned, sounding like a recalcitrant adolescent denied video games until he cleaned up his room. Berinstain turned his sunken, watery eyes on him. Reed scowled, then became deeply entranced by the need to scrape at the cuticle of his left thumb.

"It's a *fantastic* role," Maddy trilled.

"With Reed on board as executive producer and Thomson in a starring role, they should have no problem securing financing and distribution," Berinstain said mildly.

"Great," Reed said petulantly.

"You'll be fabulous!" Maddy purred.

"And she'll make the statement?" Berinstain asked.

Maddy nodded and puckered her face, as if she was sucking on a sugar cube soaked in bitter lemon. "She's agreed to say that the rumours are completely unfounded. Thomson never pressured her for any kind of favours. He's always been a perfect gentleman. And the video is a fake. Which," she said emphatically, turning to Chris, "is true, of couwse!"

"Fine," Berinstain said evenly.

Darlia's movie. A party stocked with lady celebrities demonstrating their love. It was all so transparent and pathetic. It was exactly how Krunk said it was.

"Just one more thing," Berinstain said. "Darlia proposed that perhaps Thomson receive some ongoing assistance in processing the situation. From a mental perspective."

"A shrink," Reed said glumly.

"It's a good idea," Maddy announced.

"It will be completely confidential, of course."

"I know just the person," Maddy said. "He's worked with David and Chawlee."

"That sounds like the right direction to move in," Berinstain said evenly. "Thomson, are you in agreement?"

"Of couwse he is," Maddy announced, clapping a bejewelled, tanned hand on Chris's forearm.

Berinstain's dead blue eyes, like a mounted buck head's doleful, glittering browns. The way time passed in loops and repetitions, the same things happening over and over again. Where was Alison? *What about our agreement?* Chris wondered.

TO BREAK THE TENSE silence, Chris asked Alison if she'd ever heard of the Florida study. She hadn't. A friend had told him about it, Chris said. In fact, it had come from Krunk — a neat encapsulation of how, as he put it, the world of manufactured images helped create a whole new era of zombies with credit cards. During the study, a group of undergraduates were shown a series of images. For some in the group, the pictures included ones that suggested aging and retirement. Like a beachfront sunset, a tuxedo-clad lounge singer, a sepia photo of small-town main street, a kindly doctor. After watching the images, the students were moved to another room for lunch. The group of students shown the Florida pictures took longer to get there.

Alison thought about it. "So, it's like subliminal advertising?"

"Yeah. Only everything can be advertising."

"Not everything," Alison said. "Just pictures. Images."

"Yeah," Chris said. "Not everything. Just almost everything."

"Then it's pointless? Don't resist?"

"I don't know," Chris said. He'd brought it up because he'd wanted to tell her something, something clever. "I think it's more like — just keep asking, you know?"

"Asking what?"

"Why you're walking so slow."

Alison crinkled her cheeks, gave him a quizzical stare, then tinkled a laugh. Chris laughed, too, nervously at first, then more freely. He thought to ask her if she was close to her parents. He was sure she was. But he feared what the question would reveal. He needed to tell her. He would tell her.

He'd been surprised when she'd agreed to come with him on the two-hour drive. Her presence made it feel less like a march to certain death and more like a leisurely pleasure cruise through Southern California. It was both — wasn't it? — this road trip to visit his dad.

Silently they cruised smoothly along a busy highway. Occasionally, they caught tantalizing glimpses of the Pacific as they headed to the oceanside town where his father lived.

"Alison?"

"Yes, Thomson?"

He took her hand.

"Thanks for coming. You really didn't have to. I appreciate it. And before we get there. I wanted to tell you. I need to tell you …"

She was looking at him, but her big brown eyes displayed no discernable emotion.

"I ..."

"Thomson," she said firmly, reclaiming her hand. "You're going through a lot right now. You should just focus on that. You're visiting your dad. That's great. We can talk later."

"WE'RE ALMOST THERE," ALISON said, nudging him lightly. He'd been dozing, his mind amazingly blank. Then he remembered: the trip to visit the stranger who was his father. Suicide mission, he thought with sudden clarity.

When they'd crossed through customs at Pearson Airport in Toronto, he'd gone into a sweat, realizing what he was doing — presenting his false passport, incriminating himself as an international imposter. But he'd made it across without a problem. Alison had been at his side, handing over paperwork and passports emblazoned with the golden eagle of the United States. There was a brief consultation that didn't seem to involve Chris, who shifted from foot to foot, silk socks pressing against the pads of his impossibly thin leather loafers. The customs official grimaced, looked from Chris to the documents in front of him and then back at Chris. He didn't speak. *This is it*, Chris had thought feverishly, almost eagerly. Then the official said, "Have a nice flight," stamping at the documents with a vengeance. Chris had felt let down. *You're a masochist, Chrissy. A masochist for mediocrity. The king of let's just see what happens.* Whatever, Krunk. The plane had taken off, its velocity pushing him back against cool first-class leather.

And now, a new border, a final crossing. He should have been freaking out, but he wasn't. Thomson Holmes and his father were estranged, apparently. They hadn't seen each other in years. So now he had two fathers whom he hardly ever saw, who didn't particularly care about him. Two fathers. Two absent girlfriends. Two ideologically driven filmmaker best friends. Strange how everything had a parallel, everything had its equivalent. What about the men at the centre? Weren't they both the same too? Both missing.

"Thomson? Did you hear me?"

"Yeah, cool, cool, I'm awake."

THEY STOPPED AT THE gatehouse. Security appraised them and quickly opened the barrier. They rolled into a small neighbour-hood of bungalows with white stucco exteriors and rust-coloured tiled roofs meant to evoke the New Mexican pueblo. Each house had a neatly groomed patch of lawn sporting a coconut or palm tree — Chris wasn't sure if there was a difference — and a flow-ering bush or two.

They proceeded at a stately pace down an empty street adorned with signs warning drivers to yield to golf cart traffic. Chis drummed his hands on his thighs until Alison flashed him a look. Fathers and sons. What would they do all afternoon together? What would they talk about?

They glided to a gentle stop in a driveway. They were in a cul-de-sac harbouring five of the indistinguishable faux-pueblo houses.

The driver got out to open the door for them.

"Well, I'll see you in a few hours," Alison said.

"Wait. You're not coming in?"

"Me? No. This is your thing."

"But you should meet him!" Chris said, trying to cover his sudden desperation with enthusiasm.

Alison patted his knee soothingly. "I will sometime, Thomson."

Chris turned away from the concerned, compassionate expression on her face.

The driver opened the door. Slowly, Chris stepped out. The Florida study. He breathed deeply. The air was fragrant and heavy, not exactly fresh, tinged, Chris imagined, with the chemicals that were no doubt heavily deployed on the abundantly perfect foliage in perpetual bloom. The town car circled the dead end and rolled back up the bucolic street.

THOMSON AND HIS FATHER took their lunch on the terrace beside the small pool. The lunch was simple, a chicken salad obviously prepared by someone else and left for them to help themselves. Thomson Holmes's Dad made no apologies as he served things directly from heavy-lidded plastic containers.

"Okay, then," he said. "Dig in."

Though not particularly hungry, Chris did what he was told. They ate, not speaking, Chris sneaking furtive glances at his newly acquired father. Jack Holmes was tall, taller than Chris, with a lean frame and tanned arms revealing biceps that still hinted at a life of some labour. His brown, weathered face was centred by a red, cratered nose that, along with a slight tremble of the fork and serving spoon, suggested he was or had been a fairly heavy drinker, though there was no alcohol in evidence. Thomson Holmes's Dad had a healthy looking, if greasy and unruly, sweep of white hair and overall seemed sharp enough.

"It's good," Chris eventually said as he finished his last bite.

"Yeah, thanks, made it myself." Jack grinned impishly.

"Someone brings you your meals?"

"Monday to Friday! God forbid you don't eat up! Then you hear about it."

Chris chuckled along. "Good," he said vaguely. "Good. And ..." He looked at the pool.

"Yup, still swimming. Every day. Keeps me nice and lean." Thomson Holmes's Dad laughed again, patting what Chris now saw was a pronounced belly made more evident by the man's otherwise slim frame.

"So, uh ... son?" The word *son* again, this time as a question. "How are things? How's the movie coming?"

"Good."

"They treating you well?"

"Oh, sure, they're treating me great."

"I've seen a few things about it. On the computer. It's a different kind of movie than you normally make, isn't it?"

"Yeah." Chris toyed with the water beading on his glass of iced tea. "I guess it is."

"And how is that?" Thomson Holmes's Dad leaned in, expectantly, hopefully. There was something in the way he spoke that appealed to Chris, that made him want to open up. He was reminded of his grandfather when he was still relatively healthy. He used to like to ply Chris with questions about school and friends and even what he thought about a popular TV show or song on the radio.

"It's intense," Chris said. "The character I'm playing, he's dealing with a really strange situation. He's supposed to be this superhero type, and he's trying to be that, but it's not really about that at all. It's more about the expectations he's putting on himself, and how hard it is for one guy to do anything, really, that can make any kind of difference in such a crazy world."

Jack nodded thoughtfully.

"Yeah," Chris said, riding a rush of energy. Jack was buying it, buying into the new Thomson Holmes. Sure, why not? Chris was just that good. When was the last time they'd even seen each other? "I think it's the idea of having the sense that you can do more with your life, because you're not like everyone else. But then you find out you really are like everyone else, just with this added burden. And meanwhile, everyone has an agenda for you, has big expectations, and you just aren't sure how to deal with it all, you know?"

"It's the perfect role for you." Thomson Holmes's Dad pointed at Chris's chest with his fork. "You know what I mean?"

"Sure," Chris said, smiling wryly. "I know what you mean."

Jack got himself up. "Dessert time," he said. He patted his belly. "Not that I need it."

"Let me help," Chris said, also standing.

"No, no, you're a guest."

"Please, Dad. Let me help."

"Well, all righty. There's a key lime pie in the fridge. I'll grab the plates."

Chris hadn't had key lime pie before.

"Got the taste for it down in Florida," Jack informed him. "When I was living there. After —" Jack hesitated, then realized he'd painted himself into a corner. "After I split with your mom," he eventually mumbled.

"It's really good," Chris said through a mouthful of sour-sweet and graham cracker crust. The less he knew, the better. It could be a new start, he thought optimistically. It could be a new start for both of them.

"Look at you," Thomson Holmes's Dad said. "Look at you go." He smiled paternally, served Chris another piece.

Over coffee, already made and left in a thermos, his father told him a bit about his friends at the complex. Mostly he played golf with Bob Grossman, the retired optometrist across the street.

"Grossman's a kidder, like me. We get along all right." He also played euchre and poker, and sometimes went to movie night. "But you know me," he said. "I've always been a bit of a loner."

Thomson Holmes's Dad stood up slowly, almost ceremonially. He stuck his chest out. "Look, Thomson," he said. "I know how you value your privacy, and it's not my business and all that. And I know we haven't exactly gotten along, what with my problems and all. And then after your mother passed, rest her soul. But I'm still your dad. And I haven't really been there for you. I regret that. I really do. Look, son. Can I ask you something?"

"Uh, sure." Chris knew what was coming. Maddy had drilled it into him. Just say the same thing over and over again: It wasn't me. I would never do anything like that. It's a fake. I've never even met that girl.

"Are you in some kind of trouble?"

Not what he was expecting. "Why would you ask me that?" Chris did his best to keep his voice neutral, his face impassive.

"A man came to see me," his father said gravely. "He wasn't a regular visitor. He let himself in. He was sitting right on my sofa when I came home from across the street."

"A man?"

"A man. He was asking questions: Where were you? When had I last heard from you? I said, 'Who the hell are you? Get out of here or I'll call the cops.' He just smiled at me. He had a real ugly smile."

"What did he look like? Small guy, black hair, scar on his face?"

"That's the one. You know him?"

"What else did he say?"

"He said that you'd been bad. He kept asking me if you'd told me. 'Told me what?' I asked him. But he just kept saying, 'Did he tell you? Did he tell you what he'd done?' I told him I didn't know what he was talking about, that I wasn't answering his questions. I told him to get the hell out before I called security. I think he was just trying to scare me."

"Or me."

"Thomson, he's behind it, isn't it? This whole video thing?"

Relieved, Chris nodded. He felt like crying, like someone had died or been born.

"Son, are you in trouble?"

Chris stood up too, felt himself drawing to his full, new height. The pool gurgled gently, and somewhere in the gated complex a car alarm went off then stopped. Chris stared into the red-rimmed eyes of Thomson Holmes's Dad then, finally, pulled him into a hug.

"I got it all under control, Dad."

When it was over, the old man kissed him on the cheek with trembling lips. There was a smell — egg and suntan lotion and sweat all mixed together. It wasn't a bad smell.

EXT. THE JEWISH GHETTO — DUSK
THE LOST EXPERT stands outside the rabbi's small
house. In his arms, he holds SARAH, lifeless
yet beautiful, long hair spilling over the Lost
Expert's muscled arms. The PEOPLE OF THE SHTETL,
pale, dirty, gaunt, gather around him. A MAN
begins to sing a song in Yiddish, the words
reverberating with sadness.

                     SINGER
        Veynt nit brider, veynt nit shvester.
        Veynt nit muter nokh ayer kind.

              PEOPLE OF THE SHTETL
                   (joining in)
           Az es falt, falt der bester:
           Der vos hot undz getray gedint.

ESTHER and the RABBI hurry down the street,
followed by the waddling BEADLE, somehow still
implausibly well fed. They push through the

small crowd, and a hush falls amongst the Jews
of the shtetl. The beadle and Esther begin to
wrap Sarah in a white sheet. The sky darkens,
and thunder booms in the distance. It starts
to rain. The rabbi, his face ashen, suddenly
holds his arms above his head and bursts out in
prayer.

                    RABBI
          Shma Yisreal, Adoinai, Elohenu,
               Adonai Achad!

Thunder flashes above the head of the group,
and rain mixed with hail hurtles down. The Jews
shuffle off to find shelter where they can.
Esther gently tugs at the Lost Expert, urging
him to come inside. The Lost Expert takes the
white-wrapped body from the beadle. He cradles
Sarah to his chest. The rain falls, relentless,
the white sheet turning translucent, revealing
the surprised face of his dead wife.

EXT. THE JEWISH CEMETERY — MORNING
THE LOST EXPERT stands in front of a plain pine
coffin. Beside the coffin, the GRAVEDIGGERS
prepare the hole. Behind the Lost Expert are the
PEOPLE OF THE SHTETL, shivering and starving,
revealed in the bright sunshine. The RABBI prays
silently as the gravediggers finish digging and
plant their shovels in the newly upturned dirt.

RABBI

Bring me your hungry and your wretched.
I shall not turn them away. So it is
written. Here is our friend's wife,
the wife of a man of righteous truth.
We shall not turn him away. Though we
are hungry, though we are lost, we will
not turn him away. Not on this earth,
nor in the world to come. The *tzaddiks*
have written that the greatest charity is
done in hiding, without anyone knowing.
We are all in hiding now — but we will
not turn away from who we are, from who
we must be.

The rabbi sweeps his hand to indicate the wall
in progress behind him, a foreboding half-
completed structure of concrete and barbed wire.
Behind it are several construction vehicles
guarded by men wearing dark sunglasses and
fatigues. They patrol back and forth, shotguns
against their chests, watching the gathering
suspiciously.

RABBI (CONT'D)
But let us not hide our hearts.
Let us be open and true, let us revel
in *Hashem*, in his love for us, in
the love of this man, this *ger toshav*,
and his beloved Sarah. Are we loved?

> We are. We shall be. If we die,
> then we die in love.

Abruptly, the rabbi turns to the coffin. The gravediggers begin to lower the coffin into the hole.

> RABBI (CONT'D)
> *Yitkadel ve yitkadadash …*

> PEOPLE OF THE SHTETL
> *Yitkadel ve yitkadash …*

A truck rumbles to life, and work on the wall recommences. The Lost Expert, at the lip of the grave, stands next to the rabbi and watches as one by one the Jews of the shtetl take turns slowly shovelling dirt over the plain coffin.

THE THERAPIST'S OFFICE WAS bright and angular — like an Apple store. Therapy for the stars. Chris thought of Dr. Wong's office, the giant, expansive painting that hung over his burnished, heavy maple desk. It had been rented, he recalled, from the Art Gallery of Ontario. The detail bothered him — the memory, its realness.

"Can I tell you something?"

"That's what I'm here for."

"You can't ever tell anybody, right?"

"It will be completely confidential. Unless you're planning on hurting yourself."

"No, it's nothing like that. It's something that happened when I was a kid."

"How old were you?"

"Twelve. I think. Maybe eleven."

"Go on." The therapist — a small, precise, monochromatically dressed figure of indeterminate age and gender — exuded an indifference Chris found oddly calming.

"We used to spend our summers up north. It was an unpopulated, wild area. There wasn't a phone or electricity or anything like that. It was me, my best friend K, and his uncle. I'll call him Uncle Bobby, okay?"

"Okay."

"We stayed in a cabin, more like a shack, I guess. It had barely any furniture, no kitchen, no running water, no electricity. It was practically falling down. Uncle Bobby lived there full-time. At least, I always thought he did, but now I don't know. He couldn't have lived there in the winter. He'd have frozen to death. Maybe he did. I don't know. He was K's mother's brother. But I don't think she'd ever actually been up there. I never saw her there, anyway. They sent us up there by bus. So I don't know if she knew ..."

"Knew what?"

"How run down it was. What it was really like."

"Please continue."

"Anyway, our parents sent us up there for most of the summer. It was just the three of us. We hardly ever saw anyone else. The whole area was just woods and bog and swamp and small lakes. It was mostly Crown land that was wet and boggy and in the middle of nowhere so nobody cared about it."

"Crown land? What's that?"

Shit, Chris thought. It was getting harder and harder to remember that his childhood memories did not belong to the person he was supposed to be.

"Uh, yeah, I mean state land. Nobody owns it. K and I spent our days wandering around, building things out of scavenged timber, following bear prints, looking for snakes under rocks. Sometimes we snuck up on the cabin. We'd spy on Uncle Bobby, who never really did much but sit around in his underwear smoking cigarettes and drinking beer and sometimes chopping wood. It was buggy as hell, but he didn't care.

"Anyway, that's how our days went. We developed all these patterns and rituals, things we did over and over again. Some of it was pretty weird. Uncle Bobby didn't notice. We mostly stayed out of his way. But sometimes he would get all paranoid and accuse us of stealing his stuff. He'd whip empty beer bottles at our heads as we ran away, and they'd just barely miss us. He'd dump all our stuff out of our packs and make us strip down to our underwear, and then he'd talk about what a pair of skinny little faggots we were."

"That's what he said? That you were 'skinny little faggots'?"

"Yeah. He was pretty crazy, I guess. It was just the three of us out there, the whole summer."

"Okay. Go on."

"So this one time, me and K, we were at one of our spots where we liked to hang out: a long rock ledge on the edge of a huge swamp. It was really beautiful, really quiet there. It was one of my favourite places to go. There were frogs everywhere and these big boulders that you could sit on and stare out over the water. There were always bubbles coming up through the dark grasses and different creatures suddenly appearing and disappearing. You could watch the water for hours. We built a kind of lean-to against the rocks, a shelter that we would go in, and we had some candles in there and mosquito coils and comic books and stuff, you know, we were just kids.

"This time it was a cooler day, so we'd built a little fire and we were heating up something to eat. Probably beans, we ate a lot of cans of baked beans. And there was the smell of the woodsmoke, and the sunshine through the trees was all dappled on the rocks, and we suddenly saw a real big water snake swimming in the bog. K was really into snakes at that time, so were both watching this big black water snake swim along the rocky bank, and that's when it happened."

Chris closed his eyes.

"Please go on."

Chris could not.

"Thomson, if you're not comfortable going on, you don't have to."

"No, I — I'm okay."

"Take your time."

"That's when the shooting started. Bang bang bang. The air was all stirred up around us, dirt and smoke and bits of rock. And there were shots in the water too, the water exploding and splashing — erupting, kind of.

"At first we didn't really react, we didn't know what was going on. There were bullets whizzing by us, and shrapnel from the big rocks. I got cut pretty bad on my leg, but I didn't notice.

"And then Uncle Bobby started moaning really loud: 'Boys, boys. You've gone too far this time, boys.' He really sounded crazy, completely out of his head. So then K was like, 'Holy fucking shit, he's shooting at us!' And we both started running. We ran along the rocks, but there was no cover. The bullets were whizzing along the waterline. But no matter how fast we ran, Uncle Bobby kept shooting at us. It was so loud. We were both screaming. I could hear K yelling, 'Uncle Bobby, stop it, stop it! Stop it, Uncle Bobby! You're gonna kill us!' I started yelling too, 'Uncle Bobby, stop it!' Like we were trying to snap him out of it, but it wasn't working. We kept running, and the bullets kept coming, and so did that horrible moaning: 'Boooooooys! Booooooooooys! Too far! Booooooooooys!'

"We came out of the woods at this big rocky cliff that ended in a steep drop into the bog. The shooting stopped. It was quiet. We were thinking we'd lost him or he'd given up and it was all over. We were trying to be all quiet and not breathe too loud, even though we'd been running like crazy and we couldn't catch our breath. And we're thinking it was over, he'd stopped, he'd snapped out of it. And then we saw branches rustling and bushes shaking. We froze. We couldn't see him, but he was there, he was coming. The moaning got closer and closer, 'Boys, boys, boooyyyysss.' I look over at K. His eyes are closed. He's practically crying. He starts whimpering, 'No, Uncle Bobby, no ...' Then there's a gunshot. I grab K and I pull him to the edge. One of us yells 'Jump!' but neither of us does it. It's maybe fifteen feet down into the bog covered in lily pads with lots of big rocks pushing out of it. Uncle Bobby keeps coming, and there are more loud cracks, and I realize he's not shooting at us, it's just sticks breaking under his big, heavy boots. Finally, there's Uncle Bobby, standing right behind us, close now, I can hear him breathing, I can smell his animal smell. And he's, like, right over us, and we're just standing there with our backs to him and we're holding hands and we have our eyes closed and K is crying now, sobbing, and I'm, like, just standing there, figuring that was it, we were going to die.

"Then Uncle Bobby says, 'Look at you two pussies. That one's even pissed himself.' And I looked down, and I could see the stain on my jeans, and then I felt it. 'What a bunch of pussies.' He kept saying that. And then he turned and marched back into the woods."

"That must have been horrible to experience."

"It was. But I haven't thought about it. Not in a long time."

"Why do you think it's coming up now?"

"I stayed best friends with K. I was best friends with him for fourteen more years after that. We never talked about it. Never even once."

"You never talked about it?"

"I guess we were ashamed."

"What did you have to be ashamed of?"

"The way we acted, I guess. Like scaredy-cats. 'Pussies.'"

"But he had a gun. He was shooting at you. And you were just children."

"Yeah, but — we didn't even try."

"Try to what?"

"Fight back."

"How could you have?"

"And that's why."

"Why what?"

"Why we couldn't ever talk about it. As long as we were friends, we didn't want to talk about it. It was like, if we didn't talk about it, we didn't have to think about it. I was so scared I actually pissed myself. I think there are a lot of things like that: if you don't talk about them, it's like you can pretend that they never happened."

"But it did happen."

Chris nodded.

"Yeah. It did."

"And how does talking about it now make you feel?"

Chris made a pained face. "It's like — I'm still that loser kid, all over again."

"And how does that kid feel?"

"Bad, Doctor."

"*Bad*?"

"Like he wants to …"

"He wants to what, Thomson?"

Chris doesn't answer.

"Thomson, what does he want to do?"

Chris shrugged.

"Disappear."

INT. THE LOST EXPERT'S INTERIOR OFFICE —
AFTERNOON (one year later)
THE LOST EXPERT sits slumped in his chair. A
year has gone by, but the Lost Expert looks
considerably older — bearded, with deep lines
in his face. The phone in the exterior office
rings. The Lost Expert ignores it. The radio is
on, the volume low.

                    NEWSCASTER (V.O.)
          It's been almost a year since Harold
          Allan has taken power. So far, he's
          kept all his campaign promises. We're
       heading toward a more prosperous, safer
          country, people! The ghetto is sealed,
          and President Allan is moving to close
          the borders to all immigration. Making
          our country great again, people. Jobs
          for everyone. Prosperity for everyone.
       Allan's Army has changed America for the
          good, ladies and gentlemen. Of course,
          the popular imagination continues to

focus on the President and First Lady's
little boy, adopted at the very beginning
of the Allan administration, and, by all
accounts, now thriving under the …

The Lost Expert stares at nothing. Abruptly, the
phone stops ringing.

ESTHER (O.S.)
(her voice coming from the outer office
reception area)
The Lost Expert's office, how may I
help you?

The Lost Expert, startled by Esther's voice,
jerks up.

ESTHER (O.S) (CONT'D)
Okay, I understand. Let me get back to
you once I speak with him.

The door to the interior office opens. ESTHER
comes in.

ESTHER
(holding up a scrap of paper)
A girl is lost.

THE LOST EXPERT
(sighing)
Go home, Esther. Leave me alone.

ESTHER
(sharply)
Home? What home?

THE LOST EXPERT
(looking down at the dirty floor)
Esther. I'm sorry —

ESTHER
(holding back tears)
You have to try. We're dying in there!
The rabbi sent me. He says you can help.

THE LOST EXPERT
The rabbi!

ESTHER
She was playing in front of her house.
With her dog. The next thing they knew —

THE LOST EXPERT
Esther!

ESTHER
(firmly)
It's been more than a year. It's time.
People are dying. In the shtetl, things
are bad. The rabbi is getting weaker.
Please! We need you! He says you have
to use it. Your gift. You have to
just try and use it.

The Lost Expert shakes his head in despair.

                    ESTHER
          Please. He's sick. He's dying.

                 THE LOST EXPERT
          What can I do? I can't do anything.

Esther looks at him desperately.

                    ESTHER
                   Please.

                 THE LOST EXPERT
       (a single tear sliding down his cheek)
              How old is she?

THE LIMOUSINE PICKED CHRIS up in the early evening. His pants hung off him, even though he'd tethered them to his waist via an electric blue Thomson Holmes belt. The linen jacket he'd chosen at random felt like it was billowing off his frame as he walked hurriedly from the front door to the waiting town car. He gave his driver an appraising look meant as a warning. Seemingly unaffected, the driver clicked the door shut. Chris settled against the cool leather seat and closed his eyes. He'd been up all night, lying in bed, fingering the palm-sized switch-blade that had once belonged to Thomson Holmes. In the hours around dawn, he'd drifted off picturing the assassin-turned-director Raoul Walsh and his mentor-turned-rival D.W. Griffith circling each other, going round and round.

The car climbed a ramp and began wending slowly along the congested freeway. The city up ahead, obscured by smog. On the sides, tan hills, swathed in lengthening shadow and dun vegetation.

To Krunk, it was the greatest film era — pre–Hays Code, mani-acal, exuberant, and transgressive. A nation's truth emerging. What art form would prevail in the wake of those horrific con-flicts fought with a savagery never known or seen before? Film was the only possible answer, the only art not rendered obsolete by the new madness of modern warfare — muskets levelled on grassy fields suddenly filled with the cries of *Charge!* leading all too soon to tommy guns and lung-destroying gases settling eerily over acres of muddy trenches. *Charge!* Only film, equally frenetic and just as cruel, could matter now. Chris shook his head. Snap out of it. Krunkisms. Ideas his former friend had picked up from his endless hours re-watching the remains of the silent film era and dog-earing tomb-like books purporting to be the complete, the exhaustive, the thorough history of every epoch Hollywood had known or forgotten.

"Enough!"

Reed: "He speaks! Good god! The man speaketh!"

Darlia leaned forward and put a tiny hand on Chris's knee. He jerked ever so slightly at her gentle touch, slightly stunned to find that she and Reed were both in the limo with him. "Are you okay, Thomson?" Darlia, next to him, pondering him with a luminous, puzzled gaze, while Reed, across from him, looked on stonily.

On set, Chris had felt it. Signals and portents, sudden storms passing over eerie, inviting partings in the woods. Patterns to be divined: Little Scarface hates/needs Thomson Holmes. Chris hates/loves Krunk. Reed hates/needs the money men, and Darlia loves/hates Thomson Holmes. What did it matter? The old ways were gone. The dramatic gestures of heroes dipping their wings as they took their victory laps over Paris airfields were all too easily overwhelmed by Dolby Surround, Technicolor, and the 4D experience.

"Everything is replicable," Chris blurted, channelling an inner Krunk-Reed he no longer seemed able to control. "The machine rolls on. Holmes disappears and is replaced by another, better

Holmes. Miriam Cooper leaves the aloof genius Griffith, pulled to the brooding, needy Raoul Walsh. She's looking to get back to something she's lost, but once she gets there, she finds out the truth: there's no home to go back to. 'Just one more movie, my love,' her new husband begs her. 'Then we'll settle down. Please my darling, my darling, darling girl. For me …'

"Everyone betrays everyone. Even if we don't mean to. We can't help ourselves. It's like one of those slow-motion scenes in a disaster movie. The giant wave. We all know what's coming, but we can't stop it, can't stop ourselves. It's the world we live in. It's the way we're brought up. It's what we know. What we learn, from very early on. To betray each other. To use each other."

"Thomson! That's terrible!" Darlia looked stricken. Reed tugged his ball cap lower. He made a sound, half moan, half sigh. Chris thought he was going to cry. Instead, he took a vial of pills out of his pocket, tilted three into his palm. He threw them into his mouth.

"Anyone else?" Reed rattled the pill bottle at them. "C'mon, people! It's a party!"

THEY PAUSED GOING IN. Chris stood with his arm around Darlia's slight shoulders as the paparazzi took pictures. He smiled faintly, holding his breath, steeling his muscles at the flashing cameras. Little Scarface. *Tell them. Tell them!*

Inside, the chic club was already crowded. Everyone looked up at them when they entered. Chris, waiting for his eyes to adjust, couldn't make out anyone's face. Who were these people? What did they have to do with the movie? He scanned again and thought he recognized the German's scoffing profile backlit by the glittering raised bar. Anyone else? He looked in vain for Alison.

He'd texted her this morning, his words pathetic and unrequited:

See you tonight?

Maybe?

Hope so.

Darlia returned with two glasses of champagne. She passed him one, then hooked her lithe arm through his and tugged him along. Chris let himself be led. Her glow made him disappear. Thomson Holmes, nothing more than a comma in the small talk. She introduced him to random shiny people, well dressed, tanned, healthy, physiognomies perfect to the point of freakish absence. Despite their armoured exteriors, they extended their hands demurely. You don't fuck with celebrity. Producers, agents, fixers, distributors, mid-level executives, a cluster of famous hairdressers-to-the-stars, baring teeth as they leaned into one another and showed off their tight leather pants and shirtless vests revealing glimpses of smoothly shaved pecs. The wrap party was a reward for playing ball, putting in an all-nighter, doing the studio a solid, looking away from what shouldn't be seen.

Darlia led him to a higher level behind a red velvet rope guarded by two weightlifters in tuxedoes. The rope, some-how, was enough to shield studio executives, money people, and B- and C-list actors whose faces Chris knew he was supposed to recognize. Darlia took him to a corner table. A woman stood up to meet them. She was instantly recognizable, with her quixotic smile and wraparound shades. Darlia pecked at the older wom-an's high cheekbones. Making sure the cameras were ready,

Darlia nudged Chris, shooting him a look sharp enough to cut glass. Chris leaned in to kiss the proffered cheek of the icon before him. A bona fide movie star. The cameras snapped the moment. Thomson Holmes with his long, lank arms around the shoulders of Darlia and a slightly wizened replica of Thelma — or had she been Louise?

RACHEL APPEARED, SAID SOMETHING to Darlia, who handed Chris off to her with a grateful smile that looked like a wince. Rachel led them to a nook in the back where they sat in relative darkness only very occasionally penetrated by someone asking to take their picture or just simply taking their picture. But that segment of the party was mostly over now. It was getting toward midnight, and things were loud, louder — supplicating laughter suffusing the DJ's soundtrack with wishful mania. Reed had made a brief speech, perhaps the only genuine aspect of the wrap party turned carefully staged spectacle. While Reed talked, Chris searched the fringes of the gathering for Frankie and his gang, but they were nowhere to be seen. "In this film," Reed had said, "Thomson Holmes utterly transforms himself. You will not believe your eyes. He turns himself into the most soulful, tormented, fascinating character I have *ever* had the privilege of bringing into the world." The applause had been perfunctory, many in the audience busy frantically broadcasting bastardized variations of Reed's comments over their complex array of electronic networks. Reed ended by urging the gathered crowd to get excited about the picture, because it was the real thing. "The real thing," Reed had repeated gravely before tottering off to the bar where he took the stool next to the German, both facing short glasses glinting with brown liquor, their backs to the crowd.

Rachel talked, pointing out people she knew and people she knew of. Chris nodded along, but he was tired and thought that he'd stayed long enough. He glanced around, nervously tugging at his jacket lapels.

Rachel raced into an update. She hadn't gotten any of the parts yet. Several auditions were coming up next month. Her agent had engaged a private acting coach. There was so much competition! But she was staying positive. "The only thing" — here Rachel lowered her voice. Chris saw that her hand, perfectly manicured and topped with glazed nails, was now over his. "Money is a bit — I wouldn't normally ask. God this is awkward. Do you think that —"

There was a sudden surge of excitement, phones in the direction of the door. "It's Clooney," he heard someone say.

Then came a disembodied reply: "Ah, shit, George the Bore!"

"Is he?" Chris wondered. "Is he boring?"

"Excuse me," Reed said, his heavy hand on Chris's shoulder. "Can I borrow him? I promise, I'll bring him right back."

At first, Chris thought they were heading toward an introduction — George the Bore — but instead Reed led him hurriedly through the swinging doors next to the bar, through the kitchen, down a greasy hallway, and out a side door into an alley.

The alley, lit only by the deflected streetlights of Sunset Boulevard, was intimately familiar to waiter Chris. Another alley reeking of cigarette butts and the not-so-faint odour of urine. Reed pulled out a fat cigar and his silver lighter. His hand shook, and the flame danced around the end of the stogie, haphazardly singeing the leafy skin and illuminating bits and pieces of Reed's Caligari-like expression — darkness shadowing a scowl trying to be a grin.

"Here. Let me." Chris took the lighter and carefully raised the flame. Reed drew in. The cigar glowed red. Reed's lunatic scowl steadied. Chris thought of a car's red brake lights disappearing into the night. The tender scenes he'd watched with the director. Boy Lost Expert and his harried mother. Long takes of clouds slowly turning from silver to grey and back again. The car far below, alone on an empty road bordered by blurred forest. Faded banquette seats at a diner. *It's just you and me now, kid.* Close-up of a holy mess of pancakes overloaded with sundae sauce and whipped cream. *We'll be okay. Won't we?*

"Goddamn parties." Reed's voice cracked, and he coughed a bit as he exhaled sweet, rotten smoke. "But you're doing good, Holmes. Real good."

Was he?

Reed took off his Penguins cap. He ran his hands over his greasy scalp. Then he put the dirty cap back on. Chris wasn't crazy about this weakened, anxious version of Reed. It was like Krunk in his rare moments of doubt, those end-of-month times when they were both totally broke and his friend was on the verge of being summoned to the unemployment office to discuss his job search and his chronically unsubstantiated claim that chronic back pain prevented him from most forms of labour. "Ah, what's the point," his friend would say, looking down at what was left of his black work boots, the steel toes scuffed and exposed. "Why even bother?"

"Oh, yeah, here," Reed said, suddenly animated, his voice weirdly controlled — another first, he was neither stage-whispering nor bellowing. Reed produced a half-size bottle from somewhere inside his frayed sports jacket. "We'll have a toast." He handed the clear glass bottle to Chris for inspection. It had no label obscuring its yellow brine, just a protruding cork sealed with blood-red wax.

"Smuggled it out," Reed said. "Tequila. Aged forty years. The best in the world. You can only buy it locally, and even then it's like Fort Knox. They only sell to gangsters and *presidentes* — like there's a difference." Reed giggled at his joke.

"Huh," Chris said. "I've never had really good tequila."

"Ha! Funny! I'm not kidding around! This'll make that swill you and Jackson brew at that place in Cabo taste like bilgewater."

"Ha, yeah," Chris clucked. From another voluminous fold, Reed produced two shot glasses. "But maybe we could take a rain check? I'm kinda — exhausted." Chris said the last part hopefully.

Reed was ripping at the wax. "It's just one shot."

The cork fell away. Reed kicked at it with his battered sneaker. Chris lost sight of it in the detritus of the cracked pavement.

"Here, hold these —"

Reluctantly, Chris palmed the two shot glasses. Hand shaking so violently he had to use one fat paw to steady the other, Reed poured, spilling liberally. The liquid felt thick on Chris's fingers, treacly, cold and warm at the same time. Chris tasted sour moving up his stomach to his throat.

"Reed," he tried again. "I'm really tired. Could we maybe —"

"Shit, Holmes. It's just one drink. You gotta try this stuff. We're celebrating!"

His pleading eyes, dull and rheumy in the gloom.

"You know, Holmes. What we had. What we did. That was special. You know that, right? I mean, you were *it*. The real thing. The best I've ever seen."

Reed was sloshing his drink around, half of it already spilled.

"To us!" Reed bellowed loudly. "The real thing! To fucking us! You and fucking me!"

Chris closed his eyes and drank.

"Ah!" Reed smacked his lips. "Good stuff, huh?" He nodded to himself and threw his shot glass against the alley's bricks. "Good stuff!"

"Jesus, Reed!"

Chris leaned against the brick wall. The liquid had gone down with a burn, but he hadn't really tasted it. He was just so tired. The darkness pressed in. The smells of the alley thick and tangible. Reed puffed pensively on his cigar. Chris, watching him, sensed more than he felt an onrushing dizziness — the wavering red tip of Reed's cigar starting to circle, to appear in many points of an orbit, as if he was back at the planetarium, a high school sophomore tripping on acid, *Dark Side of the Moon* pumping through the speakers, Krunk giggling. Chris narrowed his eyes, trying to regain focus. He swallowed, urgently repressing the need to throw up.

"… maybe it was worth it," Reed was saying. "Maybe it was all for a reason."

"What?" Chris managed. "What was worth it?"

Reed drew on his cigar again, exhaling with a grimace. "All the fucking carnage. All the dead. The ovens. The goddamn ovens. My mother. She never got over it, really. I owe them, Holmes. You know what I mean? I owe them!"

Reed threw his arm around Chris's shoulders. How? Chris wanted to ask. How could it have been worth it? Reed drew him down and continued in a sombre voice.

"You don't deserve all this video shit. Or maybe you do. Fuck. I don't know! All I know is you aren't like that anymore. You're someone else now. People need to know that. They need to know that the person in this movie is different. You know what I'm saying, Holmes? I'm done, Holmes. I'm done. It's my last one. It's my last movie."

Reed released him.

Chris staggered forward. His legs buckled. Reed grabbed him and held him up, his cigar tip a neon spasm in the dark night.

"I love you, man," Reed whispered.

Nauseated, Chris pushed off the director's barrel chest. With no other intention than to get away, he staggered down the alley toward the street.

EXT. EMPTY URBAN PARK, BEAUTIFUL SUNNY DAY
An eight-year-old GIRL slowly sways on a rusted
swing set. Her shoulder-length straight blond
hair flounces gently in the breeze. The girl
is dressed in the style of the day, with a
blue dress, dark stockings covered by a double-
breasted frock coat. The cloudless azure sky
sparkles under a cheery sun. A jay lands in an
adjacent tree. The girl swings, and though her
expression is neutral, there is the sense of
loss about her, as if she doesn't know exactly
where she is or where she will go next.

A MAN with side curls and a beard and a large
black hat enters the frame and stands, watching
the girl. He is smiling happily, even though
his clothes are dirty and torn and he is sickly
and gaunt. One by one, more of the shtetl Jews
enter the frame. All the Jews are filthy and
ill. Nevertheless, they begin to cheer and clap
as the girl swings. They start to dance, forming
two circles around the girl, one of the men and

the other of the women. The Jews hold hands and
dance a traditional hora, their circles moving
in concurrently opposite ovals as they sing
joyfully.

                          JEWS
               (singing at the top their lungs)
          Oy vey, I want a banana! I want one now!
          Oy vey, I want a banana. When do I want
                    one? I want one now!

The girl swings, her dark leggings cutting
straight through the true blue of the sky.

LEAVING REED BEHIND, CHRIS walked out of the lane, down a narrow sidewalk bordering a wide street. There were no other pedestrians. The traffic, moderately persistent, moved past in surges, leaving behind sudden silence, conflicting currents of hot, dry, exhausted air. Everything felt in motion even though Chris sensed himself seemingly frozen in place. It was like he was on one of those long, automated walkways he'd experienced for the first time at the airport in Toronto. He just stood there and held on. He didn't walk, but he was still moving. He got there without taking a single step. He thought of the Lost Expert. How events conveyed him forward. When to step off? A rare yellow taxi passed. Chris waved at it haplessly. It drove on. Sunset and Vine. Santa Monica Boulevard. Beverly Hills. The city was a fiction of fragments, a trailer for no specific film playing and replaying in his mind.

The real thing!

At the corner of 14th and nowhere, he felt something hard jab against his spine.

"Get in." A familiar voice.

Well, why not? It wasn't a cab, but it was better than nothing.

Chris got in and closed his eyes.

MOTION, A BODY ROCKING gently from side to side. A body. His body. His lump of slumped flesh in the passenger seat of a car. Was it real? Or imagined? A movie: camera tracking the car through the wide-open night, getting closer, catching up. Tires revolving in perfect sequence across straight asphalt bisected by double yellow lines intermittently flaring under highway lights. What make of car? Something beat-up yet luxurious, stretched out and squashed down, its frame evoking a lost world of American luxury, violence once purposeful gone cramped and flailing.

And the driver?

Little Scarface in shirtsleeves and a fedora, looking like a Prohibition gangster on a Las Vegas working vacation. Little Scarface, wearing sunglasses despite the dark. Little Scarface, window down, crook of his bare elbow cutting into the breeze. Is he alone? No. He has an associate lurking in the backseat. A second, dependably mean, with a long Lon Chaney face, impassively creased.

Nouveau California noir. *Chinatown* meets *I'm Still Here* meets *The Postman Always Rings Twice* — twice, three times, he keeps ringing! Chris, just another Hollywood dupe, no different from every other drifter who stumbled into a diner and saw a pretty lady behind the counter. The oldest story in the oldest book. You get greedy. You want things.

The car bounced. Chris felt his brain thump against his skull. Pain radiated through him. The car hopped again, lurching over some desert pitfall, Chris's body jerking around in spastic parody, a minstrel marionette, someone else pulling the strings.

A new scene: a change in the timbre of the darkness. Off the highway, driving along a rough track. Hills looming. Pale grey-green ghost pines drooping with heavy cones, lit by a big white moon. Seen from above, it would be beautiful.

Alison's wry half-smile, the look she gave when she thought

he was being funny-annoying and didn't want to encourage him. When she put her head on his shoulder. The smell of her neck. Sweat tinged with mango-coconut shampoo.

"Hey! Hey! You fucks!" Chris punched the glove compartment. He was going to throw up. "Reed! You fucking prick, Reed!" Blood pounded against his temples. He kept punching. Sweat poured off him. "Hey! Hey!"

The car swerved, dropped into a ditch, then pulled out. Chris slammed forward. Vomit surged up his throat. He threw up on his chin, his neck, his chest. He gagged sour flat champagne and Reed's Mexican concoction for gangsters and *presidentes* only.

He spit on the car floor, wiping the sides of his face against the sleeves of his linen jacket. The car slowed.

All this time, he'd focused on beginnings, on the once upon a time origin.

But what about the end? How did it end?

For the life of him, he couldn't remember. Maybe they hadn't shot it yet. Maybe they were shooting it right now? The German and Reed, somewhere in the foothills, tracking a clear night sky of abundant velvet sparkled with pearly stars. So many stars! Such beauty! Such opulent space! Far below, grains of sand shifted, just barely roiled by the faintest of winds. An animal skittered by — tiny tan pocket mouse, nervous, low to the ground, low on the food chain. Above, a hawk circled, its huge shadow looming.

It was silent in the great empty amphitheatre of the desert, waiting for the show to begin.

The car rolled to a stop.

Doors slammed opened and shut. Chris heard muttered words. He smelled the familiar bitter tang of cigarette exhale. Chris drew in eagerly. Acrid smoke: a meagre but nevertheless extant antidote to the awful reek of engine exhaust dregs and alcohol-laced bile. Memory is a taste and a smell and a need, a desire. The Lost Expert, still walking, still looking, still trudging through swamp and desert and ghetto. Not giving up. Never giving up.

They'd drive up the coast, Chris thought. They'd stop as they pleased, in San Francisco, in Santa Cruz, in Sausalito, in places he'd only heard about. On the way out of town, they'd drop in on gentle Jack Holmes, his tanned face a crow's-foot maze of regrets.

Then they'd keep going: Portland, Seattle, Vancouver, Alaska. They'd drive a convertible, a two-seater, red like the one Dustin Hoffman drove in *The Graduate*. "Hey! Hey, Alison!" he'd yell, summoning her, compelling her, arms in the air, leaning against the giant glass wall looming over La-La Land. "Alison!" Or they'd drive east, back to Vegas, the *real* Vegas, get hitched at an Elvis-themed chapel, then on across the South all the way to Florida, feet up on the dash, her small toes, nails painted pink, the wind and sun slowly turning her hair auburn.

More muttering. The crunch of footsteps. The clinking of keys. They were coming now.

Chris shivered. And then — he couldn't help it — it just happened. Heat on his crotch. He wet himself.

Someone fumbling with the door latch.

Bullets bounding into the swamp. His mom silently watching his dad pack his things. *I guess it's just you and me now.* Her brave, sad smile. *The real thing.*

The desert's dark rolled over him, cool and expansive. Chris kept his eyes closed, willed his body limp.

"Fuggin' puked himself."

"Pissed himself, too."

"Fuggin' loser."

"Big man."

"Big action hero man."

In shared disgust, they backed away. Chris opened his eyes, just a crack. A lighter flared, revealing faces pressed together, drawing on the flame then breathing out fumes tinged by shrinking fire. Little Scarface, pale, the pink slash on his face throbbing fresh. His second, the other guy, blank and laconic, exactly as Chris had imagined him. Their cigarette tips glowed. Again, Chris tasted smoke: bitter fog swirling over him and disappearing into the night. Ancient breeze stirring dormant minerals from when the deserts were oceans and the world teemed with infinite disaster.

Again, the crunch of steps.

They were coming back, bolstered, fortified, ready. They thought it was done. Nothing left to do but consign one superstar celebrity Thomson Holmes to the nigh world of dust and shadows. Another player brought down, coated in his own vomit, slicked in his own foul urine. Sordid appetites! Misplaced regret! The time for strutting over. Poor mad king! He should have died hereafter!

Ever so slowly, Chris worked a hand into the pocket of his Thomson Holmes chinos. It was still there. He could feel it.

"Fuggin' reeks."

"Uh-huh."

"You get the legs. I'll grab the arms."

"Yeah."

"You ready?"

"Uh-huh."

"On three?"

"Yeah."

"One. Two. "

"Three!" Chris screamed, launching himself, slashing wildly.

Assistant Thug jerked back. Chris fell to the soft, cold sand. Level with the work boots of Little Scarface's second, Chris stabbed his little knife at the man's oversized foot, once, twice, three times.

"Hey! My boot!" Assistant Thug half-heartedly kicked at Chris. Chris lurched forward and tackled the man around the legs. Assistant Thug teetered, landing hard on top of Chris. Chris grunted air. The switchblade went flying into the desert night, a small glittering object among many such small glittering objects. Chris slithered out from under Assistant Thug, who lay motionless, stunned by the blunted jut of rock his head had bounced off. Chris, still gasping for air, climbed on top of the man and put his hands around the back of his neck. But he was too shaky and weak to squeeze. Chris panted and swallowed, tasting blood. Assistant Thug bucked, rolling Chris back into the dirt.

"That's enough!"

Little Scarface fired, once, into the desert night. The sound was a sudden distance of orbiting echoes. Absurdly, Chris scanned the sky. Red Mars shimmered manically in a black sea of extinguished suns and satellite jetsam; planes passed in the lower spheres, their invisible plumes dispersing. A world, made and made up. Assistant Thug climbed to his feet and staggered off to the car, cursing. "Da fuck!"

"That's enough," Little Scarface said again. "Get up."

Chris stood unsteadily, facing his adversary. He struggled to swallow, still trying to wet his throat and catch his breath. Sweat in his eyes beaded his vision. The heavy pistol, wavering. Or pointing? The night a heavy blanket.

"That's enough," Little Scarface said for a third time.

"No," Chris gasped. "Wait."

He shimmied a hand into his pants pocket.

"Don't!" Little Scarface warned.

Chris grimaced in anticipation. "Wait. It's not a — Just let me —"

"The gun doesn't have to go off," he heard Krunk ramble. "Why the fuck do they think it always has to go off?"

"I'm not who you think I am," Chris said, finally getting the words out.

"What are you talking about?" Little Scarface's eyes flickered to the dark square sitting in the proffered palm of Hollywood's biggest star.

Krunk hated the saying. "Chekov shmekov," he spat in mock disgust. *But it does*, Chris thought. *One way or another*.

"Go ahead. Have a look. After, you can shoot me or —" Chris tossed his wallet. It bounced on the sand and rolled to a stop in front of Little Scarface's snakeskin cowboy boots. Little Scarface looked down at the battered wallet dubiously. He nudged at it gingerly with his cowboy boot, as if expecting it to explode.

Chris sat on the cold desert sand, luminescent under a slowly sinking moon. Little Scarface crouched five or so feet away. The gun, dull metallic black, lay on the sand between his knees.

"You're saying you're *this* guy?"

"Yeah."

"So, they, uh, brought you in? To keep that movie going? Up in Canada?"

"Yeah. Something like that."

"Huh." Little Scarface shook his head in defeated wonder. The wind had kicked up. Chris was soggy, foul in his own sorry stench. He shivered in the cold cross breeze. Little Scarface, ignoring him, squinted at what looked to Chris to be his Ontario health card and continued shaking his square head — disgusted, disbelieving, Chris couldn't tell.

"So?" Chris crossed his arms, grabbed his elbows, and steeled himself. No more shaking. He was sick of it.

Little Scarface sprung up. He paced back and forth, his lips moving silently, the gun in his left hand, the wallet in his right. He stopped in front of Chris, looming in close. Chris studied him. Poor Little Scarface, his face stuck in a leer meant to disguise his disappointment.

"You're all alone," Chris said sadly. "Aren't you?"

"Shut it," Little Scarface muttered.

"There are no *associates*."

"I said shut it!"

Little Scarface was a fake. They both were.

Scarface rounded on Chris, pointing the gun again, this time with more focussed attention. Chris stared into the barrel. It gleamed, a wet hole.

"So where is he, then?" Little Scarface demanded. "Where the fuck is he?"

"He's gone," Chris said calmly. "I don't know where he is. Nobody does. He took as much of his money as he could get his hands on, and he disappeared. He's an asshole. He's a scared, lying, raping asshole."

"Fuck!" Little Scarface screamed, the gun in his hand wavering wildly, barrel syncopating to the time of a shaking trigger finger.

"But I have an idea." Chris faltered. Then he realized it was true. He really did have an idea. "It doesn't matter now! I'm Thomson Holmes now! I live in his house. I have his phone. His passport. His bank accounts! I'm him. I'm Thomson Holmes now!"

"So what? So *what*?" Little Scarface's bared yellow teeth and beady, bulging eyes.

"No, listen. Don't you get it? It's better this way. We'll make a deal. Thomson Holmes is still worth a lot of money. He could still make millions. I'll cut you in. How about twenty percent? I'll give you twenty percent!"

"Twenty? Twenty percent?" The gun barrel wavering.

"Of everything! Everything he — I — make. There's royalties. And new movies. And commercials. Everything! It's a lot of money!"

"A lot of money," Little Scarface repeated soberly. Chris nodded encouragingly. The Lost Expert, his wife dead, his son abducted, the ghetto Jews walled in and left to die like rats in a cage. Even for him, there was something next.

"So what'll I do?" Little Scarface said miserably. It was a sudden change in the script. A new character. Who would he play?

"Security," Chris said definitively. He was standing now. He stepped toward Little Scarface.

"Security?"

Chris flashed his brightest Thomson Holmes smile. "I'll need a guy. C'mon. Put the gun away. We'll shake on it."

"Security," Little Scarface muttered.

"Sure. You and your friend."

"Thirty," Little Scarface said, slipping the gun into the waist of his dress pants. "I want thirty percent."

THEY DROVE SLOWLY OUT of the desert. Assistant Thug was at the wheel, only slightly confused by the new plan. Little Scarface sat in the passenger seat, and Chris rode in the back. All the windows were down, and the fresh air of dawn scoured the car's reek of vomit and piss and man sweat. The cool air kept Chris awake and upright, but just barely.

"So where we goin'?" Sidekick asked.

Little Scarface turned to Chris. "Where to, boss?" He flashed his trademark malevolent grin.

Chris gazed through the window. They were on a small arterial road on the desert's fringes. They passed an abandoned gas station. Heaps of garbage. An old school bus stripped of its bits. They passed a rundown shack and a globular cluster of three derelict trailers arranged around a firepit, barely smouldering. People scratching out a life on the edge of nowhere. The world was full of those liminal spaces, sparsely, unwillingly occupied. Underpasses and ghettoes.

Where to? Everywhere he'd been over the last months had been one of those places where nobody willingly lived. Swamps, deserts, and casinos. Ghettos and insane asylums. Abandoned summer camps, boggy forests waiting to be clear-cut. For most people, these weren't real places. They could only be imagined. They were scenes from the movies. When the lights come up, the theatre empties. Everyone goes home, taking nothing with them but their greasy bag of unfinished popcorn.

Where to?

He was tired.

He was so incredibly tired.

"Santa Barbara."

"Santa Barbara?" Little Scarface was suddenly suspicious. "What's in Santa Barbara?"

"My dad," Chris said.

Acknowledgements

Thank you to Emily Schultz for feedback and edits on an early draft of this book. Thank you to Sam Hiyate for enthusiasm and support. Thank you to Marc Côté for exemplary edits and fortitude. Thank you to my family for getting me through hard times — without them I would never have finished this book. And thank you to Rachel Greenbaum, my North Star.

We acknowledge the sacred land on which Cormorant Books operates. It has been a site of human activity for 15,000 years. This land is the territory of the Huron-Wendat and Petun First Nations, the Seneca, and most recently, the Mississaugas of the Credit River. The territory was the subject of the Dish With One Spoon Wampum Belt Covenant, an agreement between the Iroquois Confederacy and Confederacy of the Anishinaabe and allied nations to peaceably share and steward the resources around the Great Lakes. Today, the meeting place of Toronto is still home to many Indigenous people from across Turtle Island. We are grateful to have the opportunity to work in the community, on this territory.

We are also mindful of broken covenants and the need to strive to make right with all our relations.